YULETIDE MAYHEM

Book Two of the Jeremiah and Susanne Series

Max W. Justus

NEWMAN SPRINGS PUBLISHING
320 Broad Street
Red Bank, NJ 07701

First originally published by Newman Springs Publishing 2024

ISBN 978-1-68498-560-9 (Paperback)
ISBN 978-1-68498-561-6 (Digital)

Printed in the United States of America

One of my grandsons announced, "All I want for Christmas is for you to dedicate your book to me."

Therefore, this book is dedicated to Sam Rios.

And for those *not* in the family, an honorable mention to the many who made the book possible and to those readers with enough humor to enjoy whimsey.

Contents

Chapter 1

BACK IN BRITAIN

School pictures, ugh! *Click! Snap! Click! Snap!* Today's the day. I hate school pictures! I don't mind *family* pictures because everyone accepts my huge nose and goofy looks. They love me anyway. But *school* pictures, no way! The photos end up in a yearbook where anyone can make nasty comments by telling the truth.

My mind imagines some of my so-called friends talking together. One says, "Look at that nose, and the ears poking way out. He looks like a goof!"

Another answers, "Oh yeah, he's that tall, skinny kid. I remember him in the gym shower—big feet and long great toes, with thumbs long enough for a chimp. What's his name? Oh yeah, Jeremiah ... yeah, Jeremiah Morris, that's his name. What a nerd ball!"

A third asks, "Isn't he the one who broke his nose in gym class? Look, it's still bent in the middle. Maybe his parents hate his face and didn't get the break fixed. Ha! Ha! With that nose, what's the difference?"

Their laughter runs riot in my imagination. Nerds aren't popular kids. And, as if nerdiness wasn't bad enough, I don't read people's facial expressions at all well, which means I don't understand and don't fit in. While I have a fabulous memory and notice details other people don't, I'm so socially awkward that my parents took me to some doctors last year. They diagnosed me with subthreshold autism, called it mild Asperger's syndrome, wondered if I might also have obsessive-compulsive disorder, but then decided my near-perfect recall of details is part of the autism. *Whoopee! What a bonus.*

Many kids in grade six are downright mean. Accept my money for a wager: they will say what I imagined and gloat when they see my mug shot. Mom says I have a fertile imagination.

While she means my head is busy, she sometimes forgets how very busy. When I figure what a facial expression means, I memorize the face muscle movement for next time. That's lots of brainwork to do just to appear normal, all done to figure what people are feeling when their facial expressions remain a mystery.

Much of what the kids might say is actually true. I am very tall, and I did get accidentally elbowed in a basketball game. My broken nose had to be set. Even after the doctors finished, there's still a minor bend in the middle. *Gotta love it!* Now my nose looks even more like Dad's honker. He has a huge nose with a bend in the middle from a break he *didn't* get fixed. Dad calls us the Nasal Twins! But he is ruggedly handsome with a nose that fits his face; me, I'm ugly.

Both Mom and Dad say not to worry about my face. They say, "By the time you are twenty, you will look fine. That's when everything will be in proportion." *Well, sure, maybe!*

I once said to Mom and Phoebe, our nanny, "My face will need to be five feet long for my nose to fit!" Mom tried not to laugh! *Failure!* Then my mom said that five feet was hyperbole.

Phoebe glanced at Mom, who was stifling a giggle, and explained that hyperbole is exaggeration. She said, "Five feet is overstating it. You know perfectly well that a face three feet long would do." She said that 'cause I was feeling sorry for myself, and Phoebe doesn't like self-pity. I laughed 'cause no one has a face three feet long! Phoebe is smart. She has always been here as our nanny, so she knows that I don't feel so bad if I laugh. And Phoebe knows all about my autism. But outside the family, it's a secret.

I look in the mirror to tie my necktie. Nope, off it comes; gotta try again. One side is always too short the first try. Dad taught me how to do a Windsor knot. He gets his tie perfect first try almost always. That's probably because he wears a tie to work and knots one five times a week. Me, I'm lucky if five tries get the knot done right once.

Okay, that's hyperbole, maybe!

Looking at my face in the mirror, I think my blue eyes are okay. They look like Dad's. Mom also has blue eyes, a lighter blue. My brown hair is still straight with a cowlick at the back—that is a real nuisance. I still don't know where the cowlick came from.

On May first, I turned eleven, thirty months younger than my sister, Susanne. I am taller than most of my classmates, with lot of me to show in the bathroom mirror. A short while ago, only my hair showed in the mirror. What a change. *Come on, nose, change fast!*

My sister, who is in grade nine, turned fourteen on November 6. Susanne has gorgeous Titian red hair and blue eyes that sometimes have a slight green cast. Her nose and ears are perfectly proportioned, as are her thumbs and toes. She is taller than me, but that's not really a surprise. Mom is five feet ten and Nana, our grandmother, has shrunk down to only six feet.

For a while, Susanne started to slouch to hide her height. She wanted to be shorter than the boys. Mom told her to be proud of her height and stand straight. She does now.

When she asked Phoebe about new hair in her armpits, our nanny said Susanne is starting puberty. Her chest is starting to change shape—just a little. For quite a while, maybe a year, she sometimes gets a little grumpy. Phoebe talked to us both when she told Susanne about other things that are going to happen. Phoebe called that talk "the birds and the bees." Susanne reminded her that "those things," meaning her periods, were already underway!

I am so glad I am a boy. *Girls have too much bother!*

Susanne looks like what she is, a completely normal person, which makes me glad. She's actually rather pretty, without *any* of my deformities. The boys like her, that's for sure. But even though we are different, we are close friends.

We became even closer after our last terrifying trip to England when Susanne and I banded together to help solve a 270-plus-year-old mystery. I still get scared sometimes when I think about what *did* happen and what *almost* happened. After all, I was nearly murdered!

Susanne says she still gets scared, too, when she thinks about that trip. Shortly after we returned to the states, she told me that her life would be sad without having her baby brother bothering her. I *guess* that means she loves me! I sure do love her 'cause she always has my back. That's part of what makes a best friend!

Susanne has her friends, and I have mine, but we often hang around together, sometimes with both groups of friends all together in a bunch. We are lucky that even our friends like each other. Our closeness helps me to feel better when I have been thinking about that last trip to England and all the ghosts of dead people the whole family met. My stomach still heaves when I remember that the ghosts of my eight-greats-grandparents tried to kill me. I try to forget about what happened, but the cold-sweat nightmares still happen.

Okay! Finally, the tie is on, and the ends are proper after only two tries.

Getting better with ties! Why is my head this busy?

At school, it's time to shoot the pictures. I straighten my tie and pose like they tell me. After the camera click, I ask the photographer, "Can you do anything about my nose? Do you have an airbrush or something?"

He blushes slightly and stammers something. I guess I put him on the spot.

A few weeks later, the pictures arrive. Laughing, I jokingly hand the unopened package to my mother. "Hey Mom, these pictures are for you—a face only a mother could love." I always laugh about my face, mostly because I don't like it. I need a really good plastic surgeon, one with time on his hands.

""None of that, young man. There is nothing the matter with your face, or your nose." Mom musses and then tries to tame my hair. "Why do I always muck up your cowlick?"

"I don't know why you muss my hair. You always do, and you always ask the same question. It's a bad habit you have," I reply sourly.

"No, it's not a bad habit," she insists, "I muss your hair because I love you."

"Okay." Under my breath, I mutter, "*Geez!* Glad you don't hate me."

"Enough of *that!*"

Be smart! Don't argue when you hear that tone.

The day after school finishes, we prepare to spend Christmas with Papa and Nana, our grandparents. From our apartment on Central Park in Manhattan, all five of us pile into a limo and head for the airport where we will board a plane for London, and then take a train to South West England. The last time we went to England, I was ten. Mom was working in New York and had to come over later when they thought I was sick. But now they know I was unconscious because I was time traveling.

Like last time, we have all the upgrades because Papa insists. Fine with me. I love traveling first class. With more tact this year, I don't make comments about how great first-class travel is while looking at the passengers in coach one row back. This year, Papa and Dad split the costs after Dad said, "It's too much when Papa pays for everything as he did last trip."

After we land, Papa greets us at the airport as always. Susanne sees him first and waves her arms above her head. She gets the first hug. That's okay, I guess.

Papa is an inch or two shorter than Nana's six feet. He has thinning gray hair and bushy eyebrows with deep blue eyes that watch everything, and miss nothing, always twinkling when he plays a joke or creates mischief. His long face ends in a square jaw with ears that stick out a little, like mine do. That's another thing I got from him— just like his long thumbs and long great toes.

When she gets a chance, Mom gives her dad a big kiss and a tight hug. "I'm so glad to see you. Merry Christmas, Dad," she says as she gives him another kiss on the cheek. Her blue eyes show how happy she is to see her father.

Mom is the same height as her dad. Her short brown hair is mussed slightly from traveling. At home, she sometimes complains about carrying a few extra pounds and occasionally says, "My weight is always a struggle to control. That's why I exercise regularly at the gym."

And Dad almost always replies, "But you know, Constance, how I feel about your curves." He usually smiles in an odd sort of way when he says this.

Mom sometimes responds with a funny expression on her face too. That's when she smiles slightly and murmurs, "Yes, Sam, I *do* know what you like." Then they usually exchange *the look*, which loses me. Parents sure are odd!

Why is my noggin working overtime?

During the chaos of greetings, Papa greets everyone with big hugs. Giving each of us full, direct attention, he asks, "How was the flight?" He listens intently as we prattle on with our answers.

"Welcome to Britain," Papa says to Dad.

They both laugh. It's a running joke between them. Papa says, "Welcome to Britain," when Dad comes here. Dad says, "Welcome to America," when Papa visits us. They think this is so funny. Go figure!

Papa continues, "I've got a car waiting, and the train tickets are ready to be picked up. And there is time for a snack at the station." Papa looks toward me. "Yes, Jeremiah, it's Paddington Station." He knows I love photographs by the statue of Paddington Bear.

At the station, Papa declares, "We must have a picture with Paddington. It's a tradition."

It's probably no accident that he made that suggestion. Usually, I ask for a photo and then Susanne rolls her eyes and teases me for being such a child. *Saved!* I get a picture, and it's not my fault. *Thanks, smart Papa.*

We are rotating photographers so everyone is included in the photo when an elderly gentleman asks, "Would you like a group shot taken?"

"Oh yes, please," replies Papa.

After looking at the camera on the phone and getting advice on what to do, the elderly man says, "Now, say fuzzy pickles." He looks at the photos he has taken. "I think that's right. Took four, maybe. Please make sure they are fine before I leave."

Papa looks at the photos and says, "You have done a splendid job. Thank you."

Flushed with pleasure, the elderly man says, "Enjoy the holidays."

Taking a wild guess, Papa replies, "And Merry Christmas to you."

The man smiles with delight and says, "And Merry Christmas to each of you!" He totters away, looking very pleased.

It's going to be a Merry Christmas indeed.

Once again, we have been lucky to have a group photo with Paddington Bear. This happens every visit. I love it! Unlike Susanne, I keep all my photos with Paddington on display in my room. She put hers away in her memorabilia drawer. Occasionally, when she thinks she's alone, she secretly pulls them out for inspection. She doesn't know, but I saw her!

After our snack in a teashop, Phoebe buys the *London Times.* We board our train and settle in. Susanne is tired and trying not to let it show. Once the train starts moving, she is dead to the world beside Papa. Eventually, her sleeping head falls against his right arm. He smiles, and gazes happily down upon her. He chats away to Dad and Mom, sitting opposite.

Near the window and next to Mom, Phoebe reads her paper. Mom sometimes scans a headline over our nanny's shoulder. I'm near the window on Papa's other side, across from Phoebe. I peer out through the window at passing traffic on the roads. Later, in the countryside, I notice sheep in meadows that are separated by stone fences. I love the British countryside!

Papa's tweed jacket has familiar country smells, which always makes me feel secure and comfortable. The motion of the train relaxes me, but I don't recall falling off to sleep. When I wake up, my head is against Papa's left arm, and Susanne is pressed against his right. Poor Papa! We must be heavy. Not to worry; he seems happy despite the adults still jabbering.

At the station, the train slows and then stops. We all look for any stray items we have forgotten, pull down our bags, and disembark at our destination.

Like last time, we see Mr. Brown beside Papa's minibus. Although he is shorter than Papa, he stands very straight. He has broad shoulders, brown eyes, but his brown hair is a tiny bit grayer. He still has a pencil mustache.

Papa greets him and then says, "You all remember Mr. Brown," as he introduces us.

With a big smile, Mr. Brown greets Susanne and me. "My goodness, you two have grown since last visit—exactly as expected in a year and a half. Welcome!" He glances over to the rest of the family. "It's good to see all of you again."

Our parents and Phoebe exchange greetings with him. Still smiling, Dad helps me load the minibus while Papa talks to Mr. Brown. Like Nigel, Mr. Brown almost always makes me smile inside.

I love the drive to our grandparents' home despite the narrow roads with hedgerows on each side. Sometimes, there is no place to pull over or go past an oncoming vehicle. And once again, I don't see the turn between hedgerows that leads to our grandparents' home.

Papa explained last time that it is a Tudor-style home, built with Georgian symmetry in the Victorian period, a motley mix. If a talking bird glanced down, it might exclaim, "Look below! That house is shaped like a giant *H!*"

As we pull up the gravel drive, I momentarily gape at the house, which is actually larger than in my recollections. Susanne notices my open jaw, pokes my ribs, and demands, "Close your mouth, stupid!"

While I love Nana and being with my grandparents in their old country house, Papa is the really special fun one who knows how to break the rules. And our grands know that I'm an autistic misfit, see that my nose is too big, my ears stick out, and that my great toes and thumbs are all too long for the rest of me, but they love me anyway. Families are like that!

It's nearly Christmas time! They gotta be nice. Santa says so!

Nana's blue eyes, which miss nothing, are patiently watchful when we glimpse her face staring out from a drawing room window. As the minibus slows, the front door of the house opens. Wearing a coat and a scarf half-falling off her thick gray hair that mimics a twenties bob, she stands on the stone steps, momentarily waiting.

Nigel, their butler, is close behind. As always, he looks good in his stylish jacket over his trim figure capped with short gray hair. His brown eyes twinkle, and his lips break into a smile, as do Nana's. The winter day suddenly feels warmer.

As soon as our vehicle stops, Nana's shoes crunch on the gravel as she approaches. I jump out to be the first to give her a hug.

So there, Susanne!

When Nana looks me over after our hug, she says, "Jeremiah, I knew you had grown. I didn't realize how much."

Nana greets everyone with hugs and kisses.

Mom says, "You look very fit, Mother. I'm glad to see you. I miss you." She hugs her mom again very tightly. Mom's eyes glisten a little, like Nana's.

We all greet Nigel warmly too. Suddenly, Mr. Brown, Dad, and Nigel have most of the bags and are heading into the house. I carry Susanne's and drag mine.

Once inside the hallway, there is a pause in the conversational chaos. I butt in with, "Nana, I'm growing so fast that I have to put on my dress pants every Saturday night. Then Mom knows how much the hem must come down before church in the morning. She is a lawyer, but I am glad she knows how to sew. Otherwise, I'd be wearing *floodsies*."

Nana replies, "Oh, you poor thing. How do you know where you have put your hands and feet? They are in a different end place every week."

"Yup," I continue, "I have no idea where my hands and feet are today compared to yesterday. Forget about last week! I am always bumping into something. But if I am sitting, I have good hand coordination. Walking around, I'm a klutz. It's enough to make me nuts!"

"Poor dear boy," she replies as she gives me a sideways hug.

"My parents say everything will be better after puberty, but my voice hasn't started to change yet, or at least not noticeably."

Nana laughs. "You've been here three minutes and the topic is puberty! Not to worry. All will be well." Nana smiles, her arm still around me.

"Really?" I look at her to see if she's joshing me. She's already into another conversation elsewhere as she holds me loosely beside her.

As conversation continues among the adults, Susanne looks around, probably remembering things from our last visit eighteen months ago. As I look at Susanne, my thoughts wander.

She's taller than me—pretty, coordinated, smart, with lots of friends. Mom says Susanne has poise, whatever that is. And then there is *moi-même*; an ugly, skinny, tall drink of water, poorly coordinated, and an autistic nerd to boot. You can tell why I'm not on the popular kids' *A* team!

While I'm not a popular kid, I do have a few really good friends. They tend to be high-achieving misfits such as myself. We look out for each other. One of my really good friends is slightly taller than I am. The other is really short. Maybe because we study together, the three of us rank one, two, and three in the school, but shift our position with every set of exams. That keeps the teachers guessing. What a laugh! The difference is a decimal point, not a full-mark difference in our averages. We call ourselves the Towering Triplets! That's actually very funny, especially since one of the Towering Triplets is short. But his marks aren't. They tower over the next group below us.

My tall friend is African-American, and the shrimp is Korean. Yah, we are triplets! We also say we look alike. Then we laugh and laugh like some nerds do. We can say whatever we want because we are really good friends. Alone together, friends don't really care about what adults call political correctness.

My goodness, where did all this fluff come from? My head is too busy! Focus!

I notice that Phoebe is looking around with a strangely cautious expression.

Is she remembering our last visit too?

We are all directed to the dining room. Nana says, "Your overnight flight arrived so early that you probably didn't eat well. I have breakfast food that we will call an early lunch. There are scrambled eggs and bacon with toast, all prepared but kept warm since we were guessing on arrival time and wanted food ready and waiting for you. I hope that is all right with everyone."

I exclaim, "Great! A hearty meal with milk for us kids, but I wish breakfast had teacakes 'cause they're yummy! Anyway, I am hungry."

Papa exclaims, "Shocking!"

Glowering directly at me, Nana declares, "No, Mister Sweet Tooth. You shan't have teacakes for breakfast." Then she giggles and adds, "But that *does* sound good."

When Nana says no, she always means it.

I hear Dad stifle a laugh before he agrees, "Yes indeed." Everyone else chuckles while they attempt to concur solemnly with Nana's food rules. I glance at Phoebe as she sits down. What would we do without our friend and nanny? We don't really need a nanny, but Mom wants us to be supervised when she is at work, so Phoebe is still living with us. This makes me glad because I love Phoebe dearly. And Phoebe is a good cook! She has been with us since Susanne's birth, which is all of my life. To my way of thinking, Phoebe is part of the family.

We all gather food from the serving board. While we eat, I sit quietly, but the adults talk. I think back to the last trip here.

What a visit that was!

Suddenly, I realize why I was thinking about friends at home. *That's an escape to avoid thinking about the last visit here. Come on, buddy. Face your foe. Think and deal!*

Last visit, Susanne and I met our nine-greats-grandparents, Mortimer and Leila Wadsworth, who died in the mid-eighteenth century. What I mean is, we met their phantoms. I soon loved them both. We also met a lot of our other ancestors who were born later than Mortimer and Leila. They were residing in trunks in the attic at our grandparents' house, all trying to solve a mystery that occurred in 1744. The mystery—who robbed Walter Johnson the night he died?

My eight-greats-uncle Edgar was wrongfully accused of robbery, which resulted in the death of Edgar's friend, Walter Johnson. Poor Great-Uncle Edgar was hung in 1745 'cause they said he killed his friend!

Some of my ancestors banded together with Susanne and me to find the truth. The investigation nearly cost me my life—at age ten! While I love Leila, I never loved the ghost of my eight-greats-grandmother or her husband. She was the nasty criminal mastermind who tried to kill me to cover her tracks. But my hero, Great-Uncle Edgar himself, saved me! We tried the guilty parties so that they received justice from Saint Peter. Edgar's name was finally cleared after a few hundred years!

Their mission accomplished, my ancestors were able to leave their attic trunks for their final destination. As Nigel said after the trial, "Thank heavens, all the attic spooks have shoved off."

Most went to heaven, but two disappeared in fire, and two disappeared in smoke on the way to *their* final destination. What an ending for those four, racing down the highway to hell! The two fireballs were my eight-greats-grandparents, who still scare me, even now! Like I said, my memory of those two guilty parties won't go away. Attempted murder does that to a fella's recall! The other two smoke puffs were my seven-greats-grandparents—two unkind, self-centered snobs.

Talk about nasty ancestors!

All the family decided we shouldn't talk to friends about our experiences from our last visit. Mom glanced at Dad to verify their decision, saw him nod, and said, "We both agree with Nana and Papa. They don't think our friends would understand about spooks residing in the attic. We won't discuss that with others."

Susanne and I asked, "But all the spooks have shoved off now, so what's the difference?"

Dad replied, "People are not always as understanding or as sympathetic as you would like. You might get an unwanted and hurtful response." That's also exactly what he said earlier when my parents decided only immediate family should know about my autism.

"Least said, easiest mended," piped up Phoebe.

Well, that was a united front. Silence to others it is!

But I do talk to my sister, my parents, and especially to Phoebe when memories are making me sad, scaring me too much, or causing me awful nightmares that wake me up in a sweat. Mostly, I just try to ignore and forget. But that is difficult since there's a lot to forget. Sometimes, the harder I try, the worse it is.

At one point during that previous visit, Phoebe went to the Silver Vaults, guided without her knowledge by another ghostly ancestor from the attic—Papa's dead father. He helped her buy one of the items stolen in 1744, a silver rabbit. The rabbit originally belonged to Abigail Johnson, married to the Walter Johnson who died in the robbery.

The rabbit was half of a pair. The second item, a silver frog, belonged to Walter. It was recovered as stolen merchandise from the attic here at Papa's house. The original owners of the silver rabbit and frog had the two pieces created as a sentimental first anniversary gift in 1716. The rabbit was Abigail's since Walter called her his bunny. I asked Dad, "Why did Abigail have *that* nickname that only Walter used?"

Dad laughed and said, "I'll explain later when you are older. And the frog was Walter's, as a joke that a few frogs must be kissed before a girl finds her true prince." But he wouldn't explain about the bunny.

After they testified at the trial, the ghosts of Walter and Abigail gave Phoebe both pieces. Phoebe keeps them in a place of honor in her room. She sometimes says, "I am still looking for my prince."

I think that she has found him! Phoebe has met a young man who lives in New York City where we live. He didn't come with us for the Christmas holidays. Phoebe said, "Things are not so serious that changing holiday plans is a consideration." But she sighed when she told that to Susanne and me. I think she wishes things *were* that serious!

Hey, noggin, I get it. If I'm distracted, I won't think how scary this place can be!

I hear Nana state, "We'll have a light teatime since we have a dinner engagement tonight!" Her talk about food jolts my mind back to the present.

Goodbye, memories. Stay forgotten.

Mom answers, "Nana, I agree, but we need to unpack and perhaps rest."

As we head up the stairs, Phoebe probes, "You were quiet during lunch. Is there anything I need to know?"

"No, Phoebe," I reply, "I was just thinking about our last visit."

She asks, "Does that bother you, Jeremiah? Are you worried or upset?"

"No, Phoebe, I'm okay," I respond honestly.

"Talk to me if you need," she offers, "I'm always ready to listen."

"Thanks," I murmur as we reach the upstairs hallway.

As we progress along the hallway, Phoebe continues, "Enough happened here last time to scare off anyone for a lifetime! At least the spooks are now gone, but the recollections still scare me, if you must know."

Incredulous, I stop walking, gaze at Phoebe, and demand, "Do you *really* mean you still get scared?" My eyes are wide open as I look at her in wonder. "As an *adult*, you still get scared?"

"Yes, indeed," she murmurs with a wry smile. "Adult or not, I still do get frightened, but mostly sad when I think about what almost happened. I love you and your sister too much to lose either one." She puts her arm over my shoulder and pulls me tight beside her as we walk. Her eyes are too bright.

Phoebe is scared too. I feel better!

Susanne and I have the same rooms as last time and share a bathroom that is between the bedrooms. I'm glad Papa and Nana still live in their large old house, which is comfortable, well kept up, and full of surprises. Despite all that has happened, I love being here with my grandparents, mostly because they love both Susanne and me a whole lot and show it.

My room has a four-poster bed with a rail so that curtains could go around the bed. Nana once told Susanne and me that those curtains were called bed hangings. Fortunately, there are none now. That would be too much! But the rail still attaches to the top of the bedposts, just in case bed hangings are needed.

Mom once explained, "Bed hangings were used when fireplaces were the only heat source. Once in bed, the heavy curtains around the bed were pulled together to keep drafts away from the sleepers. The house is warmer in winter now with central heating, so bed hangings are not needed. The glass doors over all the fireplace openings keep heat from escaping up the chimneys. The glass doors can open if a fire is lit; otherwise, they stay tightly closed."

I am very glad of that—bed hangings are dust collectors, enough to make anyone wheeze!

Noggin, stop spouting everything you know, just because you're nerved up. This is such old news!

Today, all of us are going with Papa and Nana to visit their friends, Oscar and Nadia. We have met them before but not last visit. They were away during the summer when we visited last time. Apparently, we met on the visit when I was four and a half.

While they might remember Susanne and me, I scarcely remember them at all.

We will leave after teatime, drive the twenty miles to their home, and have supper there. They have an old house too. I love old houses! Old houses have character. They reveal how people lived in the past, entertained others, slept, prepared food, and kept warm.

Papa sometimes states, "An old house is a window into the past. How an old house changes is a window into the future!" Our parents agree. He occasionally adds, "It is by knowing our past that we can understand the present and shape our future."

It took me a long while to really understand his point. But I do think he is right. He doesn't mean just the immediate past, either. Papa's theory that the past influences the future was certainly true for me during our last visit. I learned how much the past could shape the present and the future. The people who covered up the facts about the robbery in 1744 certainly reached out from the eighteenth century and nearly stopped my future as they tried to silence me! Forgetting *that* takes effort!

Back on that again? Really, Jeremiah!

After I unpack my bags, I flop on the bed. I am tired from the trip but unlikely to actually nod off to sleep. Imagine my surprise when, an hour later, I startle awake from a deep sleep as Susanne knocks and appears in the bathroom doorway.

She is slender and really very tall for her age, much taller than me, but I will win that race over time. Her hair is getting longer. Right now, it falls in waves past her shoulders. Sometimes, she looks like a little girl. Other times, she looks like a young woman. Right now, she is wearing a dark-brown skirt that goes well past the knees. Over her white blouse, she wears a heavy, dark-gray cardigan. Today, she is neither a little girl nor a young woman. Today, she looks like she's dressing to audition for the part of an old maid who works in a dusty library!

"Are you going down to tea?" she asks.

I look at my clock. "Yes, it's about time. I'm hungry. Are you?"

"You are always hungry. Let's go."

I pull on my heavy sweater over my shirt. My jeans are too short. *Surprise!* My socks show above the fleece of my slippers. *Oh well!* At least the slippers are comfortable.

We walk together out of my room and along the long hall to the central stairs that descend to the main hall below. The ornate staircase in the Elizabethan style has intricately carved spindles and newel posts. During our last visit, the wood was extremely dark, but Nana has had the woodwork in the hall and staircase cleaned and the color lightened to show up the carving. The lighter color on the stairs and spindles fits with the sandy yellow of the old paneling, which reaches to the high ceiling in the hall. Nana said she is pleased with the results. I can see why.

Everyone gathers for tea. Nigel, their butler, serves. He is about as tall as Papa, but very trim. His gray hair is clipped short—no straggling hairs allowed! His brown eyes twinkle as he talks briefly to each person with a smile that always lights up the room. I'm very fond of Nigel.

Mrs. Stewart, the cook, has prepared lovely small sandwiches, crusts cut off. Then comes Mrs. Stewart's custard specialty. It's warm, sweet, and creamy. Wow! This Mister Sweet Tooth loves his desserts!

I stand as we clear away the teatime debris. Dad looks at me and says, "We leave for dinner in a few hours. Please, put on dress pants before we go, and no sneakers."

"Sure thing," I reply. Like the rest of the Americans, I head upstairs to finish unpacking and maybe have another nap.

Later, we all gather to talk in the sitting room. After a few hours, Papa eventually looks at his watch and comments, "We will need to depart in about a half hour. Nadia likes timely guests." He laughs a little as he looks around.

When the adults scatter to prepare for departure, Phoebe points and orders, "Time, you two." Phoebe and Susanne head toward the stairs.

I dash upstairs ahead of them and bound into my room to change. Fortunately, my dress pants are long enough.

Now I'm not such a dork!

In Britain, the word for pants is *trousers*. I am wearing dress trousers.

I glance in the bedroom mirror. *Not so dorky in dress trousers and dress shoes. At least this dork remembered the shoes!*

Downstairs, we all put on coats and gloves for the chilly weather outside. We need two cars. Papa drives one, and Dad drives the other. Dad and I wear matching caps, but his cap is bigger because his head is even larger than mine.

As usual, driver Dad stops in his tracks moments before he tries to get in the wrong side of the car. English vehicles drive on the left side of the road with the driver on the right side of the car, the reverse of the American system. It's confusing! And Dad often gets it wrong.

Dad drives Nana's car. Nana is the front-seat passenger, with Susanne and me in the back. This way Nana can give directions if Dad loses sight of Papa's car. With these roads, the driver needs a guide!

Like I said before, Nana is six feet tall, taller than her husband. The upper part of Nana's torso curves back because her spine does. Mom calls this Nana's dowager hump. This must have taken an inch or two off her height. And she is still six feet tall! I suddenly realize that as a young woman she must have been six feet one, maybe more, towering over most men and certainly taller than her husband. Papa, with a surprisingly straight back, has been five feet ten forever. With the height difference, it's no surprise he sometimes asks, "Have you seen my Amazon?"

Papa once explained, "As a joke, I pulled the name from Greek mythology. Amazons were tall and warlike women who were brutal and aggressive, if you believe the stories about them. They were a tribe descended from the daughters of Ares and Harmonia."

Who were those two? Maybe sometime in the future I will ask Papa. He will know without looking up anything. But when I ask, I'll need to listen. That's not in the cards tonight.

I watch as Dad slowly curls his six-feet-five frame in behind the wheel. His salt and mostly pepper hair and the top of his head almost disappear into the roofline. His dark-blue eyes flash with annoyance when he hits his knee on the steering column as he gets into the car.

That must have hurt! I just hope Dad can see adequately. He looks crammed, as does Nana.

With a sideways glance at Dad, Nana laughs out loud. "It is difficult to find a car for us tall types."

Papa drives his own car. His hair has more gray now, but his eyes still twinkle like sparkling blue seas of mischief. He has a slight paunch to his belly, but he still moves quickly and easily.

Mom sits in front beside Papa, with Phoebe in back. At five feet ten, Mom is too tall for the back seat. But at least we can see her brown hair on her head. It hasn't disappeared into the roofline like Dad's. Neither has Papa's.

Phoebe is much shorter than Mom. Her dark Spanish eyes peer out from the beautiful olive skin of her attractive face. Like Mom, she is practical and keeps her dark hair cut short. She once said to Susanne and me, "I'm five feet, six inches, which is tall for my family. Beside your parents, I look like an orphaned child."

We follow country roads with hedges along the edge of the road. These never allow much room. Going by an oncoming car is sometimes difficult. Eventually, we go through a neighboring village where we turn and follow an even narrower road, if such a thing were possible!

In a short time, we turn into a laneway and ascend a slight incline until we arrive at the home of Oscar and Nadia. Electrified entrance lanterns around the grand doorway glimmer while the gardens are sprinkled with floodlights. The windows spill warm and welcoming light, allowing us to see the large and formal house in the dark.

Earlier, when Papa was telling us about their friends, he remarked, "Their house is much older than ours. It was built in the mid-eighteenth century in proper eighteenth-century style. People at the time considered it fashionable and modern."

Nana replied to him, "I sometimes say *au courant* rather than modern. Children, *au courant* means up-to-date in the latest fashion. Their house is truly in the style of the mid-eighteenth century's latest fashion!"

Papa regarded his wife fondly and answered, "Trust a British solicitor to have the right word choice." Then they glanced at each other and both giggled like schoolchildren sharing a joke.

Above the front door is a semicircular portico with an almost flat roof. Four round stone pillars cut from the same-colored stone as the house support the portico. The façade is symmetrical. Large sash windows are regularly placed one above another along the façade, which goes on forever under a roof of green slate. The building is made of a sandy yellow stone cut in large blocks. The drive is made of small yellow gravel stones that crunch under the weight of feet. They are the same color as the stone of the house.

This is a large homestead. And I thought our grandparents' pad was big!

Nana's friend Nadia appears as the cars come to a halt on the drive. Oscar appears just behind her. Earlier, Nana said to us, "Nadia, Oscar, and I are the same age, but she acts years younger than her dear husband. Nadia is a long-distance swimmer and swims regularly."

Wow! She has big shoulder muscles and muscular arms!

Nadia is about five-eight, a little overweight, puffing out her dress in all sorts of bulges. She moves with easy confidence, sure-footed on the gravel of the drive.

Oscar is thin and appears frail and much older, without Papa's vitality. He bends forward slightly as he walks unsteadily with his neck craning upward to see ahead. He and his wife are about the same height and look at each other eye to eye. Oscar must have been taller than Nadia before he curved forward, but how much?

Nana and Papa greet their friends warmly and then reintroduce us all to them.

Oscar says, "It has been seven years since we have seen you. There have been changes in Susanne and Jeremiah since then!" He chortles happily in his recollections.

I sort of remember them … maybe. Seven years: Susanne and I *would* be different, wouldn't we?

We pile into the central hall as the enormous front door closes behind us. As in Papa and Nana's house, the ceilings are high, but here the woodwork is mostly painted. The stair has a gentle and elegant curve, with pale-yellow carpeting running down the middle of the steps. The ceiling in the hallway extends to the top of the second floor. There are fancy designs in the plaster with several colors of paint accenting the relief work on the ceiling far overhead. A banister with its spindles runs along three sides of the second-floor hall. From above, a person can look down on the central hall below from three different directions.

That would be fun. I wanna look down now!

Instead, we gather in the drawing room where the adults talk. In America, this would be called the living room or great room. Here, it is the sitting room or the drawing room. In a formal house like this, drawing room it is!

As usual, when Susanne is bored stiff, or feels a little uncertain and doesn't want to be noticed, she sits totally still. She appears attractive with her longer Titian red hair coiled up the back of her head in a French braid, a color contrast to her bright blue eyes.

Gone is the old-maid sweater she wore at teatime. Over her skirt and blouse, she has a fitted tan-colored jacket. The shawl collar, pretend belt at the back, and cuffs, which button to close like a man's shirt, are dark brown, the same color as her skirt. With her tall stature, the overall effect of her jacket and skirt is sporty and mature.

She wears gold button earrings with a not-so-small, not-so-thin, gold chain that dangles from under her jacket collar—her birthday present last November. Gone is the old maid who walked down the stairs with me for teatime. Right now, Susanne really seems to be a young-adult woman instead of a kid of fourteen. Wow! Clothes can make the person, especially for a tall girl! The bonus? She is coordinated.

In contrast, my arms and feet still don't feel like they belong. I don't know where I finish and the world begins. I've got to be careful in this lovely home. What might I knock over next? I am self-conscious of my big bent nose, so like Dad's. Without thinking, I pat down my sandy brown cowlick at the back of my head. Sometimes, it resembles a horn, especially when my hat has pushed it straight up. As usual when bored, I fidget.

I still look like a dork, even though my pants are long enough. A fidgety dork.

Phoebe notices my fidgeting and queries, "While you are talking in the time before dinner, should I take the children out to visit the gardens? I notice that the grounds are laid out for winter interest, and that you have some parts illuminated."

"Yes, indeed, Phoebe!" exclaims Nadia with a smile. "That is a wonderful idea. They will be bored silly listening to us. And thank you for noticing all the planning we have put into the garden. Summer flowers speak for themselves. Winter is another story. We have tried hard to have winter interest with box and shrubs. So please, enjoy! But come back in if it's too cold or too dark."

"Let me get you a torch," suggests Oscar. He totters back carrying a flashlight.

So that's a torch!

"Thank you," responds Phoebe as she takes the torch and turns it on. "It's very bright, even in the house."

As an afterthought to Nadia's words, Oscar remarks, "We show parts of the house in summer. The gardens are illuminated for evening hours. The garden lights are on for you, in case you wanted a tour. I turned on the garden lights for you, just in case you wanted a tour. But you will need the torch for safety on the footpaths. I don't want anyone to trip and fall."

We quickly find our coats and hats, put them on, and escape out the front door.

Phoebe comments with admiration, "Look! That cypress tree off to the side of the drive is about forty feet tall and nearly as wide, with a huge wide trunk that commands attention. I suspect the tree is ancient, perhaps a few hundred years old." We follow her gaze. Previously, I have never really thought about the time it takes for trees to grow.

Further along to the side of the house, there are lights shining on a group of tightly trimmed plants. As we walk closer, Phoebe says, "This knot garden is boxwood, which is a type of shrub that has small evergreen leaves. In this knot garden, the boxwood plants are pruned to various heights and widths to form patterns. This garden's

21

central cross, created by a stone path, makes four smaller but equal squares. The green boxwood shrubs create four separate identical knot patterns." She pauses to admire the plantings.

Apparently impressed, Phoebe adds, "This is high maintenance, but incredibly beautiful. I am fond of formal gardens. They require such hard work, but they can be spectacular!" As we walk, Phoebe continues, "This knot garden is unusual. Most have a central tree or planting area for annuals with the boxwood surrounding, which is relatively easy for maintenance. This one has larger rounded boxwood filling the center of each division, but stretching toward the middle to trim must be awkward. I like this plan, but it requires a skilled and agile gardener!"

At home, Dad, Mom, and Phoebe have taken Susanne and me to visit some gardens in America. We live on the fourteenth floor of a building overlooking Central Park in New York City. No gardens there!

But Dad insists we know a broader world than New York City. He says, "Some New Yorkers have a very parochial or narrow-minded view of the world. That is not how I want each of you to be."

We have visited working farms and done garden tours in other cities and towns, all to broaden our horizons. Gardening and farming are just a few of the things we learn about on these trips. And Phoebe clearly loves planting, gardening, and the land, even though we all live in New York City.

Phoebe's intense interest makes both of us stop and listen as she continues, "Like I said, their gardener shows tremendous skill and must put in much hard work to create such a beautiful show."

Behind the house, Phoebe points to an area of raised beds. "Oh, look!" she exclaims. "Here's the cutting garden. In the growing season, this garden has annuals and flowering perennials used for bouquets in the house. Obviously dormant in December, it's interesting to see its large size and layout, but there is not much else to see now, especially since it's mostly dark." Her torch flashes over the raised beds, all flat and empty.

The kitchen garden is next. With our bright flashlight, we see the markers for various herbs that live here in summer, mostly now missing in action or dormant. "The lavender still has its foliage, as does the rosemary. Surprise! This is temperate England," declares Phoebe enthusiastically.

We follow the path that wanders past trees and shrubs. Phoebe murmurs, "These are laid out to please the eye with their shape and, in season, probably with color and fragrance." Phoebe seems momentarily lost in distant memories.

Phoebe quietly adds, "Some of these trees are enormous, many years old. Despite the activities of mankind, the trees continue to grow. This reminder always gives me a sense of continuity and a feeling of security."

I feel it too. Sometimes, things change far too quickly.

Susanne claims, "A garden has an extraordinarily different pace from modern life. Dad says gardening allows almost no immediate gratification, and that our society encourages too much immediate gratification."

"I agree with your wise father."

As we walk along together commenting on trees and speculating about some of the shrubs, we reach a small stream and walk over a little stone bridge that is the same yellow stone as the house.

For a moment, Phoebe seems lost in admiration. Pointing, she suddenly commands, "Look back, children. Admire the beauty. The garden layout up to the house really shows that someone designed everything to be admired from all angles. What an achievement!"

The sun has long gone from the sky. The lights in various rooms make some windows glow. Susanne shivers despite her warm coat. So does Phoebe.

"I am getting cold and ready for inside—and my dinner." Phoebe glances at both of us, smiles contentedly, and asks, "What about you two? Are you getting cold?"

We both nod vigorously. All three of us head toward the house, guided by Phoebe's torch.

Chapter 2

BEFORE DINNER AND AFTERWARD

Despite Britain's temperate climate, we all feel chill by the time we are inside again. After all, the month is December. There is no snow, but the air is chilly enough to use coats and gloves.

As I warm up, I listen to the adult conversation. During their discussion, I realize Oscar is a doctor of medicine who retired with health issues the previous year.

Looking to include us, Nadia queries, "Do you two know that your nana and I work as solicitors in the same firm in London?" Her eyes brighten as she sees that this is news. "More importantly, did you know that we met when we were five?"

Susanne exclaims, "Wow! It must be fun to work together with a good friend from childhood. That's like working with a sister!"

"While there is no blood relationship between us, we are sisters in thought, if not in deed," Nana says while Nadia nods.

Nadia exclaims, "Yes! Better than sisters!" Then Nadia mutters under her breath from the side of her mouth, "Certainly, better than my own." Nana and Papa chuckle.

At another point in the conversation, Oscar states, "The maintenance of this beautiful house is a drain financially. The gardens and some of the downstairs rooms are open to the public in the milder seasons to bring in some additional income. You may have wondered why some of the trees and shrubs have labels attached. That's to educate the public. We have help for cleaning, house and grounds maintenance, and meal preparation some days a week. Nadia is doing a fair amount of the cooking, which she fortunately loves."

Nadia pipes up, "Just as well, I guess. It would be sad if I hated cooking and now had to do it full-time."

Talk comes round to some recent crimes committed in the neighboring villages. Oscar remarks, "Several robberies have occurred with high-end valuables stolen and not recovered."

Nadia adds, "One owner heard someone, raised an alarm, and stopped the robbery, so nothing was taken. But he was assaulted and his arm broken in the tussle. Others lost portable valuables, usually jewelry or small paintings." She looks deep in thought before she laments, "One does feel so vulnerable." Nadia looks around the large house in which she lives before she adds, "We could be robbed and never know anyone was wandering about the house. Even if we struggled and screamed for help, no one would be any the wiser. It is not like past times when the staff lived-in and provided protection." She appears concerned when she says this.

Oscar nods in sad agreement.

Susanne stares at her with wide eyes while the other Americans respond with sympathy. Her comments send a chill down my spine.

What a disturbing fear to have in one's own house!

Nadia glances at her watch as she says, "Well, it is time for me to start preparations for our meal."

Dad, Papa, Nana, and Mom all insist they can help in the kitchen.

Nadia questions, "Men? In the kitchen?" She giggles before she asks in a *deliberately* silly voice, "What will happen next? Votes for women?" Everyone laughs out loud.

Both Dad and Papa remain adamant that they love to cook.

"Phoebe, will you entertain the children?" asks Mom.

"Of course," replies Phoebe. She looks at us sternly before she breaks out laughing as she announces in a Count Dracula voice, "Prepare to be entertained! Did I mention that I have cards for just such an emergency? What do you think we should play?"

After laughing at her silly Count Dracula imitation, we both make several suggestions until we settle on a particularly silly game that always makes us carry on like fools. We commandeer one end of the morning room table and start our game. We hear laughter and fun coming from the kitchen nearby. They can clearly hear our loud nonsense.

There are five good cooks working together. Oscar assumes the role of supervisor, and occasional fetch man to locate items the cooks can't find immediately. He seems to enjoy the tasks, and more importantly, he certainly enjoys the company!

Since it is dark when dinner is served, Nadia wants to use the dining room. It is a large room and farther from the kitchen than the morning room. Mom and Nana both suggest we use the morning room for convenience.

With a sigh, Nadia reluctantly agrees and comments, "It's not like the old days." Her solemn face turns toward Nana, searching for agreement.

When Mom notices Nadia appearing sad, she quickly glances around the morning room before she briskly interjects, "But this room is so comfortable. It's closer to the kitchen; it's lovely and warm; and there is certainly plenty of room!"

Glancing toward her daughter, Nana replies, "Not like new places, which are usually so cut up and small." She sees her friend's persistently serious expression and answers, "The old days have gone, Nadia. We are the last vestiges. But we carry onward."

"I hate to admit it, Iris, but you are correct. And carry on we must." With a wistful smile, Nadia adds, "We are so spoiled. Plenty of room, lovely woodwork, solid construction, all left from another age, an age that is gone." She sighs sadly as she reaches for china that is soon set in place at the table. "Oscar and I use the morning room for most of our meals when we are alone, especially when help is not available."

Mom points out the windows and asks, "The windows face east, don't they?"

"Right you are," replies Oscar brightly. "Morning light usually pours in during breakfast hours." We admire the large windows that stretch up from near the floor almost to the ceiling and follow the large half-round arc of the outside wall.

Mom remarks, "The space made by the window-bow is the size of some Manhattan kitchens."

Oscar laughs. "A Manhattan rent right here? Let me put the morning room on the market immediately!"

Dad declares, "But we have a problem with location: We are too far from midtown." This makes everyone laugh, especially since Dad deliberately exaggerates his Brooklyn accent as he speaks. Susanne looks down, embarrassed at Dad's accent, till she sees me laughing and musters a half smile.

The room itself is remarkably large with a central oval table that could easily accommodate a dozen people. There are a dozen chairs, some pulled up to the table and some waiting patiently against the walls. The chair seats have plain yellow upholstery with a faint pattern, yellow on yellow. There is a sideboard set into an alcove along one wall. A door set into the wall on either side of the alcove hides china cupboards to keep china, glasses, and linens all out of sight. It's a welcoming room.

I feel cozy here.

On the walls, there are a few paintings of people in eighteenth-century attire. One is a family grouping. Another is a man standing beside his trusted horse. Family pictures, I suspect.

The sideboard has a main level for serving food. Nadia has arranged family photos in coordinated frames atop the sideboard's hutch, which makes for a friendly room.

Nadia announces, "We shall be informal today. It's family time. I'm not keen on washing up too many special fancy plates. Besides, Iris, we have known each other so long! You are the sister I never had, the one I should have had instead of the one I do. Is informal all right with you?"

"Of course, it is. Nothing better," Nana replies gleefully. "And Nigel is not here to look askance!" She laughs out loud as she declares, "I love Nigel dearly, but he is always so tidy and precise that sometimes I feel weary. I'd love to put my feet up on the dinner table, if only to see his reaction!" Everyone laughs loudly. She adds with eyes full of mischief, "Maybe while wearing a dress, just for fun!" Everyone laughs even louder.

Mom cries out, "Poor Mommy!"

Papa says, "Nothing of the sort. Poor Nigel! We're just lucky he has stayed over so many years."

"Yes, indeed, I could never manage without him." Nana looks at my sister and clarifies, "To be clear, Susanne, what I said was a joke, not something I'd actually do, granddaughter of mine."

Susanne smiles as she mutters, "Got it, Nana. All talk, no action."

Nana glances toward Papa and murmurs under her breath, "Not for public display, anyway." Discretely, Papa smiles back, eyes suddenly twinkling. Clearing her throat and speaking more loudly, she continues, "Regardless, I am grateful that dear Nigel is still our mainstay."

Nadia looks at Nana like she is saying a secret as she says, "Truth be known, Oscar is my Nigel. I couldn't manage without him either." Oscar smiles broadly as he gazes affectionately at his wife.

The dinner is superb! We have roast beef and Yorkshire pudding with smoothly delicious gravy. There are roasted potatoes with hot buttered peas.

Nadia explains, "The peas were picked from the garden and then frozen."

Dad comments, "They taste beautifully fresh."

Oscar says, "Sam, thanks for the enormous salad you have made. You've done things differently: out with the lettuce and in with the spinach. Then you've added tomatoes, mushrooms, peppers, celery, and carrots. Everything is capped with pine nuts and blue cheese tossed with a balsamic dressing. It's yummy!"

For dessert, Nadia serves a deep strawberry pie she made the day before. She serves the pie warm with vanilla ice cream.

"Is this pie made from your own berries?" queries Nana as she eats with gusto.

"Yes, made from strawberries picked from the garden, cleaned, and then frozen," replies Nadia.

"Delicious!" murmurs Nana like a schoolgirl. Like me, she is happiest with dessert.

Nadia continues, "And I did preserves. This year I did raspberries, strawberries, blueberries, and gooseberries. It is such fun when

I know I don't have to. It would be tedious were it a necessity." She pauses for a moment and then asks, "You like raspberry preserves, don't you, Iris?"

Nana nods emphatically. "Yes, indeed." Then she adds, "And what you said is very true. Things are more fun when there is a choice about doing them."

Susanne and I look toward Nana as she speaks. Her comments make sense. I think about assigned school projects versus ones that allow me a choice of what to do. When I have a choice, I have more fun.

"A choice gives more skin in the game," says Dad.

"Is that an American turn of phrase?" asks Oscar.

"From American football. That funny-shaped leather ball was originally made from animal skin," replies Dad. "It means you are handling the ball and therefore more into the game."

"Interesting how sports metaphors become part of everyday usage," muses Oscar. He looks thoughtful. "A lot of golf phrases have been adopted for common use."

"One phrase, 'Up to par' comes to mind," replies Dad.

"Or 'not up to par' as may be," states Oscar as he waves his hand down his body. They chuckle, and Dad nods his head side to side. He looks uncertain if he should laugh with Oscar.

The adults have a glass of red wine with dinner. Afterward, they have coffee while Papa, Dad, and Oscar also enjoy a glass of port.

Time passes quickly. Everyone helps clear away; and in no time, the dishwasher is loaded, the silver washed by hand, and the leftover food stored. Too soon, much too soon, it is time to leave.

Nana remarks to Nadia, "We shall see each other socially over the holidays. I am taking a few days and won't be in on Monday."

Nadia replies, "I'm taking a week. I will be in the office one day before the New Year. Everything is really on hold anyway. Most judges are away, and the Registry Office is at half-staff." She fusses with her dress pocket, pulls out a jar of preserves, and comments, "Thank heavens I didn't forget. Here are raspberry preserves to enjoy at breakfast tomorrow, Iris."

"Many thanks. We shall put your work to good use, and enjoy," replies Nana with a broad smile as she drops the jar into her handbag. "I know from past experience that this will be lovely."

Papa and Dad say, "Many thanks for the good meal."

We all echo, "It was wonderful!"

Facing Oscar, Nana proclaims, "You, my friend, are hired as *sous chef.*"

Nadia interjects, "Thanks to each of you for your help. I had fun during the meal preparation. Many hands make light work!" Nadia laughs with the others.

We all say our goodbyes and soon resume our positions in the cars. We wave at Oscar and Nadia standing by their front door. They wave in return and watch us until we leave the drive. Looking back, I glimpse them as they turn together to go inside. The house disappears from view as we wend our way home.

Susanne and I both say in unison, "I had a really good time. That game with Phoebe was fun." We laugh because we sound like a chorus.

Dad responds, "We guessed that you liked it. You nearly laughed yourselves silly. Everyone in the kitchen was laughing at you two and your antics."

After a slight pause, Nana adds, "Phoebe is in the other car. Tell her when we get home. Knowing how you feel will make her smile."

Dad continues, "I had a great time in the kitchen. I know you and Papa like to cook, and are quite expert. But Nadia really knows her way around the kitchen! It was a pleasure to work with her." Dad smiles happily as he adds, "And that meal was wonderful. Don't you agree?"

"Absolutely!" comes a chorus of three voices.

During our return drive, we obediently follow behind Papa, whose car also contains Mom and our nanny. Once home, Susanne remembers to tell Phoebe how much fun we had. She smiles broadly, regards us affectionately, and answers, "I did too."

Bed is welcome. I remember Phoebe's good-night kiss on my forehead and not much more.

I sleep deeply until a disturbing dream about Oscar and robbers awakens me with a sweaty start in the middle of the night. "What a stupid dream! There is nothing wrong with Oscar," I mutter. "Some dreams are mighty annoying!" I fall deeply asleep again.

In the morning, the winter sun peeks between the drapes and lays a pattern on the floor and bedclothes. There is real beauty in the colors and patterns of light that are exploding in the brightness. I open the drapes to the winter garden dappled in sunlight; shadows of tree branches in places, pools of light elsewhere. It's a fine December Sunday from the looks of the weather with nary a snowflake in sight.

A glance at the clock shocks me. I mutter impatiently, "You'd best hurry to dress for church."

On the dining room sideboard, Nigel has laid out breakfast in various heated pans that Mom calls chafing dishes. I serve myself eggs, thick crispy bacon, fried tomatoes, and toast, with a glass of milk to complete my feast.

Mom arrives, holding aloft the jar of Nadia's raspberry preserves given to us last night. Pointing, she proclaims, "With permission, I pilfered this delight from Nana's purse. In honor of our benefactress's informality, I am serving as is. Here is a spoon." Container and spoon weave their way back and forth through the air until they land ceremoniously upon the table. While Mom's hands open in a silly gesture of display, she exclaims, "Tada!"

She glances toward Nigel who momentarily appears annoyed. *He* would have put some of the preserves in a shallow jam bowl with a dainty spoon ready to serve small portions. What Mom put on the table literally jars his sensibilities. Poor Nigel is flummoxed but remains silent.

Mom is quietly enjoying herself as a guest, even if she is the daughter of the house. She adores Nigel, whom she has known all of her life. However, she is not above teasing his ideas on formality. She smiles up at Nigel mischievously. He bounces once on his toes. That's his version of a laugh.

When it's my turn, I use the spoon to serve generous helpings of delicious raspberry jam. "Thanks, Nadia, this is really good," I mumble between bites. When my plate is empty, I do repeats on toast and on that jam!

Like previous times sitting beside my sister during services in this church, I look at the plaques of dead ancestors, noting names, titles, and dates. Some are hundreds of years ago! I put names and faces together in my mind. We met some of their phantoms residing in their attic trunks until we cleared Edgar's name during our last visit. I have more interest now in seeing these plaques with the names of people whose ghosts I have met, whose voices I have heard, whose faces I can recall to mind.

But everything's kinda weird in my head.

After the Anglican mass, Nana joins the group Susanne and the family are talking with, makes some comment that causes a good deal of laughter, and then approaches me as I peer at memorial plaques. Along with the rest of the family and household staff, she met most of these ghostly ancestors at the trial.

That's weird too!

We pass the memorial to my murderous eight-greats-grandparents, James and Barbara Wadsworth, known as the Earl and Countess Poppycock. That plaque sends a shiver down my spine!

Nana points to the memorial plaque and asks, "Wasn't it Barbara who pushed you into the time abyss in an attempt to kill you?"

"Yes, it was Barbara. That was so scary! The time abyss was a cold, dark spinning place without time. It was hideous in there, and there is no escape without help!"

Nana adds, "My recollection is that she wanted to cover up her part and her husband's part in a robbery that caused the death of a friend of Great-Uncle Edgar."

I reply, "That friend was Walter Johnson. In cahoots with Barbara, James even allowed his own brother Edgar to hang for a crime he never committed. They knew he was innocent of robbery, innocent of harming his friend Walter! But they both wanted brother Edgar removed as heir presumptive to the title. They deliberately set up Edgar's execution. Awful people!"

Nana stares at their memorial with sadness as she attests, "Evil incarnate. What a waste, in many ways!" She inspects me closely.

Both of us know that these two evil people were also my great-grand-parents, way back. *That part hurts!* I know that Nana is concerned how I may react.

Mom overhears us. Her eyes watch my every move. I suppose she worries about my mood when there are stark reminders of what happened to me on an earlier visit here.

Touching Nana's arm, I point out, "Here is Mortimer and Leila's memorial." My heart skips a beat, and tears well up. "They were my nine-greats-grandparents, the first phantoms I met in the attic at Papa's house. Grandma Leila and I traveled back to 1744 London. It was their son, Edgar, who saved me in 1744 when he pulled me out of the time abyss."

My goodness, that seems an odd thing to think or say! After all, I am eleven, and I live in Manhattan in the twenty-first century, not in old London!

I babble ever onward. "I still remember the kindness and love I received from Mortimer and Leila. They clearly adored each other, which was wonderful to see. In life, Leila was one smart cookie and always learning something new. She could read anyone's mind, which was scary. But I shall never forget her joy in learning, her vitality, and her energy, even as a phantom."

"A good example indeed," replies Nana.

We both glance at the memorial for Humphrey and Cybil. As I point to the memorial, I announce, "Cybil was a selfish sort, and Humphrey was in love with Humphrey." I dismiss their memory with a shrug of my shoulders.

Nana chortles slightly and then states more solemnly, "I remem-ber all their punishments. At the end of the trial, Barbara and James disappeared in a burst of fire. Humphrey and Cybil disappeared in a puff of smoke. All four went to the same destination—not heaven! What selfish people! I'm glad to see you shrug them off your back and out of your mind."

I am quiet afterward. Seeing the names brings back surprisingly vivid memories, good and bad. My stomach signals slight waves of nausea but not enough to throw up. As we walk to the car, I tell Nana how I feel. She replies, "Completely understandable, dear one. You tried to help and were nearly killed. You were only ten." After a pause and a direct look at me, she continues, "We have all worried how the experience might affect you, especially with your other disability, your slight autism. You process too many details, and your memory is pathologically good. Fortunately, you are a resilient soul. We are all grateful for that trait."

As we stand beside the car that will take us back home, she puts her arm over my shoulder and brings me to her side in a sort of mini hug. Nana's love radiates to me. I love her, and Papa too. When she sees me glancing up at her moist eyes, she pulls me tight to her again. *I love that!*

In the car, I catch Susanne's eye. We are close. She knows me well, and she knows everything that happened. She may not be feeling so hot, either. Later, I must remember to ask her how she is feeling, but not now.

The rest of the day passes with a good sandwich lunch and a lovely dessert. Like Susanne, I treat myself to lemonade. Our board games and card games make everyone laugh a great deal. Too soon, it is time for a light supper and then bed.

I feel good as Susanne and I head to our rooms. As we prepare for bed, Phoebe flutters around us and asks, "Did the plaques in church bring back memories from our last visit and bother either of you today?"

We both say, "We weren't bothered."

Phoebe patters on with purpose. "I remember Jeremiah unconscious for days here in a hospital in the English countryside. But we adults knew nothing, unaware that he was unconscious all because his mind was busy visiting London in 1744. Each of us met the same ancestors that you two met. Simply meeting them and learning some of what you experienced terrified me!" She pauses to let us decide to say something, but we both remain silent. Finally, Phoebe asks again, more firmly this time, "Did the memorials bring back too many memories?"

"It's all okay," we both say but not very convincingly. Phoebe waits patiently.

Susanne finally murmurs, "The memories are vivid. I don't like them. But I know it's all over, and we are safe. It's time to move on, even when there are reminders."

My unasked questions to Susanne have been answered!

As Phoebe focuses on me, I admit, "The memorial plaques make me remember my attempted murder by an ancestor, which still flips my stomach. But like Susanne said, 'It's over now. It's time to move on.'" We three sit quietly together for a few minutes. Eventually, Susanne stands, leans over to give a big long hug to each of us, and heads into the bathroom, waving good night behind her. Phoebe and I sit in silence until the bathroom is clear, and then I head off to do nightly rituals. Phoebe seems reassured by our replies.

When I'm ready, I climb into bed. After giving me a kiss on my forehead, Phoebe flips off the light and goes through the bathroom to check on Susanne in her room. I know she worries that the plaques may bother Susanne too.

Susanne didn't time travel with me, but she was my partner. During my travels, Clive, valet to our nine-greats-grandfather Mortimer, reported updates to Susanne from 1744 London. Time travel multiple times from eighteenth-century London to Papa's house in twenty-first-century rural Britain must have exhausted his poor ghost.

Slowly, my mind empties of all thoughts.

I want peace. I want safety. I want quiet time with my dearly loved family.

Sleep overtakes me quickly and deeply, no dreams.

Chapter 3

NEARING CHRISTMAS

Christmas is three days away, and I think my gifts for everyone are organized. Are they? I am clueless. Anyway, during an earlier family conference, we decided to go to London today for some shopping, and an overnight at Papa and Nana's London place. We each have an overnight case, most with wheels. But Nana and Papa don't have luggage. They each carry a small satchel that looks like a large purse since everything they need is at their London flat.

Flat is British for *apartment*. In London, you have a flat. In New York, you have an apartment. *Same difference!*

The wind is cold and brisk as we head out to the station. I am grateful for my heavy coat and gloves. Mr. Brown drives our grans' little bus, which fits everyone comfortably for our trip to the train station. On the train ride, Papa buys sandwiches and hot chocolate. Yummy.

This is the first time after arrival at Paddington Station that we don't take pictures beside the statue of Paddington Bear.

I sadly think to myself, *Bye-bye Mr. Paddington, but it's okay. We took photos a few days ago.*

But we are older now, and the adults are too goal-focused on holiday presents to think about a trip down memory lane. Maybe photos with Paddington make the best holiday memory presents!

Once in the London Station, Nana makes a call. She has arranged for someone from her office to collect our overnight bags and drop everything at Papa and Nana's flat. That person must have been nearby, for soon a gentleman appears and asks, "Is everything here, Lady Poppycock?"

As he loads everything onto a luggage cart that he will eventually drag behind him, Nana replies, "I think that's all, Jim."

"Very good," he replies cordially. "After I drive to your location, I shall stack everything inside the entrance to the flat. Is that satisfactory?"

"Excellent," replies Nana.

"And here is something for your trouble. Merry Christmas, Jim!" exclaims Papa.

Pocketing the envelope, Jim replies, "Thank you, m'lord." He glances toward Nana and adds, "And the key to the flat will be back at the office, usual place." Nana nods in agreement. Moments later, Jim disappears with our possessions on a cart.

Susanne says, "This pickup service is wonderful. Otherwise, what a nuisance to drag luggage everywhere! But, Nana, you spoil us!" Making a gesture of counting money, she adds, "And thank you, Papa."

I ask, "And everything will be waiting for us in the London apartment ... er ... flat?"

"Right you are," says Papa.

We go to various shops that Nana knows and various department stores. Each of us is stressed about getting everything right for the holidays, even though none of us needs anything. Finally, Dad suggests that he take Susanne and me to the Silver Vaults.

Phoebe says, "I want to come too. I made a good purchase last visit that helped clear the name of Great-Uncle Edgar. Maybe I'll find an encore accomplishment!"

Eventually, the four of us head off to the Silver Vaults. With the others, we agree to meet much later to have dinner. Papa gives us a note with the address of the restaurant and the time to meet.

The London subway, called the Tube, is clean and fast. I like it better than the New York subway. One fun and easy subway ride gets us to the Silver Vaults.

Phoebe leads the way. We look at many of the beautiful and expensive objects on display. I am drawn to one item, an inkstand with a difference. The silver of the tray gleams entrancingly with a horizontal groove where a long pen might lie, but there is no pen. A glass box with an attached silver lid gleams at one end of the tray. At the opposite end is another identical glass box and lid. Both lids easily flip open, and both are engraved with the same intricate pattern that is repeated in the middle of the inkstand.

The proprietor tells me, "The inkwell is to the right, and the sandwell is to the left, for the right-handed writer."

Confused, I ask, "What do you mean?"

He explains, "The inkwell is more easily reached from the right-hand side if the writer is right-handed. The writer then poured sand on the page to dry the ink quickly. Afterward, the writer blew away the sand or dumped it back into the sandwell."

Glancing at the engraved initials and the date, I do a double take. I don't know why. The initials are M. W. J. and the date is 1732. We don't have relatives with the final initial of *J* that I know about. The date fascinates me, especially since everything is in such superb condition. What a shame that the pen has been lost. Then I realize why.

I ask, "Was the pen a quill, made from a bird's feather, whittled sharp?"

The proprietor confirms, "The quill has been lost. Organic materials like that deteriorate with time. What a pity!" He looks at me quizzically over rimless glasses with gold-colored shafts. "You are clever to realize that."

"I think Dad told me," I lie, trying to deflect attention.

Why is this tray-and-inkwell combo so interesting to me? It is not something I want to buy for myself. I cannot think of anyone who would want it as a gift. But I keep returning to it over and over. Phoebe watches me.

Dad finds something to buy for Nana as a surprise. Phoebe, Susanne, and I watch the purchase, but we don't buy anything. When I glance at the gift Dad has purchased, it looks familiar, but why should it be? Anyhow, these fancy things often all look the same to me. Susanne looks bored.

As directed, we eventually meet for an early dinner. The headwaiter greets Papa and Nana warmly since they are known regulars. We have an alcove all to ourselves.

The adults celebrate the day with a bottle of wine that Dad and Papa select together. The menu has an almost endless variety of delicious-sounding food.

Wanting to try something new, I ask Dad, "What is escargot?"

"Snails: are you going to try them?"

"I'm not sure. The thought of eating snails seems a little weird. What if I don't like them?"

"They won't be wasted," he answers with a laugh, both thumbs pointing to himself.

"All right then, I shall try them," I courageously declare.

The escargot is served with blue cheese in warm liquid butter. With fresh-from-the-oven bread to dip in the cheesy butter, I am happy, *exceedingly* happy.

As he sees me contently eating, Dad asks, "May I have a taste of one?"

I bargain, "Exchange for some calamari?"

"Done," Dad says as he pushes his dish in my direction so that I may have some of his squid.

After chewing, I observe, "Somewhat rubbery, but the taste is delicious."

"And your escargot is superb," he replies, "especially with that blue cheese added to the butter. Isn't it fun to share?"

"I love to try new foods," I reply, "and sharing makes that easy."

My veal is thicker than the usual served in the States and very tender. Susanne has a fish dish with a beautiful white cream sauce. Mom and Dad share a Chateaubriand, which is a beef loin, served medium rare at their request. Nana has scallops and Papa has a broiled fish that looks mighty good. After comments about how good the food is, silence descends onto the table as each of us digs in happily to our meal. When most of the food disappears, our happy tummies allow conversation about the day's activities, but the purchases are kept secret so that a Christmas surprise will not be spoiled.

The restaurant is crowded. Patrons at other tables contribute to the noise in their exuberant excitement for the holidays. Glancing around, Mom ponders out loud, "I wonder how many people in this crowd are stressed but must put on a show of cheerful holiday spirit when they would rather rest quietly at home."

Nana replies, "There is so much preparation that I worry if the message of Christmas is lost in the hectic activity of the season."

Mom agrees with Nana as she says, "Christmas is now too commercial."

When it is dessert time, everyone decides on a sweet from the menu's list. Nana, Dad, and I have *crème brûlée.* Susanne has blueberry pie. This is predictable. It's her favorite, and she is not adventuresome with food. Mom has tiramisu, which is a cake with coffee-flavored custard and mascarpone cheese with cocoa and ladyfinger cookies. Papa and Phoebe have carrot cake. All the adults have coffee.

Dad remarks, "This special meal should end with a glass of port."

Papa responds, "I shall join you. Anyone else?"

We hear "no thanks" and see a few negative nods.

Dad pays the bill this time. We get into two cabs and head back to Nana and Papa's London place.

I am in the same cab as Nana, Susanne, and Phoebe. Turning toward us from her front-seat position, Nana points out things of interest that we pass. She comments, "A skyscraper now stands on the site that once was the palatial family estate of the Earl Poppycock from 1750 onwards. It was owned by other members of the family before that." As an afterthought, she adds, "The residence was sold in the 1930s." She omits that in 1744, I overheard the schemes of my horrible eight-greats-grandparents in their home, that now lost building.

Moments later, Nana waves her hand and points as she continues, "Here we also pass the site where Mortimer and Leila once lived. The once large beautiful home was getting run-down but was finally destroyed in the London Blitz during the Second World War."

I see tall office buildings soaring forever skyward on the site where I visited with my nine-greats-grandparents on my time trip back to 1744 London. *Imagine!*

While we are in a cab, no one mentions my trip back in time, but I know Nana is thinking about my experience. She still worries if my near-death experience may cause ongoing anxiety or harm.

"We live much more simply in London now," says Nana.

We arrive at their apartment. It was once a large Victorian home but is now subdivided into owner-occupied flats or British apartments.

They are on the first floor. Americans would say the second floor since it is one flight or elevator ride up. The British ground floor is what Americans would call the first floor.

More confusion in language!

Susanne and I insist on taking the open cage elevator up to the first floor. What fun!

Nana and Papa may be living more simply than in the distant past, but they still have a spacious flat. There is an open living and dining area, with a fireplace in the living room. The dining room can seat a dozen people easily without feeling crowded. There are four bedrooms, two with their own bath and two that share a bathroom. Papa and Nana share a large study with two home office desks, and a pullout sofa bed for extra guests. This is my room tonight. It has its own two-piece bath, but I will share my parents' shower since Susanne and Phoebe are already sharing a bathroom, and they are girls.

As she looks around, Mom says, "I haven't been here for a very long time. The woodwork looks like it is original to the Victorian era. In contrast to the country house filled with antiques, this place has streamlined, modern furniture. This works well in contrast with the old woodwork."

Nana replies, "I am glad you like our choice. I wanted a little change of pace from our other rather more historic dwelling."

Mom continues, "Some of the paintings are modern and abstract, some are realistic, and some are very old. It's an odd mix, but it all works." As she looks around approvingly, Mom asks, "Nana, did you make most of the choices for decoration?"

"Yes, indeed I did, with Papa's approval," she replies.

Papa quietly comments, "I agreed to everything Iris suggested. She's in her own league in these matters."

Mom observes, "Nana, you have a really good eye."

Even Dad, who often doesn't notice, pays attention to his surroundings. Susanne is busy looking at some of the paintings.

Phoebe murmurs, "Yes, indeed, all beautifully done." She looks content as she gazes around her and quietly moves from painting to painting.

Nana flushes with pleasure.

In a little while, Phoebe insists Susanne and I get ready for bed sooner rather than later. We say good night to all. Once in bed, I feel Phoebe's good-night kiss on my forehead, something I have had every night of my life. I hear Nana and Papa say good night as they retire early to bed. Mom and Dad talk for a while, but I cannot hear the words. I drift off to sleep. *What will tomorrow bring?*

Chapter 4

ANOTHER BREAK-
IN AND A DINNER

It is easy to tell that it is holiday time. Gone are the usually regimented mornings we have when school is in session. We sleep in later than usual and, still in pajamas, straggle out for breakfast. Dad does try to get some order into the seven of us. Once everyone surfaces, he begins to cook bacon and eggs with toast. The smell of coffee brewing makes me very hungry. I don't drink coffee, but the aroma is wonderful.

Mom says, "If coffee tasted as good as it smells, it would be a superb beverage. Unfortunately, it doesn't." The adults all agree.

Nana always calls their apartment a pied-à-terre. I looked that up. The definition of *pied-à-terre* is a small living unit away from the primary residence. Their place is not a small living unit. It's a large living unit. Really, Nana is just trying to be funny. It's a big apartment ... okay, flat.

After breakfast and dressing, we all pack our things, tidy up, and leave everything shipshape at Papa and Nana's London pied-à-terre.

Papa states, "The underground subway is clean, safe, and very convenient. On the other hand, getting a cab can be daunting, difficult, and time-consuming, especially for seven of us, more than one cab's worth! The Tube is the way to go." We head to the train station by way of the London Tube, bags and all. Along the way, we stop for a few items Nana didn't get yesterday. Nana is very efficient when she knows what she needs to buy. We don't lose much time.

After an uneventful ride in the Tube, we soon arrive at Paddington Station. This time, Susanne acts goofy and asks for a photo by Paddington Bear. She even does her silly child impersonation as she exclaims, "Oh Daddy! May I please, please, please have a photo with Mr. Paddington Bear?"

Dad laughs at her foolishness and agrees. Soon we have shots of just Susanne and me beside the bear and some including Dad and Mom. We are just about to switch out parents for grandparents when a passing gentleman asks if we would like a photo of the whole family together.

Laughing, Papa hands him his smart phone and gives him a few instructions.

He takes two or three shots of the whole group, and then states, "You should have one good picture there. All the best of the season."

Smiling, he hands Papa back his smartphone, then disappears so quickly into the crowd of travelers that I am not sure he heard Papa say, "Thank you. Merry Christmas!"

We are so lucky! Someone always helps us out at photo time. Looking at Papa's phone, we see photos of all seven of us by Paddington Bear. What fun! I love the Paddington Bear stories and remember most of them. Thinking about them makes me feel good inside.

After Papa gets the train tickets, our dragging luggage wheels click behind us as we find our platform and board. Besides Papa's and Nana's small handheld satchels, they also now have parcels like the rest of us. We look like packhorses! Nana comments to Mom that she is returning only dirty clothes to the country so the laundry can be done there. There must be a lot of planning and forethought that goes into living in two places. Certain things are easy to have at each place, but remembering which clothes are where could be a challenge!

Soon after we board, the train starts to move. I hear the *click-clack* of the wheels as we start to roll and feel the rocking motion as we gain speed. In short order, we are moving through the English countryside with green fields surrounded by stone walls used as fences. The sight of sheep in the meadows makes me feel relaxed and content.

Papa is seated beside me. As usual, I smell the faint odor of country on his tweed jacket, which makes me feel safe and secure. I close my eyes and drift off to sleep with the motion of the train. My head falls against his arm.

Heaven!

I startle awake when Nana begins talking, clearly upset. Papa sits up straighter as he listens. He ignores my flopping sideways as his arm moves away.

Nana recites, "This text from Nadia reads, 'There was an attempted robbery last night. Oscar heard sounds and investigated. He fell in a tussle with the thieves and broke his left wrist, which had to be set by his doctor. Nothing was stolen because of Oscar's actions.' Oh dear, poor Oscar, poor Nadia!"

I remember Nadia's comments when we were there for dinner.

Nana's words echo my thoughts as she continues, "Nadia said she felt at risk in a large home with no staff. They have a security system, but there is no one nearby. This attempted robbery has made all her fears very real." Nana looks around at each of us before she continues, "I am worried. How will this episode affect Nadia and Oscar, especially with his injury? He has had medical issues and may have difficulty bouncing back from an assault." We all listen again as Nana reads the text out loud a second time, and adds, "How scared both Oscar and Nadia must feel! They are powerless against something they cannot control." Again, Nana looks lost in thought for a moment.

She resumes, "I shall call them after we arrive home. John, do you think Oscar and Nadia should come to stay with us for the holidays or until the thieves are caught?"

Papa replies, "Let's do whatever is needed for our friends." He nods in Nana's direction as he speaks. "They are good companions. I shouldn't mind a few weeks with them."

The adults talk on and on about what to do or what to offer, but no firm decision is reached. Nana eventually remarks, "I suppose it will all depend on how Nadia feels." Almost as an afterthought, she adds, "And Oscar's feelings on the subject are equally important."

Papa answers, "Let's see what they want. Let them decide."

Anxiety and worry creep into our cheery gathering. Ignoring our feelings, the train rolls merrily along through green fields and pastures, past the M1, past villages and towns.

Clouds gather in the sky. The winter sun patterns bright light here and there, contrasting to large areas covered in cloudy dark shadow. Suddenly, three enormous shafts of light appear between dark clouds flooding widening bars of light onto the fields below.

"Look!" exclaims Phoebe, pointing to the window. "Was this view painted by an artist? Utterly beautiful!" Everyone peers out through the rail-carriage glass at this marvel. Like my grandparents, I love this island called Britain!

Mr. Brown, the estate manager, greets us at the station. He has driven his little bus, which left Papa's garage to deliver us to the station yesterday. We load all our bags, clamber in, and buckle up to head home. We pass a few villages with narrow streets. I comment, "Houses are built so close to the road that doors open almost into the roadway." No one replies. The adults are too preoccupied. As his response, Mr. Brown nods to the rearview mirror and watches till I nod in reply.

Roads narrow further. Hedgerows line each side, leaving no place to pull over. Once, we were forced to pull into a laneway, which allowed a small oncoming truck to travel in the opposite direction. After the vehicle was safely past, we resumed our journey.

Talk about narrow roads!

Eventually, we turn between hedgerows and go up the long lane to Papa and Nana's home. Nigel is quickly at the door. As a good butler, he opens the bus doors and helps Nana and Papa descend. He asks about the trip. After his initial greeting, he states, "Lady Fullerton called to say she texted you. She requests you call her when you return."

Nana asks, "Nigel, when Nadia, Lady Fullerton, called, did she say what happened?"

Nigel replies, "She mentioned there was an attempted robbery. She said Lord Fullerton has an injury, but it's not serious. He has a fractured left wrist, now evaluated, treated, and 'casted.' She gave me the details because she wants us all to be on guard." He adds, "This is the fifth break-in and the second injury, all within a forty-mile radius. All involve larger homes and most with older owners." Nigel stops for a moment to pick up two parcels. He continues, "I have paid close attention to the news reporting and the local papers. A pattern is emerging."

Nana replies, "She told me the same in her text. Stupidly, I was too upset to answer her directly, which means she doesn't know her text was received. She was worried from the other robberies, and now her home has been targeted. I don't like this!"

I help Mr. Brown and Nigel take our luggage, the small parcels, and Papa's and Nana's overnight cases. Afterward, Mr. Brown returns the empty vehicle to the garage.

Soon after we arrive, but after a cup of tea, Nana calls Nadia. She wants Papa to hear so she puts her phone on speaker. As they talk, she offers, "Nadia, why don't you and Oscar stay with us until this thief is caught? It might make both of you, and me, feel more secure."

Nadia replies, "I am grateful, but we both think it best to remain here. A failed attempt means that a repeat try is not likely."

Papa says, "We would both be delighted to host you. You know that."

We hear Oscar's voice on the line. "It's a minor break without other injuries—only needed a cast. The house is safe since the thieves failed once." After a momentary pause, he continues, "Much better to stay here. They won't try again. I am armed with a cast!" He laughs out loud at his silly joke.

I stay near Nana to overhear as she chats. Papa takes the line, but their friends are still determined to stay alone. Nana and Papa are quiet for a few moments afterward, worriedly staring down at the idle phone.

Don't expect the phone to do a little soft shoe dance.

After his eyes finally lift to us, Papa states, "Oscar looks frail at the best of times. He now has his left arm in a cast and sling."

"All of this is too worrisome," adds Nana as she looks at Mom. "I hope they are making the right decision."

I doubly hope that Oscar and Nadia made the right choice.

They are friends of my grandparents. I don't know them well, but they seem to be kind people. They don't deserve this stress.

Looking toward the Americans, Nana ruminates, "Oscar has worked hard as a doctor all his life. And his hard work may have cost him his health. Nadia is one of the best lawyers in our firm. She has a moral backbone, something that is not true of all solicitors. Her competence and integrity are some of the reasons we have remained friends since childhood." After a pause, Nana utters in a worried voice, "They are our best friends. A failed break-in and a fracture. Regrettable! Frankly, the robbery at their house frightens me a little. We are equally at risk." Nana stops, lost in thought, her eyes scanning randomly during the ensuing silence.

After a few moments of quiet to gather her thoughts, Nana continues, "Admittedly, Nigel lives in-house, but he is older. Mr. Brown lives-in, but is frequently away. Altogether, we are seven—two are older and two are children. There is no team of people around for protection. I don't count Mrs. Stewart for anything except cooking. She doesn't live-in and is absent on Sundays. Her glasses are either so steamed up from her cooking or so smeared with grease, I wonder if she could tell a robber from a groundskeeper if we had one! And she cannot hear. Without knowing, she might give the thief a glass of milk and send him on his way! She is a great cook but would be a failure as a security guard."

We Americans laugh a little at Nana's rambling speech.

Papa disputes confidently, "Iris, while I agree with you about risk, it's most unlikely that anything untoward will happen." Papa smiles, hoping to calmly reassure his wife.

Later, my thoughts would say, *Wrong, Papa, so very wrong!*

Still distracted with the news about Oscar, Nana finds Mrs. Stewart and struggles to discuss preparations for the evening meal. Wow, Nana can really project her voice! Several rooms away, we all hear her say, "Ian and his wife are coming with the two boys and so is Brian. I shall have all my children present and all my grandchildren. And Brian is bringing a friend, so count him as two. I don't know her name yet. They will be here by six or so this evening. Did you get my earlier texts?"

We lose Nana's loud voice as they discuss the texts and the menu Mrs. Stewart had laid out. Mrs. Stewart understands everything when she reads. In the relative quiet, we all suspect Nana is now pointing at her own various texts and her cook's hand-written menu.

As his wife communicates with their cook, Papa smiles lamely at us and then shrugs his shoulders. Gazing at Susanne and me, he reassuringly comments, "I suspect we are perfectly safe here, despite Nana's concerns." As his eyes flit to Phoebe and my parents, he murmurs, "I see no reason to worry. We won't be burgled."

To change the topic, Dad clears his throat and then tells Susanne and me, "There are several reasons for tonight's dinner. One reason is that Brian has a new girlfriend, and he wants the family to meet her. I'll also mention that she will be with us for Christmas. When he called Nana to ask if he could bring his friend, Brian said, 'I want to break the ice before the holidays.' This might be serious, again."

With an edge to her voice, Mom asserts, "*Again* is the key word. Like we've discussed before, as a child Brian always tried to keep up with Ian and me. But being five years junior to me, it was a struggle for him to keep our pace when he was little. Brian was never an easy child and often in trouble. Unfortunately, he seems to drift with no real calling, never really finding himself despite several jobs. And he has been divorced twice, no children."

She has said this consistently about her brother multiple times. That means she means it. She continues, "Maybe this girl will be a turning point for him. The first two wives never cut the mustard in my opinion. The first one was far too selfish and the second was such a ditz!"

Nana returns from the kitchen in time to hear Mom. She chides, "Constance, that's a little harsh."

Mom replies, "Well, I happen to know that both you and Papa agree with me."

Laughing, Nana agrees, "Oh, yes, you are exactly right. I remarked only that your comments were a little harsh." She laughs out loud and then giggles. "Harsh but true. Truth sometimes has sharp edges. But I do hope you are right about this girl. I would *so* like to see Brain happily settled. He's the right age to settle down. It's time to stop playing the field." She glances toward her grandchildren after speaking. Her facial expression asks, *Did I say too much?*

Their comments make me feel a little sad for Uncle Brian. If I remember to ask, Susanne will tell me later which field game Uncle Brian plays. Cricket most likely. *Autistic me hates missing connections!*

I think about Nana's guest list. Uncle Ian is Mom's other brother, her elder by two years. Mom explained to Susanne and me a while ago that he would inherit the title, the house, and most of the money when Papa dies.

She also said, "After Papa dies, Ian will become the Earl Poppycock. Evelyn will become Countess Poppycock since Papa is the Earl, and Nana is the Countess Poppycock right now. If she is still alive, Nana will become the Dowager Countess Poppycock and will still be known as Lady Poppycock."

I really understand completely why Nana is Iris Wadsworth at work! Can you imagine your lawyer having the name Poppycock? Oh my! The merciless laughter would chase you out of court.

What did Dad call Uncle Ian and Aunt Evelyn? Oh yeah, I remember—stuffed shirts. He called them stuffed shirts. He also calls them waiters—a nasty name, really. He calls them waiters because they are waiting to inherit!

You wouldn't catch me waiting for *that* title. Avoid at all costs! Understandably, Papa rarely uses his full name with its title. *Silly name!*

Suddenly, a distant and foggy recollection comes back to me. Five-Greats-Grandmother Beatrice said, "I never thought Ian made the best choice with Evelyn as a wife." But Beatrice gave me no details about my aunt. She only enlarged upon her worries about Brian. Anyway, the details from that conversation are hard to remember, coming so soon after Great-Uncle Edgar saved me from the time abyss in 1744 and landed in a carriage with me in 1839. That whole experience left me a little fuzzy-headed!

After all, 1839 was a while ago, and time travel takes it out of you!

I snap back from my recollections when I hear Dad say, "Now, children, you may recall what I've said before about our relatives. Ian works in the financial management business sort of like me, but I have real trouble talking to him about work. He makes it seem low class to talk about money, even though money management is his occupation!"

With rolling eyes and a wry smile, Mom adds, "One of the *many wonders* of being Ian!"

Dad continues hurriedly, "If I avoid the topic of money, you will know why." He looks at us keenly. We both nod that we understand. "I'm just hoping conversation won't be uphill as I avoid a lot of topics that interest me and which Ian and I should be able to discuss since we both work in the investment field."

Mom stifles a laugh, pauses in thought, and then continues, "Evelyn completed a fine arts degree. She knows lots about art history and can tell if a painting is real or a forgery. But she has only dabbled with work and now stays at home with their two boys."

Susanne replies, "That's odd. Both boys are in boarding school and therefore are never home, except on holidays. What does Evelyn do with her time? What does she find to talk about?"

In response, Mom shrugs her shoulders as she answers, "I don't know, on both counts. I'm not one to judge since their system must work for them. But I never thought Ian made the best choice with Evelyn as a wife." More quietly, she mutters, "But I do worry about Brian."

My goodness, that sounded a lot like Great-Granny Beatrice in 1839!

Mom glances toward her parents as she speaks. Both are silent— no protests, no contradictions.

Now I know what they truly think as well.

We Americans have met the cousins a few times before, on both sides of the Atlantic. Susanne and I together have talked about them before, not always kindly. We both know what to expect. That's why neither of us is thrilled to see them tonight.

Collin, aged fifteen, is a year older than Susanne. Dexter is thirteen. They look remarkably alike; blond with fair skin and blue eyes, skinny and tall like the rest of us. They like to play tricks that are sometimes mean and nasty.

Susanne remarks sourly, "I hope Collin and Dexter behave better than the last time we saw them. I don't like it when they are nasty."

Dad responds, "That behavior was just a stage they were going through. Everything will be fine tonight."

When Dad says this, I reply, "I don't like it when they are mean, and they usually are. I don't like being around them. They've been in this stage way too long. Can't they get over it? They are okay around Susanne, probably because she is a girl. I don't think either of them especially likes me, and it shows. I don't like their *attitude*. I don't dislike *them*. I just don't want them near."

Susanne pipes up, "I don't think they are any nicer to me than they are to you, Jeremiah. Dad, you're a kind man but a totally foolish optimist. Their behavior is no phase, and I'll bet it won't be all fine tonight. They are snobs and just plain mean. I don't like that." Five adults and two children fall silent. With a faintly red face, Dad looks at his daughter with a combination of admiration and wonder, maybe mixed with fear. His face silently asks, *What sort of independent-minded being have I spawned?* No words come out.

Papa notices we are solemn, fussed about our dinner guests and worried about Oscar, Nadia, and the break-ins. He and Nana exchange a quick glance. Wisely, he decides to change the subject off our cousins.

He casually remarks, "The sun's rays are still high in the sky, but within hours, there will be lengthening shadows in the mid-afternoon followed swiftly by darkness." He pauses while we peer outside through the windows. He explains, "Since the earth is tilted on its axis as it spins, and England is far north in the Northern Hemisphere, the winter solstice on December 21st means the shortest day and the longest night for the entire year—the day of least possible sun for Britain."

We've already heard this from Dad. Boring!

Papa drones on, "It also means that the night is much longer than in New York, which is far closer to the equator than Britain. It will be dark around four o'clock. That's long before the six o'clock arrivals are expected."

Nana impatiently glances at her watch and interjects, "John, I really must head over to the church."

After a nod to his wife, Papa faces us and adds, "Many people have been assisting with the decorations. Nana is scheduled to help as well."

She replies absentmindedly, "I like to contribute but seem to do little enough as it is. The Christmas Eve service is a high point of the church year, much like Easter." Nana puts on her coat, checks that she has her purse and keys, waves goodbye, and heads out the door. She is soon followed by Papa, who has some estate business to do with Mr. Brown.

Mrs. Stewart, a wonderful cook, usually never wants anyone in her kitchen. When Mom asks about helping with her preparations, she loudly replies, "I'm glad of the help." That means she wants to finish up and go home early today! Mom and Dad spend the rest of the afternoon helping her prepare for the evening meal.

Phoebe tries a board game with Susanne and me. Susanne actually fidgets during the game, keeps looking at her watch, and sighs frequently. Phoebe finally comments, "Susanne, you look like your mind is elsewhere. And, Jeremiah, you aren't paying any attention to the game. Do you both want to stop play?"

Susanne replies, "My mind is anywhere but here. I'm sort of worried about Oscar and Nadia. Besides, I'm not keen about being with the cousins."

Looking directly at Phoebe with a sense of relief, I admit, "I am repeatedly losing track of what I'm supposed to be doing. The silliness of this board game somehow doesn't do it for me."

Susanne pipes up, "It doesn't do it for me, either. May I run away? I really don't want to see the cousins."

Phoebe laughs and replies, "No, you may not run away. And, yes, you must have dinner with your cousins. But we can stop playing." She begins to gather up the game.

When he returns from meeting Mr. Brown, Papa states, "We are dressing for dinner."

Sounding surprised, Dad responds, "I hope you don't mean black tie. My tuxedo is in the States."

Papa laughs. "No, just a sport coat and tie." As he turns away, Papa mutters under his breath, "We are dressing up for the heir apparent." Then he looks back sheepishly, hoping no one heard.

Tactfully, Dad pretends he didn't hear. I say nothing. Papa looks satisfied and moves along to the stairs.

When we get together later, all the ladies have on becoming dresses. All the men have a sport coat, dress shirt, and a tie over dress pants. I was warned again, so I'm wearing dress shoes instead of sneakers. My thoughts ask, *What difference does all the fuss make? Even dressed up, I still look goofy!*

Susanne is wearing her tan jacket, brown skirt, and low-heeled brown pumps, exactly as she did the other day. Once again, she looks mature with her hair pulled up in a French braid and knot, complemented by her lovely gold necklace and gold-button earrings—overall, pretty indeed.

At six o'clock sharp, we hear a car on the gravel drive. Four car doors slam before the front door can be opened. At the door, Nigel greets Uncle Ian and Aunt Evelyn, known by the honorary title of Lord and Lady Poppycock. They are given this name because they are in line to inherit. Collin's honorary title is Master Poppycock. Dexter is not known as anything except Dexter because he is not in line for anything. He hates not having an honorary title and no prospects!

That whole business is rather silly! I can't imagine boarding school at age fifteen for Master Poppycock! Find me a new home! Find me a new life! Find me a new name!

Papa and Nana greet everyone warmly. Collin and Dexter allow Nana and Mom to give them a kiss and a hug. Both move away quickly afterward. Seeing this, Papa and Dad simply do a handshake with each. Phoebe, Susanne, and I say hello and wave.

After bestowing their greetings, each boy, like Uncle Ian, straightens his school tie and adjusts his navy blazer. Earlier, Mom told us that our uncle was from the same school as his sons. With all three in their grey flannels and identical jackets, they could be on a school outing, master and students.

Mom gives her brother and sister-in-law a kiss and a hug. Uncle Ian acts normally and responds. Aunt Evelyn is tense and uncomfortable. She breaks away quickly. She does the same with Nana.

Aunt Evelyn's sandy blond hair is pulled back tight in a bun. Her face is long and a little full with a nose that is rather sharp and pointy over a thin slit of a mouth. Her lavender-colored full-cut dress reaches midcalf, with long sleeves and a high collar, and without any defined waist. She wears black shoes with low heels. Altogether, she has the appearance of a rather rigid and conservative matron, attempting to cover the fact that she is quite overweight.

Both Dad and Papa do give Aunt Evelyn a hug and a kiss. Her body stiffens, and she arches taller each time, which makes the hem of her dress ascend over and over. This looks really funny!

This cold behavior from Evelyn and the boys is such a contrast to the open and loving way my family always behaves. If the difference comes from being American, then good job, Brooklyn and Manhattan! Actually, I think the fault lies with Uncle Ian and especially Aunt Evelyn. Papa and Nana act the same as Mom and Dad, warm and open. Everyone is from the same family. Why don't they behave the same way? Did something happen to each one, something that no one discusses? Why is Aunt Evelyn so distant?

I remember that Uncle Brian wanted to break the ice for his friend before the holidays. When I look at Aunt Evelyn, I want to say, "Good luck with that, Uncle Brian! May I introduce Auntie Ice Cube?"

The adults start conversations about the weather and the holidays. Everyone is coming for Christmas dinner here, so they discuss the time of arrival. And everyone plans to meet at the church tomorrow for the Christmas Eve midnight mass. This will be at the local Anglican parish church. It is called Midnight Mass even though it starts at 9:45 p.m.! They discuss that there is no snow forecast, but there may be rain. Temperatures are forecast to be barely above freezing, which is colder than usual.

We hear another car on the gravel. Mom beats Nigel to the door. For a moment, he looks annoyed, then smiles at Mom's enthusiasm. "Please, proceed, Lady Constance," he comments, adding a gently welcoming hand gesture as he opens the door for her. Mom peers outside.

Calling Mom lady anything seems odd. No one stateside knows to call her by that name. But that is her British handle.

Papa and I join Mom and Nigel at the door. Dad is only part-way into the hall, standing beside Nana, all of us waiting to greet Brian's new friend. Mom watches keenly. Aided by the bright outside lights, Brian descends from the car and assists a young woman from the passenger side.

Earlier, Mom told Phoebe, Susanne, and me, "Although divorced twice, he has had an endless stream of female friends, one girlfriend after another. I wish he would settle happily but worry that he can't. This young lady piques my curiosity."

Does Mom think this one could be the one?

The young lady turns out to be about twenty-eight to thirty, which is younger than Brian. She is about five feet four inches tall. By wearing four-inch heels, she comes up to Brian's ear, but her stilettos make it difficult to walk on the gravel. Her fluffy coat is some indeterminant kind of fake fur. Some call it *faux* fur, which means something synthetic pretending to be a dead animal skin. Wearing an overcoat and gloves, Uncle Brian hunches his over-six-feet-tall frame protectively close to her and lends her his arm so she doesn't fall.

Once inside, Nigel helps them as they shed their coats.

Her black dress shows a lot of her top. There are two wide bright-red straps, each with a large black button, to hold up the top half of the dress.

I mouth inaudibly, "Do those buttons work or are they only for show?"

The upper half of the dress fits tightly, and bulges everywhere. The swatch of black material on top is skintight, straining to contain all its contents. The bottom half of the black dress has a stitched-in pretend belt that is bright red to match the straps of the top. The dress flares a little, and ends at the knee. The stiletto shoes are the same red as the dress straps and belt. Her lipstick is red, the same as her dress straps, belt, and shoes. The color combination should work. *It doesn't.*

I later overheard Mom and Nana talking privately. Mom said Uncle Brian's friend was heavy chested and called the red an accent color. Nana said *something else.*

Uncle Brian is lean and muscular with a trim torso and the sleek movements of a cat. He has thick wavy auburn hair over a long, angular face. His hazel eyes are frequently scanning his surroundings as if anticipating something bad about to happen. His eyes are flicking side to side right now. I remember Mom told us it's a habit he has, especially when he's nervous. His long straight nose is farther from his upper lip than the average.

Mom once said, "Brian has a *patrician* face. Overall, he has a handsome face that women find very attractive, if history is any guide. I am not sure that has really helped Brian!"

At the door, Mom gives her brother a big hug and kiss. He responds with equal warmth, and introduces Teresa to the hallway crowd. She is a little chubby, with dark wavy hair cut to about four inches. Her brown eyes are surrounded by a lot of eye makeup and face paint. She leans forward to adjust a shoe that has collected a stone from the gravel. Her dress top holds on tight and barely keeps her contained. I cannot move my eyes away!

Waving a finger hidden behind his other hand so that only I can see, Papa nudges me and stares at me hard. The finger tells me, *No! No!*

To stop staring, I avert my eyes and gawk at the face of everyone else. It's hard work. I just hope she doesn't need to lean over again!

Why does my groin feel heavy? Oh! Oh! Is something getting bigger?

Is this the beginning of puberty? I hope not, 'cause I'm not sure I understand about puberty yet.

Concentrating, I hear Brian's friend saying, "Teresa, without an *h.* The last name is Merlo. Same as the wine."

Papa asks, "M-E-R-L-O-T—exactly as the wine?"

Teresa, without an *h,* replies, "Almost, but there's no *t* in Merlo. But then, there is no tea in wine, is there?" Somewhat nervously, she laughs and laughs at her own joke.

Papa and Mom chuckle slightly. Nana and no-*h* Teresa exchange greetings. Standing somewhat behind Ms. No-tea Merlo, Mom flashes a brief skeptical glance at Nana and then at Dad as Nigel guides everyone into the drawing room.

Uncle Brian and Teresa greet the rest who have remained in the sitting room. Uncle Ian looks at no-*h*-Teresa with poorly disguised distaste.

Aunt Evelyn sees Teresa's dress and heels, stays seated, shakes Teresa's hand in formal greeting, and then withdraws her hand quickly. Unaware of her own actions, Aunt Evelyn involuntarily wrings her hands like she's washing them! She looks everywhere but not at Ms. Merlo.

Oh dear! It may be a difficult evening.

Papa begins conversation to cover the awkwardness of Aunt Evelyn's greeting. He goes out of his way to include Teresa, no *h*, in the conversation. Mom joins Papa in trying to break the awkwardness. Both are looking intently *not* at Teresa's chest. Her top half is bulging dangerously everywhere as her black dress top with its red straps holds on for dear life!

The meal is intended to be happy and festive. It's a time to meet someone new and become friends. I'm not sure that is happening. Papa hurriedly asks about drinks. Aunt Evelyn asks for white wine. Uncle Ian has a whiskey and soda, as does Papa. Uncle Brian has a large whiskey, straight up. Later he has another, both before dinner.

Papa says, "I have an excellent merlot, Ms. Merlo. It's just asking to be opened. Do you like red wine?"

Teresa giggles slightly and replies, "That would be lovely." Soon Ms. Merlo is clutching her own glass of merlot.

To make conversation, Papa laughs and jokingly says to her, "It's fun to choose a namesake wine, isn't it?" Teresa Merlo, no *h*, no *t*, chuckles nervously.

Mom decides to wait for dinner before having wine and has a soda water instead, just like Nana and Phoebe. Dad told me before that in America soda water is called club soda.

Language is odd!

Mom later told us that, on instinct, she expected trouble and quickly decided she would need to keep her wits about her. Nana and Phoebe both said the same thing.

Boy, were they right!

All four children have beverage choices. Susanne and I have lemonade. Collin and Dexter decide on diet soft drinks.

During the predinner conversation, Aunt Evelyn remains quiet and answers questions reluctantly with one-word answers. She steals the occasional surreptitious glance at Teresa, no *h,* and then develops the most disdainful look on her face, which she repeatedly fails to hide in time. When she isn't shooting furtive glares at Teresa, she occasionally looks sourly toward Phoebe as if the hired help had crashed the gathering without an invite.

I don't like that. Phoebe is my friend.

Aunt Evelyn clearly wants out of here, away from a badly dressed newcomer and the hired help.

This is getting ugly!

Teresa, no *h,* pays attention to her wine. She does not see the looks Aunt Evelyn has sent her way. Despite the wine, Teresa, no *h,* still seems on edge.

I hope she doesn't think booze will help with her nervousness.

Miss Teresa, no *h,* Merlo, no *t,* is soon on her second generous glass of merlot. She joins in the conversation, but she laughs nervously and too loudly when there is no need. I think that she is scared about meeting us—especially Brian's parents, the Earl and Countess Poppycock. *That's it!* That's why she is nervous. It's the silly title and the big old house! *Dah!* I have to stop my hand from bumping my forehead when I make the connection.

I'm always too slow making connections! Bloody autism.

Uncle Brian and Papa talk with Dad. Uncle Ian joins in a little, but conversation appears difficult. I don't understand why.

Phoebe stays very quiet in her corner. Her eyes are everywhere.

It's an uphill struggle for Susanne and me to make conversation with Collin and Dexter. Our cousins make it clear they have no interest in what we do at school or for fun. They start talking about their wonderful boarding school. Soon they start name-dropping by saying, "You wouldn't know about Lord so-and-so, but his son …" Then details follow about how close they are and how much fun they have with one fancy snobby name after another.

Suddenly, I notice Susanne is paying close attention to the names and sometimes asks them to repeat a name as if she hadn't quite heard, which is really strange. Susanne has great hearing! What is she up to? The cousins are trying hard to impress us that they move in exalted circles. When Susanne asks them to repeat a name, they regard her like she's too stupid to catch the name the first time. *That's a mistake!* They repeatedly declare, "Of course, you in America don't have the old families as we do in Britain."

It gets pretty tedious. Susanne and I smile, remain mostly quiet, and wish the two brats were back in boarding school where all is so wonderful! The cousins prattle on and on. Mom and Nana start eavesdropping a little, and both see that things are not going well. They try to change the topic. However, Collin and Dexter seem single-minded in their goal to be name-dropping snobs. Even Nana's diversions are ignored.

By dinnertime, there are four camps. Ian, Evelyn, and offspring are in the entitled snob corner. Next, there's the American camp, wanting to have a nice meal with relatives. Papa, Nana, and Uncle Brian are in the annoyed and increasingly frustrated group who are watching the first group behave badly. Then there is the fourth camp, Ms. Teresa Merlo. She is alone in camp oblivious, without a small *h* or a small *t* to call her own!

She finishes her second generous wine glass too quickly and now helps herself to another rather generous glass of her namesake. The first merlot bottle is gone, and she is the only one drinking red wine! Nana does not look happy! Teresa, no *h*, wobbles dangerously on her heels as she returns to her seat with her third glass of wine, which she has filled dangerously full. She still appears a little nervous and now tipsy! As Nigel announces that dinner is served, Teresa swigs the last of her third glass of wine, the true end of the bottle!

We walk into the formal dining room with its heavily carved Elizabethan-style furniture and huge windows. The gold coloring on the picture frames glows in the soft evening light of the chandelier and wall sconces. Light reflects off the gold thread within the richly colored heavy drapes drawn across the windows against the night. The room is beautiful and inviting despite its size and formality.

Nigel has carefully set the dining room table for a formal dinner. Earlier, Nigel explained to us kids, "The tall vase in the center of the table holds the flowers high up. This allows a visual sight line around the arrangement so that no one is cut off from conversation by an intrusive bouquet of posies." Susanne and I notice similar bouquets at each end of the sideboard.

Nana's best china and her sterling silver are set out for each place. The damask tablecloth is gleaming white as are the napkins folded artfully on each plate. I almost want to take a photo to send to a fancy magazine, but I say nothing. My brain imagines what my British cousins might say about their American kin if they knew my thoughts. Already, I have had enough of them. I remain silent, definitely not interested in providing them ammunition for nastiness.

Nana sits at one end, and Papa at the other end of their large dining table. Nana has place cards indicating where to sit with family members mingled in the seating arrangement to provide more conversation. Susanne and I are separated, but we are opposite Collin and Dexter. Phoebe is to my right.

We Americans compliment Nana and Papa on the beautiful surroundings and the splendid table.

Uncle Brian says, "Everything looks lovely and the table looks beautiful, Mom."

Teresa sighs, "Oh my, yes!" She clasps her hands together in a gesture of foolish amazement like a young child might, not as an adult should.

Is she a half-wit, drunk, or both?

Ian and Evelyn say nothing. I guess a spectacular setting for a meal is an expectation for them. Collin and Dexter do not notice their surroundings. Apparently, they routinely expect splendor for their exalted personages. While I am really annoyed at my cousins and their parents, I'm past it with drunken Teresa.

I glance at Susanne who has been working harder than I have to create conversation with the two cousins and has been thwarted and insulted by them. Deep inside, she is now bristling. Her watchful eyes and her clipped speech are two signs that they had best watch out!

Regardless of bad feelings, the food is wonderful. Mrs. Stewart has exceeded her usual high standards. Nigel serves fish soup, a broth with small bits of delicious fish, green chives, a few carrots cut small, ginger, and very finely ground onion. Wow, it is good! Next comes a salad of sharp-tasting greens with goat cheese and caramelized walnuts. This has a sweet oil-based dressing, which makes a delicious contrast to the sharpness of the greens. Pork loin with roasted potatoes, asparagus in a mild lemon sauce, and buttered parsnips come next. There is warm bread with melting butter. I devour several pieces.

As I do so, I see Collin look in my direction and smirk as he nudges Dexter. I have good table manners, so that's not it. Maybe he smirks because enjoying bread is too common for his superior tastes. I notice neither of the boys eats a great deal.

Are they anorexics? No, not a chance. They are too narcissistic to worry about body image.

Do only commoners enjoy their meals? Well, this commoner is determined that these cousins are not going to spoil a wonderful dinner that Nana has arranged, and which Mrs. Stewart and my parents have worked hard for many hours to prepare. The best compliment to the chef is to enjoy everything with gusto! *Stupid skinny cousins!* I eat things properly with the good manners I was taught, but I eat lots!

Susanne sees that the cousins are smirking while they pick at their food. Her neck and ears flash red. After smiling falsely through her clenched teeth, she eats with gusto too!

Dessert is a fabulous *crème brûlée* with fresh blueberries at the side. The blueberries are slightly tart, as well as sweet, with a tiny amount of salt on them. Dad often says, "Salt accents the sweetness of berries or fruits."

Collin, Dexter, and Aunt Evelyn leave half of theirs. Is that what superior beings do perhaps?

Papa serves port with after-dinner coffee. Nana, Phoebe, and Mom have had a mostly untouched glass of wine with dinner. They all decide against port. Aunt Evelyn is on her second glass of red wine. I hope it lets her relax a little. However, if anything, she is more tense. Despite saying no to port, Aunt Evelyn's lips involuntarily almost smack in anticipation. Clearly, she wants port badly.

Later, I would learn how very badly she wanted it and what it cost her to say no!

Uncle Ian seems more relaxed after his whiskey and soda and two glasses of wine. He has ignored his wife throughout most of the meal. Uncle Brian is talkative from three glasses of wine after his two whiskies. He chats amiably with everyone and keeps Ms. Merlo in the conversation. Ms. Merlo has had a lot more merlot than she should have. She has had about six glasses of wine altogether—three before dinner and three with dinner. She has finished two bottles of wine all by herself!

Occasionally, her words slur. But, yes, she would like some port, too, please, as she joins the men with a glass. Nana would usually have the men and women separate for man conversation in the library and girl conversation in the drawing room. Tonight, she is prophetically wise. Everyone stays in the dining room. Aunt Evelyn contributes almost nothing to the conversation. Ms. Merlo is obviously drunk.

Much later, Susanne and I overheard Nana say to Mom, "I was afraid of Ms. Merlo in heels with so much booze on board! She could tumble hard, especially since she's top-heavy already."

Eventually, we all head to the drawing room. Aunt Evelyn steers away from the chesterfields and chooses a chair to herself so she is not near anyone. Her legs are crossed tightly, and one ankle curls around the other so that her legs are double locked. Dad sits at one end of a sofa, and Mom sits near him. There is a gap between them that Ms. Merlo fills. With precision, Mom capably hides the annoyance that flashed momentarily across her features.

Nearly splashing her newly filled wine glass, Teresa sits down with difficulty, framed by my parents, my two roses sandwiching an unaware thorn. Opposite them on the other sofa—I mean chesterfield—Nana and Papa sit side by side. Uncle Ian also has a chair to himself. Phoebe does not want to intrude, so she finds a chair a little out of the way. She holds a mostly full wine glass, her only glass, leftover from dinner. Collin and Dexter as well as Susanne and I find seats on various smaller chairs and stools.

Uncle Brian stands by the fireplace with his hand around a newly filled large whiskey glass that he drinks quickly and refills far too full, far too soon. He paces while his words become repetitive and louder. Seemingly annoyed at times, his voice sounds increasingly aggressive. Several times, Nana tries to deflect the conversation when Uncle Brian says something that is best left unsaid.

Swaying slightly, Uncle Brian stares malignantly at Uncle Ian and prods, "So, brother dearest, how's the money business?" This is the least useful conversation opener. Uncle Ian *hates* to talk about money, and Uncle Brian knows this.

Uncle Ian replies, "Brian, we don't need to discuss money here."

Uncle Brian retorts, "Sure we do. That's what you do, isn't it? Don't you manage other people's money and your own?"

Ian again answers, "Well, yes, it is, but that is business. And we are at home now."

With an increasingly belligerent tone, Brian states, "So you manage money. I'm just trying to figure if you are any good at it."

Everyone stares at Brian who is obviously nearing the intoxication level of his girlfriend.

Ms. Merlo ignores Uncle Brian and his outburst. She has almost chugged her too full wine glass. She stands, walks a few steps, and reaches out to the serving bar. She pours another large glass of red wine. Is this her eighth or ninth? I have lost track. She does not need more. She does not need what she has had. The empty bottles are starting to line up like tired soldiers in formation. She is unaware of the most unattractive slobber trickling down the left corner of her mouth. It's very apparent because it is tinted red from her merlot and her bright-red lipstick. She sits down between my parents again. Mom sees her drool and offers a napkin to Teresa.

Ms. Merlo's words run together as she asks, "Wuz this for?" She gapes at Mom quizzically, her left eye turning in slightly.

Mom replies quietly, "You have a little wine stain on your lip. I thought you might need this."

Ms. Merlo replies, "Oooh, thank you. Happens every timb, every timb I have wine." She tries to say *time* but somehow it ends with a *b*. She dabs at her mouth but misses her lips. Her hand continues on, dangerously close to her wine glass.

Mom puts a hand around Teresa's glass to prevent red wine from landing on the light-colored sofa.

Nana is taller than Papa, even when seated. Right now, Nana appears to be shrinking, as she slinks down into the sofa, becoming smaller than Papa.

Is she trying to disappear altogether?

Papa sits up straighter beside Nana and spreads his feet slightly apart, as if prepared to stand suddenly.

Ms. Merlo looks at Mom again, her left eye turning inward slightly more. "Oh, oh, dear, I am starting to see double." She acts befuddled. "I had eye surgery as a kid. It didn't ... it didn't work," confides Ms. Merlo, definitely no *t*. "When I am tired, my eye still turns in. It's my left one." She has a giant hiccup before the word *left*. She adds, "It's okay when I am not tired. They call it an *esophobia*." The last bit was really slurred, and the last word sounded wrong. A phobia is a fear.

Fear wouldn't explain why her eye twists inward.

Mom gazes at Dad and glances toward Papa. I can tell she is trying to be patient. We all realize Teresa has had too many *merlots*, each with a *t*.

Mom quietly states, "That is unfortunate. I'm sure it is difficult to manage at times." Mom pauses momentarily, struggling to be patient. "I don't think the word ends in *phobia*, which means fear. I think it ends in *phoria*, which means latent." Mom becomes silent while she glances a little uncertainly over at Dad. I can tell she wants to say something else. Mom continues, "I think they call it *esophoria*, a condition causing the eye to turn in at times for whatever reason, such as fatigue." Again, Mom's eyes flash over Teresa's shoulder to Dad. I suspect she wants to say, "And when you are drunk," but she cannot. Mom sighs as she commiserates, "I am sorry that the surgery was not entirely successful."

Collin and Dexter have a running joke between them that no one else can hear. They make no effort to include Susanne or me in their conversation. They murmur and giggle to themselves from time to time and nudge each other, pleased with their own cleverness. Knowing that Ms. Merlo is drunk, they quietly laugh right at her.

Teresa swallows the wrong way and coughs slightly. Her skimpy dress-top valiantly strains to hold her within.

Collin giggles loudly and nudges Dexter again. Uncle Brian notices through his alcoholic fog and glares at them sharply. With loud, slow, and deliberate words, Uncle Brian asks, "What do you two find so amusing? Something you want to share?"

Both Collin and Dexter realize that Uncle Brian is also toasted. They may be unkind to others, but I'll bet that they never want anyone to be unkind to them.

Collin's eyes flit to Dexter before he speaks up. "Only a silly joke from school. Nothing of any importance."

Uncle Brian stares angrily at them and then turns away.

Dad remembers that Uncle Brian previously wanted to talk about money. Trying to start a different conversation, he innocently asks, "Brian, what company are you working with now?" *Big mistake!*

Uncle Brian listens to Dad's question, walks to the bar cart, fills his empty whiskey glass too full a third time, and then answers, "Well, since you must bleeding know, I am currently unemployed and have been for a while. I am on the dole."

Aghast, Dad gawks at his brother-in-law and exclaims, "Brian, I had no idea! I am terribly sorry and would never have brought up the topic if I had known. Forgive me, I did not mean to cause embarrassment."

Uncle Brian retorts, "So the rich bastard is sorry. That's something!"

Mom pleads, "Please Brian, Sam had no concept. He didn't mean to offend. And he has apologized. But I am glad there are unemployment monies and welfare to help anyone when they are down."

Sodden with booze, Uncle Brian suddenly becomes belligerently angry and near tears. "What would you know about being down, Miss Success Street? And married to Mr. American Wall Street. Can't spend it fast enough, can you?"

Mom turns pale. Dad's hands clutch in and out repetitively forming a fist. This is hard to do since Teresa is taking up so much of his personal space on the sofa, oops … chesterfield. I have only seen Dad make a fist once before, and that ended badly.

Oh dear! What an evening!

Mom, too shocked to speak, instinctively touches Dad's arm—her code to do nothing. Nana is as stunned as if she had been slapped. Even Papa, now pale like Mom, slouches a little.

Next, Brian attacks Ian. "And you, Mr. Important, are too fancy to deign to talk about money. Grabbed enough of it, have you? And waiting for more." With that, he nods toward Papa and Nana. "Waiting to cash in, aren't you?"

Aunt Evelyn immediately retorts, "Oh, really, Brian, this is too much!" It's her first full sentence since dinner.

Defensive, are we?

Uncle Brian replies far too quickly, "Oh shut up, you ice pick. You are such a high and mighty … Frankly, you are worthless …"

Uncle Ian stands up from his chair and interrupts Brian. "Enough of this. You have had too much to drink. So has Ms. Merlo. You are saying things you can't retract, things you will regret in the morning."

Uncle Brian becomes even more belligerent. His words slur as he proclaims, "Oh, really, big brother! Since I am to have regrets, let's have a lot to regret." Brian chugs the last of his third post-dinner whiskey and puts the glass on the mantel.

With a slight sway, he advances too close to his brother. "You are a stuffed shirt with a rod up your rear. Your icicle wife is a snob. Your kids are spoiled brats in need of a good whipping. You may be earning money, but you don't care about anyone except yourself and never have. You wouldn't help me if your life depended upon it."

Well, maybe that's what he said. The slurred words did run together a bit!

Uncle Ian stands, confronting his brother. The two men glare angrily at each other, ready to take a swing. Collin and Dexter gape in utterly stupefied fascination. Phoebe is sitting low in her chair, ready to pounce to protect her kids from danger.

For the first time in a good while, perhaps because her glass is empty again, Ms. Merlo sees what is happening. She stands unsteadily on her heels and commands with badly slurred speech, "Stop it, you two." At least, that is what she tries to say. It comes out as, "Stop zit, yous dous."

Collin and Dexter laugh out loud. Ms. Merlo abruptly squints at the cousins while she squeezes between the men and raises her arms in her attempt to keep the two men separate. Her wine glass is still in her right hand.

Staring at Brian, Ian has the presence of mind to remove Ms. Merlo's wine glass from her shaking hand. He leans over sideways, eyes on Brian, to set the empty glass on a side table.

With her hands free and her eyes on Brian, Ms. Merlo puts a palm on Uncle Brian's chest. Her other hand flaps aimlessly until Uncle Ian stands up again and her flapping hand finally hits home gently on his chest to keep the men separate.

That flapping hand needlessly searching for a chest looked ridiculous!

If Uncle Ian is paying attention to her wine glass, then he is not about to slug Uncle Brian. Unfortunately, Ms. Merlo is too drunk to sort that out. *Go figure!* Sadly, her hand flapping and arm stretching trigger a sequence of things. The strap buttons have a purpose! One button, the left one, pops off with the strain of her exertions. The button rolls under a table. *Ka-ching!* Her left strap falls lifelessly down her front, and the left side of her chest is *nearly* nakedly exposed.

Mom and Nana see this happen, and both respond immediately. Mom is up first. She grabs a lap blanket and wraps it over Ms. Merlo's shoulders.

In her alcoholic fog, Ms. Merlo still pushes against both men. As she strains against them, her dress top stretches even more dangerously. After twelve thousand glasses of wine, Ms. Merlo is unaware that she is in danger of exposure.

When Mom wraps her in the lap blanket, she misunderstands Mom's intentions. For whatever reason, she pushes Mom hard, which makes her fall back onto the sofa.

To add to the mishap, the lap blanket has a woolly surface and catches in the metal bracelet of Mom's wristwatch. The blanket follows Mom to the sofa just as Ms. Merlo's hard push is too much for her dress. The lifeless strap holds nothing when her movement causes a certain bulging body part to pop out in the gap created by the broken strap. Ms. Merlo is now *completely* exposed and *totally* naked on the left side of her chest as she stands between the two men, arms still spread up, separating the warriors.

She still doesn't realize what has happened until Nana says, "Teresa, let me help you."

Nana grabs the lap blanket, which pulls Mom's arm up 'cause it's still caught in her watch bracelet. Together, Nana and Mom desperately try to untangle the snag.

Ms. Merlo glances down and sees her naked breast. She totters on her heels as she becomes hysterical. She shrieks over and over! Forgetting the warring men, she tries to grab the blanket, which delays unsnagging it. Her copious tears make her mascara run down her face in long black streaks.

What a sight!

Eventually, Mom and Nana unsnag the wristwatch bracelet from the throw. Mom is still on the sofa. Nana is standing and covers Ms. Merlo's upper half.

Susanne looks on, speechless, mouth open, afraid to move. Phoebe has watched with a red face, embarrassed beyond belief. She later told Susanne and me, "As an outsider, I was afraid to intervene. Since Nana and Mom were taking charge, I backed off."

Collin and Dexter have tears of laughter streaming down their face. They roll in their chairs, legs kicking and arms clutching their belly, out of control with their unkind laughter at the hapless Ms. Merlo.

Dad is beside Mom who is still sprawled on the sofa. He asks, "Are you hurt?"

Mom replies, "I am fine."

Mom may be fine after that fall. A similar push could break a hip for Nana.

Papa realizes what could have happened. He now stands close to Nana, protective of his beloved wife, and poised, ready for action. He is clearly afraid Ms. Merlo may push again.

Uncle Ian looks at Teresa's glass on the side table. He sits down in his chair, red faced, angry, and laughing nastily at his brother's friend. Uncle Ian declares, "Some friend you bring to dinner. First, she is drunk, and then she bursts her seams! What a show!"

Uncle Brian doesn't know what to do about this mess. Drunk and unable to think clearly, he stands helplessly staring at his sobbing friend, partially wrapped in a blanket to cover her nakedness. Fortunately, he does nothing.

I was afraid he might start hitting. I don't like violence.

Aunt Evelyn stands up regally, a picture in lavender, looking like she just swallowed a sour pickle. "I will be in the car," she tells Ian through tightly puckered lips. "Come along, boys." She does not ask if Mom is okay. She says nothing to Nana or Papa.

Uncle Ian strides out into the hall after her, with Collin and Dexter trailing. None of them ask if Mom or anyone else is injured or needs assistance. They don't even say thank you for the meal. Uncle Ian yells, "Good night," over his shoulder as he reaches for coats from the rack. The words are aimed in the general direction of his parents.

The remaining adult family and nanny stare, their faces showing the disbelief that Susanne and I feel after an incredulous glance past our drunken uncle and his sodden girlfriend. Mesmerized, we all watch the four relatives march out together, briskly pulling on their coats as they lockstep.

Uncle Ian brings up the rear as they leave. The massive front door slams after him with a huge bang. Phoebe jumps with the noise and utters a small cry. All of us are shocked into immobile stillness and silence.

As if on cue, Nigel appears at the sound, glances toward the front door, and then stares aghast through the wide archway into the drawing room. He sees an open-mouthed group perched around the room. Some are staring stupidly toward the door, and others are foolishly gawking at the standing figure of a half-clothed, half-wrapped sobbing woman rocking on her heels, whose left breast is peeking out from under a blanket. Bright red in the face, Nigel apologizes, "Excuse me, m'lady. I didn't mean to intrude," and hastily retreats to the kitchen.

My goodness, he can move fast!

Only Ms. Merlo remains oblivious to our guests' departure. She stands whimpering, tears still streaming, poorly clutching her blanket and losing coverage, all the while swaying precariously on her heels.

All we need now is a lumberjack yelling, "Timber."

Not all my thoughts are kind! And my head is mighty busy at the moment. What's happening in my groin again? *Oops! My crotch feels really tight.*

Mom's open mouth snaps shut. She faces Teresa and orders, "Come with me, my dear. We must get you repaired." As Teresa leans to the right toward her, Mom remarks, "I'll support you. We'll go up the stairs to the second floor where I have a sewing kit and something to clean up your mascara."

Susanne sees the errant button, swoops to grab it, and hands it to Mom. "You'll need this," she mutters almost inaudibly. Mom's free hand clutches the button.

Dad stands beside Ms. Merlo, definitely no *t*, on the side opposite Mom. "Take my arm. The stairs are hard to climb."

Now, that's a lie.

Teresa nods that she will cooperate. Her left arm flaps absurdly off target again till Dad puts his arm under hers and holds on.

The stairs are shallow, designed for a dignified ascent or descent.

Dad's lie is an excuse. He's trying to help a drunken woman in tall heels who is likely to meet the floor the wrong way.

As they depart, Uncle Brian takes Uncle Ian's chair. He rubs his hands over his face, utterly defeated. Papa watches him but says nothing.

Sitting side by side on the sofa, Papa and Nana both seem small, pale, and vulnerable.

I've never seen them appear so utterly fragile!

Helplessly worried, they both just watch Brian. Nana is near tears. Phoebe stays in her chair. She looks away, not knowing what to do or to say. In stunned silence, Susanne and I sit rigidly on our chairs.

After a long and silent interval, we hear noises from the stairs. Dad and Mom help the now dressed Ms. Merlo, no *t*, descend, fully strapped in.

Without her heels, no *h*, no *t* is now shorter. Dad is almost carrying her by holding her arm tight as she wobbles while wearing Mom's fuzzy flat slippers. Mom has repaired the strap button and put the dress back in order. The mascara and face paint have been cleansed and dried. Her facial makeup is totally missing on one side, and mostly missing on the other, which makes her face look lopsided.

With the fuzzy slippers—what a sight!

When she sees Brian, Teresa starts to cry. Uncle Brian stands up and hugs her. They both start crying.

Now, her tears I get. Why his? Why they are both doing this?

Susanne stares blankly at the pair with eyes that question, *What gives?*

When we asked about their tears later that night, Mom gazed steadily at Dad and announced, "Your turn."

Dad nodded to his kids and explained, "Sometimes, someone who is really drunk has a crying spell as the alcohol level changes in their bloodstream. Usually, the person is unhappy about something anyway, but the alcohol brings out the tears. When the person is sober, they don't really know why they carried on so much."

Mom added, "Some people call it a crying jag." That later explanation helped so that Susanne and I could understand the display we all saw earlier.

The two eventually settle down. Uncle Brian stupidly says to Teresa, "Let's drive to the hotel. We have a late arrival reservation."

Papa exclaims, "Nothing doing! You both are too drunk. You will stay in the guest bedrooms."

Papa waits to see Brian nod in agreement. "I presume you share accommodations at home?" demands Papa.

Uncle Brian nods that they do.

Papa continues firmly, "Well, you may *there*, but you shall not *here*. You will have separate rooms. Ms. Merlo will be in the guest bedroom upstairs. Brian, you will be in the unused servant's room downstairs, which is the only other bedroom available. It's perfectly serviceable." Papa's words are terse and sharp.

Nana makes coffee and brings out biscuits for Teresa and the rest of us. Both drunks seem to settle with time, food, and coffee.

Papa and Dad help Brian get the luggage from the car. Wisely, Papa pockets the car keys. Mom and Nana get Teresa upstairs again and into her nightclothes. Papa settles Brian in his room downstairs. It's just as well they hadn't already checked into their hotel. At least they have their own clothes and toothbrush!

Afterward, the Americans and the grans gather in the drawing room.

"What an evening!" Nana exclaims.

"Indeed," responds Papa in a soft voice. His eyebrows twitch.

With attention on her daughter, Mom declares, "Susanne, you now understand why a woman, especially a heavy chested one, should always wear a bra, regardless of fashion. Her dress was designed to be worn without a bra. This is a bad choice of clothes on her part, in view of her figure. It would have been one thing to see her bra. It was quite another to see the full exposure!"

Out of control, I chortle, "Mom, don't you mean in *full* view of *all* of her figure." I'm gasping with laughter. The *'stop it look'* radiates from Mom and Phoebe. Nana glances my way, suppresses a smile, and hides the mirth in her eyes by turning away.

She's out of practice with kids!

Trying to redeem myself, I add, "Trust Mom to pull practical advice from a bad situation!" Again, I can't help myself as I laugh hard, which doesn't help my case for redemption. Mom appears really cross.

Since Nana understands why I am laughing, she turns her head to Mom and comments, "Trust you to say the sensible thing, daughter of mine!" Nana begins to giggle too.

Soon all of us are quietly laughing, which soon releases the tension that has built over hours. Nana snuggles against Papa. Dad moves closer to Mom, kisses her gently on the forehead, and asks, "Did I ever tell you I love you?"

With a laugh, Mom replies glibly, "No. Never."

He chuckles. "Well, I must fix that." After he gives her a peck on her cheek, his finger touches her ear as she flashes him a *look*. It's not the "stop it" look. I hear him mutter something about later. Why do adults exchange *that look*? What does it mean?

We sit in silence for a time. Finally, Nana remarks, "Tomorrow is Christmas Eve Day. Breakfast may be difficult. I suggest we regard the incident as of no importance. Ms. Merlo may have drawbacks, but she is not malicious or unkind. I don't want her to be embarrassed. Children, I insist we all be kind to her." Nana looks sternly at each of us. Surprisingly, she admonishes, "You may not behave as your cousins do." Nana pauses to think for a moment.

Open-mouthed, we stare at her after the cousin comment while she continues, "I don't know if she is an alcoholic or if she was using alcohol to cover anxiety. I suspect she was nervous about meeting *the parents*. An alcoholic would hold her booze better. I think she was tipsy after her first glass of wine. If she were a drinker, she would know when to stop or at least how to pace herself, so I think she's an alcohol novice." Nana pauses momentarily while she stares sadly at the floor. Quietly, she laments, "It's a pity all this happened."

Mom responds, "Yes. I agree. No jokes. Be kind. Talk about the incident only if she raises the topic."

Dad admits with a laugh, "It's hard to unsee all that I saw. I will do my best." He glances at Mom with a silly grin. Again, they flash a *look* between them.

Papa gazes in my direction and eyes me up and down just as Phoebe says it is bedtime. As I get a good-night hug, Papa whispers in my ear, "Well, you have had a fine anatomy lesson today, rather stimulating. Remember, all people need respect in order to thrive."

I nod that I understand. And I do. Once again, I am amazed at the kindliness my grandparents and parents have toward others. I love that about them! I'm also amazed that Papa misses nothing, and I mean *nothing!*

After hugs from all and a kiss from Nana and our parents, Susanne and I head upstairs. Trailing us, with her hand waving vaguely to the room, Phoebe says to the ether, "Sleep well, all." Clearly, Phoebe wants to be away from the scene of the crime.

Upstairs, Phoebe makes sure we complete bedtime rituals fully, and then she decides to talk to us both. She speaks quietly since Ms. Merlo is sleeping three rooms away. The walls are thick. The old solid doors are closed. Regardless, we can hear her heavy snores!

Phoebe confesses, "Tonight's display was something I have never seen here. Everyone was embarrassed. All of us are trying to make the best of a bad situation.

"Ms. Merlo is not a bad person. She might have a problem with alcohol, although I suspect Nana may be right. She could be a rare drinker who used alcohol to cover anxiety. Any worry she may have had about meeting the parents was easily made worse by the title and the family's status. However, I think Brian *definitely* has a problem with alcohol. He drank a lot before it showed. That makes me very sad for them both. And it all was so needless."

Phoebe pauses for thought and then continues, "We must forgive but not necessarily forget. The same will happen again if they overuse alcohol next time. We must be prepared for the future." She pauses again, uncertain what to say next until she finally adds, "Try to be kind and understanding tomorrow. It may be hard to do, but I know you can. Tonight, you saw firsthand what happens when a drug such as alcohol is abused. Misused, alcohol and drugs ruin lives. Tonight, booze ruined a lovely evening."

I loudly declare, "Well, it wasn't so lovely with Collin and Dexter. They are nasty." Susanne nods her vigorous agreement.

Phoebe answers, "They have been brought up to believe they are entitled. They are selfish and spoiled, and it shows. I feel sorry for them." Her anger with the cousins clearly shows. Her voice is slightly louder as she declares, "Despite their bravado, they don't have much self-confidence. That's why they drop famous names and enjoy nasty humor at another's expense. They are weak people and likely to have difficulty in their personal lives with *their* attitudes. My betting money goes on the two of you anytime!"

Both of us have such built-up anxiety from the evening's performances that the compliment makes both of us feel thankful for Phoebe's common sense and for the love she has for us.

Susanne's chin starts to wiggle and jiggle, a sign of oncoming tears. She gets a quick hug from Phoebe, and the chin slows down.

We each get a long, hard kiss on the forehead and another hug. Phoebe's eyes glisten as she commands, "Now, off to bed, you two.

We have a busy day tomorrow, starting with difficult mental work in the morning."

Shortly after Phoebe left, I felt really thirsty. In the bathroom, I muttered, "Dang, there's no cup here." I headed quietly downstairs to the kitchen where Nana and Mom are talking. It's amazing what I sometimes overhear when no one knows I'm eavesdropping. From outside the kitchen, I hear Mom's comments about "heavy-chested woman" and "accent color." Swiftly afterward, Nana bitterly remarks, "What a dress! She looked like a tart."

Why would anyone want to look like a pastry? But she did sort of look like a pastry, maybe a strawberry pastry.

I make a warning sound, and their conversation stops dead briefly and then restarts with trivia about church decorations. During the general chin-wagging, I retrieve my water. My mind still figures on Teresa's pastry-tart costume as I head back upstairs.

Strawberry or raspberry, a red fruit anyway, but why?

Despite the stress of the crazy evening, I fall asleep quickly but awaken hours later, sweating from a nightmare involving a gun and something about Uncle Brian and Uncle Ian. I can't recall the dream exactly, but it fills me with foreboding. With a sense of unease, I fall back to sleep. Stupid dream!

How will we each manage tomorrow? How will Teresa—no *h*—Merlo—no *t*—behave, or Uncle Brian, for that matter? How will any of us act?

My innermost thoughts ask, *Will tomorrow be a phony cover-up production?*

Chapter 5

CHRISTMAS EVE DAY

Welcome and reassuring sunlight creates a lovely way to wake up in the morning. I was still muddled and maybe a little upset when I drew the drapes hurriedly last night. Since I didn't close them properly, sunlight peeks into my room to spread random light patterns over the carpet and furniture The drapes askew immediately remind me of the mess last night—rather off-putting, despite the beautiful colors and patterns of light.

Then I remember what the adults said. I must forgive and be kind. That is not what I really want to show.

I'm suddenly annoyed!

What if my mom had been hurt, or what if Nana had been pushed onto the floor? Drunken behavior still can cause harm, and the drunken person is still the cause. Alcohol doesn't stop responsibility.

As I come down the stairs, I recollect that Mrs. Stewart has the day off today, so the kitchen belongs to Nana. I overhear Mom and Nana's conversation in the kitchen as I quietly creep nearer.

Time to eavesdrop again!

Mom is speaking. "I had no idea things were so bad for Brian. He is on welfare, on the dole as he calls it. His pride must really be hurt."

Nana replies, "This is not the first time. Thank heavens the system exists to help people. He has botched several good positions. Alcohol is part of the reason. But there is more I must tell you." Nana pauses as she sits on a kitchen chair. Her voice catches, and she wipes her face with her tea towel as she cries softly.

Eventually, she continues, "Drug use has been another prob- lem. Cocaine is his drug of choice. They say it is extremely addictive. When he takes it, he feels superior, almost invincible, and exhibits stupid behavior by doing and saying unwise things. He was unhappy at his last job and was using. They caught him high on drugs at work and fired him on the spot." Nana's tears start to flow.

Mom stands beside her mother as she admits with a cracking voice, "I presumed his career was floundering because he had not found the position that was his life's ambition. I did not know his taste for alcohol had become a dependency. I am horrified to learn of his cocaine addiction." She watches her mother as she adds, "But you have said nothing to me before now."

With a shoulder shrug, Nana replies in a descending cadence, "Yes, I know." She pauses, and then continues more briskly, "We have paid for rehabilitation twice. The National Health Service helps a little but not enough. We got him the best we could find—two different places at two different times." She continues after catching her breath. "Cocaine users have a high failure rate, and frequently use again. They call it a high recidivism rate. And when he drinks alcohol, he becomes disinhibited and is more likely to snort cocaine. It worries me so!"

Staring vacantly ahead, Nana begins to sob, her voice broken by gasps. "I love my children ... and ... have loved ... each of them ... equally. All received the same treatment——no favoritism. How did I fail my youngest?" Her eyes turn toward her daughter, tears streaming.

Mom starts to quietly cry too. As she stands beside Nana, she caresses her mother's shoulders. "You failed no one. For whatever rea- son, this is Brian's issue. There is something in him that causes him to do this. This is not your fault." Nana sobs while Mom strokes her mother's heaving shoulders.

I slip partway back up the stairs and start making clunking noises to warn them of my pending arrival downstairs.

Please, don't either of you tell me what I have overheard. It's too much to handle!

Maybe time will help me figure this out. My favorite uncle drinks too much and may be an alcoholic. Now Nana has confessed he is also a drug addict. Will the adults tell Susanne and me anything if they think we don't know?

Cheerily, I say, "Good morning, Mom. Good morning, Nana. Did you sleep well?"

Nana has her face slightly turned. She has a small hanky that she pulls away from her face and hides in her pocket. Mom's eyes are slightly red.

"Why are your eyes red, Mom?" I can't help myself. It's like picking at a scab. If I probe, what *will* she say?

She replies, "Something landed in one of my peepers that made both of them water. How silly! Nana helped me get it out. Orange juice?" She doesn't wait for my answer as she pours mechanically. I am handed a glass of orange juice, no eye contact.

In a few minutes, Susanne and Phoebe descend the stairs. Dad appears from the library. Papa comes in from outside where he has been talking to Mr. Brown, the estate manager. But there is no sighting of Uncle Brian from the basement, nor any sign of Ms. Merlo from upstairs.

Mom seems absent-minded. She hands Susanne an orange juice without asking if she wants one. Mom still makes no eye contact with anyone. *Not typical!*

Susanne had already tasted a little of her mandatory drink when Mom asks, "Susanne, will you help me by checking on Ms. Merlo? Call her and tell her that breakfast will be ready in thirty minutes."

Susanne senses something is wrong. She notices Nana's face remains averted so we cannot see she has been crying, sees Mom's red eyes, and hears the snuffles from her nose. I can tell Susanne wants to give a teenage quip, which will not end happily, thinks better of it, leaves her orange juice, and heaves an enormous theatrical sigh as she trots back upstairs.

Phoebe observes what we have seen. She looks uncomfortable and clearly does not want to intrude. She takes dishes and cutlery to set the table in the morning room. She stays there.

The red eyes of Nana and Mom trigger a response from Dad and Papa. Dad declares he will start cooking breakfast. Papa volunteers to help. Dad asks me to go out to check if the morning paper has arrived.

It is fairly mild outside, but I put on my coat, pull on my boots, and find my gloves as I head out the kitchen door. Walking around the side of the house, I glance back through the windows to see the adults talking earnestly.

Papa seems sad and Dad appears solemn. Nana is receiving a shoulder hug from Mom. I guess that Dad and Mom are getting the full lowdown on Brian.

Normally, it's a bit of a hike to reach the post box at the roadside far down the drive. To give them more time, I dawdle a little. Hopefully, the adults have had a chance to talk.

When I return with the local rag in my hand, Phoebe remains in the morning room slowly setting the table. *Please, let Susanne be upstairs.*

After putting the newspaper on a side counter, I take off my gloves and put them in my coat pocket, slip off my coat, and hang it on its peg. Finally, I slide out of my boots and into my slippers.

Susanne stomps heavily down the stairs. She is muttering under her breath. She never mutters.

Why is she muttering?

When she comes into the kitchen, Susanne is rather red in the face and avoids eye contact. In this kitchen, avoiding eye contact is really easy right now. Everyone is looking somewhere else and trying to appear busy. Nothing has yet been done toward breakfast, which confirms my suspicion—adults were sharing secrets.

Absentmindedly, Mom asks, "Is Ms. Merlo up?"

Susanne says nothing for a moment and then blurts out, "Yes. She is awake. She will be down after she and Brian are finished." Susanne's face is now scarlet. She stares at the floor.

Mom is holding a bowl that drops with a clatter. Fortunately, it does not break. The egg in Dad's hand drops, hits the bowl rim, breaks, and drips down the outside of the container. We hear a quiet, "Darnation." Nana starts, looks at Susanne, then at me, and then at

Papa. Papa flushes with rage. He leaves the room and heads for the stairs. From the sound of his speedy footsteps, he is taking them two at a time.

Wow! He can move!

Nana calls after him, "Care with what you say. They are adults. I know you don't approve, but ..." The rest of the words are forgotten when she realizes he is no longer in earshot. He wasn't listening anyway.

We hear raised voices. Brian's voice is angry because of interrupted privacy. Papa's voice is loud with indignation.

Papa yells, "This is my house and your mother's. I set the rules last night. You were to stay in separate rooms. Could you not restrain yourself and show some respect for your parents' wishes and morals? What sort of example is this for the children?" There is more conversation that is not heard as the tone calms down.

Dad has cleaned up his egg mess by the time Papa, flushed and angry, returns to the kitchen. He tries his best to act normally, but we can see his struggle. His effort is forced.

"They will be down shortly." After speaking, Papa slams the cutlery he was about to use.

We are all seated in the morning room and have begun to eat when Ms. Merlo and Uncle Brian join us for breakfast. Uncle Brian is sulky and gruff, trying to hide his anger. Ms. Merlo says a pleasant "good morning" to all. She wears no makeup, but she is well put together. Her dress, which descends well past her knees, is conservative with a high collar and long sleeves. She is wearing flat-heeled shoes, so she looks short beside Brian.

Nana explains, "It's self-serve this morning. Coffee and food are all laid out waiting for you in the kitchen." The late arrivals collect food and coffee before they return to the table.

Nana tries to make conversation. Since money, work, estate projects, and careers are all forbidden topics, she is limited to the weather, the midnight mass tonight, and plans for the next day, which is Christmas. Mom helps her in this uphill struggle. Much of the time we eat in silence. I am glad Nigel has a day off today.

We would be even more embarrassed if he saw all this. Eventually, breakfast finishes.

Uncle Brian remarks, "We should be leaving."

Nana appears worried. She may be disappointed with his actions, but he is her son, whom she loves. Besides, she always wants good feelings between all family members. She asks, "Will we see you at church tonight? The midnight mass begins at 9:45 p.m. Will you and Teresa be there?"

Realizing how hard his mother is trying to smooth things over, Brian replies, "We will be there."

"And Christmas. You both will spend the day with us?" Nana asks.

Uncle Brian glances at Teresa, who has been quiet and subdued. From her demeanor, she clearly wants to be friends with Nana and all the family. I don't know about her intellect. Can anyone guess if a drunken person has brains? However, she seems to be a well-meaning person.

After her eyes flit to verify Brian's head nod, she faces Nana squarely and states, "If the invitation is still available, we would be delighted to spend a family Christmas together."

Interesting! She searched for his agreement—a code between them. Does that mean the relationship is serious? Autism leaves me out of the loop!

Nana audibly sighs, "Oh good. That is wonderful. Christmas dinner is at 6:00 p.m. But you are welcome any time before that. Here's an idea. Since you are at the hotel, why not come for breakfast and open presents with us? It would be fun."

Papa glances at his wife with his face flashing annoyance until he realizes what an effort at reconciliation she is making. Papa adds with false cheeriness, "Yes. That would be wonderful. You are welcome to spend the day here. Far better than wasting time in the hotel." He looks to the side immediately as he realizes what they may do to waste their time.

Teresa flashes a smile of gratitude at Papa. "It's settled then. What time is breakfast?"

As she points to Susanne and me, Mom answers, "These two will be up any time after eight. We have breakfast before gifts. Does eight-thirty suit you?"

Teresa smiles at Mom. "Couldn't be better."

This conversation puts Uncle Brian in a better mood. He smiles for the first time as he says, "Goodbye. Till later. And thanks for breakfast." He hugs his mother and his sister, shakes Dad's hand, hugs his father, and waves cheerily to Phoebe, Susanne, and me. Perhaps the incident of the morning will be forgotten.

Nana and Papa see their son and his girlfriend to the door and watch while Brian puts their luggage in the car. They wave farewell as the car moves down the drive. The door closes softly.

Nana and Papa gaze at each other and say nothing for a moment. Nana moves closer to her husband. His arms reach around her in a long hug. We give them a little alone time. She dabs away tears as she returns to the morning room. We all continue fiddling with the last of our food. Dad has another cup of coffee. Mom nods yes to his question about a refill. Susanne glances at me from time to time, still slightly flushed and totally embarrassed. Phoebe has remained unusually quiet throughout breakfast.

Papa pours himself more coffee, sits quietly for a moment, and then remarks, "I want to make something clear to the children. Brian and Teresa are of an age to understand consequences and to make their own decisions. Perhaps I am an old fuddy-duddy, but I do not approve of casual sex. Brian has had two wives and two divorces. There has been a string of girlfriends—all short-lived affairs—not good for anyone. In the world of HIV and other diseases spread by sexual contact, I worry about Brian."

Then Papa utterly surprises Susanne and me. "If Ms. Merlo were his one and only, his betrothed and soon to be wed, I would not have insisted on separate rooms." He pauses before he admits, "I am upset that he could not follow house rules even for one night out of respect for Nana and me." Suddenly pensive, he pauses again before he continues, "But he is our son. I do not want to drive him away because I disapprove of his lifestyle. That is why Nana and I are making an attempt at reconciliation."

Nana looks at her husband and agrees, "Yes, John, you have said it well. I am willing to overlook this incident, but what happened is not a good example for you two children. Sexual intimacy is for a committed relationship only. In an age of deadly disease spread by intimate contact, monogamy is the safest, whether married or not. Besides morals, my concern is safety."

Susanne and I are red-faced at the candor of our grandparents. The same conversation from our parents would never have had the same impact. But here are respected older adults, successful people, loved by us, who are wise to the ways of the world. They are dispensing advice to a teen and a preteen on the topic of sex! Both of us pay attention!

Dad and Mom both state, "We agree with Papa and Nana. We wish Brian could find a committed relationship. He needs to get his career act together, as well as his personal life."

All of this gives Susanne and me a lot to think about. We help clear the dishes and load the dishwasher. Phoebe directs us, if only to keep us busy.

Nana confides, "I must help out at our church to assist with last-minute details." Mom decides to go with her to help, an excuse for conversation time with her own mother.

Dad decides to go with Papa when he says, "I have a few things I need to do related to the estate. Would you care to help?"

"Absolutely," Dad replies with a chuckle.

Suddenly alone with us, Phoebe solemnly states, "Well children, we three need to talk."

Again, we find places in the morning room and sit comfortably, even without food. Sunlight streams in, marking patterns of light on the furniture and carpet. This adds warmth and a sense of hope and well-being.

Phoebe asks, "What exactly did you see, Susanne?"

Susanne turns red as she answers, "I knocked, but there was no answer. I opened the door and looked in. Brian was lying on top of Ms. Merlo, but it was pretty clear what was happening from their thrusting movements under the blanket. They were having sex."

Phoebe replies, "I am sorry you saw that. Intimacy should always be private. And it should occur only in a committed relationship. This is not how I expect either of you to behave. Like his excess alcohol, this episode shows bad judgment on Brian's part. Ms. Merlo is not blameless either."

In the silence that follows, I decide that it's my turn to come clean with what I know, especially since problems may come up later.

I admit, "I was quietly heading to the kitchen this morning when I overheard something else that Nana told Mom. They didn't know I was listening, and still don't. Afterward, I retraced my steps and pretended to clunk down the stairs so they would not know I had listened."

Phoebe and Susanne both look at me intently. Susanne mutters, "Aren't you the devious one?"

I smirk back at her. "Nana told Mom that Uncle Brian has been in rehab twice for cocaine abuse. He can be triggered by alcohol, and he does stupid things when he snorts. He has no job because he got fired for drug use at work."

Phoebe gazes down sadly while her head slowly moves side to side as she listens.

Susanne queries, "Are you sure you heard correctly? I can't believe Uncle Brian, our favorite uncle, is a coke-head." Susanne stares at me as if I have two heads and spout fire.

"I know what I heard." My shoulders shrug with my answer. "Papa and Dad came into the kitchen the same time as you two. You all saw Mom's red eyes and Nana with her face turned away. She had been crying."

Phoebe observes, "I did notice and knew something was wrong. That is why I busied myself setting the table in here."

Susanne recites mechanically, "I didn't have enough time to notice much, what with following orders to troop upstairs again to awaken the copulating couple. I did see things were tense."

I add, "I was dispensed to get the morning paper from the postbox. After I left, I looked back. Nana and Papa were talking earnestly to Dad and Mom. All of them were supposed to be preparing food, but nothing started until after we returned. I'll bet that they were telling our parents the details about Uncle Brian's addiction and rehab episodes."

Phoebe continues, "There was quiet conversation ongoing in the kitchen. I didn't even try to overhear. You are probably right, Jeremiah. Your guess fits with what I saw."

Susanne still looks stunned at the news. She says quietly, almost to herself, "It is so hard to believe Uncle Brian could be that stupid."

Phoebe replies quietly, "Take this as a lesson to you both. Excess alcohol and drugs lead to bad judgment and bad actions. Be better than that, you two. Always be able to look at yourself happily in the mirror as you clean your teeth in the morning. If you are not happy with what you see, fix it, and stop what is wrong. Better still, don't make the mistake in the first place. Think first!"

Susanne suddenly exclaims, "What pain his cocaine addiction and alcoholism have caused for Nana and Papa! What a mess drugs have made of Brian's life! I will always remember."

"Me too," I declare emphatically.

Fortunately, years later, we could still truthfully say, "We both remembered to think first!"

Susanne appears thoughtful as she adds, "This makes Uncle Ian and Aunt Evelyn's response at dinner the other night a little more understandable. It was not only what happened, but also their knowledge of the cocaine and rehab episodes that triggered their unsympathetic response."

Now things are starting to make sense for me too.

I add, "My guess is that Collin and Dexter don't know about the drugs. They are just nasty enough to find last night's situation a bit too funny."

Susanne nods with Phoebe and adds, "That's my guess too." We all sit in sad silence before we disperse.

After a while, Papa and Dad return with an enormous tree attached to the roof of the car. They hail us to help them. Tightly wrapped in twine, the tree enters the drawing room on their shoulders.

All of us are recruited to work. Papa, Dad, Susanne, Phoebe, and I each carry a box or two of Christmas decorations from the storage area in the basement. It takes very little time to get everything assembled in the drawing room. The tree stand appears from its storage container. Soon the tree is upright; lights are on, decorations hung, with an angel sitting at the top. A porcelain Santa guards a side table, and the stockings are all hung. After returning all the empty boxes to their storage cupboards one floor below, we check the lights again and admire our handiwork. Even competing with daylight, the enormous tree looks splendid.

"That's a beauty," declares Dad. All voices agree.

"Time to celebrate with a cup of tea," suggests Papa. We trail after him into the kitchen and eventually end up in the morning room drinking tea and snacking on leftovers. As we laugh and joke together, Papa says, "Once again, a task has been fun by making it a game with many hands to help."

When Nana and Mom return, we leave our cups and dishes on the morning room table and head to the hall to greet them.

Susanne announces breathlessly, "We've decorated the tree, and then Papa suggested tea. There's plenty for you two, but maybe, well, do you want to see the tree first?" Susanne smiles expectantly at Nana and Mom.

Nana gleefully replies, "That would be splendid."

We troop into the drawing room to show off our handiwork. Both appear surprised and delighted.

"It looks wonderful. In the darkened room, it will truly be splendid," remarks Nana.

"I can't wait for nightfall," responds Mom. "And I won't need to wait long," she mutters as she looks out through the windows and shrugs her shoulders.

Nana bats her eyelashes at Papa and adds, "But I think your idea of tea is still a good one." We all head back to the table for more to eat and drink.

Chapter 6

CHRISTMAS EVE

In the afternoon, Nana states, "So we are not rushed for church, tonight's Christmas Eve supper will be a little earlier than our usual seven or eight o'clock. Nigel is away with friends for a few days, so we are serving ourselves. Mrs. Stewart is with her family. Various food items have been prepared in advance, which I can serve with a little help."

Around six o'clock, we assemble in the dining room. Nana announces, "It's self-serve from the sideboard. Papa and Sam may lead off. Tonight's meal is a salad with cold meats and shrimp."

There are slices of various breads, sliced turkey breast and sliced ham, cold potato salad, egg salad, celery sticks stuffed with cheese, olives of several varieties, and an enormous bowl of salad sitting beside a gigantic platter laden with shrimp.

Previously, Mom said to Susanne and me, "For future reference, shrimp are simple to prepare. They can be either quickly cooked in boiling water till opaque and then chilled under cold running water to remove any debris, or they may be sautéed in butter or olive oil. Boiling is tonight's planned cooking method. They will be served beside a bowl of red dipping-sauce made tangy with horseradish. Use the large spoon to ladle servings into individual. bowls."

I see the empty smaller bowls she mentioned, all of them awaiting an individual serving of shrimp sauce. Pointing impolitely to the red bowl, I enthuse, "I can't wait to taste that sauce! And I love shrimp."

Dad corrects, "Jeremiah, you *like* the shrimp. You don't *love* shrimp; they cannot love you back."

Laughingly, I reply, "I think they might."

Everyone takes some of everything. I take multiple shrimp. Nana glimpses my plate and giggles. "I am sorry you despise shrimp. Poor lad." She points to the mounded heap of curved bodies on my plate, shrimp ready to be eaten.

Mom adds, "I don't think Jeremiah has met a food he doesn't like." She and Dad laugh with Nana.

After his eyes scan me, Papa shrugs his shoulders and observes, "By the look of it, your parents will need more lucrative employment to keep you fed." He laughs too.

I furtively glance toward Susanne. She hasn't skimped on anything either. But I don't even want to tease her. One of her friends at school has an eating disorder called anorexia. I am glad that Susanne is normal and is not following the "I must be too thin" crowd. One of her casual friends at school starved herself into a really significant illness.

After the main course, we have sliced the fruit that Nana and Mom prepared earlier; apples, oranges, bananas, grapes, and blueberries all mixed together with lemon juice squeezed overtop to keep everything fresh. A sprinkling of candied walnuts gives a crunch to the sweet. *Yum!*

There are conversations about the church decorations and who worked this year in preparation, all with a sense of anticipation for this service. Nana declares, "The church is always beautifully done up."

Papa says, "The major services at Christmas and Easter are as much good theater as anything else, always wonderful to see and share."

I can't wait to see what has been prepared.

After dinner, we stack dirty dishes in the kitchen and then load the dishwasher. Phoebe, with Dad and Papa, makes sure all the food is placed back in cold storage. As we head out of the kitchen, I hear the dishwasher kick in. It is an older model and is a little noisy. But it works!

Two cars are needed to transport us, Papa in one and Nana in the other, in case directions are needed. In the back seat, Phoebe sits between Susanne and me. Dad is driving, and Nana is his front seat navigator.

Phoebe asks, "Are each of you excited for Christmas to arrive?"

Susanne replies, "Of course! It is so good to be here with Papa and Nana. Christmas is different from when we were little, but I love the magic of the holidays."

I add, "And we have good company and wonderful food. Everything is very different than in America, but I love being here at Christmas."

Phoebe asks, "What do you want for Christmas?"

Susanne responds, "We have enough stuff. Gifts are fun, but I'm not burning for something new."

I pipe up, "Shrimp! Now we're done."

After Dad laughs out loud, he mutters from the corner of his mouth, "What besides food?" While he awaits my reply, he exchanges glances with Nana, who nods and grins.

I finish with, "I don't need anything." Phoebe seems satisfied with our responses.

We soon reach the village church with its surrounding graveyard. The building and its partially enclosed porch in front of the main door are made of a brownish-colored stone. The entrance to the porch is an arch but with limestone edging.

As we park, Susanne says, "That porch with its arch is very pretty."

Still seated, Nana replies, "This porch arrangement keeps down the drafts in winter. That's an important feature, since there is no heating, central or otherwise. Children, you may notice that all the windows are topped with gothic arches, and most windows have stained glass. The stained glass was added in the seventeenth, eighteenth, and nineteenth centuries. The original building is old, dating from the fifteen hundreds. I am told the porch arrangement was added much later, early nineteenth century."

Phoebe comments, "That porch addition was cleverly done. It blends in seamlessly, as if original. While not large, the church is exceedingly attractive. The boughs of evergreen placed around the stone arch of the entrance are a beautiful touch. And I see a lovely large evergreen wreath on the door to the church proper! With the fruit and red berries, it looks like a Della Robbia wreath." Her seat-belt release clicks.

Nana replies, "Right you are! Clever, Phoebe!" Nana turns to smile back at Phoebe and then continues, "The men put up the arch-way evergreen. I did the wreath. It began with a wire frame that we use each year."

Susanne exclaims, "It's beautiful! You *are* a clever gran."

"Yes, indeed," echoes Phoebe, "and you did a splendid job with the wreath. That type can be difficult to properly balance."

Nana flushes with pleasure.

Inside the crowded church, we see upright wooden rods attached to the pews along the central aisle. Each ends in a burning candle. Each of these rods is covered in evergreen so that the candle appears to rest in green boughs. Each windowsill has an evergreen arrange-ment festooned with ribbon and holding a hurricane lamp over its candle. Poinsettias are arranged in various parts of the sanctuary and near the altar.

Nana says, "We don't adorn the Communion rail. Some people need support as they get up from kneeling during Communion."

Off to the side is a small crèche scene donated by some pros-perous soul. The figures are beautifully done, finely detailed, and the wooden stable is finely crafted.

"That crèche is beautiful," I whisper.

Practical Nana replies, "And it all comes apart for storage!"

With the candles burning and the lights dimmer than usual, the mood is set for the Christmas celebration. It's magical! The festive decorations are also a good distraction from the many plaques on the walls naming the dead. Most were former members of the church. Many of these people named are my ancestors.

Like I said before, I met many of their phantoms in Papa's attic during my last trip. Some of my ancestors were wonderful people, and some were killers. I'm glad there are festive garlands distracting me from that recollection!

On arrival, the ushers hand a candle to every member of the congregation. The music starts as we wend our way to sit together.

The church is nearly full, but two people graciously shift sideways to give us seats a few pews behind Uncle Ian and his family. Those four relatives must have arrived early to be seated in splendid isolation near the front in a pew to the right of the main aisle. Since the service is starting, we will greet them later.

Odd to have no one else in their pew. Several available places stay empty!

At the beginning of the service, I crane my neck to look back. Tardy as usual, Uncle Brian and Teresa are searching for a seat. They find two available spots they can cram into in the last row on the left side of the aisle beside the opposite wall, farthest from the exit. At least they arrived and found a place to sit, even if nearly late!

A few minutes later, I twist around again. The place is packed! At the rear of the church, new arrivals are clustered together, forced to stand throughout the proceedings—no place to sit. I discretely wave my hand. Uncle Brian and Teresa respond with a smile and return a small wave.

The seats beside Uncle Ian and his family are still vacant. Perhaps latecomers don't want to walk that far forward, which might intrude on the ceremony. Instead, they remain standing at the rear of the church until the end. That's hard on the feet!

Is their courtesy part of British understatement? Who knows.

There are many hymns and the choir performs two anthems beautifully.

Late in the service, an acolyte lights the candle of each person sitting along the aisle. The flame is shared neighbor to neighbor along the pew. When all the wicks are glowing, the church is plunged into darkness as everyone sings "Silent Night."

The quiet beauty of the scene deeply affects our emotions. As we depart, I feel uplifted and filled with hope—as intended.

We wait as Uncle Ian and his family approach. They stop to greet us. As we talk, we wish them a Merry Christmas. They quickly head down the aisle. Aunt Evelyn walks to the right of Uncle Ian, with the boys on Uncle Ian's left, the same side as the exit. Uncle Ian and the boys are looking in that direction.

Aunt Evelyn is blocking their line of vision, so I am not sure if Uncle Ian and the boys notice Teresa and Uncle Brian lingering against the far wall at the rear of the church. But my aunt definitely does. She slows her walk. As Ian and the boys exit, she turns abruptly to directly face Teresa and Uncle Brian, who both look expectantly at Aunt Evelyn's disdainful face.

This is Aunt Evelyn's chance to mend fences. Instead, she makes eye contact, deliberately moves her head sharply away, and abruptly turns her back on Uncle Brian and Teresa. Task completed, she follows rapidly behind the rest of her family.

I wince. *What an obvious snub!* A moment of talk might have healed much.

Uncle Brian and Teresa wait for us at the back. We talk briefly. The events at the house are never mentioned and no one says anything about the brutal snub.

Papa, who has seen the snub too, goes out of his way to be kind and show interest in Teresa. He is desperately trying to make her feel at ease with us.

Following his lead, each of us gives them hugs as we say Merry Christmas and again extend a welcome to spend the next day with us.

Once we are in the car, there is a brief discussion of the beauty of the church with its decorations and the beauty of the service itself. On the way home, all of us become quiet, burdened with the great unsaid.

Finally, in the heavy silence, Dad looks in the rearview mirror, nods to Phoebe, glances at Nana, and comments, "It was painful to watch Evelyn's snub. Teresa was hurt. So was Brian."

Nana replies firmly, "Thank you for that opening. I was afraid to speak. Yes, that was dreadful, so unkind." Nana turns back toward us and clarifies, "That kind of behavior is not right. I am disappointed with Evelyn but not entirely surprised. I can't change *her* behavior, but *we* can control our own. All must be kind to both Teresa and Brian. We shall not follow Evelyn's lead, understood?"

If we didn't understand before, we sure do now!

Phoebe smiles slightly as she listens to Nana. I suspect that she was hoping to hear those words.

When we arrive home, everyone gathers in the drawing room. Each person has a stocking hung. Some are old and embroidered, while others are make-do ones——altogether, an odd assembly of mismatched socks as they hang in an irregular row.

Dad announces, "We must leave something for Santa." Susanne rolls her teenage eyes while I keep my mouth shut. He enthusiastically asks, "Do you think Santa is tired of milk? Should we get him some orange juice for a little variety?"

With a sideways glance at Dad, Susanne replies, "Why don't you leave him a nice little glass of scotch whisky?"

Dad gazes sadly at Susanne before his eyes slide quizzically to me. "Oh, I guess we could. At least it *would* be a change from the usual milk." Then he gets a small glass and puts in a small amount of scotch. It sits beside the Christmas cookies and the carrot for Rudolph. Dad frowns down at the plate, glances first at Susanne and then me, pouts at the plate, sighs deeply, and then forces a smile as he declares, "Now, we are all ready for Santa." His voice is not yet quite cheery.

Susanne and I say good night to everyone, get Christmas hugs all around, and head upstairs with Phoebe. We hear a chorus of "Merry Christmas" as we go.

As usual, Phoebe supervises the nightly rituals and tucks each of us into bed. It's my turn to go first tonight.

The same as every other night of our lives, she gives each of us a kiss on the forehead once we are in bed. This nightly ritual provides a constant for us, a reassurance that the world is a safe place. *Not everyone is so fortunate.*

After a goodnight kiss on my forehead, I bid them, "Goodnight and Merry Christmas." Susanne and Phoebe echo my words in reply, head out of my room, and quietly begin to talk once inside the adjoining bathroom.

I hear *Santa* and *believes* mentioned a few times. The sounds are quieter as they go into Susanne's room. I'm too tired to eavesdrop! They are still murmuring together in Susanne's room as I fall deeply asleep. I dream of Santa munching on cookies and drinking scotch.

Chapter 7

CHRISTMAS DAY MORNING

The sunlight is brightly streaming into my room through cracks and openings between the drapes. Patterns of bright light illuminate spots across furniture and the carpet alike. The slowly moving patterns are pretty in themselves, but when the bright light hits the old oriental carpet, blue patches and patterns glow with new life. Already, so early in the morning, the sun patterns are enough to make life seem good.

But it is not so early in the morning! After a late night, I have slept later than expected. The midnight mass Christmas Eve service began at 9:45 p.m. but didn't finish till well after 11:00 p.m. It was long after midnight when I finally "hit the hay," as Dad would say.

I open the drapes and see a faint dusting of snow on the gardens and walkways. It rarely snows here, so this little bit is something to admire and crystalize in memory as it glistens and sparkles in the sunlight. This all reminds me of Christmas at home, where snow is all too common. Sometimes, it is welcome right at Christmas if it doesn't cause traffic problems.

It is past 8:30 a.m. by the time I clean up, dress, and quietly, almost stealthily, head downstairs. I overhear Dad tell Mom, "I was so sad when Susanne suggested scotch for Santa. My guess: She knows who always ate the cookies, drank the milk, and chewed on the carrot. Do you think Jeremiah knows, too?"

I make a noise before I enter, which kills the conversation. Mom and Dad are starting preparations for breakfast without actually beginning to cook. Papa is here, too, but Nana still hasn't come down. Teenage Susanne is yet to be seen.

Phoebe appears from the morning room after setting the table there. She waves to me in greeting as she says, "Good morning. Merry Christmas, Jeremiah." My hand flaps in her direction.

"Merry Christmas to all," I reply and wave to all.

Mom proclaims, "Merry Christmas and good morning, Mr. Lie-a-Bed. I expected you up crack o'dawn. I am glad you slept in—that gave me a little respite. Breakfast will be coming soon." She pecks my cheek with a flitting kiss.

As I pass near Dad, he says, "Come here, you. I need a Christmas hug." As I lean into him while he sits, his long arms hug me tight. His stubble, which has grown since yesterday's shave, tickles and scratches my face. He has his own characteristic smell, different from Papa's, one I remember from forever. It is a scent I associate only with Dad and love, just as much as I love the faint smell from Papa and his tweed jacket. Neither wears cologne so their smell is a constant. Mom and Phoebe are always trying various perfumes, which makes things different with them.

Shortly after my arrival, Nana arrives fully energized. As a natural leader, she starts to direct preparations. She asks, "Jeremiah, will you rouse Susanne?" She looks for my answer.

I nod, giggle, and reply, "Your wish, my command."

Laughing, she jokingly orders, "Beard the lioness in her den. Wake her up. I know she is a teenager, but I want to open presents, and we eat first! Now, give Nana a kiss."

After she receives her kiss, her arms wrap around me and hug me tight. "Nana loves Jeremiah. Now off you go, my dear."

Who could grumble with such a request?

Heading up the stairs, I review my parents' overheard conversation in my head. I know what I could say about Santa, but why change things? Say nothing, and nothing changes. That's my plan; let well enough alone. Besides, change is not my thing.

Santa still needs his cookies and milk.

Susanne lies on her bed, almost face down, sprawled on her left side. Her right foot sticks out from under the covers. Drool has mostly dried on the left side of her mouth and chin. It is a pity my phone is in my room. A photo would be a good source of teasing, maybe even threatened blackmail.

Who would marry that?

"Good morning, Miss Sunshine. Rise and thud!" I open the drapes to let sunlight pour into the room. Colors flare everywhere—on her coverlet, on the carpet, and on the wall where the sun hits part of a painting, making a lady's dress glow scarlet.

She mumbles almost indistinguishable sounds. "Muuumph. Wha …" Obviously, she's not awake.

I project more loudly, "Good morning, Ms. Sunshine. Time to rise and shine." I clunk along noisily. Holding her book high, I return it to the desk with a thud. "You failed the thud test!" I sing a silly ditty louder and louder. She moves a bit, then wiggles more.

Finally, she responds sleepily, "What are you doing? It's the middle of the night."

"Silly girl. It's the middle of the morning. It's almost 9 a.m."

She answers, "That was yesterday's clock, not today's."

"Whatever do you mean?" I ask.

She mutters something about yesterday and rolls over. I sing louder, then hand a tissue in her direction. "Time to clean the drool off your chin."

Suddenly wide awake, she sits up, grabs the tissue, wipes her face, and calls out, "Oh gross … I hate that."

She squints at me sideways through sleepy eyes, nods, and mumbles, "Thanks." She then pushes the covers to the side and points her long legs toward the floor as she sits up on the side of the bed. "Okay. You win. I am up."

With a lilting voice, I remind her, "Merry Christmas, Susanne."

"Oh, yes, it is. Merry Christmas to you, Jeremiah." Her sleepy words sound a little fuzzy, but she is now clearly awake.

"I will see you downstairs. Nana is supervising breakfast's creation, so don't take long," I advise as I leave the room. "You know she's a mover and shaker."

I hear her babbling agreement as the hallway door shuts behind me. Dad always says teenagers need more sleep, and Susanne sure proves that point!

Back in the kitchen, the phone rings, which Nana picks up. "Hello," she says to the receiver as she puts the phone on speaker.

Uncle Brian says, "Teresa is still tired and is going to take it easy for a few hours more. We will eat something at the hotel and see you later if that is okay."

Nana agrees. They talk a little more before the line disconnects. Afterward, Nana admits, "Perhaps, just as well. I think Teresa needs time to get her thoughts straightened out. Last night's snub must have been most painful."

Phoebe quietly suggests, "Teresa has had a lot happen. She wants to be at her best. It's always hard to be on cue all day. Anyone can see why she might need a little extra rest."

Nana regards Phoebe quizzically and affirms, "You are remarkably perceptive. And, yes, I think you are right."

When Susanne arrives a little later, she seems a different person. Again, her hair is swept up and away from her ears and face in an adult style, accenting her pearl earrings. She wears a dress that is conservative but flattering to her tall and slim figure. She has almost become a young woman, no longer a kid like me. It is good to see, but, deep down, I don't like it.

Susanne and I are in the same schools. She knows my friends and I know hers. Sure, we fight sometimes, but we always have each other's back. We have had wonderful times together, and we worked hand in glove during my scary time travel that helped obtain Great Uncle Edgar's pardon after his wrongful execution in the eighteenth century. That sure brought us closer together; after all, I was nearly murdered!

We have always been best friends, but now she is growing up and away from me. She is becoming an adult, while I'm still a dorky kid. That makes me sad. I'd rather be a kid with my sister forever. Despite all that has happened, our childhood together with our family and with Phoebe has been too magical to ever leave!

Suddenly, I feel momentarily overwhelmed with sadness and pressured by the passage of unkind time.

However, I soon feel better with that wonderful thing called breakfast. We have bacon and eggs, fried tomatoes, a small pancake each, and toast with homemade preserves. The adults drink coffee; Susanne and I have milk. We talk during the meal, but I try to hurry since I want to open presents. No one else seems to mind if the meal takes forever.

When we finally go into the drawing room, the drapes have not yet been opened. In the dark, Papa turns on the tree lights. The effect is magical! The tree is over ten feet tall and almost reaches the high ceiling. At the top, there is an angel in a cloth dress with a halo light that is a yellow-orange color shining above a beautiful ceramic face that smiles down, happy with what she sees. Her wings are silver and look like they could let her fly. She has watched many Christmas seasons come and go, and many people. Glass balls are everywhere on the tree. They reflect light from the many bulbs burning bright. Old ornaments collected over many years are scattered among the branches. Anyone could look for hours and still miss things tucked between the needles.

"I regret opening the drapes," confesses Papa as he slowly lets in the windows' bright sunlight. "The tree lights lose their intensity."

He is right. The lights on the tree become insignificant. Moments before, they were intense and magical.

Earlier, we all agreed that there was to be only one present each, especially since we are traveling. But the stockings hung on the mantel have old-fashioned gifts from Santa typical of a previous century. There is a fancy chocolate bar in each. We later learn this is from one of Nana's frequent trips to Switzerland. When asked about this, Nana deftly replies, "I am one of Santa's helpers. There are many of us, you know." She giggles when she says this. In each stocking, there is also an orange, a candy cane, and a whistle for every person in the family.

Everyone is quizzically fiddling with his or her whistle when Nana declares, "There have been break-ins. I thought this could be a way of making noise to communicate with each other and to scare away burglars if the need should arise. The whistle noise will go farther than the voice can carry."

We all make sounds of agreement, but I can tell some feel skeptical.

Mom states, "Nana, I'm not sure everyone will want a whistle around their neck all the time. With any luck, it will never be needed."

I notice that while every whistle is made of a stainless-steel type metal, the metal loop holding its neck-string is painted a different color for each person. Each neck-string matches the color of its loop. Mine is blue, Susanne's is pink, Mom's is red, Dad's is black, Phoebe's is yellow, Nana's is purple, and Papa's color is turquoise. Altogether, there is almost a rainbow!

Phoebe laughs. "I rather like the yellow color. I shall wear mine."

After the stockings are emptied, we open the main presents.

Susanne opens a large box containing a dress she had admired in a shop. She laughs with excitement as she opens her gift. Mom and Dad smile and appear relieved that she is happy.

I receive a tie and a dress shirt with French cuffs from Mom and Dad. Perfect!

Nana and Papa give me an envelope with a check and a wrapped box containing cufflinks for my new shirt. The cufflinks are a fleur-de-lis shape, enameled black over gold, which shows along all the edges.

Papa comments, "The cufflinks are a reminder that the Normans conquered the Anglo-Saxons in 1066, making French culture part of the English. That would be hard to tell now, but it is part of our history." He glances toward my envelope and adds, "Use the check to get something you want when you have returned home." I give both parents and grandparents a thank-you hug.

Nana gives Papa a useful new sweater. He is obviously pleased since he is always wearing one in this drafty old house. The color is sapphire blue, which makes his eyes seem to dance even more than usual.

Nana especially likes her bottle of a perfume from Papa. He knows what she prefers, which made his shopping easier!

Mom gingerly opens her beautifully wrapped gift box and gushes over a blue dress that she liked when she was shopping with Dad. In the store, she said that it cost too much, but Dad replied it looked lovely on her. She held off; apparently, Dad went back to the shop anyway. She is thrilled with the gift even though she thinks it is too expensive. Mom is funny that way. She has enough money, but she is still thrifty and always thinks twice before she spends her cash, or Dad's.

Mom's gift to Dad is a new dress shirt and tie for the office, with his initials monogrammed on the pocket. The collar buttons down, which he prefers. There are button cuffs, not French cuffs. Mom knows what he likes to wear—Dad is pleased. He gives Mom a thank-you kiss on the cheek.

With an eye on me, Dad remarks, "French cuffs are for fancy, not for the office."

"I am especially pleased with my French cuffs and first pair of cufflinks—perhaps *because* French cuffs are for fancy." I don't say that sometimes I want to feel like an adult despite my massive nose overpowering my silly-looking face and despite my autistic social stupidity!

Mom reaches for a box that she hands to Phoebe. "I remember what you admired when we were out together and looked into a store in the village. I hope it is okay."

With big eyes, Phoebe looks at the box and reads the label with our four names signed. She takes off the bow, unties the ribbon, slowly undoes the paper, and folds it carefully. She gasps with delight when she looks inside. She holds up an attractive deep-scarlet blouse with a shawl collar and long sleeves, which puff a little at the shoulders. It is unusual looking and rather pretty. Then she pulls out a black skirt. She stands and holds it in front of her. It falls below the knee, slightly fuller at the bottom in what Mom calls *A*-line. It looks like it will fit perfectly.

"Dad and I got you the blouse, and the kids insisted the skirt was a must-have. I hope you like them."

Phoebe answers, "They both are wonderful. But you said we were not to exchange gifts especially since we were traveling."

Mom points to her children and answers, "Your gift to us is your looking after those two." Phoebe smiles back with moist eyes.

Papa comments, "Nana and I made no bargains about gifts." He looks at my parents and confesses, "We had no idea what to give you, and then you said, 'No gifts. They are too much to carry back.'

Instead, please accept this." Papa hands an envelope to each of our parents. Inside each card is a check.

Papa laughs. "Green is my favorite color, and money is green. You said not to get you anything, but you really must buy something you truly want, either here or in the States."

Mom replies, "Papa, I said having us here for such an extended period was gift enough."

"Ditto," echoes Dad.

"Nonsense," quips Nana. "Use the money for something you will enjoy. And think fondly of us as you do."

"Thanks, many thanks," our parents echo as they hug the grands.

Nana hands Phoebe an envelope and adds, "And we made no bargains about gifts for Phoebe."

Phoebe slips it open, reads the Christmas message written by Nana and signed by both, and then gasps when she reads the check that Papa signed. She exclaims, "Oh my!" and then looks toward our grandparents. "This is very generous! Thank you." She goes to each, hugs both, and gives Nana a peck on the cheek.

Phoebe reaches under the tree and pulls out two wrapped presents. "I think this is for you two," as she hands Susanne one and the other to me.

Each is a book. I picked out Susanne's, as instructed, and she picked out mine the same way. But Phoebe went in on each so she also signed each card. Both are books we really wanted. We all exchange thanks.

Mom motions to Dad, who finds a long thin gift hidden behind the Christmas tree. It looks sort of silly, wrapped in gaudy paper and tied with an enormous bow, but it is our gift to Papa. He looks at it, eyes twinkling, and reads the label signed by the four of us and by Phoebe. I think he suspects what it is. Like a kid happy in a candy shop, he looks at the long thin object, takes off the ribbon, and tears back the paper.

Inside is a long walking stick made from a single piece of beautifully smooth wood that was once the trunk of a young tree. Slight bumps where branches have been cut away show its natural shape. A brown stain highlights light and dark streaks running along its length. The handle is sturdy brass, with an engraved pattern, and comfortable in Papa's hand when he tries it out. It is also tall enough that Papa can grasp the upper section of the wood instead of the handle.

Papa says, "Now everyone will stay in line. Papa has a walking stick and knows how to use it!" We all laugh, mostly because he thinks this is exceedingly funny. After a pause, he continues, "This is a wonderfully practical gift for there are often holes in the ground and uneven areas in our wild fields. With this excellent probe to find those holes, I'll be less likely to have a twisted ankle when I'm out walking."

Mom remarks, "I'm so glad you like it. We heard you talking to Nana about searching for one. When we saw this, it seemed to be the one you needed."

"Right you are," replies Papa, while using the stick to pull up from his chair. He returns to the tree and hands a present to Mom and one to Dad. The labels say from Susanne and Jeremiah.

Mom is thrilled with the long wide scarf we found in a local shop. When she slings it round her neck, it is long enough to fall to her waist, despite her height.

Hallelujah! It's long enough.

Dad seems delighted with our gift, a sweater with a wide shawl collar, wooden buttons all the way down the front, and pockets on each side. The wool is a smooth but sturdy weave, designed for use and comfort.

Dad and declares, "I love the dark brown color. It looks so comfortable that I'm putting it on now." He stands, modeling his gift. "This is perfect. And it's long enough! Thank you, children."

We each receive a thank you hug and kiss before he returns to his seat.

Phoebe hands Papa his present and hands one to Nana.

As Papa starts to tear the paper, Phoebe comments, "I heard you say that your brown belt had recently died when the buckle broke. I also heard you say you like brown and not black. Nigel helped me get the right size."

Papa presents his gift of a soft leather belt for inspection. "Thank you, Phoebe. That was truly thoughtful. And you are right on all counts. Bless Nigel! Where would we be without his help?"

Like a schoolgirl with a sweet tooth buying candy, Nana deeply concentrates as she opens Phoebe's package. Her expression changes dramatically to utter surprise when she discovers red leather gloves made by a well-known glove maker. Her delight increases as she tries them on. "Phoebe, you purchased the correct size!"

Phoebe giggles. "Nigel was a great help again, especially for the size. I was dithering about the color, but he told me to go for broke. Some of the blame goes to Nigel."

Nana continues, "May I tell you, I have always secretly wanted a pair of red gloves? Do you read minds like Leila?"

Leila was the name of my nine-greats-grandmother who could read others' thoughts. Her name brings fond memories and then a shiver down my spine. It was her daughter-in-law who tried to murder me to cover her own tracks. I shiver again and try to quickly dismiss my thoughts, block the flooding images, and concentrate on matters at hand.

Nana furtively glances at my sweaty and anxious face. Then her eyes dart from person to person uncertainly after her careless comment as if she needs emotional reassurance herself. Nana's face tells me she wishes she hadn't mentioned Leila's name. Moving past the mistake so that we *all* move along, she stands up and goes to Phoebe, who also stands. Nana hugs her hard. "I love you dearly for many reasons. The gloves are only part of the story."

Enough with the flooding images and sweaty anxiety! Back to normal, idiot.

Mom reaches under the tree. "This is for you, Nana. It is from the four of us. Sam found it in the Silver Vaults when we were in London the other day. It is an estate piece, but I suspect you may like it."

Nana looks at the box and smiles. "I didn't realize you had purchased anything in the Vaults. My, but you are a clever sneak!" She giggles as she looks at Dad. She adds, "You too," as she glances back at Mom.

She rips the paper, opens the box, and gasps, "Oh my. This is exquisite!" Inside is a beautiful old brooch, with a central emerald and surrounding diamonds. The overall shape is slightly elongated, almost a teardrop shape. "Oh my, there is also a chain. The brooch can be pinned without the chain or worn as a pendant." She puts it on. It dangles down her upper chest, flashing in the light and looking beautiful. She notices the brooch is heavy and, used as a pendant, tends to swing as she walks. "I shall use the chain but pin it in place. That will end the pendulum!" Her moist eyes dart to each of us as she remarks, "I am thrilled. But you shouldn't have. It is too much."

Dad answers for all of us. "Nonsense. After all you do for us? And you two are feeding us for several weeks. You should have three of these and a halo!" He laughs.

As Nana gives each of us a hug and a kiss, the sincere emotional warmth of her touch tells us she is thrilled with her gift. When it's my turn, she kisses me and whispers, "Feeling better?"

I nod and whisper back, "Yes. All okay now."

"Good. Sorry about that, dear one."

She leaves the chain around her neck and pins the pendant brooch where she wants it to rest. For some reason, my mind flashes to Leila and then to Jemima in the attic as I gawk at Nana's beautiful pendant.

Why does it seem familiar?

Nana reaches for the last gift under the tree. There is an envelope and a box wider than an adult palm and maybe longer than two palms together. "This is from Papa and Nana, dear Susanne. Open it. I hope you are pleased."

Susanne opens the envelope and gets a check from Papa, the same amount I received. She glances fondly toward each in turn. "Thank you very much." After they respond, she slowly unwraps a nineteenth-century jeweler's box. She gently undoes two restraining tags and pulls out a beautiful long string of rather large pearls. Susanne's eyes become big indeed as she exclaims, "Oh, my!"

Seemingly lost in dreamy thoughts while gazing directly at Susanne, Nana explains, "These were my grandmother's, a gift from my grandfather on their tenth anniversary. Throughout all their many decades of marriage, the gift was regarded as special, a token of their life-long devotion to each other. You will soon be of an age to wear them. Remember, this as a special gift from another generation, long gone, through your Nana. Enjoy them." Nana's pensive eyes fall to the floor for a moment before they return to Susanne. Then, more briskly and all business, Nana continues, "I had them restrung for safety. The last time they were restrung was about fifty years ago, when *my* mother gave *her* mother's pearls to me." Emotions flit across Nana's face. She remains silent for a moment.

After a pause, Nana quietly adds, "I offered them to your mother years ago. But we were helping with student debt, and she insisted that was enough. At the time, she said, "If I ever have a daughter, you will know when they should be gifted.""

Mom glances at her mother and then at her dad. Her gaze rests momentarily on Susanne and then back to her mother. "I remember that conversation so well. I never regretted the decision. It was not that I didn't want them or didn't value them. But I'm big, active, and a klutz. I'm always at the gym. Pearls would have a short half-life with me." Mom starts laughing. "I was actually guarding their welfare!" We all smile and giggle.

Afterward, Nana continues with a solemn voice, "And now my granddaughter shall have the pearls and understand the meaning and the love. The strand is well over a century-and-a-quarter old. These are completely naturally occurring, not cultured as we see today. They are a true gift from nature, found by happenstance, not farmed."

Fascinated, Susanne handles the almost-white strand. There is no clasp; it is long enough to go over anyone's head. Each pearl is uniformly large with a luscious luminosity shining iridescent in the light, each and every one perfectly matching in color and size.

The strand dangles to her midchest. With the pearl earrings she is wearing by chance, and with her hair piled high, she indeed looks like a lovely young woman. My sister is no longer a kid like me.

I wonder if I will ever look like an adult instead of a dorky kid.

I touch my nose without thinking! Susanne is growing away from our childhood together and leaving me behind. It's an effort to dismiss the sudden sadness I am feeling once more.

I'm afraid of tears, and I don't want to explain.

Susanne is quietly smiling with bright eyes as she hugs and kisses Nana and Papa. She is utterly thrilled to be wearing the necklace that once belonged to her two-greats-grandmother.

Nana eyes are moist as she responds, "You are welcome, my dear. Treat them kindly. Wear them in health."

Mom pipes up, "Key words: treat them kindly." She laughs. "You're less of a klutz than your mother. That's why I'm glad they are yours. If I owned them, something bad would happen—fractured pearls, a broken string. And they look great on you, my dear. Enjoy." Mom smiles contently and gazes at Susanne with great affection. "My grown-up daughter, when *did* you grow up?"

Is Mom sensing the same loss that I feel?

There is a moment of quiet as everyone looks at mature-ly-dressed Susanne. I sense that all the adults are asking themselves the same question. "When did she grow up?"

Finally, Papa queries, "Did everyone receive their gifts? Any unopened ones remaining?"

There is a chorus "Nothing left for us."

"Is everyone satisfied?" asks Papa.

Again, multiple voices reply "yes, indeed," and "Santa toppled his sleigh over right here."

Papa starts the cleanup of paper overflowing from the bin he had in place to collect debris. "We are having a crowd over later. Let's run gifts upstairs or wherever to clear the room."

There follows the activity of sorting gifts, keeping cards, and throwing out paper until some people decide to climb the stairs to stow presents upstairs.

I notice Nana wears her brooch, and Susanne keeps touching the necklace around her neck. *Those two gifts sure were winners!*

"Does anyone want tea?" asks Nana's voice.

"Yes please," echo adult voices everywhere.

"I'll make a light teatime lunch. We have a big meal scheduled for later."

As the chaos settles, I ask Dad the difference between a natural pearl and a cultured pearl. He explains, "A cultured pearl is produced when a shell nucleus, usually a bit of mollusk shell, is artificially introduced into the oyster, usually by hand. The oyster responds by secreting a material called *nacre* to cover the irritant.

"In contrast, a natural pearl occurs when a parasite or bug lodges inside the oyster and won't leave. Or the nucleus may be sand that the oyster cannot expel. The oyster secretes *nacre* to cover the invader or foreign body. Layer after layer builds up until the pearl is formed." I nod that I am following and still interested.

Dad continues, "Pearls were once very expensive because consistent size and color were hard to find, making it difficult to find matching pearls for a strand. Now, culturing makes the process easier and faster. And removing the pearl doesn't necessarily kill the oyster. Many oysters undergo the implant procedure time after time. Older oysters create better pearls, so oyster farmers protect their producers."

Dad pauses thoughtfully and then adds, "Pollution of any kind, however, stops pearl production cold. Pollution may one day kill off pearl production completely. But that hasn't happened yet."

In a little while, we assemble in the morning room. Nana has tea ready with scones, butter, and jam on the table. She has included Nadia's preserves, informally in their jar with a spoon beside. The jar is only half full now because of the devouring hordes. We discuss our bounty and start to assign tasks for the dinner we are all helping to serve later in the evening.

Nana announces to the ether, "Brian and Ms. Merlo will be here. So will Ian and his family. Nadia and Oscar are also coming. We need places for fifteen, but check my math! Dinner will be about six o'clock."

Susanne and I are assigned the task of setting the table in the dining room. At the start, we talk about Nigel and how he works. He measures the placement of plates and cutlery with a ruler, and he places water and wine glasses in rigid order. When we decide that we will obey his rules, we scrounge in the sideboard drawers till we find his ruler and several layout diagrams, one labelled "formal dinner party." This shows how everything should be placed——the one to use!

The flowers on the table have stayed well in the cool house. After we hoist them off the table and make room on the sideboard, little snips here and there make them appear new. Today's tablecloth is red, a Christmas color. With a little difficulty, we spread it over the enormous table and add the green runner to the center. Then we return the flowers and sweep stray petals and leaves from the floor.

We arrange place settings and labels with Nana at one end and Papa at the other. Six chairs sit on one side and seven along the other. Exactly as Nigel explained earlier, the vase holds the flowers high enough to easily see past the arrangement to Susanne seated on the opposite side of the table's midsection.

Carefully, the china, glasses, silverware, and finally a heavy red napkin are in place for each setting, exactly as in the instructions. The process is tedious, but we make it a game. Following his diagram, we use Nigel's hidden ruler to measure exactly where each silverware piece rests. Soon we are laughing at nothing in particular while we complete the tasks and return our implements, both ruler and paper.

This time, I do take a photo because Collin and Dexter are not here. I ask Susanne to pose at the table head where Nana usually sits. Afterward, my eyes are glued to her photo on my phone. With her pearls still on, Susanne appears grown up. Because their hair color is so different, I have not realized how strikingly Susanne looks like Nana. Good for Susanne! I think Nana is beautiful.

Susanne and I have a bad case of the giggles. This sometimes happens if we are a little overtired or feel unsettled about some upcoming event. Clearly, both of us are a little anxious about the evening dinner especially since neither of us likes Collin or Dexter's company. We take more silly photos of each other with our handiwork, and laugh so hard that our anxiety about the upcoming evening falls into another world and is forgotten.

When Nana appears, she announces "I came to inspect your handiwork, especially after I heard giggles." Her eyes jump from one of us to the other with a silly exaggerated stare like a detective in a pantomime, and then she starts laughing. "Can you tell me if things are obviously going well, or *shall I* make a determination?" She laughs again before she peers quizzically around her and exclaims, "Clearly

Nigel helped you with this. You must tell me. Where have you hidden Nigel?" She laughs out loud at her own foolishness.

We both giggle with pleasure. In unison, we answer, "Nana, he isn't here. He's away for Christmas. We followed his rules, and we put back his ruler and written instructions!"

She smiles broadly as she replies, "Well, you both have done a marvelous job. Here is the cloth for the serving board. It matches the tablecloth."

We lift the flowers from the sideboard, the serving board as Nana calls it. We trim up dying flowers as we did with the table bouquet, tidy up the sideboard top and the floor, set down the cloth as instructed, and replace everything back in order. Delighted, Nana is beaming.

Nana glances at each of us. "Beautifully done! Thank you." Her eyes happily roam around the room before they return to us. "Mrs. Stewart, Mr. Brown, and Nigel are away for Christmas. Have a little rest. I may need your help tonight!"

She wanders off towards the kitchen. We stay in the dining room for a few more minutes, continuing to admire our handiwork. Susanne asserts, "Well done, if I do say so myself."

As we head out of the room, I reply, "Well done, indeed."

I'm still dreading some of our guests!

Susanne whistles a show tune. She usually does that when she's really happy about an accomplishment or when she is really well prepared for a test.

Why is she whistling?

Chapter 8

CHRISTMAS DINNER

I find Dad alone and sit down near him. Without saying anything, I glance at him a little uncertainly.

He puts down the book he was reading and asks, "You are rather quiet, Mr. Jeremiah. What's going on? Do you need to tell me something?"

I reply, "I dread seeing Collin and Dexter 'cause they're just plain mean! They act like they know better than everyone else but don't ever need to bother proving it. I know Susanne feels the same."

Dad responds, "Everyone has noticed that they try to put others down. They exploit any weakness in others to make fun of them. They provide a good lesson of how not to behave."

"So what do I do to make them nicer?"

"Jeremiah, you cannot make them nicer. Only *they* are responsible for how they behave. Perhaps someday, something will happen to change their behavior, or maybe they will always be nasty."

I ask, "So there is nothing we can do to wisen them up?"

"Nothing that will work," Dad replies as he shrugs his shoulders slightly. "Don't stoop to their level, be unkind, or laugh at the weaknesses of others, unless you want someone to laugh at your own." He pauses for a moment and looks off into the distance. Eventually, his eyes wander back to his feet on the cassock. He solemnly adds, "Remember, all of us are subject to human frailty. We all have feet made of clay!" He looks at his own slippers and laughs. "Even if those feet are rather large." He chuckles again when an afterthought suddenly strikes home, which makes him exclaim, "Like mine!"

I look at Dad's enormous feet and joke, "Are your clay feet heavy?"

With a silly pretend southern drawl, Dad jokes, "Dunno! I declare, ain't never took 'em off! Can't call me Mr. Stubbs."

With a slight smile, I mostly ignore his silliness. Quietly mulling over his comment about feet made of clay, I reply, "You are right. No one is perfect at everything. Everyone has a weakness somewhere, a gap in their armor."

I flash to a previous episode of my recent eavesdropping on our parents when they were talking together. I figured Mom agrees with Dad about the cousins when I overheard her say, "Both boys are capable of modifying their behavior, and they alone are responsible for making those changes." She sounded annoyed, maybe angry, and then she added more quietly, "I'm not expecting big changes ever." She appeared sad and went to Dad for a reassuring hug. That sent this eavesdropper tiptoeing away.

Moving past those recollections, my attention returns to Dad who is gazing at me to see if I am paying attention. Dad continues, "What goes around will come around. Maybe something will happen to make them *both* reasonable and kind human beings. But I'm not holding my breath! Such behavior is a shame. Sadly, it has been taught, or at least accepted!"

To this day, I remember Dad's humor when he said, "Everyone has feet made of clay!" and laughed at his own big feet.

I never want anyone to make fun of my weaknesses and mistakes. Heaven knows, there are enough of those! With Dad's good advice, I unconsciously made a lifetime decision that day on how I should treat people, partly because I realized Dad was right—none of us is perfect, especially me.

At some point, Nana asserted, "Guests were instructed to arrive at five o'clock for pre-dinner drinks, conversation, and gift exchange." I remind myself that previously we all decided not to exchange gifts with our cousins and uncles and aunt. That would be too much to cart back with traveling. But Nana and Papa will exchange gifts with their guests.

Well before four o'clock, Nadia's car appears with Oscar as passenger. Fortunately, the outside lights were already on. Nadia holds her husband's right hand since poor Oscar's gait is unsteady on the gravel. From his injury during the robbery, his left arm is in a cast supported with a sling. All this is hidden beneath his coat, leaving his left coat sleeve empty. He seems even weaker than on our last visit. Once safely inside, the new arrivals remove gloves and coats while exchanging the usual greeting with us all. Papa gives both a hug, and Nadia and Nana exchange a kiss on the cheek.

Nadia focuses upon Nana and asks, "Do you need kitchen help? I came early on purpose." Not waiting for an answer, she exclaims, "But I must see your tree first!"

Despite being a muscular, heavyset woman, she moves briskly as she starts the procession into the sitting room. Nadia's dark-blue silk dress with long sleeves rustles as she moves. Her dress is becoming, if noisy.

Oh dear! Oscar is not steady walking inside either! And he is carrying a decorated bag. Papa notices, takes the package, and supports his good arm as we walk. Oscar suggests, "Leave that bibelot on a table till later."

We are all smiling broadly as we enter the drawing room. Nadia's rustling stops in front of the illuminated tree. The drapes had already been drawn against the dark outside. Once again, the tree lights dominate the room, despite the low electric lamps. The effect is truly magical.

Like a schoolgirl, Nadia exclaims, "Oh how beautiful! I do so love a Christmas tree!" Her hands clap together in delight.

Oscar nods approvingly. "You have outdone yourselves as usual. It's beautiful and makes me remember many happy memories of Christmases past."

Phoebe gazes at the tree and agrees, "You are right. It is beautiful! I feel happy just looking at it."

Facing our gran, Nadia says, "We have something for you two. If you don't mind, I'd rather exchange before the guests arrive." She notices Nana and Papa's expression. "I know … I know … we talked about this before." She smiles disarmingly. "We agreed not to exchange with everyone, but you are not … *everyone*." Her lashes flap coquettishly.

Nana replies, "I thought we were not exchanging at all. Although I did get you and Oscar a bibelot—just because." Nana hands a package tied with a blue ribbon to Oscar and another gift with a pink ribbon, identically sized, to Nadia.

They tear them open and start laughing. Inside are cooks' aprons that cover from the neck down to the knees. There is a strap that slides over the head and a long cloth belt in a solid color that could tie around the sturdiest cook. The aprons have a matching pattern of wine bottles, bread, and grapes. They are high quality but designed to be fun. One is blue and one is pink, exactly like the ribbons.

"There are different colors so that the cooks never get the wrong apron," observes Nana laughing. Oscar and Nadia are still giggling as they hold up their new aprons.

Oscar adds, "And we will know who is the boy." He puts his apron on with a little assistance to get the strap over his head and then to fasten the belt. "Am I fetching?" asks Oscar in his cast, sling, and apron.

My, he is a good sport!

Nana replies, "Always, Oscar. I can't think *why* I haven't stolen you away." Everyone roars with laughter.

When the laughter settles after a thank-you-hug, Nadia digs into a pocket and hands Nana a small package. "This is from me. Well, from both of us really, since we needed to agree. Please, enjoy this special gift."

Nana catches her breath. The package is small enough to be jewelry, and she knows Nadia too well. Consternation passes across her face as Nana handles the package.

Nadia notices her friend's expression and exclaims, "None of that, young lady! I will tell you now." Nadia's hands enclose Nana's over the package. They lock eyes as Nadia resumes, "These belonged to my mother. I remember your conversations with her about them. You always admired them whenever Mummy wore them."

Nana is suddenly near tears. Has she guessed what the box contains?

Nadia continues, "I have a sister, and she has daughters. I am not close to my sister, and her daughters are prigs." Nadia laughs loudly. Afterward, eyes still focused on Nana, she declares, "I want you, my real sister, to have these." She releases Nana's hands. "Oscar and I agree. Both of us want you to have something left by the one person who I knew always loved me and who dearly loved you from childhood too. We grew up together like loving sisters, always in each other's house. I should have given them to you years ago."

Slowly and carefully, with her hands trembling slightly, Nana unwraps and opens the box. Inside are gold earrings with a large emerald at the bottom and three medium-sized diamond stones in a line above. The earrings are a teardrop shape, meant to hang down slightly, with another diamond over the stud for a pierced ear.

Nana bursts into tears of happiness. As she recovers, she utters in delight, "Oh my, how I *do* remember your dear mother wearing these. They were an anniversary gift, I remember. Your mother had such a beautifully long neck. They looked superb on her. And she wore them every time she could." Nana's eyes move away from the box to engage Nadia. "Are you sure you want to part with them?"

Nadia answers, "I have more than I can ever use. Oscar has been overly generous, and my father was exceptionally good to Mother in that department. After her death, even when we split things up between siblings, there was too much. But I remember how you enjoyed these. And your neck is longer than mine. They will look wonderful when you decide to wear them."

Nana faces Nadia to give her a big hug. "All right, your opportunity is gone. You may *not* have them back!" Nana laughs as she wipes away a few stray tears.

She takes out the gold studs she was wearing and puts on the earrings. They dangle but not too far. The flashes of light from the beautiful diamond stones are eye-catching, while the emerald beckons with its green flashes. They look wonderful.

Nana points to a side table and quietly asks, "Phoebe dear, you are standing near the drawer that holds a hand mirror. Will you pull it out for me to admire this wonderful gift?" Phoebe finds the mirror and holds it for Nana. As our gran turns her head slightly to see the earrings from several angles, she is silent, almost unable to speak. Her eyes brim with near tears. Eventually, Nana clears her throat and confides, "Nadia, I feel close to your mother as I wear them. And that is a wonderful thing." Several happy tears fall.

It's Nadia's turn to cry. She grabs a tissue, dabs her eyes, and blows her nose, which is never elegantly done. Nadia adds, "I am happy I gave them to you. I've been thinking about doing so for several years, and for some reason, a voice in my head said that this was the year to do so. The giving is such pleasure when the gift has meaning!" They both nod in agreement as Nadia gets another hug.

Nana turns to the mirror again. A hand touches one earring. Then she abruptly stares at the brooch and chain she received this morning. She breathes in sharply.

Susanne is the first to expose what everyone is now noticing. "The brooch and the earrings are similar in shape, and the gold is the same color. In fact, the design is almost identical. Are they a set?"

Nana stares hard, as does Nadia.

Nadia responds, "If I didn't know better, I would say they were a set. The designs are really identical."

Nana nods in agreement. "Well, that is a happy accident. Who would have thought such a thing possible?"

Phoebe puts the mirror away. She swallows hard, and her eyes are bright. Clearly, she is moved.

Nadia peers again at the pairing of the earrings and the brooch. She asks, "While the brooch is new to you, is it an estate piece?"

Nana replies, "The family bought it at the Silver Vaults. So, yes, that is correct."

Nadia ponders for a moment and then states, "I have a vague recollection of my mother and father discussing the myths surrounding estate pieces when she received these earrings. I wonder. Were they an estate piece way back then when my father made the purchase? Imagine a set divided so many years ago and now reunited! Wouldn't that be something unique?"

Nana answers, "Well, my dear, we shall never know." The air is silent for some time. Nana wipes her eyes and smiles brightly.

For some odd reason, my mind flips back to Great-Aunt Jemima and the emerald pendant she wore just before she and Great-Uncle Edgar followed Saint Peter to heaven. The images flit by, but I'm not sure why. At the time, I didn't pay much attention to Jemima's pendant. Too much was happening all at once.

Painful images surface, random and useless recollections that lead to worse thoughts. I frantically try to dismiss the ugly memories. *Please, let me forget!* Ignoring my plea, my mind recalls Leila, our time travel when I was ten, and my near murder in the time abyss by eight-greats-granny Barbara. *Enough with all of it; the flashbacks, nightmares, and night sweats!* They spoil my otherwise most wonderful childhood. My childhood must remain magical and good, not painful.

Out of my control, I see images from the time abyss with Great-Granny Barbara smirking at me and cackling, "Welcome to the time abyss. I hope you enjoy your eternity in nowhere." I feel the thump as Great-Uncle Edgar and I landed safely in the carriage of Marcus and Beatrice.

I can't keep doing this. I want to scream!

Regardless of my wishes, I see Great-Uncle Edgar talking to the ancestors, explaining the case against Barbara and James. I hear the voice of Saint Peter dispensing justice.

Stop. Please stop. I am going to scream!

I see Edgar and Jemima after they had a choice in how they looked once Edgar had been pardoned. That's when Jemima was suddenly wearing the same pendant.

Who cares if she was wearing the same pendant? *My head is bursting.* It makes no difference if this is the same pendant and the earrings that also once belonged to Great Aunt Jemima. *I don't care!*

The images in my head must stop! I shall go mad. I'm dizzy and sick to my stomach.

I concentrate on my relatives and our guests to get rid of my useless thoughts. Sick and overwhelmed, I swallow hard to avoid vomiting while anxiously gazing around. Fortunately, I'm standing behind most of them, and no one is paying me any heed. If no one notices, there will be no explanations. Too slowly, the nausea lessens.

With a glance toward his old friend, Oscar points with his good right arm to the fancy beribboned bag that our grandfather courteously carried to a table as instructed. "On a lighter note, that bibelot is for you—a little something to be enjoyed now that it's a few years out from the vineyard!"

Papa deftly opens the bag. "Oh, Oscar, what an extraordinary vintage! Thank you muchly." He gazes approvingly at the bottle of fine red wine he has received. "The four of us together shall enjoy this over a meal after the holidays." Papa nods to Oscar with pleasure.

Beaming with satisfaction, Oscar jokes, "Oh, goodie!"

Nadia puts on her apron as she and Nana wander into the kitchen. Oscar totters after them. He and Nadia look like matched bookends in their aprons. Oscar remains a little unsteady, so Papa hovers beside him as they walk, and touches his good arm.

Good! They were too preoccupied to notice me. They won't ask anything. And I'm better now.

Chatting in the kitchen, Nana puts the final touches on the food preparation that she, Mom, Dad, and Papa have done during the afternoon. Susanne is too enamored of her necklace, Nana's brooch and earrings, and much too busy teasing Oscar about the silly aprons to notice me.

Safe!

At some point, Nana says, "You must know about the incident the other night."

Oscar and Nadia suddenly become concerned. Nadia exclaims, "Not you, too!"

"No, not that kind of incident, not another robbery. But there was a problem related to Teresa, Brian's new friend."

Nadia orders, "Tell all to your sister."

Soon Oscar and Nadia are wide-eyed and fully informed about everything. Their responses indicate that they previously knew about Uncle Brian's alcohol problems. Oscar giggles when he hears about the copulating couple. Afterward, he steals a glance at us kids and puts on a solemn face, a day late. They clearly understand when Nana confides, "We have forgiven Teresa and Brian. We hope it was nerves in a nondrinker that caused the problem for Teresa and anxiety about unemployment with Brian. While we wish the best for Brian, we wanted you informed in case there are further problems. Who knows what might happen tonight?"

Nadia and Oscar nod. "Worrisome," asserts Oscar, "but not the end of the world."

"Right you are," agrees Papa cheerily, as he helps Oscar take off his apron.

Oscar fixes his eyes hard on Papa and queries, "More important than the alcohol slip up, is Brian using cocaine again?"

Papa briefly returns the intense stare before his eyes flit around frantically until they rest on his grandchildren. His mouth opens once and then closes. Desperate, he almost whispers, "The children know nothing at all about that."

Poor Oscar turns pale, stares vacantly at Papa, and declares, "I've really stepped into it. Apologies!" His helpless gaze turns to his wife, whose annoyed eyes travel past him to Nana and then latch onto Papa.

Phoebe rapidly and firmly interjects, "There is no need for an apology, Oscar. The children and I already know most of Brian's problems, including his two rehab admissions for cocaine."

Stunned, our guests, parents, and grandparents stare at the three of us. Eventually, Papa squeaks out, "How did you learn of this?" A moment later, he appears almost angry. More assertively, he repeats, "Tell me how you three learned of this."

Phoebe's eyes move uncertainly from person to person until they fix on Papa. "Simply put, you were overheard. That's how we know. You were overheard quite by accident."

Her simple statement knocks the wind out of Papa's sails. Suddenly, everyone but Papa seems relieved. Nana touches his arm and quietly but firmly states, "And we were worried about sometime needing to explain to the children. That work has been done. Be grateful, John."

It takes a few moments for Papa to regain his composure and eventually laugh. "Duly noted, Iris. As usual, you are right. Thank goodness for acute hearing!" As his tightly held tension breaks, he laughs again before he adds an afterthought. "It shouldn't be a secret in the family anyway."

Oscar gazes intently at Papa and repeats, "I was careless and never asked if everyone knew. That was thoughtless. I most sincerely apologize."

Nana declares, "Nonsense, Oscar. Your apology is accepted but not needed. You opened the window and cleared the air. I, for one, am relieved." We see the look of relief on all the adults, especially Mom and Dad, who are nodding vigorously in agreement.

Papa glances at each of the adults, fixes his eyes on Susanne and me, and quietly confesses, "I'm glad you both know." He turns to Oscar and replies, "Your question was, 'Is Brian using cocaine again?' My answer is that I was told no. I was angry enough to ask, and I *did* ask when they were *in flagrante delicto*.

"When he is using cocaine, Brian acts stupidly because he feels invincible. And his actions here were arrogantly stupid and inconsiderate, in my humble opinion. Hence the question." Papa's anger toward Brian's weakness for drugs and his son's flaunting the house rules has returned even now as he talks. He is once again really mad!

Nana glances at Papa, nods her head, and squints her eyes briefly. Then she briskly says, "We have finished in the kitchen. Let's head into the sitting room." She nods benignly toward us kids, glares briefly at Papa, and whispers into his ear, "Change the topic, *now*!"

I don't know what *'in flagwhatever'* is. Susanne is beside me and notices my lips open. She pokes my ribs hard while all of us are walking into the drawing room. I face her to complain as she mouths the words, "He means when they were having sex."

Now I do understand what Papa was actually talking about, even though I don't know the spelling. I'll figure that later. At this moment, I nod my head and shut up, right quick-like. Susanne's innocent eyes focus elsewhere, away from me. My hurting ribs are a good distraction. My nasty recollections and my nausea have now completely gone, thanks to my dear sister's assault.

Eventually, Mom and Dad find a place on a sofa as Susanne and I find side chairs. I look with wonder at the glowing tree. It's mesmerizing! The tree makes me forget about everything bad.

At exactly five o'clock, we hear crunching on the gravel drive as Uncle Ian arrives with his family. Papa greets them at the door and helps them with the coat rack while Uncle Ian struggles with a thick-handled bag containing their gifts.

Once again, the cousins and their father look like master and students on a school outing. All three wear an identical white shirt, blue blazer, and gray pants, sporting the same school tie. But Uncle Ian is wearing his favorite tweed overcoat. The colors go well with his old-school tie.

In a high-collared, long-sleeved dress with sheer material plummeting overtop, Aunt Evelyn is a picture in brilliant pink. This two-layered tent could conceal the worst figure or an atomic bomb! The hideous color makes her long face appear flushed. Her shoes and handbag unfortunately match her dress. *So … much … pink!*

Her blond hair is pulled up mercilessly tight and tied with military precision in a small bun. The severe hairstyle makes her nose appear sharply pointed above her thin, tightly drawn lips.

A bit later, when they *thought* they were alone, I overheard Mom tell Dad, "Evelyn dressed like a caricature of a conservative matron from fifty or sixty years ago!" As I eavesdropped, my thoughts ruminated, *If that is how they dressed, I'm glad I wasn't alive then!*

After exchanging greetings, everyone gathers in the drawing room. Uncle Ian deposits his bag of presents beside the magically gorgeous tree. Collin and Dexter pay no attention to anything in their beautiful surroundings. They already have some running joke between them that they don't share. Aunt Evelyn gives the tree a nodding eye sweep and mumbles, "How nice." She then changes the topic of conversation as she sits deliberately isolated in an armchair.

Mom and Dad return to their spot on one sofa. Collin and Dexter find side chairs. Papa and Nana have chairs awaiting them. Nadia and Oscar sit side by side on another sofa. Phoebe slinks off to a corner to be inconspicuous, on guard, and out of the way.

Papa serves a glass of white wine to Aunt Evelyn and whiskey to all the men except Dad. The rest of the adults have iced tea; we kids have ginger ale. My wandering thoughts ask, *After last time, are they choosing iced tea to stay clear headed?*

About twenty minutes later, we hear another car on the drive. Papa goes to the door.

Uncle Brian is there with Teresa beside him. Papa helps them with their coats. As Brian hands over two bags, I notice him warn, "Care, Dad. That one is heavy. Shall I take it?"

Papa takes one and leaves the heavier for Uncle Brian. Both end up alongside the cousins' bag near the tree.

Uncle Brian is dapper indeed, casually dressed in a dark turtleneck sweater, brown tweed jacket, beige khakis, and light brown shoes.

Teresa's black dress with its high collar, sleeves almost to the elbow, and a flared skirt that finishes well past the knee, is surprisingly conservative. A wide pleat on each side below the waist allows a flat black panel to show down the front of the skirt—almost like a take on one of Leila's voluminous dresses from the eighteenth century.

A black velvet band at the neck anchors a sheer over-layer to the upper half of her dress. This comes to a velvet band at each wrist, allowing sheer material only to cover the lower arms, and ends at a wide black velvet band around the waist. The dress adroitly hides her bulky upper half.

Her low-heeled black shoes will keep her steady no matter what happens. A long strand of blue lapis lazuli beads between gold balls, deftly knotted below her neck to control their motion, gleams in the light.

Either she has improved in the makeup department, or someone helped her. With her lighter lipstick, her makeup looks far more natural. In fact, it is perfect. Her wavy brown hair is restrained with a black velvet band keeping hair away from her face. Altogether, she looks stunning!

Teresa glances around somewhat uncertainly. Still standing, Uncle Brian and Teresa greet each person who momentarily stands in return. Remaining seated, Uncle Ian and Aunt Evelyn say a curt hello and nod in the arrivals' direction. We hear a choked chuckle from Collin. Teresa gazes directly at Uncle Ian and then fixes her eyes on Aunt Evelyn. She fleetingly glances at Mom, Nana, and Papa. She nods briefly to Dad, then she returns her gaze to Ian. When her eyes fix again on Evelyn, Teresa admits, "I feel bad about what occurred the other night. I was so anxious about meeting Brian's parents that I had a shot of liquor with Brian before we arrived. I rarely take alcohol. I was not in control and drank far too much. That was my first time becoming drunk. I do apologize."

Aunt Evelyn's mouth is open. I can tell she wants to say something mean to Teresa and now she can't. She glances away before her gaze returns to contrite Teresa. "Oh, think nothing of it," she ekes out with a forced and insincere smile. Aunt Evelyn wrings her hands together unconsciously while her stiff body shows she doesn't want to hear what Teresa has most humbly said.

It's hard to snub someone who apologizes.

Nonplussed, Uncle Ian gawks silently at Teresa. Her eyes flit toward Mom and Nana. Then Teresa stiffens slightly as she stands as tall as her frame allows and stares at Ian. The room is silent, deathly silent.

He was mean last time. He stomped out in disgust, and he didn't even ask if Mom was hurt when she was pushed onto the couch. Maybe he should be the one saying sorry! Uncle Ian glances around quickly, realizes all eyes are on him, and finally capitulates with a nod. "Apology accepted."

Collin and Dexter appear confused as they watch.

They were anticipating nastiness.

Swiftly following, Uncle Brian declares, "I was wrong and apologize for everything I said." He looks intently first at Evelyn and then Ian.

Ian mutters, "Just a spat between brothers. Apology accepted."

Evelyn begrudgingly whispers, "Yes, accepted." Her eyes flick to Brian before staring at the floor, as if she had been tricked into speaking.

Nana sighs audibly, and her shoulders relax visibly. As peacemaker, she comments, "Not to worry. Each of us has done something we wish we hadn't. Mustn't worry. All is forgotten."

Nadia gives Nana a knowing nod. Oscar's eyes twinkle. He pretends not to understand and says nothing.

Nana stands again, then reaches over to pat Teresa on the shoulder. Papa, Mom, and Dad all mumble something like "All is forgotten." While Papa asks about drinks, he smiles at Teresa with admiration and affection. This is another time I realize how big are Nana and Papa's hearts. I also understand that Teresa means she doesn't drink frequently or a lot—except for last time. No wonder she didn't know how to control her booze.

Teresa notices the iced tea pitcher as cool drops of condensation trickle down the glass. "I would love some of that wonderful iced tea—my favorite."

Looking peeved, Aunt Evelyn has another glass of white wine. Uncle Brian asks for iced tea. Mom visibly relaxes as she hears this. As she sits beside Dad, she snuggles slightly closer to him and touches his knee. Collin says something to Dexter under his breath which makes them both laugh. Papa notices; his eyes flash to his grandsons, but he remains silent. The rest pretend not to notice.

Nana inquires, "Since there is a little time before dinner, shall we exchange presents now?"

Uncle Ian concurs, "Yes. Good idea."

Aunt Evelyn's head nods yes. Collin and Dexter smirk and eye each other as if something really funny has been said but cannot be mentioned.

Mom watches Susanne and me as she reinforces, "You two know we agreed not to exchange gifts. We already have too much to cart home."

Susanne and I both respond, "We know. We are not expecting anything."

Phoebe adds, "We are heavy laden as it is. You certainly don't need more."

Oscar clarifies, "And everyone knows we all agreed not to exchange. We shall simply have a good time together."

Collin smirks more while Papa presents gifts, signed by our grandparents. One goes to Aunt Evelyn and the other to Uncle Ian.

Aunt Evelyn's present is beautifully wrapped and tied with a fancy bow. She roughly tugs away the wrappings and opens the lid of a high-end gift box. Inside is a stunning sapphire-blue leather hand-bag with gold trim. I know from Mom that this is the hot color for this year. The maker is well-known and the purse is pricey. Aunt Evelyn appears bored.

Nana comments, "Papa and I went in on this together. We wanted you to have something special." Nana looks at Evelyn eagerly, hoping Evelyn is pleased.

Evelyn regards her mother-in-law with indifference and answers flatly, "Oh it is lovely. But it is not really my color."

She couldn't get at Teresa, so she's taking it out on Nana!

Nana flushes with embarrassment. Mom's mouth opens, but no words come out. Papa stares at Nana. His eyes don't leave her face. Nana recovers and stammers, "That *is* too bad." Then she says something I never thought to hear from her. "I was so hoping you liked it. But from a lifetime of experience, I obtained a return receipt, just in case."

Here my jaw drops because Nana rarely mentions price. She continues somewhat coldly, "It was so expensive that I didn't want the money to be wasted. That's why the return receipt is in the box. You may exchange it for something else. They also guarantee the full cash back if you are not pleased. You may take the cash to keep or for a *different* purchase."

She pauses as if she is deciding to continue. She sighs deeply and lets her cold rage push her onward. While Nana's eyes bore into Auntie Evelyn, she clips her words. Flushed with rage, her head involuntarily bobs in anger.

"Perhaps you may wish to take the proceeds and travel comfortably to Paris to stay for a long weekend at an *extremely* good hotel."

Wow! Obviously, this was an *exceedingly* expensive gift. Aunt Evelyn's response has been in poor taste. None of us has ever heard Nana be so direct about what a gift cost.

Even autistic me knows Nana is really mad!

Mom glances at Dad. She suppresses a snicker by pretending to sneeze. Papa looks admiringly at his wife and smiles slightly.

As she finishes speaking, Nana regards Evelyn steadily and coldly. Despite feeling hurt, she is trying to be calm and to keep good relations. Frankly, I am wondering why she bothers. But then, Auntie Evelyn controls two grandsons.

Evelyn's eyes flit sideways to the floor and then return toward her husband.

Nadia had gazed fixedly at Evelyn with an open mouth, which she closed abruptly, fighting back words. Now she stares at the floor and fiddles with her hands absentmindedly.

Oscar tries to pretend that nothing is amiss. As a result, he looks empty-headed.

Susanne and Phoebe appear to be recovering from a stun gun while the cousins quietly snicker. My befuddled head is pivoting from one face to another.

Hurriedly, as if on a salvage mission, Uncle Ian rips open his gift, which is a cap matching the tweed of his favorite overcoat and a pair of beautiful leather gloves in a compatible color. Trying to make up for Evelyn's nastiness, the usually reserved Ian is effusive in his thanks. Afterward, while he bounds to the hall, he remarks, "Wait. Let me find my coat. Hold tight." At the coat rack, he dons his tweed and the exact-match cap. Modeling the hat and gloves, he actually does a little dance as if he were a young peasant trying to impress his girl.

This makes Nana and Papa laugh, mostly to relieve tension, I suspect. Nadia and Oscar are surprised and delighted that he is trying so hard to please. They clap in rhythm to Uncle Ian's little dance. Or rather, Nadia claps and Oscar bangs his right thigh with his good hand to make a clapping noise. Phoebe is uncertain about what is happening and looks to others for cues. Mom relaxes and joins Uncle Ian in his little dance. Dad giggles at the pair. Embarrassed, Collin and Dexter now look like they want to be in another county. Aunt Evelyn's livid red face silently screams, *Don't be undignified!* Uncle Ian looks at his wife, understands her completely, and smiles broadly. Meanwhile, he prolongs his dance with Mom. She hugs him at the end, and he responds with another brotherly hug.

Papa brings over the three bags while Uncle Ian doffs his coat and cap. Gifts are distributed. Nana and Papa open the gifts from Uncle Ian and Aunt Evelyn and the boys. They all went in together on each gift according to the card. Nana and Papa say, "Thank you."

After unwrapping the sloppy thin paper held with quantities of tape, Nana looks awkwardly at a plate that Aunt Evelyn, Uncle Ian, and the boys have given her. It is three-tiered, with a central rod supporting the layers. The pattern is gaudy, and the central portion has metal curls that are meant to be ornately classy but come across as poorly designed and cheap. It has a pedestal as well, which makes it tall and extremely top heavy.

Nana's face struggles to cover annoyance and disappointment. Her eyes flit side to side amid rapid thoughts puzzling how to avoid a socially awkward situation! Even autistic me notices! What about everyone else?

Is she envisioning the same top over teakettle spill I am imaging as I look at the prize? By the way Nana regards it, I suspect there is another story. Later, I learned that Nana labeled this plate at the church bazaar in the summer. She saw one of the other parishioners sell it to Evelyn. She was surprised Evelyn had made the purchase, cheap though it was. Now she knows why. Nana refrains from telling Aunt Evelyn that she put the price tag on her own Christmas present!

Imagine the response if Nana spilled those beans! Staring harshly, Nadia suddenly appears flushed while her mouth opens and closes silently, making me suspect she was also at the church bazaar when the plate was labeled and purchased. She looks everywhere except at Evelyn and Nana. She is desperately trying *not* to speak.

I hope her tongue doesn't bleed!

Papa regards his gift; an out-of-date tie, wider than the current fashion, gaudy in its pattern, and made of a synthetic fiber. Did it lie forgotten in the back of a drawer? He remarks, "Thank you all. I'm *certain* to wear this soon." He quietly places the box on the farthest portion of a nearby table.

I know he will never willingly wear it, unless maybe to the pigsty.

No one in the family says anything. We all try not to stare at the tie or the three-layered plate—gifts that are thoughtless, trivial, and cheap.

When Collin and Dexter are given beautiful books from Nana and Papa, they say a quiet and insincere sounding, "Thank you, Nana and Papa." Both boys place their beautiful books aside, never opening a cover. I later thumb through them and discover fascinating and beautifully illustrated county histories.

They also receive new shirts and proper ties to match, not school ties. They check the size labels to make sure they are correct. Without sounding either excited or grateful, they murmur a soft, "Thank you," before pushing these gifts aside too.

Nadia watches the boys intently while Oscar stays silent and deliberately gazes off into the distance.

Papa peers into the bags Uncle Brian carried in and pulls out Teresa's wrapped present, which turns out to be a bottle of exceedingly fine scotch. He stares at the bottle in surprise and delight.

Oscar announces quietly, "Aren't you the lucky boy?" Nadia and Phoebe laugh.

Papa exclaims, "Thank you muchly, Teresa!" His eyes drift down to the lovely bottle, which he caresses absentmindedly with a finger, before he focuses again on Teresa. He softly questions, "How did you know this is my favorite?"

She smiles broadly and seems to relax for the first time. After she glances toward Uncle Brian, Teresa's gaze returns to Papa. She replies, "I have my source. I wanted something special for you. You are so kind to me." She glances sideways at Aunt Evelyn and then at Uncle Ian, flashes a smile to Nana, and then returns her gaze to Papa. She continues, "You are very welcome. I hope it is the first of many such gifts." She lowers her eyes slightly before looking Papa right in the eye. With another smile, she nods toward Nana, but returns her gaze to Papa.

Papa eyes her quizzically.

I think he realizes there is more to Ms. Merlo than was visible that first visit.

Nadia and Oscar smile for the first time since gift opening began. Nadia's shoulders relax slightly.

Papa remarks, "I thank you again. I shall enjoy this slowly over a long time, small aliquots only. The taste is exceptional."

Bursting with happiness, Teresa murmurs, "I'm glad you are pleased."

Uncle Brian hands a long, flat package to Nana with a card that reads, "From Teresa and Brian." He comments, "We did this one together."

Nadia exclaims, "What fancy wrapping paper! That ribbon is lovely."

Nana carefully opens the beautifully wrapped present. She sets the gorgeous ribbon aside and carefully tears the beautiful paper, as if to salvage some for another gift.

Inside is one of the most beautiful shawls I have ever seen. The beautiful woven print is peacock feathers in vivid and accurate colors on an intricate brown and tan background. The shawl is longer and wider than the usual, almost large enough to substitute for a child's bed blanket, and descends far down her back when Nana wraps it around her shoulders. It looks cozy with a long fold of material hanging from each arm even after she wraps it once around her forearm. As Nana inspects the gift, she smiles and inquires with real interest, "Teresa, did you choose this?"

Teresa replies, "Yes, I did. Brian and I needed to go in on it together. But from what Brian told me about you, I was certain you would like it, so we thought carefully and then splurged."

I don't think she realizes that she has referenced cost by what she says. Clearly, she badly wants to please.

Nana realizes that Teresa wants her to know that the gift is well-thought-out and precious in the mind of the ones giving it.

Nadia teases, "That shawl is exquisite! Teresa, I have determined that next year you and I will exchange gifts. Maybe I'll get a shawl too!" She bursts out laughing.

Uncle Ian glances at his wife and sons. When Auntie Evelyn and the boys remain stone faced while the rest of the group laughs, Uncle Ian breaks into raucous laughter. Tension in the room eases, at least for some.

Regarding Teresa with new eyes, Nana comments, "My dear, you are an expert. I love shawls and this silk is spectacular! I shall treasure it." Nana is now near tears.

Teresa stands up, comes over to Nana, gives her a little kiss on the cheek, and murmurs, "You are so welcome." She touches the fabric and adds, "There is nothing like the feel of good silk." Nana reaches up and hugs Teresa tight.

This gift, with the thought and effort it represents, blots out the grandsons' ingratitude, Evelyn's bad gift choice, plus her nasty response to Nana's gift. It lets Nana even now ignore Aunt Evelyn, who glares at the shawl bitterly, her lips tight with rage, her mouth silent. I remember Mom saying, "Nana is always quick to forget a slight." Mom is right!

Uncle Brian hands Papa his gift. There is bright paper and a bow. Papa rips it off like a kid in a candy store. Inside is a warm sweater, cabled with thick wool, and exactly the sort of thing Papa would use. Papa is delighted.

Oscar declares, "You have a sweater to keep you warm on the outside and Scotch Whisky to keep you warm on the inside. You are a lucky boy indeed!"

Papa laughs out loud. He reaches to a table where there are two envelopes. One is marked "Teresa," and one is marked "Brian." Each opens their envelope.

Teresa appears surprised as she looks at the cash and then has a tear in her eyes. "This is too kind. You needn't have."

Papa retorts amiably, "But Santa is here only once a year."

Nana adds, "We don't know your likes and dislikes yet, my dear. But there must be something you want or are saving up to do. Enjoy."

Teresa notices the word *yet*. Her eyes widen and brighten. She gives Nana and Papa a sincere hug.

Uncle Brian looks at the cash he has in his envelope. He says, "Thank you, Mom. Thank you, Dad. You are the absolute best. This will be an enormous help."

Nana replies, "There is cash, not a check, so no one can snoop into your business." She glances at Susanne and me before she whispers to Uncle Brian with a stern face, "I don't want you to lose welfare payments because of a little extra cash. We want to help, not create a problem." She is overheard by all.

Nadia and Oscar smile at the grandparents. Nadia comments, "Clever you to use cash. Always thinking, you two."

Uncle Ian pays little attention to this interchange. With a furiously red face, Aunt Evelyn watches like a hungry vulture searching for carrion.

130

Brian hands Ian a package. Ian seems startled as he quips, "I thought we were not exchanging this year."

Brian replies, "It was something I found quite by accident. It was in a used bookshop—a token, but it's for your whole family."

Uncle Ian opens the wrapped book after examining the note card. Inside is a book of the peerage. He appears utterly surprised and asks, "Where did you find this? It has been out of print for years. It is one of the few books on the subject that is really authoritative, complete, and accurate."

Uncle Brian answers, "I knew you would know its value. It was in a local bookseller's bin ready for the dumpster. It was discounted—the bookseller was hoping to get a little for his efforts. I thought of you and knew you would enjoy."

Uncle Ian remarks assertively, "I shall indeed. This book is very hard to find. It is also actually fairly valuable to a collector." There is a distinctly greedy look on Ian's face as he smacks his lips like a hungry child while mental wheels calculate the dollar value. The gesture is most unappealing. He mentions in confidence, "Just as well the bookseller was apparently not well informed."

Nadia looks away, hiding her disdain, and Oscar appears embarrassed by the unabashed greed he has seen.

Uncle Ian collects his thoughts and conceals his emotions. With an ordinary expression, but eyes keenly looking at Brian and then at Teresa, Ian says, "Many thanks. And I shall make sure I explain the contents carefully to the boys."

Aunt Evelyn almost snorts when she hears this and then turns her face away. When her gaze returns to the others, she looks passive, not engaged, and slightly amused in a superior sort of way. Her face suggests she knows something secret. It's clear she has no plans of sharing anything.

Both Collin and Dexter are busy whispering between themselves, sharing a private joke and laughing quietly. I don't think they even heard what their father said to Uncle Brian.

Uncle Ian continues, "Yes, we all shall enjoy this enormously."

Aunt Evelyn remains silent. She looks like her mind is far away, simply not part of the events going on. Occasionally, she glances toward her husband with a smirk. Her expression is hard to read, but her anger seems to have faded.

I suspect that her thoughts are not kind.

Papa collects bits of ribbon and paper, puts them all in a trash bag, and then asks about refreshments. Uncle Ian has another scotch. Papa is more relaxed and has another small one. Teresa and Uncle Brian stick to iced tea. Aunt Evelyn has a refill of her wine.

We try to make conversation with Collin and Dexter. Whatever we say they find amusing but not in a nice way.

Susanne flushes slightly. She is more and more a young woman, exceedingly bright, widely read, and far more mature than either of these two. To be treated like an American country fool is not playing well with her.

When Susanne is bored, she remains quiet and still, but not today. She regards the two cousins intently, and her jaw moves silently in tiny movements that are almost invisible. Susanne rarely becomes angry, but when she does, watch out! She has words, and she knows how to use them!

I know my sister well enough to know her neck and ears become red before she lashes out. Her hair is pulled up, allowing me to see that the back of her neck and her ears are now a scarlet fire! This is a sure sign of danger, the same way that the chin quiver signals tears.

I am most interested to see what happens next!

First Nana and then Mom stand, preparing to go into the kitchen. "Let me help, too," offers Nadia as she puts on her apron again and follows after them. With Papa at his side, Oscar, carrying his apron, totters in that direction too.

When Uncle Brian offers to help, Nana suggests, "You keep everyone amused. We have sufficient cooks." Afterward, we hear distant kitchen noises.

Aunt Evelyn remains seated, volunteers nothing, says nothing. Uncle Brian and Teresa exchange the briefest of glances as Teresa tries to engage Aunt Evelyn in conversation. She gets monosyllabic answers, and everything Teresa says seems to fall flat with Evelyn. Bless her heart, Teresa keeps trying.

Uncle Brian tries to make conversation with his brother. Ian is not interested until Brian requests, "Now tell me more about the book. I know nothing of its origins."

This piques Uncle Ian's interest. We all listen as he begins to talk about why the book was written, its purpose, how much it was used in the nineteenth century, and the rights and privileges of male primogenitor.

This last reference is somewhat without tact, since Ian's right of male primogenitor leaves Brian penniless. Uncle Brian shrugs his shoulders and moves the conversation along. I, for one, am glad Uncle Brian has no alcohol onboard. In different circumstances, the conversation might have gone rather differently.

Susanne stops the near-invisible jaw movements and begins asking the cousins about school life. They sort of snicker and say words to the effect that an American *girl* wouldn't understand about their school.

I see a deeper red flash on the back of Susanne's neck, like a controlled lightning bolt! As red flushes from her cheeks down her neck and onto her upper chest, her jaw juts out slightly. Her head tilts while she says so calmly and coldly that even Aunt Evelyn pays attention, "Just try me."

The cousins stop still. The laughter ceases. They stop smirking, confused by the danger they sense. They start babbling something about activities. What they say is not thought out, and the thoughts expressed are not clear.

Susanne interrupts, "I do not understand what you are saying. Do you not know what you do at school?" She questions flatly, coldly, and without blinking.

Uncle Brian suppress a chortle. Teresa looks at Susanne with admiration. Suddenly, Aunt Evelyn seems a little nervous. Other than angry distain, this is the first emotion I have seen from her. Uncle Ian seems really amused, ready to watch a good fight. Phoebe stays quiet in her corner, carefully watching her eldest.

Susanne continues, "So let's start again. This time, try to make sense." Like an angry schoolmistress, one with authority, she fixes them in the steady, hard gaze of a cobra ready to strike. The severity of her gaze matches the cold tone of her voice.

Collin, the elder brother, starts to talk. When he says something about school, Susanne listens intently. Then she questions him. She drives for details. She cross-examines with real skill. When he says something that sounds like the facts have been stretched, she quizzes him relentlessly until the stretcher has been unmasked and the truth laid bare. She makes him out to be a fool who lies when he can. He tries dropping names. She quizzes him for details about the names he drops. She paid attention to the name-dropping last time. I remember noticing that she played deaf the other day so he had to repeat the names.

Now I understand. She was making sure she had the correct names. Susanne has done her homework by researching all the names they dropped. She catches Collin out several times. Somehow, she remembered the lineages mentioned and knows details of the lives involved. *She's a quick study who knows her stuff.*

She talks about the relations of the people they reference. She knows more about the families that the two cousins talk about than the cousins do. I stare in wonder and admiration.

Go, sis, go!

Dexter offers to answer for his brother by way of explanation. He gets the same grilling too. He actually starts to sweat.

Lovely!

Then she asks about the subjects they study, what is required in the course material, and how they are marked and graded. When she has a grasp of this, she starts in on content. This is their downfall. She quickly finds out from their answers that they are in the regular school program and doing no advanced work. She also discovers that their grades are passing but not in any way exceptional.

As I ponder her future as a prosecutor or lawyer for the criminal defense, she suddenly attacks. She approaches the topics in one of the courses that they have studied. She asks a few deadly, tricky questions. They fail in their answers. Then she mentions that she did one of the same courses in the preceding years in an advanced program for the gifted—younger though she is. She gives them the answers that they failed to provide. With one verbal axe blow after another, she exposes their weaknesses academically while she politely references the right answers that she has learned from her studies.

She casually mentions, "I was a year younger than you, Collin, when I did this course. One of my classmates, my best friend, was only twelve as she did the same work, but she is now ahead of me by studying work that is over a year above my level. Ivy League schools are already courting her for admission—US schools that are on par with Oxford and Cambridge. While I am only fourteen, I am doing advanced work that will provide easier access to Harvard, Yale, Stanford, or Princeton, exactly like my friend."

She pauses to let this sink in. Then she asks, "What do you plan as an occupation?"

Collin, heir presumptive, walks into the trap as he asks, "You mean, to actually get a job?"

"Yes. That is what is customarily meant when you are asked about a career choice." Susanne now sounds like a career counselor dealing with the village idiot.

"Well, I inherit. That should be enough."

Susanne sizes up her prey with satisfaction as she quizzes, "And if that fails or the money runs out, do you plan on the dole? Or do you have a backup idea for an occupation? You know, something to train your mind and maybe bring in some money."

She has obviously hit upon new territory. A glance at him makes me realize he has never thought this through. Somehow, the arrogant boy with so much snickering and bluster seems rather pathetic and clueless.

Collin suddenly realizes how lame he sounds. He tries to return the attack. I smile. At this moment, that is *not* a good idea.

Collin snickers, "So I suppose you know what you are going to do? I suppose you have early acceptance already?"

Susanne smiles disarmingly. In a calm quiet voice, she explains, "University acceptance is still some time away. However, at the present time, I am mulling over two things. Surgery fascinates me. With my superb hand-eye coordination, I am thinking about plastic surgery, perhaps maxillofacial reconstruction. The thought of helping accident or burn victims return to real life thrills me." She pauses for effect.

"But then, I may go into law. Our family has a pattern there already. There are so many faces to the law. Besides trial or criminal law, there is estate law, financial law, and then the whole useful environmental law that is now crucial to save the planet." She flutters her eye lashes at the cousins and jokes, "After all, we must save the planet. It is the only one with chocolate." She laughs. "And I like chocolate."

Even autistic me realizes that this cat has finished playing with her mice. She is giving them a way to retreat.

How long will it take before they realize she has thrown them their escape keys? Their cell door is now open. Collin and Dexter are the only two who do not realize they have been released from the interrogation room.

Uncle Brian jokes with her, "Susanne, I do agree. Saving chocolate is a top priority." He chuckles. "We can include the planet as a tagalong." He laughs heartily, which breaks the palpable tension.

For the first time, we hear voices giggling in the kitchen. Uncle Brian glances at Susanne and asks, "Shall we check up on the kitchen help?"

Susanne is no longer flushed. Her ears are still red, and they will be for hours. But the neck-and-chest flush has receded, and the back of her neck is an almost normal color.

"Uncle Brian, what a good idea!" She stands as Uncle Brian offers his arm. For a moment, she stares directly at Aunt Evelyn. Her expression shouts, *Don't mess with me.* Far too sweetly, she asks "Aunt Evelyn, you don't mind if I help with things in the kitchen, do you?" In an almost snub, she doesn't wait for Evelyn's reply. Rather, she turns her head away and shows her back abruptly to Evelyn as they head off to the kitchen.

Nice touch with Evelyn! Kitchen tit for church tat!

Pale and angry, Aunt Evelyn's mouth is slightly open long after she recognizes Susanne's reference to the church snub. She glances at her boys and then stares at the vacant space where Susanne had been sitting. Her shoulders shrug slightly before her eyes move past me to gaze at the ground thoughtfully, in a silent sulk. Imitating her, both boys appear as sulky as their mother. Aunt Evelyn holds up her glass for Uncle Ian to refill. He says nothing as he fills her wineglass, her fourth drink. Without eye contact, he hands it back to her and taps the glass four times.

Surprise! Uncle Ian has a code to try to control her drinking. Wow!

Almost with contempt, Uncle Ian glances at his boys. He says nothing to them. Collin looks toward his mother who is staring at the floor, and then he stares fixedly straight ahead. Dexter looks wistfully at his dad. He wants some reassurance. None is to be found.

Uncle Ian seems like a schoolyard bully who has just watched someone else do the bullying. It appears that he enjoyed what he just heard. He deliberately ignores both sons.

Deep inside, I am concerned. He doesn't seem to like his boys much. That makes me sad, even though they don't seem likeable in the least. I cannot imagine missing the unconditional love of both my parents. But that lack would explain a lot. It makes me especially unhappy when I notice Dexter near his dad, watching him for signals of affection and finding none. Collin doesn't seem to care. Is Uncle Ian missing each of Dexter's signals for affection?

Phoebe tries to make conversation with Evelyn about the weather and general topics. Evelyn responds in monosyllables, seemingly forced to converse with someone clearly beneath her. I pitch in to keep the conversation going.

Uncle Ian watches with unkind amusement. I am starting to dislike my uncle, almost as much as his sons, but not so much as my aunt. She is in her own category.

Papa enters to announce that we should all gather in the dining room. With the drapes drawn against the dark and chilly evening air, the room invites us to admire our dinnertime surroundings. The chandelier and wall sconces shine softly, making the gold around the picture frames softly glow. The carefully groomed flowers look lush and almost exotic. The setting is splendid!

All but four guests comment on the beauty of the room. Our Brit-snob relatives don't seem to notice. After we are all seated with Nana at one end and Papa at the other, Papa says grace.

We start with a leek soup, which is delicious. Then comes salad. It is so good I am afraid I will fill up on that alone. We have turkey and ham, sweet potatoes, string beans with almonds spiced with lemon, and a new bread recipe that Nana has tried. All is delicious.

Nana has made a special dessert called Christmas pudding. It is similar to fruitcake but far thicker and denser, filled with plums, dates, and dried citrus bits. I learned later that the pudding is heated by steam. A clear brown sauce, essentially brown sugar and butter, is poured over each individual serving so that the sauce remains clear, without bits of broken pudding mixed in to destroy its clarity. This is a Christmas treat only, and I love it.

Yummy! The Americans, Uncle Brian, and Teresa murmur that the Christmas pudding is scrumptious.

Aunt Evelyn stays sulky throughout most of the meal, until dessert time, despite the large number of glasses of wine she drinks. The cousins remain glum, on cue with their mother, clearly unhappy that a foreign American girl-cousin has bested them. Uncle Ian remains in good spirits, easily amused, and oddly sociable indeed, talking to everyone *except* his wife. Teresa keeps up a running conversation with all and shows that she has an intelligence that I certainly missed on her first visit.

Mom later said to the family, "Teresa's conversation shows she is both well-read and observant. Her opinions may not be always the same as everyone else's, but they are well thought out and very articulate."

Another time that I wrongly judged the book by its cover!

Uncle Brian is witty and fun, a joy to be near. Mom relaxes because Brian is sober and Teresa is turning out to be a friend. As Teresa relaxes in her company, I can tell Mom likes her. Mom laughs and jokes, especially with Dad and Brian. Nadia and Oscar are good at table. Oscar has hundreds of funny stories, which he says are mostly true. Papa just has a good time all-around. Every attempt is made to include the three grumps in conversation.

Oscar has trouble cutting his food since only one hand is working. Mom is his nearest neighbor and assists him. She asks laughingly, "Shall I spoon feed you, too, Oscar dear?"

Oscar chuckles. "However tempting, that isn't necessary just yet." He laughs out loud. "We shall leave that for another day."

Everyone laughs at this, especially Nadia, who proclaims emphatically, "A distant day, I do hope!"

Each adult has a water glass and two other glasses, one for red and one for white wine. When I asked Papa earlier about the different glass shapes, he told me, "The white wine glass is smaller and narrower. The red wine glass is fatter, more balloon-shaped, which helps to bring out the wine's aroma." The adults are served white wine with their soup, then red and whites for the main courses. Fortunately, most everyone drinks only moderately. I notice that Teresa and Brian have only one glass of red wine each and then stop.

Good for them! I think they are trying to make up for the previous episode.

Aunt Evelyn is the only one with several glasses of wine with each course. She says little, but what she says is clear. Drinking a lot of wine has no apparent effect on her.

About dessert time, the wine finally helps. Aunt Evelyn starts to relax. Amazingly, monkey see, monkey do, the cousins follow suit. Or, maybe the three sulking ones simultaneously became bored showing that they are irritated. I wish Aunt Evelyn could accept people for their innate worth and not fuss about their status. She would be so much happier.

With time and a full stomach, the group becomes animated and happy. As we clear the table, everyone, including Aunt Evelyn, helps put food away and stack plates and cutlery in the dishwasher. There is laughter, teasing, and fun. Each person recounts funny stories from long ago. Even Collin and Dexter look on with interest; that really surprises me.

Maybe they learned something from my smart sister.

After all debris has been tidied, Phoebe suggests cards. Surprisingly, everyone agrees. Even Aunt Evelyn joins after she fetches another glass of wine. We choose a game we frequently play that is more fun and more unpredictable with more players. It's the right time to become noisy and silly.

Like my grandmother, I forgive easily. After a bad beginning, it has been a wonderful Christmas dinner. My bad feelings toward my Uncle Ian and Aunt Evelyn and the cousins evaporate. Maybe we will be friends after all. I hope that happens.

Too soon it is time for Nadia and Oscar to depart. They leave with hugs and kisses and plans for a reunion soon. Papa escorts them to their car and makes sure Oscar is safely buckled.

Uncle Ian and Aunt Evelyn and my cousins quickly follow them. Surprisingly, there are hugs freely given, even from our aunt. I hope this isn't just the result of her wine. There isn't anything wrong with Evelyn if she would just loosen up a bit.

Dad later said, "She needs to pull out the poker." I wasn't quite sure what he meant, but I guessed that she just needed to relax.

Surprisingly, even our cousins hug both Susanne and me. Dexter asks, "May we get together later in the week?" Susanne's startled eyes momentarily rest on me.

Before I can answer, she speaks up. "That would be a great idea. Let's talk tomorrow."

If the invitation was only a social comment, they are in for it now! Immediately, we all arrange a time to get in contact.

Uncle Brian and Teresa stay after everyone else has gone. Phoebe says, "Good night. Merry Christmas," and disappears into the kitchen. I think she wants to give the family some privacy.

Brian faces Papa directly as he states, "Thanks, Dad, for being so good about things the other day. Teresa already apologized. But I am saying it again. You always are there for me when I mess up. I love you and Mom. I am trying hard."

Papa focuses intensely on his son and then pulls him into a big bear hug. "You know I do love you. So does your mother."

Papa's index finger motions to Teresa. "You are an interesting young lady. We are off to a new footing. I hope we see more of you." When Teresa starts to laugh, he suddenly realizes his wish was badly phrased.

Teresa giggles. "Lord Poppycock, you have seen *quite enough* of me! Shall we say 'more frequently' instead?" She makes a silly hand gesture of display and laughs out loud.

Teresa is a very good sport!

Papa hastens to add, "Consider that rephrased." Fortunately, Brian laughs as heartily as Teresa and Papa at the *faux pas.*

Teresa's big smile is lovely to see as she laughs and says, "Frequently indeed, minus any encores."

With new insight and increasing affection, Papa adds, "Brian needs a rudder. He is not an easy boat to sail."

Teresa locks eyes with Papa as she replies, "It's easy when you feel like I do about him. There is something special about Brian."

All of us, minus our nanny, crowd into the doorway or spill onto the stone of the front entrance to say good night and wave goodbye. Uncle Brian opens the car door for Teresa, closes it, and then seats himself behind the wheel. They fasten their seat belts before Uncle Brian starts the engine. The car heads slowly down the drive.

After any celebration, there is always a letdown at the end. I know the others are feeling it too. Standing in silence for a moment by the closed door, we silently gawk at each other before we head back to the drawing room. Phoebe joins us again.

"That was an interesting evening!" exclaims Papa. "Susanne, you are becoming an interesting woman. You handled your snob cousins well."

Papa's candor generates a general discussion, during which he says, "My one hope is the cousins will come round and become nicer."

Mom contends, "I have less optimism about Evelyn."

"But she was so much more relaxed later in the evening," Nana reminds us.

Papa queries, "Did you see how much wine it took for her to relax?" He pauses and then adds thoughtfully, "And none of it showed at all. That is worrisome."

I ask, "Papa, why is it worrisome?"

He looks at me and at Susanne, then glances to the other adults until Mom nods. He continues, "It is a sign that Evelyn may drink so much so often that she is tolerant to the effects of alcohol."

"You mean she may be an alcoholic?" I ask.

Papa replies, "The word *alcoholic* has many associations. I would say a tolerant, heavy drinker instead."

Mom adds, "Indeed, a practiced drinker. Some might call her a functional alcoholic."

Phoebe's head nods yes. Nana's eyes flit from Papa to Mom before she comments, "Functional alcoholic is a worrisome diagnosis."

Papa glances at his wife and nods in agreement but remains silent.

Mom flashes her eyes briefly at Susanne and me before she quizzically focuses on Dad and then speaks. "I hope it wasn't the wine controlling her actions. I hope she can finally relax with us. She is family!" She nearly chokes on the word "family" and coughs afterward.

Dad appears deep in thought and silently peers at his shoes. He shrugs his shoulders slightly when his eyes flit back to Mom. He volunteers nothing and again stares blankly at his shoes.

Soon it is bedtime. Susanne and I wish everyone good night, dispense our hugs and kisses, and precede Phoebe up the stairs to our rooms.

After our nightly rituals, Phoebe kisses me on the forehead and says good night. Off goes the light. In bed, I think about the day.

I recall Nana's offhand comment as we opened presents. Phoebe's gift of the red gloves made Nana remark, "May I tell you I have always secretly wanted a pair of red gloves? Do you read minds like Leila?"

But Leila was a very real eighteenth-century person, my nine-greats-grandmother, who certainly appeared to be able to read minds. The comment reminded me of meeting Leila in the attic of this house when I was ten. After her death in 1752, she resided in her trunk, first in the London house attic until that house was sold, and then in the attic here. With some of our other ancestors who died after that date, Susanne and I tried to solve the mystery of a robbery and a death in 1744. Leila and I time traveled together to 1744 London, found the guilty parties, and, using Leila's words, "exonerated the innocent Edgar, wrongly executed in 1745." Edgar's name was cleared and the case finally settled.

The guilty parties were Barbara and James, my eight-greats-grandparents! Both wanted to stop me from exposing the truth about them.

Barbara nearly succeeded in her attempt to kill me! The unwelcome, recurrent, and intrusive recollections around those events, and any recall of the spin in the time abyss vortex make me feel uneasy, restless, anxious, and sometimes nauseated. Recurrent mental images and the anxiety they create are horribly real.

As I slowly drift off to deep but restless sleep, I recollect the nightly kiss from Phoebe that I have had every night of my life. I love those moments of touch, comfort, and reassurance. That nightly kiss means all is right with the world …

Sometime during the night, I awaken enough to fitfully listen to a new sound. Recognizing the pattering, I mutter sleepily, "Oh, rain—not a big deal. At least we don't get ice storms here like we sometimes do in New York."

Boy, you are wrong again!

I drift off to sleep, more soundly than before.

Chapter 9

HELLO, LEILA

I don't know how long I slept again before the dream began with Leila's voice saying, "Wake up, dear one. I must talk to you." I roll over in bed and pull up the covers, nestling into the comfort of my bed.

It's a dream. I must be having a dream.

Still asleep, I see my nine-greats-grandmother, Leila. I don't see her husband, Mortimer. But I see her son, Edgar, my eight-greats-uncle, wrongfully hung in 1745. Like all the other ancestors who resided in the attic until my last visit, they mostly, well all but four, went to heaven when Saint Peter cleared Edgar's name.

Grandma Leila is wearing a mid-eighteenth-century dress. It's canary yellow with sapphire-blue embroidery on the bodice and sleeves. The top has a sapphire-blue inset panel in the front with a square neckline. The sleeves cover past the elbows and end in rather fancy lace. The skirts are voluminous, canary yellow, and with several vertical lines of fancy blue embroidery. Her hair is piled very high—artificially high—and powdered white. A few stickpins protrude slightly, as intended, I suspect. Her sapphire-blue shoes are embroidered in canary yellow, the opposite of the dress, which is blue on yellow. She is already tall, about six feet. Her funky heels and her idiotic hair make her appear even taller!

And poor Edgar! Wrongfully hanged in 1745, he was pardoned by Saint Peter the last time I was here, a year ago last July. A few minutes after that pardon, Saint Peter damned the guilty parties, Edgar's brother James and his wife Barbara, my eight-great-grandparents, killers both.

Like his mother, Edgar has always been tall, but no one else has such remarkably crooked teeth. In my dream, he is fuller in his body but still trim. His thick, naturally dark hair pokes out in spots from under his white wig. Apparently, he doesn't care to fit it properly himself, or he is sticking with his untalented wig maker! He wears an eighteenth-century waistcoat that is mostly white with black. His breeches that reach below the knees are dark red, with black silk hose tight on his legs. Bright brass buckles shine against his black shoes. He smiles at me broadly, showing those hideous teeth, and nods as we regard one another.

He needs an orthodontist!

I love Leila and Edgar. It feels good dreaming about them. Lovely! I shift a little deeper under the covers and move my comfortable pillow. What a nice bed! Lovely dream.

Odd! I feel the covers pulled back. I feel a hand against my forehead. Leila's voice says, "Jeremiah, we must talk."

I flip to my back and open one eye. Leila is in my bedroom! Despite closing that eye and then opening both, she's still here. *This can't be!* I close both eyes tight and then open both wide. There is Leila, my nine-greats-grandmother, standing near me, with Edgar in front of the window drapes! *Yikes!*

Shocked, I yell out and jump straight up from my bed. My head crashes into the rail intended to hold hangings along the side of the bed. That throws me backward. With a resounding crack, the back of my head smashes into the wooden headboard of the four-poster bed.

I grab my head and ask, "What are you doing here? Why aren't you both in heaven?" Clutching my aching head, I glare at both and demand, "What have you two done that you are back in the attic again?"

Leila looks at me with bemused eyes and replies, "We are not back in the attic again. No! Of course not, dear one! What a silly thought!"

"Then how can you be here?"

Leila replies repetitively, "Day pass. I have a day pass. I have a day pass from heaven. We both have a day pass … from heaven."

I stare at her in astonishment. We hear footsteps in the hall and from the adjoining bathroom.

Leila's fingers go to her lips as she makes a slight hissing sound. She is telling me to keep a secret.

Mom, Dad, and later Papa with Nana appear from the hallway. Susanne and Phoebe both appear from the door to our shared bathroom between our rooms. Clearly, Phoebe checked on Susanne on her way to me.

There is a chorus of "What happened?" as multiple pairs of eyes focus on me anxiously.

I glance toward Leila, but she has disappeared. At the window drapes, I see a crooked grin with crooked teeth almost six feet up, where Edgar's mouth is when he is standing. The mouth is smiling at me broadly, but the rest of his tall frame is nowhere to be seen. My head is spinning. And it hurts!

I don't know what to say. If only I can see Edgar's smile, they must be hiding. I peek at the drapes again, but the teeth have gone away.

Yes, they are hiding.

I view the crowd and stammer, "I must have jumped up and banged my head during a bad dream."

Mom comes over, kisses my cheek, and feels my head with her hands. "Oh my goodness. You have a goose egg. Is this sore?" She touches the spot where I hit the headboard so hard.

"Ouch. Yes. That hurts. Stop touching the sore spot!" I exclaim.

She asks, "Any headache?"

"No, Mom. Only when you touch." My grumpy answer is not really the truth. My head is spinning, and I do have a headache, whether from the blow or from my visitors, I don't know.

A fuss, probing questions, trip me up—no thanks!

Looking concerned, Dad asks, "What was the dream?"

What can I say? While everyone has met Leila and the rest of my ancestors at the trial in the attic, I don't really want all of us involved—involved in who knows what? Perhaps it was only a dream.

With a willful lie, I reply, "I dreamt about spinning in the time abyss, just before Great-Uncle Edgar saved me. It was a scary experience, so no wonder I jumped up in my sleep."

Without thinking, my eyes dash toward the window drapes. Six feet up, a mouth with crooked teeth is smiling broadly at me before it disappears again. A faint thumbs-up sign suddenly vanishes into the drapes. Involuntarily, I glance toward Papa who is focused on the window drapes while he taps his nose with his index finger. He remains mute while he fixedly stares at me, as if he is making a calculated decision.

"I will be all right after I go back to sleep. Sorry for the noise," I declare earnestly.

Mom announces, "I will stay for a few minutes." There is no arguing with Mom. I know that from experience.

Phoebe comes over, kisses my forehead, touches the side of my face, and kisses my forehead again.

Her nightly kiss on my forehead reassures her as much as it does me.

"Goodnight, again," she whispers into my ear. She turns toward Susanne and briskly commands, "Now off to bed with you." Susanne waves good night as both return to their rooms through the open bathroom door.

Papa and Nana say, "Good night. Sleep better," and leave through the door to the hallway.

Dad comes over, kisses my cheek, and comments, "I figured you would have dreams about that eventually. Not to worry. You are safe. All this will pass from your mind and eventually be mostly forgotten." He enfolds me gently in his long arms as he murmurs, "Good night. I love you."

I return Dad's hug. Thankfully, for a big guy with a powerfully muscular physique, he is an incredibly gentle person.

With a glance toward Dad, Mom asserts, "I shall return to bed after a few minutes here." Dad nods in agreement, waves to me, then exits into the hallway.

Mom sits beside me. "Do you want to talk?"

I understand the kindness that she is offering. She quietly asks, "Any anxieties you want to talk about or something you want to get off your chest?" Her fingers touch the side of my face.

The one thing I don't want to do is talk in case I say too much. That's why I lied about my dream. Did Leila and Edgar really get a day pass from Saint Peter to come see me? I'm still hoping that maybe, just maybe, I had a dream, no, a nightmare.

"No thanks, Mom. I'm good," I mutter while pretending to get sleepy as Mom pats my forehead and my hands. As she sits patiently beside me, she affirms, "I love you, dear one." My eyes open wide at "dear one," the same words that Leila spoke to me after I banged my head.

Are the words we use genetically encoded? Leila is also my mother's eight-greats-grandmother.

I deliberately close my eyes to slits. Mom eventually decides I am drifting off to sleep. The bed shifts as she stands. She walks on the thick Persian carpet toward the door, but I notice she pauses. Through my eyelids, I notice that she watches me for a long time. Deliberately slowing my breathing as if sleeping, I don't dare move. After a time, the door to the hall swings open as Mom leaves. She quietly closes the heavy door after her.

I wait, but hear nothing. There is no extra person moving or breathing in the room. My eyes open slowly, scan the room and see nothing, even at the window drapes. Was this a dream? Or did Leila really come with Edgar because she needs me to do something or to tell me something?

Nana's comment, "Do you read minds like Leila?" made me think about them all. Perhaps thinking about them made me dream. I have great affection for Edgar, Leila, and her husband Mortimer, my nine-greats-grandfather.

But why would I specifically dream about Leila and Edgar?

I owe my life to Edgar. He used his thoughts to pull me out of the time abyss. He will always be a beloved relative and my hero.

But why dream about him, and why tonight?

As I lie pondering with eyes open, I look over to the window drapes again. Almost six feet up, I see Edgar's crooked smile and his crooked teeth. Soon a translucent image of his wig and his shoulders appears, followed by the rest of him.

He grins at me and mentions, "As Mother says, it takes energy to fully materialize. If you don't mind, I shall give you only an *outline*."

Reminded by his words, I reply, "That's what Leila said to me when we first met." Recollections from that first attic meeting flood over me. Some memories are good, some awful.

Leila's voice asks, "Have they gone?"

Edgar's replies, "Yes, they have. I am already visible."

"In that case, here I come." A moment later, Leila has fully materialized to become a real person, apparently real flesh and blood. She eventually sits on the side of my bed facing me, her weight denting the mattress and moving me. She leans over me slightly, one arm on the far side of the bed to support herself.

This is in contrast to Edgar who remains semitransparent. I can see through him, but not to his insides. He is the translucent image of a mighty tall and trim eighteenth-century man with crooked teeth and a bad wig. *My hero!*

Leila seems more relaxed and happier than when I first met her in the attic a year and a half ago. The canary yellow and blue of her dress and shoes is fetching and flatters her tall frame, which can handle the multiple yards of fabric in her copious skirts. She looks like a rich and happy early-eighteenth-century woman out for the day! Too bad the hair still wants to touch the ceiling!

Lordy! That hairdo is high!

I can't contain my questions. "How did you get out of heaven? Saint Peter didn't kick you out, did he?"

Leila starts to laugh loudly. So does Edgar.

By struggling to a sitting position in my bed, I avoid knocking Leila to the floor. I hiss, "Shh! Someone will hear you."

"Nonsense, dear one. They may hear *you*, but they will never hear *us*. Hearing *us* is by invitation only! Seeing us likewise."

That I do remember. If I can keep my voice quiet, then we will be safe. Then I have an image of Papa looking at the drapes. I ask, "Was Papa in on the invitation?"

"Yes, dear boy. I think he should be informed, as a courtesy, if nothing else," replies Leila. "He has done so much for us."

Again, I ask quietly, "How did you leave heaven?"

With her enormous blue eyes smiling coyly and her long lashes fluttering, Leila nods her head happily and repeats, "Day pass. I have a day pass."

I peer at Edgar, the question written on my face.

"Ditto," he says.

"Why?"

Leila answers, "I get them regularly. Formerly, I liked to seep out of the attic trunk to travel, look, listen, and learn. I told you all that before. Do you remember?" Leila looks at me fondly and watches me nod yes. She continues, "Well, at first Saint Peter said I needed to stay put. But I felt I was getting out of date too quickly. I kept asking him questions. He was very patient at first, but eventually, he did remind me I was not his only client. Finally, he said I could have a day pass. At first, they were restricted. Now I believe Saint Peter prefers me to travel—a lot. Isn't that marvelous?"

I stare at her, my mouth gaping.

Does she really understand what she has just said about herself?

Her insatiable curiosity has made her into a real nuisance. Saint Peter wants her to go away! He's probably sorry that we solved the case so that she is there in heaven instead of residing in the attic. To know Leila is to love her; to love Leila is to know her. Neither makes her easier. She has too much energy and a mind that never stops. I pity Saint Peter. Then I recollect that he was saved from his task for a few hundred years while she resided in the attic! She is making up for lost time, I guess!

My eyes go from one to the other with a fixed stare for each. Leila wiggles slightly. "Why are you here?" I ask pointedly.

Leila gazes steadily at me. Edgar glances toward his mother, sees her head nod yes, and replies, "I am going to let the most knowing one answer." He waits.

"Why am I here? I am here to warn you, dear one, to warn you," laments Leila, suddenly appearing sad. Edgar nods yes.

I am bewildered. "Warn me about what?" My voice pitch is way up.

"Well, you know how I am. I travel. I look. I listen. I learn." Leila stops talking, waiting till I nod that I understand.

"That's what you often repeated to me when I was ten," I sputter grumpily.

Leila declares, "I have discovered something." She gazes at me with big eyes, lashes fluttering.

In reply, I expectantly gape at her. *Is Leila stymied?* In exasperation, I demand, "Well, what have you discovered? Tell me what you know, please."

She replies smartly, "But I don't know with certainty." Then, with clipped speech, she declares rather tersely, "And for your information, young man, I never get stymied!"

When my thoughts suggest, *Tread carefully, Jeremiah*, she nods a vigorous yes. *Oops!*

I am tired. My head is spinning. My cranium hurts. And the headache from the smack on the headboard is larger because of the frustration I am feeling right now. I control my words. That is not something I want to do, but I must. Smiling as best I can, I ask, "Leila, what is it that you don't know?"

That sounds like a very stupid question.

Looking at me a little sadly, but with reconciliation in her voice, Leila quietly says, "I am sorry about your frustration. And it's not a stupid question!" A worried expression passes over her kindly eyes. She regards me intently as she quietly adds, "Don't be so hard on yourself."

Oh dear, Leila the mind reader!

She continues, "I have only my suspicions to tell you. But the bad feelings are very strong." She stops speaking and looks down sadly. Finally, she admits, "I am very anxious."

In my sleepy state, I forgot she reads minds like I read books— very well. She knows how annoyed I feel.

Careful, or you'll put another foot in, Jeremiah! Or another thought!

I plead, "Leila, I am tired. I have a headache from my head bump. Sorry I'm cranky. Please tell me what is going on."

She responds, "It's happening again. Once more, it will happen!"

Totally lost, I ask, "What on earth are you talking about? I don't understand."

I may not understand, but she suddenly has my attention in a most frightening way.

She continues, "I still travel almost every week and more often around the big holidays. There are many people I like to see and find out how they are doing." She pauses, then rambles along on a tangent, "I wish we could do Christmas cards!" She pauses for a moment, lost in memories and reflections before she adds, "But they weren't invented for nearly a hundred years after I died."

My goodness, she is easily distracted! But she never forgets anything! That is a gift and a curse! She pauses, her eyes moving back and forth under her beautiful long lashes as she gathers her thoughts. Finally, she says, "That's when I saw it."

"Saw what?" I quietly ask.

"The car." She pauses as if I will understand everything.

I demand firmly, "What are you talking about? What car?" Since she can read minds, it is best that she understands her answers are creating real annoyance because her answers are not clear.

"Oh yes, let me be clear." She focuses on me and confesses quietly, "Apologies that I get distracted. It is *too busy* inside my head!"

Oh dear, she has read all of my thoughts again.

"Your uncle's car," she replies matter-of-factly.

"You mean Uncle Brian's car?" I ask.

"Don't be silly, dear one. Uncle Brian is unemployed and on the dole. He is hard up and lost *his* car. It went back to the dealership. He may have the use of Teresa's car, but it wasn't Teresa's car at all. I know what her car looks like. No, not hers, nothing like."

Well, her knowledge of the family is up to date and far ahead of anything my parents or I might know. I really must take my hat off to Leila.

"Thank you, dear," she says, as if I have said my thoughts out loud. "But it is more difficult with your Uncle Ian. He is wealthy, with a real little fleet of cars."

I remember his Mercedes from the meal before Christmas and the Bentley he used for Christmas day.

"I don't know how many he has," I confess honestly.

"Well, dear, besides the two you were momentarily thinking about, he has a red Jaguar, a green Corvette, a pickup truck for work relating to the house and land, a tractor, and an old sedan which is falling apart. The sedan was his first car. He's sentimental about that one. It's not much use and won't run, which is why it stays put under covers in the garage." She pauses. She passes a quizzical sidelong glance in my direction and asks, "Do you know if Collin drives?"

Surprised by the question, I reply, "Collin is fifteen. I don't think he may obtain a license yet."

Leila answers, "Yes, I know he is not eligible for a license—he's too young. I was asking about driving. He learned to drive using the tractor—all perfectly legal on one's own farmland."

A chill goes down my spine as I reply, "I don't know."

Leila continues absentmindedly, "It was the Jaguar. It seemed so out of place."

Lost again, I mutter, "What do you mean?"

Leila focuses her lovely eyes upon me and responds quietly, "There have been robberies. In an early robbery, one elderly man was pushed and broke his arm. Only easily portable high-end things have been taken, and not a lot has been stolen." Her words stop for a moment before she continues, "Even Nadia and Oscar have been victims. Oscar was injured as he stopped the thieves, and now he's using a sling because his left arm is in a cast because of a fracture." Leila pauses again.

I interject, "Have you been observing us closely?"

Ignoring my interruption, she resumes, "These things worry me. There is something about the robberies that disturbs me."

She pauses in thought, and then speaks again. "There is a car—a red Jaguar—near each crime scene. It parked to the rear of Oscar's house the night he stopped the robbery. Yes, Jeremiah, I have been watching. The person who comes out of the car wears bulky clothes with a hoodie and moves easily and quickly. On each occasion, not even *I* have been able to see the face timely or tell if the person is male or female. But it is happening again."

"Leila, you are losing me again. What is happening again?" I ask in desperation.

Leila stares directly at me while she slowly and deliberately foretells, "Someone is being set up. I feel there will be another death, like Walter Johnson's."

While cold chills make me shudder in terror, I stare at her and then at Edgar. It was Walter Johnson who died in a robbery in 1744. His demise signed my great-uncle Edgar's death warrant and made him a spook too young!

Edgar confirms, "She is right to be suspicious. We recently discovered there is a handgun in Ian's house. We don't yet know who actually owns it or how it got into the house. One thing is certain. Ian doesn't know it is there. But the car with its travels, always near the crime scene, and now a gun. We are suspicious that something is amiss."

Deeply intrigued and increasingly horrified by what they have said, I ask gingerly, "Do you have any idea who has driven the red Jaguar?"

Edgar replies, "No. In the dark, we have missed the features each time. As Mother said, the driver always wears bulky clothes and a hoodie, as you call it. The person is of uncertain age, could be male or female, and moves smoothly and rapidly. Unfortunately, that describes everyone in the house, even Ian, when push comes to shove."

Befuddled, I ask, "But what motive could anyone in Uncle Ian's house have to steal from prosperous elderly people? Why would anyone in that household chance getting caught committing theft for a little money?" I pause in total bewilderment before questioning, "They must have enough money. Why would they push people and break their arms?"

Edgar shrugs his shoulders as he gazes at me. Leila's eyes are transfixed by the carpet. After a pause, she raises her eyes to me, traces her hand along the pattern on my bedclothes blanket, and quietly asserts, "As a cover for what is planned next."

My wide-open eyes stare at Leila. Both Edgar and Leila's expressions exude intense and sincere sympathy. My eyes flit from one to the other. I don't know what to say.

Edgar breaks the awkward silence that hangs over us as he remarks, "Like Leila, I get out more often. Certainly, more than when I resided in the attic. When we found the gun, I started investigating Ian and Evelyn's finances."

I interrupt, "Excuse me, but how did you find the gun?"

Edgar almost giggles as he replies, "It was totally by accident. Leila and I were doing a usual sweep to make sure everyone was well and happy. It was on a chest in the bedroom. Only Evelyn was home, and she had no idea about us nearby. She hid it in a drawer. We both saw her put it there." He looks at me for a moment before he adds, "Now, why would she need a gun? So I decided to snoop around. She didn't get it legally for it is not registered to her name. In fact, it is stolen property."

This news creates more shudders. I recollect how Aunt Evelyn appeared at Christmas before dinner, at times so distant. *What was going through her mind?* I am lost in this thought as Edgar finishes and his mother begins. Her voice startles me back.

"Yes, she seemed distant indeed," agrees Leila. My mouth *again* falls open in surprise.

Why am I surprised?

She always reads my every thought! Hello, my name is Mr. Open-Book. Suddenly suspicious, I ask, "Were you observing us tonight?"

With her eyes stuck on me, Leila replies, "Yes, dear boy. In view of the circumstances, I thought direct observation might be best. In fact, I've been rather cautious. For some time now, I've been in the room during every family interaction with Evelyn."

Fascinated at what she might have learned, I ask, "Did you read Evelyn's mind?"

"Yes, dear one, I did. She's difficult to follow when she's drunk, which is often, but other times she is logical and unbelievably sinister. I'm worried," Leila replies matter-of-factly, "especially now that she has a firearm. Edgar will explain more."

My attention is riveted to Edgar who states, "We decided to follow the money. Despite being a money manager, Ian is not on a good financial footing. He has made a few mistakes and has lost much, leaving his business and clients in jeopardy. Financially, he is in real peril. Evelyn knows this, and she is frightened. She married for status and privilege. I am not sure she is willing to lose that." Edgar pauses for a moment to let my sleepy mind catch up.

He continues, "He is covered with insurance, *heavily* covered with insurance. The policies are old enough that an apparent suicide would not be a problem. If she had those proceeds, she would be financially safe, even where she presently lives." Edgar pauses again for a moment and then continues, "If he dies, she will never become Countess Poppycock. But she will have a lifetime of security."

There is a long pause. I am dumbfounded by how much snooping these two have done!

Leila ignores my thoughts. Instead, she briskly states, "It is very like Barbara and James framing Edgar and letting him hang. The robberies are the frame. A break-in and shots fired, ending in a death, all easily explained away. Like Barbara, another killer who wants money and position has joined our family."

After Leila finishes, almost as an afterthought, Edgar pipes up, "And if not a death during a robbery, a backup plan of staged suicide is always a possibility." They both become quiet and wait for my response.

My room is not cold, but I feel frigid and shiver with fear. In the momentary silence, I think back to Barbara and James, my eight-greats-grandparents. I recollect her long-standing schemes, and what she did to persuade my eight-greats-grandfather to agree. The plans included my murder to cover their tracks when they were in danger of discovery. Heartless actions, cruel and pointless, that all backfired. I feel cold, weak, and overwhelmingly tired as I listen and recollect.

Why must I be involved in something so awful again?

I remain silent. What can I do against such horror? The only sound in my room is something hitting against the windows. The sound becomes louder, which rouses me from fear to action. When I glance at my clock, it is after one in the morning.

"Leila, I need to check what is happening outside." From her seat on the side of my bed, she stands and moves slightly away. I swing my legs out of bed, don my heavy robe, which warms me up, and peer out through a gap between my drapes. It is snowing heavily with a sleet snow, icy like hail, pounding down after the rain. This may cause a big problem in a country where snow seldom falls. There is little readiness for rare snowstorms or ice storms. This is now a true ice storm, the kind we sometimes have stateside.

I open the drapes on one side. Edgar stands beside me, shocked at what he sees. Soon Leila is peering over my shoulders. Seemingly enthralled, she exclaims, "Oh how wonderful! Snow at Christmas. Almost the same as a Christmas card. We didn't have them in my time."

Back on Christmas cards again!

In a dreamy voice, Leila prattles on, "It was Sir Henry Cole in 1843 who had the artist John Horsley design cards for his friends. It caught on as a nineteenth-century invention that became a tradition. And snowy scenes are so picturesque!" Trust Leila to include a history lesson in her rapture over the garden scene below.

I am less enthusiastic as I observe "But it rained first." I glance knowingly at Leila.

"Well, yes, it often rains in Britain, dear one."

Leila has not made the connection.

I knowingly gaze at Edgar and then shift my eyes to Leila as I articulate with emphasis, "The rain freezes as the temperature goes down to create snow and sleet. Freezing rain sticks to roads and power lines. I suspect many houses will lose power today as the lines come down under the weight of the ice."

Leila stares at me vacuously for a moment before she finally comprehends. "Oh, my! Clever boy. You mean electricity. I forgot about that. You are telling me people will not have electricity. Oh, dear. That's not good!"

She pauses, still slightly blank, but eventually continues, "You see, I never had electricity. That was invented … oh, let me see … yes, late nineteenth century when Edison was backed by J.P. Morgan." While she pauses, the enormous hairdo bobs. She gives me an empty-headed smile, clearly satisfied by her recollection.

Shortly thereafter, Leila appears slightly troubled. She quickly questions, "But surely they can simply light the fire and use their candles?" As Leila speaks, she regards me with consternation, then with a question mark on her face. "Or … have they moved past that?"

Edgar answers for me. "They moved passed that stage a long time ago, Mother. Many don't have a working fireplace. They need to plan ahead to buy candles, which are used rarely now—special occasions only."

Leila replies, "Yes, Edgar. I do know that. But it is hard to let old habits die. I so loved beeswax candlelight, such a lovely light!"

I let them carry on talking about the old days and life as they see it now in modern England and America and wherever else they travel. Time passes and they are still chatting about candles.

Finally, I interrupt and ask pointedly, "So what are we to do?"

Leila asks, "About the candles?"

Unable to help myself, I laugh out loud, which feels good and relieves my horrible tension. Too late, I shush myself. With a silencing finger to my lips, I listen, eyes flicking side to side. I whisper, "No sounds. No one heard me." I drop the finger. Eventually, I reply, "I'm not worried about people's candles. I am worried about a possible upcoming murder."

Leila suddenly gathers her thoughts and quietly confides, "I don't know what to do except observe. We extended our passes to keep you informed."

I recollect the first time Leila materialized in the attic to greet me and talk. I remember my steep learning curve and my confusion while meeting the other ancestors residing with her in that not-so-empty space. Marjorie, my two-greats-grandmother, left a handkerchief and cigarette holder as my clue that the interaction was real and not a dream. Those objects convinced me that I had actually met my ancestors and that everything I recalled from that rainy Monday afternoon was not a bad dream. Those objects spurred me to get

Susanne involved and led me to act with Leila to solve the ancient case against Great-Uncle Edgar.

With a quiet and uncertain voice, I ask, "Do you still have your residence in your attic trunk?"

Leila replies, "Indeed, I do! If I need to stay there, I can, as may Edgar."

I hear my unlikely answer, scarcely believing that my voice utters, "Yes, Leila. That is the best idea. You have given me information I had no opportunity of knowing without you. You need to be close by to help. And you need to keep investigating and telling me what you find."

Edgar nods. "Got it."

Leila avows, "We're glad to help. We shall never forget what you did for us. We are eternally grateful."

There is no way I shall ever forget either!

I say nothing.

She pauses, flicks her eyes side to side, and laughs. "That joke about eternity was unintentional. Still, it is *extremely* good."

I deliberately ignore her joke.

Leila asks, "I do hope the worst memories are not too bad?"

My goodness, she is right on target tonight! Read my thoughts straight up!

"As always, dear one," she replies.

She never stops!

I face her but say nothing, my mind deliberately blank.

After a minute or so in silence, we discuss how to communicate since trips to the attic may not be timely. Finally, Leila suggests, "One of us will come when you summon by thought or call out either name."

Leila pauses for a moment before she adds, "Don't daydream about us. Be careful with your thoughts; otherwise, we will be yo-yos coming back and forth."

I understand her concerns, especially after her demonstration that she is aware of my every thought.

I love Leila dearly, but sometimes she scares me. Edgar is just my best friend ever.

Edgar suggests, "Get some sleep. We will talk tomorrow." He materializes fully to give my shoulder a pat, tousle my hair, and give me an embrace that lifts me off the floor.

Newsflash! He is mighty tall!

Suspended mid-air with dangling toes, I hug him back, hard.

Leila embraces me tightly and kisses my cheek firmly. She pushes me away to inspect me closely before she hugs me again.

She remarks, "Till tomorrow. Oh, I do love my nine-greats-grandson! But, silly boy, I would never willingly frighten you!" Her eyes lock mine as she quickly adds, "And you are taller!" Her eyes move their intense focus from one of my eyes to the other. "I shall never forget your help."

Again, I recall why I also shall never forget.

Leila counsels, "Try not to dwell on the bad things that happened. You are safe now. The images will become less with time."

Busted again!

They both vanish. Plopping back into bed, I close my eyes. I think sleep will be impossible.

When I awaken hours later, last night's open drape allows light to pour in through the window whence Edgar, Leila, and I watched the storm last night. Reluctantly, I climb down from my bed, open the second drape wide, and stare down in awe at the gardens below.

The scene is not one of England at all. It is one from an American Snowbelt region. Snow covers everything, at least eight inches deep, which is unusual. But under the snow is ice. I can see it covering the tree branches and distant power lines. Tree branches are bent down almost to the breaking point from the weight of the ice, which looks like glass and glistens in the sun. I suspect there are power outages and downed power lines. How will the local community, which is not used to this harsh weather, be able to manage?

What will the day bring?

Chapter 10

THE MORNING AFTER THE STORM

Wow, I feel groggy! Soaping up in the shower, I think back to the night before. Right now, I feel as uncertain as I did when I was ten and first met my ancestors. Was last night's encounter real? Are there tell-tale signs left to prove that my encounter with Granny Leila and Uncle Edgar was real? Last time, Marjorie left her handkerchief and cigarette holder to prove we had spoken. I don't think there's a crutch like that this time.

After dressing, I dawdle in my room. A few strands of long white hair, the same color as Edgar's ill-fitting wig, are on the carpet near where Edgar stood last night. At the desk, there's a tiny piece of canary-yellow fabric with blue thread caught in the edge of a drawer handle. So, this wasn't a nightmare after all.

Too soon, it is likely to be a nightmare, a living nightmare!

Heading downstairs, I notice the house sounds quieter than usual and feels different—slightly chillier. The voices from the kitchen are Nana and Papa talking with my parents and Phoebe. At first, they don't see me as they discuss widespread power outages.

Papa persists in his commentary. "The power generator is working. It will keep us safe and warm." He pauses to glance out through the window, then resumes, "The generator will provide enough energy for the furnace, power for the appliances, and for hot water. And the furnace is set to drop a few degrees to conserve energy.

Everyone will need a warm sweater." Papa turns slightly, peers at me sideways, and asks, "How are you today, Mr. Goose Egg?"

I reply, "My head feels fine, but I'm a little tired, that's all. What a stupid nightmare!"

Each briefly faces me as they echo, "That's okay. You will recover," but Papa recurrently glances at me oddly while they resume discussions about electricity and outages.

Britain usually doesn't have snowstorms or ice storms that disrupt power. This is a big deal for all concerned. Everyone in the family is questioning how long before power returns. I listen in as I start breakfast of toast and jam with milk to drink.

Nana mentions, "Brian and Teresa likely have power at the hotel. Ian and Evelyn do not have a generator. Their section is without power. They may need to be here."

Perhaps it's just as well Nana didn't see the look I flashed. Papa does see me but says nothing as he hides a slight smile.

Mom says, "I will check with Brian first. I hope your guess is right."

She calls him and gets through on their cell. Brian confirms, "We do indeed have power. We are cozy and fine, and our hotel has a restaurant. The roads are impassable so no one is going anywhere until the roads are clear or the ice has melted. We can eat our meals at the hotel." They chin wag for a few minutes more and then agree to talk later.

Nana then calls Uncle Ian. The calls fail the first two times. The third time is successful. After initial greetings, she puts her cell on speaker while she asks about power.

Uncle Ian states, "We are without power, eating a cold breakfast together, and thinking of registering in a hotel."

Nana replies, "There is no point of a hotel. It costs too much, and everyone else wants a room. Come here instead."

I watch Nana as she listens patiently. It seems discussion is occurring at Ian's house. Eventually, we hear her say, "We will expect you when we see you. Take care on the roads. Plan to stay a few days until things clear."

Papa requests, "I want to talk to Ian." He gets right to the point. "Ian, there is a likelihood of falling temperatures. Your house will get too cold without the furnace. Shut off the main water line before you drain the water systems. Open the taps so pipes don't freeze and burst. Don't forget to drain the hot water heating system too."

Uncle Ian gratefully responds, "That's something I had not thought about. Thanks for speaking up."

Papa replies jovially, "No need for the mechanicals of the house to wreak havoc while you are with us."

Ian and Papa review details on how to do everything that must be done. "See you around late lunch," affirms Papa as he listens for a reply. He nods when he hears confirmation. Nana now knows expectations.

As a practical and capable hands-on man, Papa mutters quietly after he hangs up the phone, "Ian is not mechanically minded. He needs guidance on everyday things." Papa appears slightly displeased or at least dissatisfied. In a slightly more audible voice, he continues, "Ian relies too much on others to do everything for him."

During my breakfast, Papa requests, "Jeremiah, I will need your help after we eat. Do you mind?"

Excitement rises. Helping Papa is the best thing! He is so smart and sensible that I always learn something. I love to be beside him.

"Yes, Papa. That will be fun." He gazes at me and returns my smile, but there is something distinctly odd in his look.

After he finishes his coffee and I swig down the last of my milk, Papa remarks, "It's time. Come help me check the generator. You need to know how it operates."

We walk along to a door behind the main stairs to descend to the basement, past the servants' quarters and bedrooms, to a section below the kitchen. Behind the laundry is another room hidden behind a locked door.

Papa gets the key from a hook above the door, unlocks it, and returns the key. This is something I have always noticed about Papa. He always puts things back immediately. He often repeats, "I don't want things misplaced."

I point to the key back on its hook and remark, "Good idea!" He nods in return.

This room contains hot water heaters, three in number. There are huge sinks to handle industrial-type cleaning. There is a huge furnace that is working away to keep us warm. There are several electrical panels with multiple lines extending from them. Nearby is a generator, permanently installed.

Papa explains how the generator works and what triggers it to start, how it is fueled, identifies the proper venting to the outside, and tells me some of the things that can go wrong. He points out various gauges that must be inspected to know that all is right. Even though this is clearly a routine for him, he poses questions to verify that I understand what he is saying.

Learning mechanics side by side with Papa is heaven!

He seems satisfied and about to finish when he abruptly fixes his gaze hard upon me. His mouth opens to speak, then closes. His eyes shift toward the furnace and generator again, but finally, they return to me. With a heavy blink, he inquires, "How is Leila? And how is Edgar?"

Previously, my mind was debating about telling Papa the details of the visit last night, but I didn't know if I should. Now I have my answer!

My first thought is to say something stupid like, "She's fine." *Really?* She has been dead for 266 years. That would be like answering, "Oh, she's still dead!" Instead, I ask a question. "How did you know she was in the room?"

Papa chortles and admits, "I saw the crooked teeth nearly six feet up and the thumbs-up before they both disappeared. Only Edgar is that tall, and few have teeth that awful. He was laughing when you mentioned him as part of your dream. And if Edgar was there, so was Leila. Was Mortimer with you, too?"

There's my answer. Last night when he looked so quizzically at the window drapes, Papa did see Edgar's smile and figured I had visitors!

I respond, "No, Grandpa Mortimer was not with his wife last night," and then I spill everything I know. He listens through it all before he asks probing questions.

"They don't know why the gun was purchased?"

"No," I reply.

"And they are not certain for what purpose?"

I repeat, "No."

"But they saw Evelyn put the gun away in a drawer?"

"Yes."

As he searches for facts, he queries, "We don't know who else knows about the existence of the gun?"

"No, we don't."

He questions again, "But they think Ian knows nothing?"

"That is what they said. I'm not sure why they think that."

Papa states, "Probably based on his history. Ian dislikes guns, and is the only country squire I know who knows *nothing* about firearms and *does not* shoot." Papa seems sad as he answers.

"Why is that, Papa? Didn't he learn how to shoot safely?" As I look at Papa, I tentatively ask, "Didn't you teach him properly?"

Papa gives me a sidelong glance, sighs deeply, and explains, "When Ian was young, his best friend was accidentally killed when an older brother was cleaning a shotgun and didn't realize it was loaded." He pauses to see my reaction. Fascinated, I stare as he talks. "The shot hit the youngster directly in the chest, killing him immediately. It was no one's fault, but the older brother was devastated." Papa stops talking as his memories flood back.

I keep silent, horrified at the images that suddenly loom in my head. After a long pause, I ask quietly, "The accident itself must have been awful, but did Uncle Ian actually *see* what happened?" Papa stays quiet for so long that I am frightened by what he might say.

Eventually, Papa continues, "Fortunately not. But the accident still scarred him deeply. I still remember poor Ian at the funeral. In some ways, he really has never recovered." With a sad tone in his voice, Papa resumes, "Ian refused to ever touch a gun. He became withdrawn for a time, and he became more aloof. He focused on school, planning for the future, and money. He lost a part of his social self. He developed a wall around himself that no one could break through." Papa sighs softly. He faces me directly and sadly presses onward. "He refused to be close to people. Perhaps he feared the pain of loss again." Papa stops for a moment, and then adds quietly, "But by doing so, he guaranteed the loss of close friendships and shared experiences. He is still that way, which must be lonely. It breaks my heart, but that is the way he is."

After another long pause, Papa continues, "When choosing his bride, he married a woman who wanted money and a title. She demands a certain style, but she is not a loving person. What he really needed was a woman who was so outgoing her nickname could only be Bubbles. Instead, he married a 'gimme, all in proper form, gimme more.' Papa pauses, and then fixes his eyes on me as he admonishes, "This isn't to be repeated, but Evelyn reminds me of Barbara, always has."

I am dumbfounded by Papa's candor and horrified by what he has said!

I met Barbara, my eight-greats-grandmother, during our last visit when I was ten. During her lifetime, she wanted money and a title, demanded a certain style, and would stop at nothing to get what she wanted. She set things up so that Great-Uncle Edgar would be executed. That made her husband heir to the title and its monies. Her ghost tried to murder me when I was close to exposing her misdeeds. Right now, I am eleven and a bit. This is too much information to have at any age.

Papa's eyes search mine as he warns, "This conversation is our secret—not to be shared with anyone, not even Susanne or Phoebe! Do you understand?" Papa appears stern. His words fall heavily upon my ears.

"Yes, sir."

"Good." He says nothing more for a few minutes. We look at the generator as if it is about to break into a soft shoe dance to entertain us. Nothing happens.

Finally, Papa concludes, "If too many people know something is up, events may be altered."

He pauses, then recaps, "I know you will communicate with Leila and Edgar. Despite being watchful, we will still need their information. When you know something, tell me. You can't do this one alone. It's not like last time." Papa's eyes are bright with a near tear that I see. He seems anxious, worried, and utterly tired. His eyes remain on my face while he adds, "We need to do this one together."

I go over to Papa and give him a squeeze. He hugs me tight. "You are very special to me, young man. We both need to keep everyone safe." He pats my shoulder as we head upstairs.

I feel old as we mount the stairs, extremely old indeed!

Upstairs, when we enter the kitchen, everyone looks at us expectantly. Susanne is now with us, finishing her cereal and milk. It takes a moment for me to force myself to become bright and cheery.

Papa announces, "Jeremiah was a big help in checking the generator and will soon know how to operate it." His charitable comment makes everyone laugh.

Susanne notices I am solemn. I deliberately brighten up to avoid any questions, mostly because she knows exactly what to ask.

Phoebe decides that we are all bored and need entertainment. "Since we can't drive anywhere, let's play in the snow. Come on kids. Dress for the weather."

Yup! This is exactly what I need. And Susanne could use a little fun outside after her struggles with the cousins yesterday. Soon we are outdoors where the weather is below freezing but not really cold, at least by North American standards.

Phoebe jokes, "This is Canadian beach weather." She wings a snowball that whizzes past my noggin.

I demand, "What do you know about Canadian beach weather?" as my snowball misses its mark. "You aren't Canadian."

"No, I am not. I am an American from a Spanish family, but my Uncle emigrated from Spain to Canada, north of Winnipeg. I always tease him because he hates winter, yet he lives in the northern part of Canada. Living around Toronto, I could understand. That area is milder. Winnipeg, not so much." Phoebe laughs and laughs. We both start giggling too.

"I tease him about enjoying himself at the beach in winter and playing with a beach ball deflated by the cold." With a few chortles, she continues, "I gave him a Frisbee for sport because there is no air inside to contract and deflate. He didn't think my gift was funny! Me? I thought it was hilarious." Phoebe giggles helplessly. "I crack up whenever I think about his frisbee."

We laugh uncontrollably as we play. Building a snowman is hard to do when the snow is icy, but we try. A rise in temperature helps; the icy snow melts enough to be sticky. Our silly lopsided snowman is leftward-leaning, ready to fall over at any moment.

Phoebe takes out her cell phone to photograph us by our creation. She sends the photos to our parents' phones later with the title "Children with Parson Brown." She is always thinking up fun things! I think Susanne loves Phoebe as much as I do. Certainly, we both adore her lively company! After the snowman, we make snow angels and then chase each other as we throw snowballs. Eventually, as the wind picks up, it starts to feel colder.

"I think Parson Brown is safe for tonight," I declare, pointing to our tilting creation.

A moment later, Phoebe asks, "What about hot chocolate?" She looks mischievously at my sister. "Susanne, you know that brown stuff, *chocolate*, the reason we must save the planet."

The reference to her verbal fight with our cousins makes my sister weaponize snow. Phoebe laughs and runs moments before a snowball makes contact with the middle of her back. Susanne yells, "Yes, you had better run!" She chases our nanny all the way to the house. The three of us have a huge case of the giggles by the time we are inside.

We take off boots and gloves in the porch enclosure by the kitchen door. Inside, we hang coats on their hooks to dry and let melting snow drip onto the tile. We line our boots and gloves on drying trays designed for wet boots, not snowy boots. Mom, in her wisdom, has already started warming the milk for hot chocolate.

Could anything be better?

Chapter 11

THE REST OF THE DAY

Nana reminds us, "Your cousins will be staying. Their house is only a dozen miles away, but our wonderfully narrow and winding British roads will be treacherous. They are expected in about an hour or so, but it may take longer. I just hope they don't get stranded."

Before long, it is after one o'clock, and I am getting peckish. The sounds of a car struggling up the icy drive and stopping before the house bump thoughts of food out of my head. Uncle Ian struggles out of the car and nearly slips on the ice despite the gravel underneath. He goes to the opposite side to help Aunt Evelyn. He gets her to the house and up the steps before he returns for their bags.

The cousins do nothing to help till their father commands, "Look sharp and start carrying things in." They do so begrudgingly. Dexter seems more eager to help than Collin, but neither is enthusiastic.

My goodness, they are spoiled!

Nigel is not here to help. He was visiting friends and family for Christmas and is snowed in. The same happened to Mr. Brown and Mrs. Stewart. Since all landlines using telephone wires are down around us, they have each used their cell phone to let us know that they are safe and warm. Nigel is staying with friends who have a generator. Mr. Brown's house has power. Mr. Stewart called, "We are here with Mabel's sister. Not so much ice here, but too much snow. No problem with power, not like you. We're cozy and warm, we are. But we can't get back." I'm glad *he* called. I cannot image Mrs. Stewart struggling to hear using any phone!

Once inside, the new arrivals shed his or her bulky coat. Aunt Evelyn's bulky coat looks warm with its hood that tucks away to be hidden. This is the first time I have ever seen Aunt Evelyn dressed casually, wearing trousers and a blouse. Over this, she has a bulky sweater for warmth. She has slip-on flat-heeled shoes. I notice that she is really overweight with quite a belly sticking forward. No wonder she prefers copious dresses without shape. She needs a good exercise program!

As Uncle Ian removes his new gloves and new tweed cap, he exclaims, "See this! I'm wearing my new presents."

I'm glad he likes them, and even better, he's also still trying to make up for Aunt Evelyn's cold nastiness!

Under his tweed coat, he wears jeans with a sport shirt and sweater. He doesn't look like a stuffed shirt today. He looks sporty and fun despite his receding hairline and his little paunch. I remember his behavior when Teresa embarrassed herself. What a contrast with his attempt to make everyone feel better when Aunt Evelyn was so cruel to Nana over the handbag present! Since he knows how to make up for Auntie Evelyn's behavior, why can't Uncle Ian *always* be the nice man I have seen and not the cruel snob that he is sometimes? I want to dare him to friendship, even if that makes him vulnerable. His friend's death was years ago. It's time to heal. But I remember Mom saying, "Behavior habits are learned early and hard to change."

Uncle Ian comments, "It took nearly an hour and a quarter to do the twenty-minute trip, and we skidded twice, but we are finally here safely. Thank goodness we are here at all!"

There is general conversation about the roads, the power outages, the weather that is so unusual, and neighbors with generators and those seeking shelter elsewhere. When each person receives a room assignment, my aunt and uncle are allocated the remaining guest room upstairs. The cousins are to share the only unused servant's room in the basement. All of these are so far out of the ground that none seems subterranean, each furnished with modern comfortable furniture.

Will the cousins pull a face about being in the basement? Who else is wondering?

For some reason, Collin says, "That's really cool. Don't you think so, too, Dexter?"

I suspect Dexter was about to follow his brother's lead if he made a fuss. Instead, he senses his brother's enthusiasm and blandly replies, "Yeah, that's cool."

Looking relieved, Nana says, "And there are twin beds." I guess she was also having misgivings and expecting complaints.

We gather in the dining room for lunch. Nana has made a wonderful potato-and-ham soup with warm bread that melts butter. There are sandwiches—egg salad, ham, and turkey. Sweet pickles, dill pickles, and olives make me content. There is tea for the adults and lemonade for the kids. Yum!

Even the boy cousins seem happy. Both share jokes with us with the occasional explanation about British customs, making sure everyone is on the same page. They seem to be trying hard to be friends. What a change! This dreaded lunch turns into a happy affair. Surprisingly, Aunt Evelyn appears relaxed. What has changed that makes her happy? She laughs and tells stories from her childhood that not even the grandparents have heard. Everything seems wonderful.

Later, I might say, *Looks can sure be deceiving!*

Uncle Ian sees the change and smiles easily. *I like that!*

Time passes quickly. This is how time with relatives should be. After lunch, Phoebe suggests games. We decide on one of our usual card games. Soon everyone is laughing hysterically at the silliness.

A little later, darkness has fallen, and the temperature outside is dropping. Papa draws the drapes in the dining room and drawing room. Nana turns the tree lights on, then comments, "I shall start dinner." Mom, Dad, and Papa all volunteer to help. It's not long till we gather for food again.

Nana frets, "I'm sorry it is leftovers." But what she serves is wonderful. There is Christmas pudding still left, and the brown sauce has been saved separately so it remains clear when it's served.

I am in heaven again. I do love to eat!

Papa serves wine with the meal. Nana and Mom both have a glass, Dad and Papa have two each, Phoebe has one but half remains in her glass, and Uncle Ian finishes two. Aunt Evelyn has been drinking steadily. I count five but may have missed a predinner drink or two. She seems sober, speech clear. Uncle Ian pays no attention to her alcohol consumption. Once again, I wonder if this is usual for her? I recall her wine consumption last time and that she never seems intoxicated.

Everyone helps with cleanup, putting dishes in the dishwasher, and putting food away. When the dining room has been cleared and cleaned and the kitchen set to rights, everyone moves to the drawing room. Papa serves more wine, and most of the adults except Phoebe help themselves.

It is nearly bedtime when I realize neither Edgar nor Leila has contacted me. Maybe they know that there is no news. I make eye contact with Papa. Shortly thereafter, he says, "I'm heading to the kitchen to get more ice." He nods to me and commands, "Give me a hand, Jeremiah." I follow him.

In the kitchen, he whispers to me, "Have you heard from Leila or Edgar?"

"No, I haven't."

"Let me know if you do," he insists, looking like he means it.

I nod in agreement and trail after him as we return to the drawing room with enough ice to build an igloo.

Aunt Evelyn is finishing another glass of wine. She is now talkative, but some of her stories are repetitive. The alcohol may be hitting her despite her marvelous tolerance. She has had at least seven glasses of wine, and only the last seems to have affected her. That's well into a third bottle and she is still drinking!

Soon Phoebe says, "Time for bed, you two."

We give hugs and a kiss to Mom and Dad, then Papa and Nana. Uncle Ian gives Susanne and me a warm and friendly hug, like a proper uncle. I approach Aunt Evelyn who accepts a kiss and puts her hand on my shoulder when I hug her, an improvement over pulling away. Susanne gets the same response, a half hug but better than before. Even that little change is refreshing!

I hope she can change to be more loving.

We wave good night to Collin and Dexter. We have had a pleasant evening, but neither of us wants to push boundaries.

Upstairs, Phoebe waits for us to complete our nightly rituals and then tucks each of us into bed. Susanne is first tonight. She always gets a forehead kiss, same as me. Afterward, Phoebe follows me to my room. She gathers the covers and pulls them back as I pile into bed. I feel the wonderful good-night kiss on my forehead. I close my eyes but sneakily watch as she disappears through the door to the hallway.

After a short time, I hear adult voices drifting up from the hallway below, all saying goodnight. First, it's Uncle Ian and Aunt Evelyn heading to their room, and then my parents. Finally, my grandparents are overheard talking as their feet patter toward their bedroom.

Doors close. The house becomes quiet. I'm still awake and waiting for my spook relatives to appear. Eventually, I sit up to whisper, "Leila," and then "Edgar," but hear nothing. I repeat their names.

"Coming, dear one," answers Leila's voice. Suddenly, she appears, fully materialized. "I was listening to Evelyn and Ian. They are fighting quietly, in whispered voices, about Evelyn's drinking."

I reply, "Mom thinks Aunt Evelyn is a 'functional alcoholic' since she drinks steadily and daily, but she hides it well enough that she can keep up appearances."

"Appearances are important to her," asserts Leila as she gazes fixedly at me, "but she sometimes makes exceedingly poor decisions."

I nod that I understand. *I really don't but can't figure what else to say.* "Is the gun here or did she leave it at home?"

Leila replies, "I don't know yet."

"Where is Edgar?"

Eyes on me, Leila whispers, "Still eavesdropping on the fight."

At that moment, it becomes clear that we don't need Edgar's reconnaissance. Everyone hears Aunt Evelyn's enraged voice yelling at her husband, who cannot placate her.

I jump out of bed, open my door, and peer out. In response to the ruckus, Papa appears in the hallway and walks toward Ian and Evelyn's closed bedroom door. Papa knocks and asks, "What has happened? Are you both all right?"

With slightly slurred words, Aunt Evelyn angrily retorts something like "Go away and mind your own business." It is not said nicely. She swears and uses bad words. Her excess alcohol now clearly shows.

Their loud fight alerts Collin and Dexter to dash upstairs. Dexter asks rhetorically, "Are they at it again?"

"Shut up," commands Collin.

Dexter demands, "Why?" His eyes scan along the heads appearing in the corridor as he continues, "They'll all know in a minute if they haven't already figured."

Papa asks, "What do you mean?" Nana has appeared from their bedroom doorway and stands in the hallway, clutching her dressing gown closed in front of her.

Mom and Dad have popped out of their doorway. Phoebe is in front of her bedroom door, alert but immobile.

Dexter answers, "Papa, you saw her tonight. She drank triple what everyone else did, and she still appears sober. You don't do that without practice."

His words sound like an adult, not a young teen.

Knowing next to nothing at that moment, I suddenly feel sympathy for my two nasty cousins. The ugly words continue but less loudly than before. Uncle Ian attempts to reason with Evelyn, who is *not* in the mood.

After Papa knocks again, he asks, "We heard loud voices. What's wrong?" The bedroom door opens part way, and Uncle Ian's head pops out.

Ian glances at his father and mother nearby, both with worried expressions. His eyes sweep down the hall to his sister and her husband, showing concern and pity. He notices Phoebe, anxious and uncertain, as she stands immobile in front of her bedroom door, assessing the situation and deciding the danger level for her children, and what she must do next. Eventually, Ian's searching gaze fixes on his sons near the stairs. Dexter's face shows a mixture of concern and love. Collin's inscrutable expression confuses autistic me.

Ian opens the bedroom door wide. "You should all come in. Meet the real Mrs. Wadsworth," he proclaims sarcastically.

Papa inspects the room with Nana now standing beside him. I crowd in between them.

Aunt Evelyn is sitting in an armchair near the fireplace. Her face is turned away, glaring at the cold, empty hearth. She rubs her hands through her messy hair, scratches her scalp in anger, and then rubs her hands together in agitation. Her head turns; she stares at Nana and Papa. With an irritated voice, she demands, "What are you two birds looking at?"

As she tries to regain composure, she admits, "Ian and I were having a spat, that's all." Her attention returns to the lifeless fireplace. She remains silent and motionless, eyes staring straight ahead.

Nana steps toward her. Evelyn puts up a hand in a "stay away" signal. Nana stops dead in her tracks.

Mom and Dad are now moving in from the hall doorway. Mom notices Aunt Evelyn's gesture and exchanges glances with Nana, whose expression screams, *What do I do to make this better?* Papa doesn't know what to do either, and it shows.

Ian regards his wife with a face that registers concern and contempt, an ugly mixture. But how often has he witnessed a mess like this? He peers toward the hall doorway where Phoebe now stands—face worried, hands clutched. His eyes search past her. "I don't see you, boys. Are you still there?"

Dexter rushes past Phoebe to reach his Dad. Uncle Ian holds his son close beside him.

Dexter says, "I'm sorry this happened again, Dad." He looks at his mother. He quietly and simply asks, "Why?"

When Aunt Evelyn regards Dexter, a smirk curls her open mouth. She glances at Papa and then at Nana before her mouth closes; she decides to remain silent. Her drunken gaze returns to the empty hearth.

As Collin struts into the room, he stands tall. His chin juts forward beneath his angry face. While Uncle Ian is looking toward his wife, Collin glances at his mother, and then he glares at his father with an expression full of hate.

He quickly scans the room and realizes all eyes are upon him. As if a magician waved a wand, his features change to concern and embarrassment as the anger and hate magically disappear. The change is so fast that I doubt myself and ask inaudibly, "What *did* I actually see?"

Collin glances at his father and asks with apparent concern, "Are you okay, Dad?"

Oblivious to the prior look, Uncle Ian nods yes while his eyes remain fixed on Aunt Evelyn. Collin gazes at his mother and asks, "What about you, Mom?"

Without moving her eyes, she answers, "I became angry and yelled. That's all." She shifts in her chair and scans the room. "This is all a tempest in a teapot. Go to bed, everyone. The show is over!"

Nana says, "Well, Evelyn, if you are certain. Remember we are all here to talk as you need."

"Yes, indeed," says Papa.

Mom and Dad murmur in agreement. Motionless and angry, Evelyn ignores everyone. Dexter approaches his mother for a hug. Her body stiffens as she suffers his touch. She does not respond with any gesture of welcome or love.

Collin goes over and touches her shoulder. Her hand reaches up and grasps his tight for a moment. When his arms slip around her shoulders, her lips touch his hand. As she releases him, he turns away from the others. He makes no eye contact with anyone and avoids his father as he leaves the room. His feet patter on the stairs.

Dexter returns to his Dad whose arms enfold his son. Uncle Ian bends to kiss the side of his face before he hugs him tight again. Afterward, Dexter is near tears, his eyes fixed on the floor, as he heads down the stairs to the room he shares with his brother.

So Aunt Evelyn loves Collin and has no use for Dexter. How awful!

Papa reaches for Nana's hand, holding tight for reassurance and mutual support. Departing, they murmur "goodnight." Speechless, Susanne and I follow them out.

Phoebe has already disappeared down the hallway and stands before the open door to her room.

Mom and Dad are still hanging back by Ian and Evelyn's open bedroom doorway. They jointly utter "goodnight" before they close the door behind them.

Papa motions to Mom and Dad to come to their room. Susanne and I follow. Phoebe's dark eyes scan us before she goes into her room and shuts the door.

Papa closes the bedroom door firmly and motions to speak quietly. He admits, "We both have known there was a problem, but we did not know it was escalating this far. No wonder Ian has seemed distant and distracted recently."

Nana nods in agreement.

Mom asks, "How do we handle things in the morning?"

Nana replies, "I suggest we take cues from Evelyn. If she wants to pretend nothing happened, then nothing happened. If she wants to talk, then we talk. Let's not reference anything from tonight."

Our parents nod agreement. Dad suggests, "Hopefully, all this was alcohol talking. Perhaps their fight was truly only a tempest in a teapot."

Papa proposes, "Yes, let us be optimistic. 'Tempest in a teapot' it is."

We exchange glances. Then Mom commands, "Now back to bed, everyone."

Nana and Papa whisper, "Good night," as we straggle out of their room. Dad and Mom both come into my room with Susanne. Phoebe appears in the bathroom doorway. She is so quiet that I sometimes think she is a phantom!

Is she taking lessons from Leila?

I remember Mom asking, "How much of Dexter's bluster is the pain of dealing with a distant father and an alcoholic mother who dislikes him? The poor kid is only thirteen! What else has he had to deal with at home?" Then she adds quietly, almost to herself, "Collin is the older and probably feels he should be able to fix things. But he's only fifteen. It's too much for each of them. No wonder their personalities can be difficult."

Susanne quietly speculates, "I think Uncle Ian was mightily embarrassed." She looks around to see that all nod in agreement. Still appearing pensive, Susanne ponders, "How many times has Uncle Ian been hurt like this?"

"Some things we may never know," quips Dad.

Susanne persists, "I realize we will never have that answer but guaranteed it's more than once. Dealing with crap like this, it's no wonder no one can get close to him. His social status among strangers may be the only thing left to him."

As she touches my sister's shoulder, Mom remarks, "That's perceptive, Susanne."

Mom tucks me into bed. I get a forehead kiss from Mom, one from Dad, and then one from Phoebe.

Mom comments, "Sleep well, if you can. Remember we love you."

Susanne waves and then leads the way to her room through our bathroom. My family leaves the communicating doors open. I hear the same go-to-sleep ritual occurring with my sister. Afterward, her hall door opens, the light turns off, and the hallway door closes. Our rooms are now dark. Susanne's breathing slows as she falls asleep.

I am nearly asleep when Leila's familiar voice whispers to me, "Are you awake, dear boy?"

I open my eyes. Fully materialized, she stands beside my bed and leans over me. As I sit up, she straightens to her full height. She is wearing the same dress as last time. The fabulous sapphire-blue embroidery on the canary-yellow silk fascinates me. My thoughts ask, *Where in heaven does she get this wonderful material?* Then I realize I have answered my own question. I look to the side and see Edgar's smile show first as he also materializes standing tall beside the window. Gazing at both, I whisper, "Did you see tonight's performance?"

Leila replies, "We were there before you were. We saw all."

I ask, "What does all this mean? You were concerned about robberies and a possible upcoming murder. What everyone saw tonight was a drunken word fight."

Leila's eyes probe mine. She responds, "Did you see Collin as he came into the room?"

I answer, "I thought he flashed anger and hate toward his father. But the expression changed so quickly that now I am uncertain what I saw."

She affirms, "You saw correctly. You saw anger and hate. I was shaken by what I read in his mind."

I feel a chill when Leila says that she is shaken by the thoughts she read.

She has seen much and not much fazes her.

She continues, "He is capable of almost anything, including murder. It must come from his mother's side."

I think back to our ancestry, laugh out loud, and instantly regret the sound. Too late, I cover my mouth with my hand and listen carefully. Susanne's regular breathing means she's still asleep.

Reassured that I'm safe to talk, I blurt out, "What do you mean, his mother's side? Barbara married into our family. She was Collin's eight-greats-grandmother and mine. Her genetics are part of the makeup of every generation since. And she was a killer."

Leila looks at me knowingly as she smiles. "Yes, dear one, that is true. But Barbara had a brother. He married and had offspring. The brother carried on his father's title, as have his first-born male heirs. Evelyn is the daughter of one of those descendants."

Surprised, I ask, "You mean Uncle Ian married a cousin?"

Leila replies, "You must remember that the British aristocracy, despite its pretense, is a limited number of people. She is a sixth cousin. Neither the geneticists nor the church has an issue with such a distant connection. In fact, many in the family don't even realize the connection exists." She smiles with satisfaction.

Fascinated, I gaze at Leila again as I affirm, "But *you* know."

"Of course, dear boy, I follow such things. That is why I think the psychopathic behavior comes from the mother's side. No one else in Barbara's line seems to think and act like that."

I think of what it takes to be successful financially. Withholding judgment, I say nothing.

Edgar pipes up with news, "Collin knows about the gun. He asked his mother about it earlier today. He asked if it was ready."

I feel cold as I ask, "Ready? Ready for what?"

Edgar looks at me steadily with concern on his face as he states, "That is what we don't know yet."

I ask them, "Did you find out anything else?"

Edgar replies, "Nothing that you don't already know. Collin seems to love his mother and hate his father. Dexter loves both and is rejected by his mother. It's not clear why. Maybe because he loves his dad so much?" His enormous shoulders shrug with his unanswered question.

Leila interjects, "That interaction with Dexter and Evelyn tonight broke my heart. I wanted to materialize and just hug him tight."

Facing her, I laugh. "Just as well you didn't. You would have scared him out of his wits." All of us giggle with this image. As an afterthought, I add, "I don't think either Uncle Ian or his family knows about you."

They exchange glances. *Are they deciding what to say?*

My voice rises slightly as I demand, "All right. Come clean. You both know something I don't."

Leila's eyes flit to Edgar before she states, "Well, they certainly know nothing of the trial of James and Barbara. They know you were ill in the summer you were ten but not the reason why. They were told that you had some odd virus and then healed without *sequelae.*"

"What are *sequelae?*"

Edgar answers, "Something that is a consequence or a result of a previous injury or disease."

"No side effects of the illness," I muse.

"Righto!" he proclaims too cheerily.

With eyes on each of them, I persist, "There is something you are still not telling me."

Her eyes move down and to the side as Leila continues, "We didn't want gossip about the trial in the attic. Your cousins are of an age and temperament to say the wrong thing. The neighbors don't need to know there was funny business in the attic." Her eyes return to mine.

"That sounds like only part of the truth. The rest of the story, please. No lies!" I wait, jaw thrust forward.

Leila confesses, "Oh my, you are as insightful as I am, more is the pity! All right, here it is. Ian does know that we and other ancestors used to reside in the attic. So far as he is aware, we still do. He came up when he was about twelve. We met and we talked. He was not a trusting lad, maybe from losing his friend when the brother accidentally shot him. Although he thought about helping, he returned to tell Mortimer that he had decided to decline." Leila glances down sadly as she acknowledges, "Afterward, Ian wanted only security and calm. Beforehand, his cautious temperament did not like adventure and risk. The death reinforced that attitude. I can't hold it against him!"

Pondering what she has recounted, I mutter almost to myself, "Well, at least he has some information. Who knows if he will ever need to know more?"

With a smile, Edgar responds, "Only time will tell."

While I'm sitting on my bed, my eyes head north to both my favorite ghosts. I ask, "What about my other uncle? I know Mom didn't know about the attic ghosts until we told her. Does Uncle Brian know?"

Leila appears solemn and remains silent as Edgar answers, "Neither your mother nor Brian came up to find us. Ian never told them about us because he didn't want them to know he decided not to help."

Leila states, "Your mother has always had a lot of spunk. I once thought she might have succeeded. But, like Brian, she never knew to try." Leila looks at me fondly as she adds, "So I was not surprised in the least when you, her son, jumped in with both feet, as it were." She stops talking and giggles out loud.

Suddenly, Leila exclaims, "Oh my! Look at the time. You must get your rest. We shall talk tomorrow." I stand as she bustles over to kiss my cheek and hug me tight.

Edgar's enveloping arms pull me to his chest. Wow! Feel the power in his frame. Once again, I marvel at his tall stature as my toes dangle far above the floor! However, we should give him the name of Susanne's orthodontist. His teeth need help!

Edgar releases me in a heap on the bed as Leila disappears into an outline of yellow and then is gone. All of Edgar disappears except the smile and a thumbs-up sign that disappears last.

With such love shown me, can anything be wrong with the world? Yup! Sure can!

Chapter 12

BAD WEATHER, BAD DEEDS

When I look out my window in the morning, I think the light is playing tricks on me. Darn! It snowed again! Clearing the paths and shoveling the driveway were for nothing. Everything glistens in a new layer, a deep layer, of icy snow.

Britain has a temperate climate, and heavy snowfall is not part of a temperate climate. In America, we know snow is going to fall, so we prepare, especially in the snowbelt areas. Not so much for the Brits!

This means Auntie Evelyn will remain our guest. Dang! Unhappy thought!

I prepare for the day and dress. Downstairs, Mom and Nana are talking quietly in the kitchen. Nana has had recent cell phone calls so she knows that Mr. Brown, Nigel, and Mrs. Stewart must hunker down where they are because travel is impossible. Fortunately, the pantry and the fruit cellar are full. We will not go hungry. We may run out of milk, but there are worse things!

Phoebe appears from the morning room where she has been setting the table.

As he comes in from outside, Dad says, "Well, everyone, I've shoveled the sidewalks to the kitchen door, the front door, and a path to the car in the driveway. We are clear for travel, maybe!" He laughs, "But according to the news channel, non-essential travel is forbidden." Nana suddenly appears worried. Dad notices and adds, "Travel for heat and safety is essential, if anyone asks."

Papa appears from the basement. He reassures, "All is right with the generator and the mechanicals. We still don't have full power, but we won't run cold. And there will be plenty of hot water."

Nana reminisces, "When Papa was thinking of that generator, I thought the odds of needing it were slim. I griped about the expense for a while. Then we had a freak sleet storm. Even though we didn't lose power, I capitulated. Now, I am mighty glad I did." Nana glances admiringly at her husband. "I married one smart man." She laughs, reaches out, and touches the side of his face. "There you are, my smart man!" She leans toward him and kisses his forehead. Papa smiles back happily.

Nana's phone rings, which surprises her. She looks at the number. "Oh, it's Nadia." When she picks up, I hear the two talking away as if they haven't seen each other for weeks instead of two days. After reassuring each other that both are safe, they discuss the weather, the lack of traffic as reported on the news, and the closure of various roadways.

Nadia says, "We are on generator power too. It's working beautifully. Hats go off to Papa who explained everything to Oscar and convinced him we should have one. Otherwise, we should be begging for lodging."

Nana replies, "You would be welcome, but you might have a devil of a time getting here. So stay put and be safe." They chat for a while until they finally agree to catch up later.

Not long after that call, the phone rings again—Uncle Brian on the line. "So many unfortunate people without heat or hot water are looking for a room at the hotel. We are hoping we can stay with you to help out someone else who needs our room."

Without a pause, Nana answers, "Of course, you may. Come over directly. Mr. Brown and Nigel are stranded elsewhere. You can use their rooms. I will phone them to ask permission, but I know they will agree."

Brian interjects, "Check with them first."

"I shall call now," she replies, "and ring you back." With a successful lawyer's efficiency, Nana makes two calls, gets reassurances that she may use the rooms, and then punches in her son's number.

When Uncle Brian answers his phone and hears her "all clear," he responds, "Teresa and I will be at the house in an hour or two. Not to worry about breakfast for us. We were up early and have already eaten."

Nana seems surprised but says nothing except, "See you, whenever you arrive. Be safe on the roads. Bye for now."

Shortly after Susanne enters the kitchen, Nana orders, "Beds need new sheets. And the boys need to surface for breakfast. Rouse them up."

After brief explanations to Susanne and instructions to us both, Susanne and I are in the basement rooms with clean linens. Nigel's room is arranged with the same military precision used to set a formal dinner party table. Nothing is out of place. Mr. Brown's room is also tidy but more humanly so. A few magazines are scattered about, and a dirty shirt covers a chair since it missed the laundry basket in the bathroom.

In a few minutes, both rooms have fresh linens on the bed, fresh towels, washcloths, and hand towels in the bath. Fresh soap and shampoo are beside each bathroom sink ready for use. Once again, I marvel that the windows are large and let in lots of light. There is at least a foot from the windowsill before the ground is seen, even with the snow. This is a basement with a difference!

The boys hear us moving around. As we dump dirty towels and sheets into the laundry basket, they trot over and ask what is happening. Susanne and I explain. Dexter seems very happy at the news. Collin is more thoughtful and subdued. *Why?*

His reaction confuses me.

Collin remarks, "This is a curious place. Past the bedrooms and laundry, what's behind the door at the far end? I mean the one near the window that is beside the door to the outside."

Without hesitation, I answer, "That's the mechanicals room. It has the furnace, the water heaters, the electrical system, and the generator."

Collin replies, "That's interesting. So the generator is in there, vented to the outside I presume?"

If he has an interest in mechanicals, then this can be a way to friendship. I volunteer, "Let me show you."

He follows me to the door. I reach over the door millwork, pull the key off its hook, undo the lock, and open the door wide. Susanne and Dexter tag along behind us. I explain the workings so far as I understand them. Collin seems fascinated with the explanations I have learned from Papa. As I carefully secure the door afterward and return the key to its place, I miss something, something that would come to mind almost too late.

By the time Susanne and I are upstairs again, Uncle Ian is in the kitchen. Dexter quickly gives his father a big hug. Collin comes over to get a hug, but he is not as enthusiastic as his brother. He looks like he is trying hard to show affection, but the effort seems forced.

I'm confused again.

We gather food from the refrigerator, and Papa scrambles eggs for everyone. We each make toast, and Mom makes a carafe of coffee. Aunt Evelyn appears as food preparation is finishing. We all head into the morning room, which is warmer and cozier than the dining room. The sunlight reflecting off the snow makes the room incredibly bright.

"I almost need sunglasses," declares Aunt Evelyn.

I stop myself from asking, "Do you have a hangover?"

We all eat eggs, toast with jam, and drink juice; the adults have coffee. Conversation flows easily. Like the rest of us, Aunt Evelyn pretends that nothing bad happened last night. Ignoring the past helps the day begin easily and allows everyone to relax. All is going well. Everyone lingers over breakfast. Conversation with the cousins is easier. A real camaraderie is beginning. *What a relief!*

After breakfast debris is cleared away, we all think about playing cards but decide against. We bring out the monopoly game, which is new to our cousins. It's fun to see them quickly learn strategies as we play. The moment it finishes, we hear a car struggling hard on the uphill part of the drive. Papa opens the door for Uncle Brian and Teresa. The trip took longer than estimated.

The two struggle on the icy snow to bring in their bags and belongings. Once safely inside, they greet everyone warmly. Teresa is happy with Nigel's basement room and Brian with Mr. Brown's.

Off to the side, Papa quietly requests that the lodgers remain in separate rooms. Brian says, "Agreed, Dad." Teresa nods yes.

Papa whispers, "We really must set a better example for the children."

The rest of the day passes in snow shoveling and then playing outside with Susanne, Collin, Dexter, and Phoebe. Uncle Brian joins us, and Teresa comes out too. It turns out that Teresa loves the snow. She asks, "What do you call the little thing rolled up from snow?"

"A snowball," replies Susanne.

"Oh my, who knew that's what they were called?"

Like she didn't know!

"Teresa exclaims, "Well, look, I have one!" She begins firing one after another from her stockpile with each of us as a target.

"War," I declare. Unfortunately, we never chose sides. Teresa is soon chasing each of us in a snowball fight. And we end up chasing each other as well until uncontrolled laughter has us gasping and plopping in the snow covered in white splats.

Phoebe remarks, "We need another snowman to match our leftward leaning creation from yesterday." We are laughing so hard we can scarcely start building. Our prior snowman is covered in snow and looks like he is snuggling in a white blanket. Soon, there are two, but today's snowman is taller and straighter.

"We could build an entire village of snow-people," suggests Dexter.

The wind picks up as the sun's shadows quickly lengthen. The temperature drops suddenly.

"Maybe not," contradicts Susanne. "I'm getting too cold."

"I'm blue about the fingers despite my gloves," contributes Collin.

Uncle Brian yells, "Sissies," as he pegs a snowball at Teresa and runs toward the house.

Teresa cries, "Revenge is mine!" as snowballs hit smack in the middle of Uncle Brian's back. Without looking back, he continues running, despite hit after hit. For the record, Teresa is a crack shot!

Inside, we all declare, "It's getting a little cold out there."

Mom replies, "You'll warm up soon," as she makes hot choco-late by the gallon. Most of us have two cups. Eventually, we warm up.

It has been fun, really unexpected fun, with the cousins. Teresa is a good sport who loves to act like a kid!

We really like Teresa! And Uncle Brian always loves to play, which is one of the reasons he is our favorite uncle.

The cousins have never amused themselves in snow like this before, so they have all sorts of questions about how we manage this kind of weather in America.

Susanne and I realize our cousins have had a hard time. Despite their previous behavior, we have more understanding and empathy for them than before. If the bond with our cousins becomes stronger, that may help them.

We young folk retreat to the informal sitting area off the kitchen and talk about school in England and school in America. This time there is no competition, no one-upmanship—only relaxed informa-tion sharing and companionship. This feels good.

When it is time for supper, we load our plates from the array of leftovers in the kitchen and then head to the warm morning room, which is large enough to accommodate the thirteen of us with ample space. There are fourteen chairs, so that works well with one chair left over! There is laugher and foolishness, jokes and banter—truly a wonderful family gathering. Papa has a small whiskey, as does Dad. They are the only ones who have any alcohol. Aunt Evelyn seems relaxed and smiles often. What a change!

Later, we would realize that this was the reaction of someone who has made a decision and is happy with the choice.

After our wonderful meal of delicious leftovers, we clean up the morning room and the kitchen. While we are settling in the draw-ing room, several of us grab a heavy sweater because it is cool. Once everyone is seated, Papa asks if anyone wants a drink.

Collin announces, "It's about time I learned how to serve from the bar. If I move to America and become a bartender, I'll need to know useful things like fixing drinks." He laughs as he says this with

MAX W. JUSTUS

the warmest of smiles and such an abundance of charm that everyone is captivated and giggles. Every person agrees to be his guinea pig.

He starts with Nana's iced tea and then Teresa's. Mom asks for the same but with extra lemon, which is also Uncle Brian's choice. Both say their tea tastes wonderful with the extra citrus flavor. Papa requests a scotch, small with ice. Aunt Evelyn orders a small scotch with ice, which she cradles for a long time. Dad's choice is a neat scotch. Susanne and I have club soda with lemon, which is what the cousins and Phoebe also have.

As we finish sipping our drinks, Susanne says, "I don't know about the rest of you, but I want an early night. I'm tired after playing outside play in the snow."

"Yes, indeed," comes as a chorus from everyone. "Let's hit the hay early tonight."

Mom suddenly remarks, "My goodness, I am overwhelmingly tired. I didn't do much exertion today, and I wasn't playing outside in the snow, but I am pooped! It's this girl's bedtime. Too much Christmas!"

Uncle Brian answers, "I did a lot of shoveling today, and we played in the snow. No wonder I'm tired. Hopefully, there's not another layer of snow to shovel tomorrow."

Collin answers, "You won't be shoveling snow tomorrow." When eyes regard him quizzically, he scans the room, laughs, and adds, "It's not supposed to snow any more tonight."

Everyone responds with, "Well, that's a good thing."

Odd! Collin seemed so certain about the forecast. He must have looked it up.

We all head to our rooms. Phoebe tucks me in and gives me a kiss on the forehead. I hear Susanne and Phoebe in Susanne's room, and then the hallway door closing as Phoebe leaves.

I feel uneasy as fitful sleep overtakes me. Something that was said tonight brings fear to my gut but what? Why am I so uneasy? My anxiety-laden dreams frighten me briefly awake, then vanish from memory.

At some point, I feel my shoulder touched, then shaken, and hear Edgar's voice. "Wake up! Wake up *now*." Edgar's anxious voice pleads, "Please, wake up! You need to act!" I start to move in my sleep. Edgar almost yells, "Wake up. It's urgent!" His enormous hands shake my shoulders vigorously, which wakes me up right quick! He has my full attention as he stands beside my bed, fully materialized.

Groggily, I sit up and swing my legs off the side of the bed. I ask, "What time is it?"

Obviously frightened, Edgar regards me sternly. "Nearly 1:00 a.m."

"Oh, no wonder I am still so sleepy." I glance around. "Is Leila here too?"

Edgar answers, "Yes. She is with your mom. Mortimer is with Brian."

"Why?" Wide-eyed and bewildered, I stare at him. "What is going on?"

Edgar articulates firmly, "Something is wrong with your Mom and with Brian. Both are breathing too slowly. It looks to me like a sedative has been given. But it's not like the sedative dose that Barbara gave Leila that put you in the time abyss vortex. That dose allowed Leila to wake up. This time, I'm not so sure that they will wake up!"

While his huge hand touches the side of my face, his eyes bore into mine to make sure he has my undivided attention. He continues, "This dose must be much higher. Both are breathing too slowly. This looks like the intention is murder—the murder of your mom and Uncle Brian."

I am shocked speechless. I stare at him in disbelief, paralyzed with fear.

What can I do?

Edgar registers my confusion. Just then, Leila appears.

She frantically pleads, "We must get help. Mortimer says that Brian is breathing too slowly, and your mom is too deeply asleep. They both are pale and off-color. Something must be done, and it must be done quickly!" Her eyes frantically scan side to side. Wringing her hands, she emphasizes, "But it must be something that can be explained to outsiders. The police will need to be involved. They will not understand the three of us." She stares at Edgar.

I ask stupidly, "You mean you, me, and Edgar?"

Leila glances at me and realizes I am not fully awake and clear minded. She articulates patiently, "No, dear boy. I mean Mortimer, Leila, and Edgar. We have been dead for centuries. The police simply *will not* understand."

My palm hits my stupid forehead as I utter, "Oh yeah! Duh!"

Edgar speculates, "There must be some way of attracting attention, which would incidentally find that the two of them are in trouble."

My mind is in a whirl. What to do?

I think out loud. "If there were a fire …"

Leila almost screams, "No. The house would go like a tinderbox. You cannot set a fire."

I focus directly on her and almost giggle from anxiety. "No, Leila, not set a fire. Set off the fire alarms."

She pauses, moves her head from side to side as if to clear away her fears, and agrees, "Of course! Fire alarms! We never had those. What a clever dear boy. We trigger the fire alarms." Staring at me in confusion, her head and all that hair bob while she asks helplessly, "How do we do that?"

I reach into the night table beside my bed. "In case the power fails, these matches can light the candles that are on the chest opposite my bed."

Holding the matches and grabbing one of the candles, I look Edgar in the eyes and challenge, "Edgar, there is a smoke detector in the hallway outside my door. Heat will trigger it. Can you somehow reach to it to set the alarm?"

Edgar's wide toothy lopsided smile shows all his crooked teeth. He partially dematerializes except for his right arm and hand. "Ready for action," he declares through his silly grin.

I light the wick and hand the burning candle to him. He opens my bedroom door and floats up near the smoke detector to hold the flame underneath it. It seems to take forever, but eventually, a loud screeching sound recurrently beeps. Oops! I forgot to tell Edgar that any fire alarm is incredibly noisy! The sound startles poor Edgar. He jumps back, which is hard to do when you are levitating in midair. He drops the candle, but his enormous arm swoops down so rapidly that his huge hand firmly grabs the middle of the taper as it falls. He descends to the floor, everything intact, wick still burning.

"I forgot to tell you that it's loud," I whisper.

The noise makes Edgar scrunch up his face. With his free hand over one ear, he asks, "How long does this painful racket continue?"

"Until the alarm is reset. Come in here now," I command, motioning him into my room and closing the door behind him. He hands me the burning candle. I blow it out and return it to its holder.

My frightened eyes turn toward Leila as I suggest, "Go to Mom. Keep her safe while Mortimer keeps Uncle Brian safe. Edgar, watch what everyone is doing. I need your eyes on everyone."

They nod assent, and both disappear without a sound.

I rummage in my night table drawer, grab the whistle, and pull the blue string over my head. Non-stop, I blow into the whistle, open the door to the bathroom, and charge toward Susanne's room. She is already struggling to wake up. The whistle makes her sit bolt upright!

When Phoebe appears in the hall doorway, she asks, "What is going on? Is there really a fire?"

My shoulders shrug with the safest answer. "We don't know yet."

I head down the hall blowing hard on my whistle. Papa is talking to Nana as both appear in the hallway.

Further down, I see Aunt Evelyn and Uncle Ian standing by their room. I see Evelyn holding a small satchel and her purse.

"What should we do?" asks Uncle Ian.

I shrug my shoulders and reply somewhat sarcastically, "It's a fire alarm." What other information can I give as I move past them?

Susanne is right behind me. She asks, "Aunt Evelyn, what are you carrying besides your purse?"

Evelyn appears annoyed as she answers, "My jewelry, in case the alarm is real."

Susanne nods and agrees, "Probably wise."

I am not sure that Susanne is sincere. She doesn't sound sincere.

Near Mom and Dad's room, I overhear Dad talking to Mom, but without reply. She won't wake up.

Suddenly, I hear Dad's voice booming, "I need help in here! Now!"

Susanne and I burst through the door as Papa rushes in behind us. Dad is frantically trying to rouse Mom, but he can't. Her color is odd—pale and slightly blue.

Dad exclaims, "Something is wrong! Constance is limp and won't respond. She is barely breathing." His fingers touch her neck for a moment. "She has a pulse." Then he yells, "Someone call whatever the British have for 911!"

Papa moves to the phone to dial, but the line is dead. "Damn this ice storm!" He races down the hall past his wife and returns, already talking on his cell phone. His voice is calm and slow, but the tension in his voice is as thick as bridle leather. He uses his full name, omits the title, gives the address, and declares that the call is urgent. He describes what we see. He is advised to start artificial respiration by breathing into her mouth with her nostrils pinched shut.

Dad began this before being told. Phoebe stands nearby, watching intently. She asks, "Do you need help?"

In rapid fire between breaths, he retorts, "No. Take care of the children."

Mom's color is already better. Dad rechecks her pulse and continues to breathe into her mouth regularly and deeply. He focuses only on Mom. Never have I seen him look so scared. With her mouth open and terror on her face, Susanne stares at Dad as he gives Mom air. Like Susanne, I want to cry in relief now that I know that Mom will be safe. As long as someone helps her breathe, she will have a pulse and will probably live.

Uncle Ian and Aunt Evelyn stand near the doorway to the hall. Evelyn calmly says, "You have everything in control. We shall go downstairs."

Ian tentatively asks Dad if he needs help. Dad abruptly responds, "No." Ian's shoulders shrug, apparently relieved. Dad ignores him; his focus is Mom. I don't think Dad will remember Ian's question.

Nana announces, "The fire trucks will be here soon since the alarms are connected to the fire department in the village." My eyes flick toward her when I realize she is not accustomed to ice storms.

I remind her kindly, "No Nana. The fire department will know nothing. They are only connected by landlines, which are down from the ice storm."

Totally baffled, Nana momentarily gapes at me before she comprehends. "Of course, you are right. I will call now." Out comes her cell phone from her dressing gown. She glances at Papa and orders, "John, go with Jeremiah and check on the boys, Teresa, and Brian. They are downstairs, and I want to be sure they are awake in case the fire alarm is real. I am calling the fire department," she says, pointing to her cell phone. She has to raise her voice to be heard over the screeching alarm from the hallway.

Immobilized, Papa has been staring at his limp and unresponsive daughter. There are tears in his eyes and overwhelming anxiety and fear on his face.

He is terrified he may lose his daughter.

He shakes himself slightly, makes sure that Dad can keep doing what he is doing, and watches as his wife begins her call. He touches my shoulder as we both descend the stairs past Uncle Ian and Aunt Evelyn and continue down to the basement.

My thoughts flash to Uncle Brian.

When we get downstairs, I see Dexter's head poking from his room. I yell over the fire alarm, "You're awake. Is Collin up yet?"

Dexter answers unthinkingly, "He was gone when I woke up. He must be upstairs already."

Why didn't Collin awaken his brother?

I dismiss the thought as quickly as it flashes through my mind. When I see the gleam from Nigel's nameplate on the door that Teresa has left ajar, I glance inside the room. Her bed appears used but empty. The outside window in the hallway is ajar, and cold air is blowing inside. I register this, but I make no connections, at least not until later. I follow Teresa's voice to Mr. Brown's room. Standing by the bed, she is desperately trying to awaken Uncle Brian. Suddenly, she screams.

Papa rushes to his son sprawled on the bed and feels for a pulse. Involuntarily, he nods yes while his hand touches his son's chest, which confirms extremely slow breathing. Like Mom, Uncle Brian's color is pale, but he is starkly blue around the eyes and mouth.

Papa glimpses me, nods, and yells, "Tell Nana and Phoebe that we have another patient." He pinches Brian's nostrils and begins breathing into his open mouth, exactly like Dad is doing for Mom two floors up. After a few puffs, the skin color is better. Papa checks the pulse again and mutters, "Stronger now." He sees me still locked in place and yells, "Please! Go!"

Despite being startled, I sigh in relief and dash up the stairs two at a time. I understand the emotions behind Papa's response. *Am I mastering autism? Later, think about that later.*

In the central hallway upstairs, I notice Collin off to the side. His parents are still talking on the stairs, unaware he is nearby. There is something odd about his slippers, but nothing fully registers until later because of my anxiety.

I run up the next flight, tell Nana to call 911 again, and explain why.

Poor Nana goes pale, grabs the table next to her to steady herself, reaches automatically for her cell phone, mutters something I cannot hear, and connects. She gives a clear history and reinforces emphatically, "There are now two critically ill people. Help is needed *urgently.*"

Desperate to remain outwardly calm, she stands beside me trembling in fear, pale and sweaty with anxiety. But outwardly, she acts like one cool lady!

It seems to take about a year for the two ambulances to arrive with the EMTs. They come after the fire truck, a forever gap. However, the ambulance personnel are prepared for the worst. Directed by our hand gestures and babbled instructions, one group efficiently heads to Mom and another to Uncle Brian.

I watch Mom from the foot of the bed as they set up an IV, and document her physical findings. Initially, they allow Dad to continue rescue breaths. He must be doing them well. But in short order, they gently but firmly remove him and take over completely.

Susanne holds Mom's hand until she is directed to move away. She goes to Phoebe who hugs Susanne around her shoulders from behind. They both watch in utter fear.

Last night, both Brian and Mom were tired, but Mom remarked, "My goodness, I am overwhelmingly tired. I don't think I did much exertion today…" Now I know why I was so anxious. She sounded like Leila the night Barbara poisoned her!

As I stand at the foot of the bed, I suddenly and irrationally expect to spin in the time abyss vortex again. I grab the bedpost in terror. The similarity of her words, my position at the foot of the bed, people trying to help the unconscious victim—all these recall the poisoning in 1744 London. Mom and Uncle Brian have been poisoned. Suddenly, my mind is certain, but who did it and why?

Surprisingly quickly, Mom is placed on a gurney. She now has an IV and a tube from her mouth going into her lungs. A bag is squeezed regularly by one of the responders. This gives Mom enough air to keep her alive since she is no longer breathing on her own! Dad is clearly told where she is going, but Nana makes sure that she also hears. Reading his face, Dad could never repeat any instructions given to him right now.

After Mom's gurney is wheeled down the hall, the legs collapse on command at the stairs. Uncle Ian and Aunt Evelyn are still loitering on the stairs so that *both* ambulance personnel must direct them to move away.

Are they in shock, self-centered beyond words, or stupid?

The gurney and its custodians descend the remaining stairs. Uncle Ian finally sees Collin and asks, "Are you all right?" He seems reassured by the reply.

Once on the main floor, Aunt Evelyn nods to Collin. A peculiar expression passes between them. He approaches his mother, who puts her hand on his shoulder in a sort-of hug, but oddly, she holds her purse in front of her belly.

The look confuses me. Why doesn't she put her purse down while she hugs her child?

After they carry Mom down the stairs on the now short-legged gurney, the legs come to full length again on the lower floor. She is wheeled to the waiting ambulance, the gurney legs shorten again on command at the ambulance's rear entry door, and she rolls into the first ambulance.

Two of the responders stay with her. A third person closes the rear door tight and then drives. As they disappear, the slippery ice on the drive makes them slide a little sideways.

The same events must have happened in the basement. A gurney with short legs appears in the main hall from the basement stairs. The legs descend and Uncle Brian is wheeled past us.

Like Mom, he has a tube into his lungs and an IV running. A woman in uniform is compressing the bag regularly to give him enough air. The tape holding all in place distorts his face slightly. It is clear he makes no spontaneous respiratory efforts whatsoever. Without the artificial ventilation, he would be dead!

I hear one ambulance person mutter to another, "*That* was a near thing."

Papa is told again where they are taking Brian. It is the same hospital that has accepted Mom. As Brian, unconscious and ventilated, passes us, Papa touches the shoulder of his son. Papa's silent tears stream down his cheeks. His nose drips. I give Papa several tissues to clean up his mess.

The fire department has finished their inspection. Two firemen come to Papa as he finishes honking his nose. One of them says, "Lord Poppycock, we find no reason why the alarm was triggered. The house is secure. There is no fire."

As the fireman scans his surroundings, he continues, "I regret that the fire alarm seems the least of your worries. Good night to you, Lord Poppycock. Good luck." He touches his helmet, as does his mate, before both men disappear through the front door. Papa nods silently. His wobbling voice spurts out a "thank you" to the disappearing figures.

Aunt Evelyn stands to the side, slightly away from Uncle Ian. She clutches her purse and satchel tightly as if the rescue workers or the firemen might rob her. When she glances at Collin, he comes to stand beside her again, but he seems slightly annoyed. With fear in his eyes, Dexter comes to his dad and leans against him.

With tears streaming down her face, Teresa comes upstairs into the main hall to stand beside Papa. My brain flashes to her first dinner with us. I am thankful she is not wearing mascara. The recollection of streaming eye makeup is the first comic relief I have felt. Not funny at the time, it is funny now. *I need funny desperately.*

Phoebe is hovering near us as Dad embraces Susanne and me. He holds us tight and kisses the top of Susanne's head and mine.

He murmurs, "It must be all right. Please, let it be all right." He hugs us tighter as he repeats, over and over, "Please, let it be all right." His chest heaves as he sobs, "I thought she was going to die. She was barely breathing. I love her too much to lose her."

Dad eyes Teresa, who is supporting Papa's arm and holding his waist to prevent his collapse. Dad reaches for Papa's other arm and guides him to a chair in the hallway. Nana is soon beside him. Teresa sticks to Papa's side.

Uncle Ian and Aunt Evelyn stand aloof with Collin beside his mother and Dexter tight against his father. Ian leaves Evelyn and comes over to Papa. Dexter trails after him.

Uncle Ian says, "They are both alive. They will be well cared for. We will take two cars and follow them to the hospital. Evelyn will drive mine and I will drive Papa's car. Is that all right with you, Dad?"

This is the first time Uncle Ian has tried to do anything useful. Since he did not consult Evelyn, she fleetingly appears put out. Her eyes scan her surroundings before the expression quickly vanishes. Politically savvy, she does agree.

Everyone takes a few minutes preparing to depart. To sound cheery, Nana announces, "I am bringing a thermos of tea and some biscuits. We may be there for a long time." She wipes away a tear so she can see straight and heads to the kitchen. "You don't want NHS food."

I ask Papa, "What is NHS?"

He replies with a faint smile, "National Health Service."

I laugh, which makes me feel better. Susanne glares at me and then realizes the joke. She smiles, despite her chin wobbling hard enough to trot away. Tears are not so silently trickling down her face, and she needs to blow her nose. I hand over a tissue box. Her hands fumble for the prize.

Through her tears, Susanne mumbles, "I am amazed at Nana. She has two children who were found near death from an unknown cause. She kept her cool on the phone when she wanted to scream instead. And now she is planning a menu to keep us fed regardless of what may be in store." Susanne dries her tears and blows her nose while mumbling, "What a gran!" She smiles sideways at me and makes a sound that is a cross between a sob and a giggle.

Eventually, all eleven of us squeeze into two cars. Fortunately, Papa's car has a bench seat so three may sit across the front and three across the back. Uncle Ian drives. Teresa sits between Uncle Ian and Papa in the front. Phoebe sits between Susanne and me in the back seat.

Aunt Evelyn drives Uncle Ian's car. Dad is in the front passenger seat since his legs are so long. Nana sits in the back between her two grandsons, Collin and Dexter. Nana looks squished.

The road is slippery and dangerous. We see the occasional car that has been abandoned after sliding off the road. Sometimes, we have difficulty with hills because of the underlying ice. By all appearances, neither of the Brits who are driving knows how to handle ice on the road. The trip terrifies me! Susanne is completely still and quiet, but her jaw is almost invisibly moving. I can tell that she's terrified too! *Is she praying?* It seems like years before we finally arrive at the hospital to find both Mom and Brian in the intensive care unit.

We are directed to a small ICU-specific waiting room, which we fill. Fortunately, no other unknown family is also waiting. When we are allowed to talk to the doctor in charge, Dr. Jones explains, "Something has caused them to be sedated and need artificial ventilation. They are stable now, with normal vital signs and reflexes." She asks questions of all of us. After she goes over their medical history, she asks, "Tell me again how they were discovered."

When she learns that the fire alarm was the only reason that each was found, she whistles softly. Her enormous eyes open wide, showing a lot of white, in stark contrast to her extremely dark skin. She sharply inspects Dad and Papa after she learns what they did before the ambulance arrived.

She asks, "You say the fire department found no fire?"

Papa answers, "They found no reason for the alarm's trigger."

Dr. Jones states in a matter-of-fact tone, "You are lucky the fire alarm went off. Ambulance personnel reported that these two had nearly stopped breathing when they were found. Without oxygen, the heart would have stopped beating. The fire alarm and your interventions saved both of them. Both will be okay in a few days. The male, Brian, was closer to death, according to the responders. He may take longer to recover."

We remain solemn and silent. Quietly, Papa says, "May I speak to you privately?"

Surprised but curious, the doctor agrees. Papa nods for me to come with him. Dr. Jones pushes her security badge over a door lock. We follow her through the door and into a little cubicle where we may speak in confidence without being overheard. Dr. Jones sees a nurse gesture to her through the glass in the door and remarks, "Excuse me a moment. There is something I must do before we begin. I shall return." Papa nods to her in agreement. Her large muscular frame moves away quickly.

When we are alone for the moment, his face close to mine, Papa demands, "What do you know? Tell me quickly."

I reply, "I saw Leila and Edgar. Mortimer was with Brian." I spill everything I know. "Edgar set off the fire alarm. He is snooping around the house and may have more information later."

Then I emphatically declare, "Mom and Uncle Brian have been poisoned. I'm certain! The scene in the bedroom with Mom looked like what happened when Barbara poisoned Leila in 1744. It's the second time I've seen the results of a poisoning!"

The doctor returns carrying two files. Stray pieces of paper stick out. She asks medical history questions which Papa can answer for Brian and which both of us answer for Mom. I'm suddenly glad our parents have discussed their medical history honestly with their children. My autism helps me recall the answers to almost everything she asks.

When the doctor has finished speaking, Papa admits, "I am not sure what investigations you are doing." His eyes fix piercingly on the doctor as he asks, "Do you know what caused the coma?"

Cautiously, she replies, "We will run drug screens. Both will be tested." She suddenly seems a tad anxious, perhaps wondering what His Lordship will demand next.

Papa regards her squarely and speaks slowly. "I think you had best run forensic testing. Perhaps the police need to be notified. I suspect foul play."

After the doctor suppresses a gasp, she regards Papa with renewed interest, then thinks for a moment before she inquires flatly, "Have either of them done drugs, now or ever?"

Papa swallows hard. "My daughter has never done anything of the sort. She is a successful lawyer in Manhattan." One hand gestures toward me. "This is her son." Papa stops talking as his gaze lands on me.

The doctor's eyes scan me. "I thought you might be an American from the accent." Her beautiful dark skin contrasts against her perfect white teeth when her mouth opens wide in a kindly smile.

Appearing slightly flushed, Papa quietly adds, "My son has been in rehabilitation twice for cocaine abuse and alcoholism. His last alcoholic drink was at Christmas dinner. He says he has stopped cocaine. His drugs of choice are stimulants, not narcotics, which he has never abused." He pauses and then adds, "But this is different. I suspect this was something intentional against the two. Their pupils were midsize. They were breathing slowly, and they were blue."

The doctor replies, "Those observations are helpful and fit with the report from the ambulance personnel. I suspect each had a barbiturate or sedative overdose, but we will look for opioids as well."

Papa asserts quietly, "Neither has any interest in tranquilizers." They did not take anything willingly or for fun. This was attempted murder."

Again, Dr. Jones inhales sharply through her full lips. She looks at Papa and asks, "Do you think your family is at future risk?"

Facing her with a sad expression, Papa replies, "Honestly, I do not know."

Dr. Jones responds, "Thank you for your candor. I will keep you up-to-date and shall notify the police when appropriate. Meantime, I suggest that your suspicions be kept between us until we have more facts. Do you agree?"

Papa states, "Yes. We don't know who made the attempt." His anxious eyes focus on the doctor as they exchange a most peculiar look. Papa's next words echo in my mind. "It could be anyone, even someone from the house." He stares hard at the doctor.

I shudder from the cold chill running down my spine.

Dr. Jones nods and adds, "Best to allow only a few to be aware of the investigation." Her hand gestures to the door as she states, "You may return the way we came in." She walks away briskly on wide swaying hips. And with that, Papa and I are alone in the cubicle again.

Quickly thinking, Papa tells me, "You must say that the doctor's conversation was about the medical history and treatment only. Say nothing about the investigations and the police. Someone in the house is responsible. Be silent, please." Papa commands me sternly, but he appears to be pleading.

"Yes, Papa," I reply.

With no door code required to exit, we return to the others to find Dexter tired and confused. Collin steals oddly furtive glances at Papa and me. Susanne does a straight forward and direct search of my eyes, as does Phoebe. I act as dumb as I feel. Nana fusses about everyone's comfort and welfare. Like Dad, she hasn't thought about the cause yet. Uncle Ian is bored now that the crisis has passed, and says he wants his bed. Aunt Evelyn, like Collin, seems very pensive indeed and perhaps annoyed. Both seem to be reviewing and planning. *Their reaction seems odd.*

We are directed by a medical technician into the inner sanctum. Time passes very slowly as we mill between the two adjoining rooms, one with Mom and one with Uncle Brian. Except for Evelyn and Collin, who stand together outside the rooms looking bored, each of us wanders from one room to another. Frightened, we stare at the unconscious person on the bed, barely recognizing them under their appliances and machinery.

Each patient is connected to a ventilator, a cardiac monitor, and an IV going through a regulating pump. There are wires and tubes everywhere. The quiet of each room is disturbed by whirrs and beeps—extraordinarily distracting. *How do people work amid this noise?* The rooms are mirror images, which is easy to figure out because the inside walls are moveable glass. Dr. Jones ignores us as she returns repeatedly to reassess each patient until she knows they are truly stable without new surprises.

As she passes, I ask, "How did we get rooms side by side?"

"Well, the two rooms side by side was luck, not good planning." Dr. Jones laughs a little as she stands near me and remarks with a smile, "But none of this was good planning." She advances closer and briefly looks directly into my eyes to reassure me. "Don't worry, son. They will both be okay." She notices that this cheers me up and almost makes me smile. I stare after her as her wide hips waddle away.

I think to myself, *Her kindness makes her easy to like. Remember that, Jeremiah.*

A heavy-set nurse with stovepipes for legs interrupts us as we meander from room to room. "We've broken the numbers rules in view of the circumstances. Now it's time to return to the waiting area. We will keep you updated."

After we are shepherded back to the little waiting area, Nana pulls out her thermos and biscuits. The staff gives us plastic coffee cups. Soon we are forcing down tea and British biscuits, which we Americans call cookies. For maybe the first time in my life, I am not hungry.

In a few hours, Dr. Jones reappears in the waiting area. She states, "I have reassessed both patients again. The effects are lightening, both are improving, and soon both will be off the ventilator. It's time to go home to get some sleep. You may return later in the day. I have your home and mobile numbers to keep you informed." She gazes directly at each of my grandparents, but her eyes fix on Papa as she adds meaningfully, "You will be called if anything develops." Papa nods that he has understood.

My tired brain asks, *Does she mean anything medical or anything for the police?* My shoulders shrug, but no one notices enough to ask why.

Reassured, we nod that we agree. Like bedraggled ducks, we drift back to our two cars as before and slowly find our way home over icy and slippery roads, with a few near skids thrown in for added excitement.

I hate ice storms, especially in Britain! Brits don't know how to drive on ice!

Hello, welcome bed! Phoebe's good night kiss given in the not-so-early hours of the morning becomes a vague recollection as I tumble into deep and dreamless sleep.

After awakening in the late morning, I head downstairs. Dad is finishing a phone call with the hospital staff. He waves as he tells me, "Constance and Brian are still ventilated but much improved, according to the latest report." Despite the good news, Dad still seems anxious. "Both patients will soon lose the breathing tube," Dad adds as an afterthought.

Nana seems exhausted, but she prepares a late cold lunch, which she leaves in the refrigerator with a sign that reads "food here" above a black arrow. She always has a sense of humor, for which I am grateful. She is sipping tea with Uncle Ian and Teresa when I find them in the kitchen.

Aunt Evelyn remains upstairs. Collin is downstairs in his room alone, and Dexter mopes between his father and Nana in the kitchen. Papa comes downstairs. He is unshaven and scruffy. I have never seen him appear so tired and unkempt. I recall the thoughts that he expressed to the doctor and the reasons.

I suspect he has not slept much.

Susanne appears eventually, looking pale and haggard. She talks to Dad, who quietly gives her his update. Susanne replies tearfully, "That's good news. But last night, I could not stop thinking about what happened. I kept breaking into tears, silently, and all alone. I didn't really sleep.

"I tried to figure why the fire alarm went off with no fire. Thank heavens it did because that's what saved Mom and Uncle Brian. Did someone know what was happening and trigger the alarm to save them? But who would do that? And why won't they explain?" Her eyes quizzically flit between Dad and me when she asks this. I play dumb. Clearly, she didn't overhear conversations whispered in the night.

My sister is way too smart.

Dad replies, "Susanne, no one triggered the alarm. We're just lucky that it happened."

Completely in the dark, Susanne still searches for reasons. She repeats her comments about the fire alarm and adds, "I am confused. How did that alarm get triggered?"

If only I could safely tell her all that I know. Her smart mind thinks differently from mine. She might find the right answer. But Papa said no—don't tell Susanne and don't tell Phoebe. He is afraid the murderer might overhear and do some new horror.

Is excluding Susanne the right answer? Despite uncertainty, I'm following orders. My shoulders shrug, apparently without a reason. My sister regards me suspiciously.

Papa commands, "Jeremiah, help me with the generator." I gladly agree. Moments later, we walk down the stairs together. The faint and gentle smell that I associate with his tweed jacket is now unpleasantly strong from anxiety and sweat. He needs a shower. I move closer and inhale deeply. I still like his smell, which calms me, despite its intensity. All will be right with the world, even though he stinks! It's Papa's stink.

Once we are alone in the mechanicals room, Papa pleads, "I know that you have told me all. But is there *anything* that you have recalled since we last talked? Please tell me, has Edgar come to you?" Papa looks at me earnestly.

I think back using a mighty foggy brain. "There's no news from the ancestors," I murmur while I think. I try to recall all the events in order. Frustrated, I recite mechanically, "Yes Papa, there are a few things. Let me clear my head to create order." My foot taps impatiently until words come. He waits silently.

Finally, I begin. "First, the outside window in the basement hallway was cracked open, which is an unusual breach of security. I didn't remember that until just now. Second, when we got to the boys' room, only Dexter was there. He said that when he was wakened by the alarm, Collin had already gone upstairs. But why would

Collin not waken his brother to make sure he was able to get out if the alarm was real?"

Papa looks like he is cataloguing this information.

Suddenly, Collin's slippers come to mind. Pensive, I muse, "Third, there was something odd with Collin's slippers. What was it?" I pause to dig deep into jumbled recollections.

Papa probes, "What was odd?"

Suddenly, my mind has it. I assert, "There definitely was snow on the edge of Collin's slipper when he was in the upstairs hallway. If he came from his room to the upstairs, where did he get the snow?"

Papa asks, "Snow? Snow on his slippers? Are you certain?"

"Yes. I am certain. The image is in my mind," I reply confidently and then stop to think more about my next statement before I continue. "You know that Collin does not seem to like his father. Dexter clearly adores his dad. All that showed when Aunt Evelyn was drunk the other night and had a row with Uncle Ian." I pause to face Papa. "I don't know if any of this is important." We stand together in silence while Papa tries to piece things together.

After a time, I add, "I wish Susanne was included. She has a good noggin and loves puzzles."

Papa looks at me kindly. "You are such a generous soul. I do love you for that!" While he tousles my hair, we both hear footsteps on the stairs.

As Susanne's beautiful Titian hair appears, her eyes scan the mechanicals room. "I came to check on you both. You have been away a little while. Is all working well?"

Papa nods to me when our eyes meet. Now that I have permission, I say, "Funny thing you should ask, dear sister. Let me explain."

Papa watches silently as I tell her all.

Susanne listens quietly. She asks no questions as I talk, but her eyes do roll when I tell her all about Leila, Edgar, and Mortimer. She nods occasionally when I confirm her suspicions that we had help. After I explain, "Edgar triggered the fire alarm," and describe both his startled response to its screech and the near mishap with the lighted candle, she laughs out loud.

"That is such a visual," she declares with a smile. "I can see his giant arm swooping down fast to grab the candle." Her smile quickly fades, and she falls into silence. Finally, she states, "No wonder we are having such trouble again! I'm not going to say what else I'm thinking."

Suddenly, we all hear a quiet female voice saying, "It's not our fault that you are having such trouble again!" A moment later, Leila, in her wonderful yellow dress, stands in our midst. She glares momentarily at Susanne and declares, "And those were unkind thoughts, child."

Edgar is behind her. He is wearing his mostly white with black waistcoat and his dark-red knee breeches over black silk hose. The buckles on his shoes gleam despite the scant light in the mechanicals room.

Mortimer tags after both, apparently having a good time acting as lookout for his wife and son. He smiles broadly as his head rotates side to side to keep a watch on the hallways. Mortimer has a green-and-white waistcoat, with green breeches over dark silk hose. As Edgar-the-son and Mortimer-the-father stand near each other, they seem dressed for Christmas in red and green. It nearly makes me laugh. There is a new food spot on Mortimer's waistcoat. Obviously, his paunch is always in the way during meals.

Like Leila, I get lost in other stray thoughts, maybe because my head is spinning.

Do phantoms need to eat? What do they eat? And where do they get food? After they eat, do phantoms need to go to the bathroom? Random thought! Stop it, Jeremiah. Get a grip!

Leila stares at me oddly.

Really, stop it, Jeremiah.

Papa and I wave to Mortimer, whose fingers blow a kiss to Susanne and me. I pretend to catch it. Papa says, "Good morning, all."

Susanne turns bright red as she stammers, "Hello, Grandma Leila, Grandpa Mortimer, and Uncle Edgar. So you are helping us?" She pauses, notes that each of them nods yes, searches out Leila's eyes, and asks, "Still reading private thoughts, Leila?" I detect sarcasm in her voice.

Leila adds, quietly and pleasantly, "Not to worry, dear. Were I you, I would think the same things. But no one would know *my* thoughts."

If this is Leila's attempt at making things better, she missed the mark!

"But, Granny, you just made mine public!" exclaims Susanne in a frustrated voice. "Really, must you?"

Leila smiles sweetly and responds, "Not really public, dear girl. Shared only amongst those who need to know. Insincere apologies for the disclosure!"

Susanne unhappily nods that she understands. I giggle. Irritated, Susanne stares at me and slides her finger down her nose.

Is she threatening to ski down my big nose? She does that when she's annoyed with me.

Leila gazes directly at me and remarks, "And as for your thoughts, Jeremiah, our food has no substance. The issues you raised in your mind are of no concern. But, yes, your mind is very like mine—everywhere at once." I turn scarlet.

Busted again!

Leila looks past Susanne to Papa and me as she announces, "Edgar has information." She turns to Susanne and admonishes, "And there's nothing the matter with Jeremiah's nose. He will grow into it. Kindly leave that topic *alone!*"

Now both kids have bright red faces again! Papa smiles briefly at his busted grandchildren.

The mechanicals room is already cramped. Edgar moves his big frame and impressive height in slightly. He is heavier than when he was executed for murder and now takes up a lot of space. We all stand small and still as we listen.

Edgar begins quietly, "I have tried to figure the reason for framing anyone with the robberies or causing the robberies as background noise. Because Leila caught some of their dreadful thoughts, I have concentrated on Evelyn and Collin." Edgar smiles a crooked grin at his mother.

Edgar continues, "I saw Collin go to his mother yesterday, earlier in the day. She gave him the gun and palmed him something I couldn't see. Now I realize that must have been a pill bottle. Evelyn was alone with him in the bedroom when the exchange occurred. The transfer was obviously prearranged and swift. There were very few words exchanged except for Evelyn saying, 'You know exactly what needs to be done.' Collin replied that he understood."

Edgar continues with more spirit, "While Leila stayed with your mother and Mortimer stayed with Brian, I wandered everywhere. I discovered that Collin was not in his room with Dexter. He was outside in a bulky coat and hoodie. He was making tracks in the snow to make it look like he came in through the window, which he previously unlatched."

Edgar pauses, then continues, "From conversations I overheard, we know that Evelyn wants Ian dead. I do not understand why Collin wants your mother and uncle dead." He points the index finger of his enormous hand in the direction of his mother and father. "None of us saw that one coming."

No one answers. After a moment, Edgar continues, "Collin's plan was to stage a break-in, during which two people were shot and killed. He drugged them so that if the burglary failed, they would die anyway."

Leila interrupts, "He thought a careless autopsy might even miss the overdose, especially if the victims had a conspicuous hole in the head."

Edgar continues, "Why would anyone ever believe a fifteen-year-old kid was the responsible party? He would never be suspected in a robbery gone wrong. But why do any of it?"

The living regard Edgar and Leila with horror. Then Susanne, who has been quiet, pipes up, "I think the answer is clear. It has something to do with inheritance. Collin had no plans for a career except inheriting the title. But I don't know the legal side of all that."

Leila adds quietly, "I have read Evelyn's thoughts. She finds Ian distant and work-obsessed. He is in a financial mess and is worth more dead than alive. Like Barbara before her, she wants her style, her comfort, and social prestige. She doesn't need Ian."

Turning to face Leila, Susanne asks, "But Barbara lived in the eighteenth century. She and Evelyn are not related. Why did you bring up Barbara?"

With her beautiful eyes focused on Susanne, Leila answers with long eyelashes aflutter, "Barbara had a brother. Evelyn is his seven-greats-granddaughter. And he was a successful sociopath in his day. He never got caught with his misdeeds. In his way, he was as evil as Barbara."

Susanne appears astonished, and then notes, "Poor Dexter. Collin is as bad as Barbara! Ouch!"

Leila adds, "And he is an equal to his mother. She is the brains behind the future murder of her husband. But Collin has his own big ideas to expand what comes to him."

Leila pauses, looks at each of us, and then comments, "I have read Collin's mind as he daydreams. Susanne is right in her assumptions. Collin wants the title at any cost. I have overheard conversations between mother and son, and I have read their thoughts. Collin wants to remove heirs presumptive so he is free to plan his inheritance in a more leisurely way. It does not bother him to murder. With Brian and Constance dead, then it's just a matter of timing for Papa and Ian."

Susanne stares incredulously at the living and the dead, one after another. Papa winces visibly at Leila's words, his eyes full of pain as they dart from one person to the next.

Leila continues, "Evelyn is party to everything. She approves and encourages Collin in his actions."

I feel uneasy, realize why, then petulantly assert, "It's fine to know all this. We have nothing we can prove in court. We don't even know how Uncle Brian and Mom were poisoned."

Leila answers, "You will figure this out soon. We will assist you. Think back. Who volunteered to serve from the bar last night?"

Before we can say anything, three dead people, two nearby and one standing in the hallway, answer in unison with a singsong voice, "Collin." The rest of us are stunned, gawking with an open mouth. The phantoms' attempt at humor falls flat, but the point is taken.

I think back to the charming bartender. As a Victorian toy maker might say, the penny dropped.

But how do we go from knowing to showing?

Chapter 13

THE PLAN: WHAT PLAN?

We stand there stupidly while Papa asks, "What we can do to prove how the poisoning was done? How do we get evidence that will play in a court of law?"

Susanne mutters, "The verbal testimony of dead people probably won't work." Even the dead ones smile, chuckle, and nod.

After much discussion, Papa and Leila agree that our three ancestors will keep a watch while we all carry on as if we know nothing. We must carefully stop any new murder attempts. Not much of a plan!

I feel as anxious as Susanne looks.

Papa repeats vehemently, "I don't want to tell anyone else. At some future date, my wife will need to know what the ancestors did. Right now, she is stressed enough with what is happening. I don't want to be overheard or for someone to make a slip comment. Ditto for your parents and Phoebe. We must play this close to the chest."

At least Susanne is now included in the inner circle.

When we go upstairs, I try to act normally. Collin glances oddly at Papa, Susanne, and me, but his expression disappears so quickly that, once again, I almost miss it.

Nana announces, "Even though it is only mid-afternoon, darkness will be falling in no time." She sighs. "Regardless, we must soon visit the hospital. Let's have a quick tea-time here before we go." With Teresa's help, she moves edibles from the refrigerator. Even Aunt Evelyn, Collin, and Dexter chip in.

I watch Collin like a hawk, hoping he doesn't notice. Watchfulness is harder to hide than you think. *Will he poison someone else?* That's a terrifying thought!

Nana notices that Colin is solemn. She assumes he is worried about his aunt and uncle. Trying to provide comfort, she remarks, "Don't worry, Collin. They will both recover and be fine."

He looks even more pensive after she says this.

I wonder what new horror he is planning?

After eating, there is general discussion about who will visit. Aunt Evelyn and Uncle Ian decide they will stay home with their children, who seem relieved. Collin appears moody and cranky, although he tries to hide it.

What is he up to next?

Teresa is clearly anxious to see Brian, but she graciously states, "We should first visit whichever patient is awake and off the tube."

Papa looks at her with affection. He realizes she is desperate to see Brian but cares for both patients. After he goes to the garage to get the little minibus—because it can seat nine and we are seven—Papa plaintively asks, "Sam, will you drive please?" Poor Papa looks so tired that Dad readily agrees.

Surprisingly, the weight of the little bus holds the road better than the cars. The arrival at the hospital is uneventful, without sliding and skidding this time. But then, an American was driving!

When we graduate from the general waiting room into the locked inner sanctum, we stand near the nurses' station in the central area of the ICU. Surrounded by glass door after glass door, the entrance to room after room, we peer at both patients in their cubicles. As Dr. Jones leaves Uncle Brian's room, she smiles toward us, lifts her hand in greeting, and comes closer to update our group. "Mr. Wadsworth is not ready for the breathing tube to be removed, but his vitals and reflexes are stable. We are weaning him off the ventilator, and expect his tube will come out early in the morning. He is not yet aware of his surroundings."

Concerned glances fly back and forth among the adults. They understand more than Susanne and I do.

Dr. Jones notes the anxiety this news creates. "We did an EEG study that shows normal brain wave activity. He will recover without neurological injury. It will take a little longer. Please, rest assured that all will be well."

The adults visibly relax with an almost audible sigh.

When Teresa remains visibly upset, the doctor directs attention to her and asks, "How are you related?"

"I'm his girlfriend," replies Teresa, trying to fight back tears.

Dr. Jones smiles warmly and reassures, "I understand your deep concern. He will be much better by tomorrow."

Teresa almost cries with relief when she hears this. Papa puts a comforting hand on her shoulder and comments to Dr. Jones, "Thank you. That is good news for us all." In response to his touch, Teresa faces Papa and lets her anxious tears fall. She leans against him for a moment before she straightens up and dries her eyes.

The doctor continues, "Mrs. Morris's breathing tube was removed earlier than we expected. She is doing well, almost back to normal. The key word is almost, which means *not* completely. She is looking toward you all. Why don't you visit her first?" With a smile, she focuses on Susanne and at me. "Remember, she will tire easily. Don't wear out your Mom."

When we all follow the doctor's advice and troop into Mom's room, Teresa's eyes repeatedly flit toward Uncle Brian, comatose in the adjoining room amid machinery. Mom's cardiac monitor and her IV with its pump are still in place. She is awake and hugs us tight but remains rather groggy and confused by what happened. She explains, "My throat hurts from the tube. That's why my voice is husky." Her questions are repetitive, perhaps from the drugs still in her system.

Dad notices what she is doing and sternly commands, "Constance, stop fiddling with your monitor leads."

Mom looks down at the wires she has been twiddling in her hands. Befuddled, she mumbles, "Oh yes, the nurse did say to leave them alone." She glances up at Dad. "I didn't realize. I must have forgotten. *What* did you call them?"

Dad repeats, "Monitor leads. They connect you to your cardiac monitor. Please, Constance, leave them be." Mom nods and moves her hands to her lap. A moment later, we have the same conversation, but this time it's about her IV line, which she is absentmindedly twisting around a finger.

Dad finishes with, "Stop with the fiddling, Constance." Papa and Nana face her with real concern.

Like the doctor said, she is much better but not there yet. We decide to give her an abbreviated version of what happened. Her hands become still as we tell her that she and Brian got sick from something they both ingested.

She repetitively asks, "Is everyone else all right? I have trouble understanding what we two ate that could have caused such a problem. And no one else got sick! This isn't like a usual food poisoning."

At the end of our visit, Mom says, "I have never felt so out of it nor so tired! What did Brian and I have to eat that affected us so? One would think we had been poisoned!"

Papa, Susanne, and I cannot look at her when she says this. Fortunately, ignorance is bliss. Nana's clucking, Teresa's genuine reassurance, and Dad's responsive hugs dismiss this from her mind. We each get a hug and kiss goodbye. As we leave, I see her head lie back. She appears to be falling asleep again, cardiac leads and IV intact.

Next, we troop in to see Brian in the neighboring room, still unconscious and on the ventilator. Standing beside his unresponsive body, Teresa starts to quietly cry.

Papa reassures her as best he can. "He will recover. The doctor said his brain was not injured and that the tube would come out tomorrow."

Teresa leans against Papa's chest and sobs uncontrollably. "I know he will be fine, but I ... am ... frightened. And the worst part, I don't ... I don't ... understand why this happened."

Papa says nothing in reply. What can he safely say? He looks over to the room where his daughter is asleep again, blissfully unaware of Teresa's sobs.

The road home is more difficult because the ice and snow on the road melted a little during the day. But with nightfall, the temperature has dropped, and ice has formed again. There is a slight drizzle now, and the misty rain freezes immediately. The roads are treacherous. The trip home takes twice as long as usual. Saints be praised, we finally reach home without major mishap. Thanks for driving, Dad!

Once in the house, Uncle Ian asks, "How are the patients?" Papa gives everyone a quick update.

Aunt Evelyn watches as Papa speaks but remains uncharacteristically silent about the patients. Eventually, she says, "I've opened a bottle of wine, if anyone wants some." We don't know if Uncle Ian had any. Holding her wine glass, Aunt Evelyn comments, "I didn't know when you were returning, so I didn't prepare anything."

"Quite so, hard to know what to do," replies Nana good-naturedly.

As Susanne turns away, she rolls her eyes. Apparently, she doesn't agree with Nana.

Nana, our mover and shaker, insists we need to eat. She declares, "I will make sandwiches."

Papa responds, "Considering our anxiety level, sandwiches sound like a good comfort food. Does everyone agree?" We nod yes.

Nana proclaims cheerily, "Sandwiches for supper it is. You had best eat up. That's all there will be!"

When my sister, our nanny, and I are in the morning room setting the table, Susanne whispers in my ear, "Auntie Evelyn is too bloody lazy to bother helping out. Wants to be served, she does, and to drink booze while she's at it."

From the other end of the table, Phoebe hears and whispers, "Shh! You might be overheard, even if you are right!"

Frustrated, Susanne continues, "Did you notice? She is working her way through a second bottle that she opened."

Whispering, Phoebe replies, "Yes, I did. But I don't want words with her because she overhears." She regards us sternly, puts a finger to her lips, and hisses, "Shh!"

We look down at our work, but Susanne and I smile at each other, mostly because Phoebe agrees with what must not be said.

As all eleven of us find places around the morning room table, Nana notices the two conspicuously empty chairs and another beside the wall. Upset, she counts the chairs and remarks, "I should have known something would happen. There were thirteen at table last night. That brings bad luck!" She stops speaking, glances around, and then bursts into tears. She wipes her face and apologizes, "Oh my! Silly superstitious me! Too much tension."

Papa stands up from his end of the table, comes over to her, and holds her shoulders from behind in a gentle hug as she sits. She holds his arms tight to her and rests her head against his torso. With closed eyes, she holds him tight for an endless time. He kisses the top of her head and waits till she releases his arms before slowly coming back to his end of the table. His shoulders slouch.

Always the good host, our grandfather asks about drinks. No one wants alcohol except Ian, who already has a small whiskey, and Evelyn, who swirls her wineglass coquettishly. Tired and fed up, Papa notices the second wine bottle is now dry. Surprisingly, instead of a small whiskey for himself, he opens another of the same vintage, pours a tiny portion, and leaves the rest of the bottle on the table. Moments later, Evelyn's presents her now empty stemware. Papa nods. When she quizzically smiles happily, he fills her goblet to the brim.

This surprises me.

She has already clearly finished the second bottle, and this starts the third. I am afraid she may become belligerent again.

What is Papa doing so deliberately? What's his plan?

Uncle Ian is nursing a miniscule amount of whiskey, which makes me think he didn't start with wine. Whiskey comes from grain and wine from grapes. Previously, Nana attempted to educate her grandchildren about alcohol. Her quote? "Wine before liquor, never sicker! Now remember the slogan, children. Never mix grain and grape, unless you want to be ill." My guess? Auntie Evelyn alone is responsible for the empty wine bottles.

Nana and Teresa have tea, while we kids have lemonade and slowly eat our sandwiches. Seemingly absentminded, Collin sullenly and silently eats more than usual. I'm clueless: What is he is planning? Aunt Evelyn has a few sandwiches while she drinks wine steadily. She gradually becomes cheerier, talking with everyone instead of remaining silent and cold. As she does so, Dexter seems relieved. Collin responds by becoming cheerier himself.

Is Collin using charm so he can harm some of us?

After eating, Phoebe suggests a card game. She has been silent throughout most of the dinner. She has asked no questions about *how* two people in the house became ill. As I am wondering if she is wearing blinders, I see her eyes follow Collin as he moves around the room. Collin goes downstairs to get something and returns. He pauses near his mother's purse that she has left in the hall. Is he hiding something? I can't figure how to find out unnoticed. Suddenly, I realize Phoebe is scrutinizing his every move.

Why? My thoughts ask, *Has she guessed something? Has she figured out what he did!*

All but Papa and Aunt Evelyn join in the card game. Papa pretends to read the paper but is actually spying on everyone. Aunt Evelyn quietly becomes totally toasted. After all, she has swilled three bottles of wine! Please, Papa, doesn't open another. When the game finishes, Aunt Evelyn states, "I'm going to bed even though it is relatively early. Last night was too much, and sleep time was too short."

Uncle Ian yawns and comments, "I'll join you soon. It was indeed a short night!"

Aunt Evelyn waves a hand to everyone, including Dexter, and heads up the stairs. She neither hugs nor kisses her sons.

Collin complains, "Mom, I'm tired and need to go to bed, but I have a headache.

She replies, "Come up with me. I will get you a headache pill." Collin hands Aunt Evelyn her purse and follows her up the stairs before Nana can volunteer the medication she has in the kitchen. A few minutes later, he comes down. He waves goodnight and heads to the basement.

Dexter is beside his father and doesn't want to move. I am happy to see that Uncle Ian recognizes Dexter's anxiety over the events of the day and stays put in his chair. With a slight smile, Dexter moves over to sit on the arm of his father's chair. Within moments, he leans in tight against his dad, making Dexter and Ian seem glued together. For the first time ever, I see Uncle Ian smile with affection toward his son, which makes me happy.

The one topic that is never mentioned hangs like a large shadow over everything, a shadow no one admits is there. That topic is how the two family members became sick at the same time.

After a while, Uncle Ian remarks, "I must get rest. You too, Dexter." He hugs Dexter tight, kisses the top of his head, and declares, "I *do* love you, young man. Now off to bed."

Dexter looks like he wants "I love you" repeated many times over.

"I love you too," he replies quietly with glistening eyes. Clearly, Dexter seldom hears "I love you." He heads downstairs to join his brother while his father climbs the stairs to be with his wife.

I am glad that this mess is waking up Uncle Ian. He must recognize Dexter's love for him, but, as a good father, he needs to return that affection.

Everything plays over and over in my mind. *I still don't understand Collin.*

Eventually, everyone decides that bed is a good idea. It is a sooner bedtime than our usual, but everyone is exhausted and worried. We say our good nights. In a short time, Phoebe plants her nighttime kiss on my forehead. Susanne waves good night and leads the way to her room with Phoebe following.

I sleep fitfully until Leila wakes me with a hug while Mortimer stands beside her, both fully materialized. Quickly wide wake, I say, "Hello, good to see you, I think," and sit up immediately without bonging my noggin. This is the first time I have had a chance to see Mortimer to give him a proper greeting. The basement encounter doesn't count. He smiles warmly and declares, "Oh, it *is* good to see you again, too. More fun at home, I see!"

I stand to give Mortimer a big hug, who leans in to kiss my cheek. "I don't need to bend so far to give you a peck. Thank you for growing." With twinkling eyes, he laughs. "That saves my old back, although I don't think it matters, being dead and all." I giggle with him and give another tight squeeze.

Uncle Edgar appears, nods to me, and quietly announces, "Collin returned the gun to Evelyn." He dropped it into her handbag when he came up from the basement. I am worried that something may happen."

As Edgar speaks, we hear an argument starting between Aunt Evelyn and Uncle Ian. We cannot distinguish the words, but the tone is cold, sharp, and nasty.

Uncle Ian utters the words "your drinking," but the rest is lost in her loud diatribe of bitter complaints against him.

Suddenly, Uncle Ian's voice is louder and slightly higher. "What are you doing, Evelyn. Put that away!"

At that moment, nine people know that a gun is involved in what is happening. Six are living, and three are dead. I just happen to be standing in my room with the dead ones, but no one new needs to know about them!

I head to the door. Susanne is poking her head out of her doorway, Phoebe from hers. From the other direction, I see Papa in the hallway and Nana leaving their bedroom. She slips her cell phone into a pocket and then fastens her dressing gown closed with its belt as she comes along the hall.

I hear Dad getting out of bed. A moment later in the hall, he questions, "What is happening?"

Papa and I exchange glances. We race to the door of Uncle Ian and Aunt Evelyn's room. Papa tries the handle, but the door is locked.

Papa yells, "Unlock the door."

Evelyn pauses in her loud complaints against Ian. Her voice caustically orders, "Don't move, hubby dearest. The door stays *locked*." We hear Ian trying to reason with her, almost pleading. The noise has roused the basement dwellers. Collin is now near me and Dexter is trotting up the stairs. Teresa doesn't know what to do. She finds Phoebe along the hall and stands behind her. "Stay right there beside the window, Ian. Don't move." Evelyn's voice is uncertain and panicked. Susanne, Papa, and I know that she is holding a gun.

Standing next to me, Dexter announces anxiously, "Mom bought a handgun. I hope she didn't bring it, but how can she force him to stay against the window without something to threaten him? She must have the gun."

Okay, make that ten people who already knew that she has a gun—seven living and three dead. Soon everyone will know about the gun but not that the dead are watching.

Wow! Talk about weird!

Glaring angrily at his younger brother, Collin asks, "How do *you* know she bought a gun?"

Dexter replies, "I saw her putting it away. She never mentioned applying for a permit, so it has to be illegal."

The latch turns and the door opens. Papa, Collin, and I rush into the room. Keeping the gun pointed at Ian, Evelyn glances around. "How did you get in?"

No one volunteers anything. Fortunately, no one else questions, either. I know the answer and want to thank Edgar, but I remain silent. Near the bedpost, a lopsided smile vanishes about six feet up.

Dexter's voice implores, "Mom! Stop!" as he enters the room and moves slowly toward her.

She sees him and pivots slightly. She turns the gun in his direction and then returns her aim toward Ian. "Stay back or I'll shoot you both."

Dexter stands still. Collin is beside him with an odd and angry expression on his face. Papa orders, "Boys, don't move."

Uncle Ian, transfixed by the gun, is forced to stay near the window. Aunt Evelyn dominates the middle of the room. Collin and Dexter are halfway to their mother while I am immediately behind them, looking at Collin. Papa remains near the door to the hallway, deciding.

Aunt Evelyn's hands are shaking. Obviously drunk, clearly angry, and apparently confused about what to do, she repetitively berates Ian for his cold personality, his lack of ambition, and his inadequacies in keeping her happy. Her words slur. Strung together, the words make sense, but most of her complaints sound like alcohol talking. I shudder when recollecting Papa said a drunk with a gun is extraordinarily dangerous indeed.

"I need to finish this now!" Her eyes bore into her husband's.

From the corner of my eye, I see a tall outline materializing, which distracts me from seeing Dexter rush forward to tackle his mother.

They fall together in a heap, arms flailing as he reaches for the gun that she holds tight. The gun disappears between them as Dexter pushes her arm down. Uncle Ian looks frantic, uncertain which way to move to protect his son.

Bang! Aunt Evelyn howls in pain. Silent Dexter seems stricken. He rolls away from his mother, his pajama bottom covered in blood. Has he been shot? No! Unharmed, he holds on tight to the gun clutched in Evelyn's hand.

Collin runs forward. He yanks the gun from Evelyn and Dexter's grasp. Aunt Evelyn reaches for her badly bleeding leg and, moments later, pulls back her bloody hand. Pain distorts her face.

Enraged, Auntie Evelyn yells, "You little bastard. What have you done?" She glares at Dexter and screams, "You little bastard!"

The expression of despair that crosses Dexter's face could break the hardest heart. He mumbles through streaming tears, "I am sorry, Mummy. I never wanted to hurt you. I didn't want you to hurt Daddy."

In her drunken stupor, Aunt Evelyn focuses on Collin and belligerently admits, "This wasn't part of the plan."

Collin glares at his mother and commands, "Shut up. You are drunk. Just shut up."

She yells back, "Afraid they might find out? Afraid they might know?"

Suddenly, we *all* realize that Collin holds the gun. *Some* of us realize that *none* of us is safe.

Nana's face is a question mark that beseeches Papa to act as they stand in the room near the doorway to the hall. Susanne and Phoebe remain near the doorway closest to the bathroom, with Teresa cowering behind, all locked in place. I move slowly and quietly toward one side of Collin, still too far away. Papa moves in slowly and noiselessly toward the other side. We make eye contact and nod.

Uncle Ian stands motionless, confusion and worry over his face, as he pleads, "Collin, put the gun down. There is no danger now."

Collin answers, "This is not how it is supposed to work. It's all wrong."

Uncle Ian appears confused and confesses, "I don't understand."

Collin declaims loudly, "You wouldn't. You never had enough time for us, to pay us any attention. Why would you understand now?"

Papa commands, "Drop the gun, Collin. We need to look after your mother."

Collin ignores his grandfather. He points the gun at his father. *Oh boy! We need another plan.*

Clutching at straws, I demand, "Why did you commit the robberies, Collin? Homes invaded and arms broken, that was you and Aunt Evelyn, wasn't it?"

Collin turns his face toward me but keeps the gun aimed at his father. "Why do you think I was involved in those silly robberies?"

I reply, "The red Jaguar was seen at every robbery. No one knew if it was involved, but it was present." I pause. Collin becomes irritated while his father seems utterly bewildered.

"How do you know that?" Collin demands.

"I just know." Then I ask, "Did you drive each time or did Aunt Evelyn?"

He laughs. "I don't have a license. I am not allowed to drive."

"You are not allowed, but you know how. You learned at the farm using the tractor." I ask again, "Did you drive, or did Evelyn?"

Incensed, he viciously retorts, "You think *you* are so smart. Like I said, I don't have a license." He shifts his weight from foot to foot, still aiming the wildly waving gun at his father.

That's really dangerous!

I ask, "Who pushed the two old people during the robberies, you or Aunt Evelyn?"

Wildly looking around, Collin exclaims, "Damn Oscar. Stupid old man!"

I state, "You poisoned Uncle Brian and Mom. What did you put in their special iced tea?"

Seeming to regard me as an all-seeing monster, he asks, "Why do you think that?"

With a shrug of my shoulders, I reply, "I have my reasons." My deliberate smile infuriates him. "We have figured it out, Collin."

He sneers, "If you figured it all, then you know. But you don't know and you haven't figured it out, have you, Yankee cousin?"

"Why did you want them dead?"

He acts as if he has nothing to lose as he waves his gun between Uncle Ian and me. He replies, "Well, smart American, you've got the wrong end of the stick. You'll never get anything right."

His callous eyes fix on his mother. "But you … you stupid woman! You had to get drunk again and get ahead of yourself, didn't you? You stupid cow!" For a moment, the gun points at her chest while he glares at her.

Aunt Evelyn first fixes him with a steely gaze, and then her head slowly and silently turns to the side. Her red-stained hands return to her bloody groin. Her face is deathly white.

Is that white color from rage or blood loss?

As Collin returns his aim to Uncle Ian, he momentarily stares at his father indecisively. In that pause, Papa and I rush him from each side and knock him over. The gun fires again, but the aim is wide and shoots through the drapery rod attachment. On one side, the heavy drapes plummet to the floor in a pile.

Collin lands in a heap as we tackle him. Papa holds him tight; Dad takes the gun, and I grab the closest drapery tie from the intact side to keep Collin restrained. Like a hangman's noose, the remaining tieback persistently swings ominously from its attachment halfway down the window frame while the darkest night peers in through the naked window.

Nana reaches for the phone to call for help. The phone is still dead. Nana loudly swears, "Damn it all to bloody hell." She reaches into her dressing gown for her cell. She sounds really angry as she calls for an ambulance and then calls the police!

Aunt Evelyn has turned ghostly pale. A pool of blood on the carpet oozes out widely from her groin. *Her color is from blood loss, no matter if she's angry.* Phoebe goes to Evelyn as Dad rips a pillowcase into strips for a pressure dressing. With her twisted mouth wide open, Evelyn curses as she screams, "Let me die!"

Incensed, Phoebe yells, "Shut your mouth, or I'll slap you into a bleeding pulp!" Over Aunt Evelyn's bitter protests, she vigorously ties a pillow case strip as a tight tourniquet, then applies a dressing, but blood is rapidly oozing through. In fear, I stare at the enlarging stain, shocked by Phoebe's never-before-heard display of fury.

Dad watches Evelyn and Phoebe as he rips a second pillowcase.

Phoebe pulls the first bloody dressing off, leaves the first tourniquet, and ties the second around the leg so tight that Evelyn cries out. Phoebe glares at her with dark eyes flashing and almost screams, "Warning!" She raises a bloody hand with red fingers pointed at Evelyn. She is poised to hit! This shocks the patient into silence. Phoebe uses the entire second ripped pillowcase before the saturating flow slows. Evelyn is now incredibly white.

With this much blood loss, I wonder if Aunt Evelyn will get her wish?

When the ambulance arrives, Aunt Evelyn is stabilized with two intravenous lines, a new pressure dressing, and quickly bundled off to hospital and surgery in the same hospital we visited earlier for our first two casualties.

The police arrive to question everyone. Fortunately, I am not questioned first. That gives time to put a story together.

The police politely ask Papa if they may search the premises. Papa replies, "I insist that you do. You do not need a warrant. Do I need to sign a waiver?"

"No," answers one of the officers.

Papa, Susanne, and I have a problem. We obtained information from ancestors, but court officials would never understand. Too bad Leila cannot be included. I'd love to see her play with and twist the mind of some stodgy judge!

Gotta watch our statements!

I whisper to Papa, "Where did we hear about the red Jaguar?"

Papa's eyes scan as he replies, "I thought that info was in the papers. Yes, I am sure that is where we found that information. Remember, no words about ancestors."

I nod. I find Susanne and repeat Papa's warning about ancestors. She replies, "Duh," and insolently rolls her lovely eyes.

Uncle Ian receives a call notifying him of Aunt Evelyn's urgent need for surgery. The surgeon tells him the risks. Aunt Evelyn may lose her leg because the femoral artery was severely damaged! It will be a long night for everyone, especially the surgeon involved.

My goodness, we are keeping hospital personnel busy!

With the arrival of the police, Collin quickly goes from curtain ties to handcuffs. After a brief preliminary questioning, Collin is taken into custody, escorted to the back of a police car, and driven to the police station for formal interrogation.

It takes hours for the police to get all our statements. After gathering his facts, the senior officer states, "Lady Evelyn Wadsworth and Master Collin Wadsworth are both under arrest. Both are charged with attempted murder." The officer looks at Papa and Nana's stricken faces and sadly adds, "So sorry for the trouble you are having, Lord and Lady Poppycock."

Papa makes strong eye contact and answers, "Thank you for your kind words." Nana nods in acknowledgement, tries to answer in return, but words fail. Her chin is giggling like Susanne's does before tears. *Oh, dear!*

The officer adds, "We must serve a warning that you and all of the family must stay in the country until all inquiries are finished. That includes Lady Constance Wadsworth Morris and all the American family." The officer smiles slightly, perhaps hoping to avoid a confrontation at this news.

Papa smiles back and replies, "That's okay. Right now, all we want is sleep!"

The officer's tightly held shoulders relax slightly in relief.

My guess is that some privileged people aren't so nice!

Susanne and I stare at the officer for a moment. It's so odd to hear our mom called by the name Lady Constance Wadsworth Morris, but that is her proper name.

I'm glad we Yanks don't bother with titles!

Eventually, in the wee hours of the morning, the police depart. After they leave, Papa mutters to Susanne and me, "Collin won't give much away. His type neither takes responsibility nor admits mistakes." Nana didn't hear him. As soon as the police left, she and practical Phoebe busily tackled the bloody carpet upstairs, despite everything.

Cleanup done, Nana later asserts, "Collin must have gone mad. What other explanation do we have? I know Ian is distant, but this rage came from out of nowhere." Nana's head shakes slightly in disbelief. "And how did this firearm get involved? Where did it come from? I don't understand." Her head moves side to side as Nana frantically tries to make sense of all that has happened. Eventually, Nana admits, "And Evelyn was in a drunken rage and didn't know what she was doing. In her right mind, she would never have intended to harm Ian." She quietly cries beside Papa, who holds her. "I don't understand," she sobs. He looks away to the distance, his face very solemn. What can poor Papa say?

Dad and Phoebe quietly gawk at the floor.

A while after the police leave, Uncle Ian's phone rings as he walks into the sitting room. He almost jumps at the sound, fumbles with the phone, listens to the voice at the other end, and replies, "Yes, this is Ian Wadsworth. Thank you for calling, Dr. Mehta."

On speaker, the surgeon's rather bass voice says, "Your wife's femoral artery was severed, but it has been repaired. She lost a lot of blood and has received multiple transfusions. It's fortunate your family acted so quickly to control the blood loss, for she could easily have bled to death. I worried that if the repair didn't go well enough to establish good blood flow, she could lose her leg. Fortunately, a graft to the artery has salvaged the leg, and all is well." He pauses long enough to let us understand his words.

His kindly voice continues, "Do not come to see her till much later. The roads are dangerously slippery. Besides, she is sedated and doesn't understand what is happening. She will probably sleep the rest of the night. The painkillers will help with that too. Rest easy that she is fine and remains in stable condition." Uncle Ian and the surgeon speak a little more. Finally, we hear the surgeon ask, "My apologies, but I must enquire. Do you know that your wife is under arrest?"

Uncle Ian nearly chokes on his words as he answers, "Yes, we do know. The officer made that crystal clear."

The surgeon continues, "One wrist is handcuffed to the bed. I don't want you surprised when you see her."

Uncle Ian murmurs, "I thought as much. Thank you for your time and candor. I am grateful to you."

Uncle Ian stares blankly at his cell phone afterward. He shakes himself slightly, notices his son, and extends his arms. Dexter immediately clings to his side in a tight hug. They stand close together, each seeking comfort and both crying quietly.

Wake-up call, Uncle Ian. I am very glad to see this closeness, but I don't know why. Wait! Here's the answer. Dexter has feelings of empathy for other people. That means he's not a screwball like his brother.

Repeat good nights are longer, and kisses on the cheek are harder all around this early in the morning. Later in my room, Phoebe kisses my forehead. After she says, "Good night," she gives me another hug. My eyes close. She flips the light off and closes the bathroom door. I am alone and asleep instantly.

Sometime later, a female voice says, "Good night, dear boy. I love you dearly."

My eyes open to find Leila sitting beside me, fully materialized. Her right hand slips into mine for a sweet moment before disengaging to turn on the light on my bedside table. Her other hand lovingly caresses my forehead. Grandma Leila continues, "We are returning to our destination. This is goodbye." There is tear at the corner of her eye.

I reach up to hug her tight. Her lips kissing my cheek feel wonderful. The weight of her torso against my chest as I lie in bed is comforting. She loves me, and I love her, ditto for Grandpa Mortimer and Uncle Edgar, and all the gang who helped me last time.

Leila gently moves away. I sit up and then quickly stand as Mortimer approaches. "My pleasure, as always," he remarks. He shakes my hand and then hugs me tight. "Goodbye, my grandson. I love you, my dear boy."

I murmur, "And I love you, too, Grandpa."

My eyes search for Uncle Edgar. First his crooked smile and hideous teeth appear, followed by a thumbs-up sign. A moment later, he fully materializes.

I joke, "Is this order of appearances a new party trick?"

He laughs and affirms, "Yes, it is, courtesy of my reading *Alice in Wonderland.*"

I state, "Thanks to all of you, including Mr. Cheshire, for your help. You saved Uncle Brian and Mom. I shall never forget."

Uncle Edgar hugs me to his giant frame. As always, this lifts me from the floor. He exclaims, "You saved my soul, proved me innocent, and obtained my pardon from Saint Peter." He hugs me again. I'm still at his eye level, toes dangling.

I reply, "And *you* saved *me* from the time abyss vortex." He puts me back onto the floor.

He glances at me sheepishly and adds, "That was harder than I expected." Then he laughs. "But we survived to tell the tale together, with only one of us dead. And I was already predead, so no harm to either."

We both laugh. Then I ask, "Did you say goodbye to Susanne? She loves all of you too."

In unison, they reply, "Yes, dear. She has said goodbye."

I watch them closely as Leila heads towards the door in her canary yellow dress with the blue embroidery and blue shoes with canary yellow embroidery. Mortimer follows after, shorter than his wife, even if you exclude her high hair and her heels. He wears his green knee breeches and dark silk hose with a green waistcoat that still has last night's dinner spattered on the paunch up front. Their son towers after them, fuller in figure than after his execution, striding confidently, and waving his hand back to me in a fond goodbye. There is so much to his red breeches because his legs are so long! Once again, I marvel at his height.

All three become outlines before they reach the hallway door. They turn back for a last look, wave a hand, and then vanish. Suddenly alone, I feel sad and a little lonely for a moment. Then I think of Dad, Phoebe, and Susanne. Mom and Uncle Brian are recovering in hospital! Gratitude fills my heart and happiness returns.

I look up to see Susanne at the bathroom door. She asks, "Did they say goodbye to you too?"

Susanne sees my nod and stands beside me, arms outstretched. In response to her hug, my hands hold on tight. When I sit on the edge of my bed afterward, she joins me.

She declares, "I do love you, baby brother."

"I love you, too, old girl." I giggle.

Calling my fourteen-year-old sister "old girl" is entirely too funny.

We sit side by side, holding hands in silence for a few moments. The silence is comforting. We are simply two ordinary children sitting together, hand in hand. Eventually, she whispers, "Goodnight, sleep well," and stands.

"Good night, and you too," I reply.

She nips back into her room through the open bathroom door. Once again, I am alone.

After I crawl into bed, turn off the light, and shift to my side, I instantly fall asleep.

Chapter 14

THE NEXT BLOW

It may be late morning, but it's still far too soon when I awaken to see the sun peeking in between cracks in the drapes, spilling patterns onto the floor and furniture. On the carpet are spots of color, bright yellows and blues, where the sun tickles sparks of brightness. I may be tired, but the blotches of sunlight make me feel secure again.

Reviewing recent events, I ask, "How could all of this have occurred?" *Without the ancestors' warning about the poisoning, what might have happened?*

The answer to my thoughts makes me shudder. Would we have ever known why we lost two members of the family? Still pondering, I clean up and shower before dressing for the day.

Downstairs, Nana and Papa are fussing in the kitchen. Both are dressed but appear rather haggard. Nana's pale face has no makeup; her eyes are bloodshot, and her hair needs work. Papa is unshaven; he hasn't found his hairbrush. I suspect that neither grandparent has slept much.

Teresa is trying to help. She finally decides making toast is her niche for this morning. Phoebe floats watchfully nearby, setting cutlery at each place in the morning room.

Uncle Ian sits at the kitchen counter solemnly drinking a coffee.

His arm encircles Dexter who is glued to his father's side. Both Uncle Ian, and especially Dexter, need the reassurance of touch, one from the other. When his father shifts, Dexter separates and then leans in toward him again. Dexter has lost a mother and a brother to the legal system. In one sense, this is the day that Dexter first learned he never really had a true mother or brother. He is a badly frightened and lost soul in need of much reassurance.

Dad surfaces in a little while with unshaved stubble that colors his lower face blue from the thick black hair poking through his skin. The bags under his eyes make him look as haggard as Papa and Nana. Dad waves and murmurs, "Greetings to everyone," as he pours a coffee. He sits silently in a chair not far from Uncle Ian. When I stand beside him, he reaches to me, puts his hand on my back, pulls me to him, and then silently hugs me tight. I half sit on his knee, although my legs are easily touching the floor. His hand stays on my back or shoulder at all times for reassurance as he glumly drinks his coffee.

Susanne is last to appear, still in her pajamas and housecoat, with slippers that flap against the stone of the kitchen floor. She stands on the other side of Dad. Only when he hugs her does his hand leave me. He ignores his coffee, sits touching each of us, but says nothing. He fights tears unsuccessfully as he holds his children. All are silent.

Nana pragmatically decides that business must be as usual. After Uncle Ian has had a coffee and starts a second, she directly interrogates, "What legal representation do you want for Evelyn and Collin?"

Uncle Ian shakes his befuddled head and then admits, "Sorry, I haven't thought that out. I'm glad you asked. I've must leave this deep funk and deal with the pressing issues at hand." Frowning, he ponders for a bit, and then tentatively questions, "If I said, 'That's her problem,' would I be a monster? After all, she was about to murder me." No one answers. He pauses and shakes his head slightly to gather his thoughts in the silence.

Before anyone can comment, Uncle Ian continues solemnly, "I shall pay for my divorce lawyer, not hers. I doubt divorce grounds will be contested. For her criminal defense, she may find whomever she pleases and pay for representation herself." He sounds angry.

Papa and Nana act suddenly surprised. This is perhaps the first time in a long while that Ian has shown enough backbone to stand up for himself. He has been deeply wounded emotionally, with appropriate anger now directed at his assailant. Nana and Papa smile slightly in relief.

Phoebe reappears after duties are done in the morning room. Now everyone can hear. Nana persists, "And what will you do for Collin?" She sits down at the table almost across from her son.

Uncle Ian thinks for a moment and then confides, "I shall start with a psychiatrist and a lawyer. His behavior and his plans are those of a psychopath." He pauses sadly. "What will happen to him, Mom?"

Nana's eyes flare as she exclaims, "Surely not a psychopath, Ian!" She queries, "Don't you think it is some form of mental illness, perhaps a psychosis? Isn't there some medication that can make him into a normal person again?"

Uncle Ian gazes sadly his mother and quietly confesses, "I have watched Collin for years. He has *never been* a normal person. He can be charming because he knows how to play to his audience. But he is a bully at school and is sometimes cruel to animals. He finds inflicting pain amusing. I am concerned he does not feel emotions as we do. I fear he is truly a psychopath."

Almost in tears, Nana cries out, "Oh, Ian, surely not! That is too horrible to contemplate in a grandchild, or any member of the family." A tear trickles down as she pleads, "Ian, please be mistaken. A psychosis can be treated. I *want* him to be normal."

Uncle Ian stares straight at her, reaches for her left hand, holds it tight, and asks, "May I tell you something I have kept hidden for years?"

With wide eyes staring, Nana whispers, "Yes, tell me now." Dexter appears transfixed by his dad, Papa stricken. We all anxiously watch in horrified fascination, afraid of what is coming next.

Uncle Ian asks, "Do you remember when we had the little dog named Buddy?"

With a glance at his wife while Nana nods in agreement, Papa declares, "Yes, we do. She was a sweet young spaniel that ran away. I recollect you seemed attached to your little pal who was always with you."

Dexter responds, "I remember her. She was the only pet we were allowed, and I really loved her. She loved to cuddle with me, more than Mommy did."

Uncle Ian unhappily recounts, "We got the dog for the children when Collin was about five and Dexter about three. Dexter clearly loved the animal. But I noticed that Collin sometimes pulled her ears or tail until she yelped. I explained to him over and over all the reasons that gentleness is required with animals. Another time, I caught Collin viciously kicking the animal. She was cowering in fear, so I suspected this was not the first time she had been beaten."

Uncle Ian pauses to collect his thoughts. Riveted by fear, we stare blankly, dreading the next revelation.

"Then one day I caught him going too far," confesses uncle Ian. "Collin, a five-year-old, had a damp, almost wet, cloth in one hand while he had one arm encircling the dog's neck and jaw, holding the jaw closed. The dog could only breathe through her nose. Then he was covering her nostrils with the damp cloth till she wiggled frantically, desperate for air. He was doing this over and over when I found them. I grabbed the cloth as I tried to snatch the terrified animal from him. The dog ran to cower behind a chair and out of reach.

"When I tried to explain to him the harm he was doing, Collin smiled up at me and confessed, 'It's fun to make her wiggle. Besides, she's a dog. She can't tell on me.' And then he laughed."

After a horrified silence, Uncle Ian continues, "That's when I knew there was something wrong with Collin. But I could not accept what was wrong until much later."

Shocked, my dad almost whispers, "Ian, I am sorry, so sorry." My wide-eyed grandparents watch Ian, waiting for the next blow.

Uncle Ian continues, "I was worried about what to do. That evening, I told Evelyn all the things I had seen. She regarded me with a cool expression and remarked, 'Well Ian, he was just playing. He's only five. And it's only an animal.' That's when I knew that there was something wrong with both of them. Psychopaths do not feel empathy and may sometimes hurt animals for sport. I watched my son and eventually realized he is a psychopath … like his mother." Uncle Ian's eyes focus on the floor, his face stern and sad.

Gasps of horror kill the silence. Under her breath, Phoebe mutters, "Like mother, like son." She briefly glances at the floor before she tearfully peers out through the window.

Shocked, Teresa appears incapable of speech. Susanne and I, like the others in the room, are stunned.

Papa seems afraid of the answer to his next question. "Ian, you were fond of the dog and took it everywhere with you. What happened? Did she *really* run away?"

Uncle Ian replies, "After that near-suffocation incident, I was terrified Collin would maim or kill that helpless creature. She was a lovely spaniel with an affectionate disposition, an animal that just wanted kindliness. Dexter adored her, and I didn't want him to lose his little friend. But she was too trusting and dreadfully vulnerable.

"Personally, I'm not overwhelmingly fond of the responsibility involved with pets, but I decided I had to protect her. I tried to never leave her alone with Collin after that. She came with me to work and stayed by me in the house at all times. Evelyn named me Mr. Dog-Walker. Dexter and I would play with her together. I loved that, especially since Collin never bothered with me unless he wanted something."

Uncle Ian pauses again to swallow hard before he continues, "Evelyn always ignored the animal. I noticed Buddy always ran happily to Dexter, paid no attention to Evelyn, and was increasingly wary of Collin. I suspected Collin was still harming her the few times she was away from me. The dog needed protection even though Dexter might be unhappy. Repeated brutalization might make her vicious. There was a chance that she could be killed.

"Eventually, I spoke to the vet on the QT and told him some of what had happened. He made enquiries and found her a good home in a different county where she would never be seen by Evelyn or Collin. The vet awaited delivery.

"It wasn't long after that encounter before Evelyn wanted to visit her parents with the children. I said business delayed my going for a day. That's when I handed Buddy over to the vet to spirit her away to safety. I made up the story about her running away. And I forbade any future pets." After a slight pause, Uncle Ian finishes with a grimace and a near sob. "This is so bloody painful!" His face is now a little sweaty and his chin wobbles as he fights tears.

We all realize that Uncle Ian is right. This story is bloody painful.

Dexter exclaims, "So my rotten brother is the real reason I lost my dog!"

Uncle Ian replies, "Dexter, I am sorry. I hope you understand why I couldn't tell you what I had to do."

Dexter faces his dad and almost smiles. "At least Buddy was safe in a new home."

Uncle Ian fondly watches his son while briefly patting his shoulder. "Thanks for understanding, Dexter." Then Uncle Ian looks squarely at his mother and apologizes in a soft voice, "I am sorry, Mummy—incredibly sorry!"

Suddenly, Nana's face turns to stone. In a matter-of-fact and quiet voice, she affirms, "You do realize that if the psychiatrist says he is of sound mind and a psychopath, then, at best, he must be in an institution for the criminally insane, possibly for the remainder of his life." Shocked silence fills the next few moments. Nana's voice catches as she adds, "But he must have gone mad, a psychosis of some sort. It must be so. It must be!"

Susanne's eyes lock mine while her face says, *Nana doesn't want to accept the obvious.*

Uncle Ian holds his mother's hand tight as he again apologizes, "Sorry!" He begins to softly cry like a large frightened child, his expression pleading for *her* understanding. *He* understands reality.

Poor Nana! She's fighting the truth.

Through tears, Uncle Ian looks toward his father. Papa mouths almost inaudibly, "I understand." Ian returns his gaze to his mother.

With her free hand, Nana touches Ian along the side of his face, cups his chin, and again strokes the side of his face. She commiserates, "Yes, I know, Ian. I know. It's not your fault. This will get sorted out. But you have Dexter, whose personality is distinctly different from that of his brother."

Does she realize what she has admitted? My money says no.

They both look to Dexter. He is quietly crying real tears that trickle down in a relentless stream. His nose is dripping down onto his lip.

Nana hands Dexter a paper towel. He dries his eyes, honks his nose, and moves over to lean in tight to his father.

I am glad to see this. At first, I don't know why, but then I do.

Papa notices the confusion on his three grandchildren's faces. He begins, "Susanne, Jeremiah, and Dexter, let me explain something to you. Sociopaths and psychopaths don't have real emotions and true empathy. They show only pretend emotions that they have learned to fake in order to get what they want. But they *are* responsible for their actions."

Papa's words confirm why I'm relieved. Dexter missed the psycho gene. His tears are real.

We continue to talk in the kitchen while Papa makes scrambled eggs. Teresa silently becomes his assistant and actually does most of the work. Phoebe flutters nearby to help. Bacon sizzles; and soon we assemble in the morning room with bacon, eggs, toast, and jam. Susanne, Dexter, and I have milk as the adults consume large quantities of coffee.

Eventually, most feel that we can cope with what's left of the day. As we prepare for our trip to the hospital, we know we will see Uncle Brian and Mom. The great unasked question: what to do about Aunt Evelyn?

Finally, Nana asks Ian directly, "Do we visit Evelyn? What are your wishes?"

His jawline hardens as Ian grits his teeth. He replies truthfully, "I don't know the answer to the question."

Dad appeases, "Ian, your feelings are completely understandable. We all accept whatever you decide and will follow your lead." I notice nods of agreement everywhere, especially from Phoebe.

As we prepare for departure, Dad optimistically claims, "If all goes well, we will need more seats for the way back, eleven instead of nine." He regards Nana's satchel and the small bag Teresa is carrying. He chortles, "And we need room for baggage."

After a little discussion, Dad drives Papa's car and asks Nana to come with him in case he becomes lost. At Papa's direction, the remaining seven of us pile into the little minibus that can hold nine. The snow and ice are melting, leaving the roads still tricky, but the temperature is above freezing. The trees, which recently shone like glistening creations in a fairyland, are now bare. Broken branches show raw wood here and there. From time to time, we see an old tree lying on its side, pulled to its death by the weight of the ice.

At the hospital, getting through the locked doors is now a routine. Inside the inner sanctum, Mom is awake and mostly back to normal. She is still confused by what happened.

Uncle Brian has had his tube removed, but remains on a cardiac monitor and still has an intravenous line. Unlike Mom, he has no sore throat and is definitely back to normal. "I want to get home as soon as possible," he declares, "and I'm starving."

When Dr. Jones visits us, she states, "Mrs. Morris, you are up and unhooked from our machines. Perhaps we could walk into Mr. Wadsworth's room? I'd like to talk to all of you together but only once."

After we assemble, she briefly focuses her big eyes on Papa while she states, "You were right, Lord Poppycock. Both patients were indeed poisoned. The drug used was a barbiturate in a high enough dose to cause death."

Both Mom's and Uncle Brian's eyes wildly dilate with anxiety at this news.

Mom stammers, "But why ... who would ... whatever for?"

Uncle Brian appears stunned into silence until he mutters, "How did you know, Dad?"

After glances at both patients, Papa responds, "We have answers we can share later."

Dr. Jones continues, "The good news is that you were found before you had complications. When the fire alarm went off, neither of you awoke. Apparently, the fire alarm was a false alarm, but your illness was not. That false alarm saved your lives." She sighs and her large frame almost shivers when she speaks. She fixes her eyes on Susanne and me and smiles slightly as she repeats, "Remember, kids, the fire alarm saved your uncle and your mom. So you two can relax a little. They both are now safe."

That close call frightens Dr. Jones! Even autistic me can tell.

Her face turns back to her patients as she continues, "You both have recovered without complication. And I can hear that your voice has fully recovered, Mrs. Morris. Is that right?" Mom nods yes and gives a thumbs-up. The doctor adds, "I shall get your discharge papers shortly. You have no new restrictions."

Dr. Jones glances at Papa and states, "Lord Poppycock, the police were notified after we determined both patients had been poisoned with the same drug, although my call turned out to be redundant." She almost chuckles.

Flashing a furtive glance at Uncle Ian, she continues, "By law, the investigators have access to our full medical documentation on all three patients." Papa nods to her with a knowing half-smile, which she returns. Uncle Ian's expression remains blank—his thoughts are elsewhere.

After a shoulder shrug, she gazes at each of us in turn and then focuses on her two patients. She asks, "Any questions for me?"

Mom and Uncle Brian are too confused to ask anything. Nana is the one who speaks up. "I think all will be well. Thank you for your care, Dr. Jones. We are all extremely grateful."

Dr. Jones again glances briefly toward Uncle Ian and almost undetectably shakes her head side to side before she departs to the central area near the nurses' station and talks to a nurse on the other side of the counter.

Suddenly Papa taps his forehead, seemingly annoyed, and mutters, "Think ahead, John. Don't be such a fool." Papa nods to Uncle Ian and audibly remarks, "I forgot to ask her something." Papa trails the doctor with Uncle Ian and me in tow.

When she has finished with the nurse, Papa asks, "May the family use Brian's room to talk privately? We won't take long."

Dr. Jones smiles slightly. "I happen to know you have a plateful to discuss. Take your time." With her eyes again on Uncle Ian, she quietly explains, "Mr. Wadsworth, your wife is in another bed at the far end of the hallway to the left as you exit the ICU, number 14F, in case you need to know." Her face appears sympathetic and slightly sad. After her eyes rest on the floor for a little time, they return to Uncle Ian with the expression, *I have finally done my duty despite your silence.* She is also telling him that she understands if he ignores Aunt Evelyn!

Wow! I'm finally getting this British understatement nonsense.

The doctor adds, "If you do head that way, you will find the room easily. A constable is stationed by the door." Her timid smile softens her news. She waits for questions, but none are asked. She nods goodbye while she gestures with a hand and then slowly moves away.

I know my aunt is under arrest, but reality hurts! Dr. Jones was kindly enough to prepare us.

From the nursing station, Dr. Jones briefly watches the family in Uncle Brian's room. Then her full frame and wide hips glide along the unit to another patient's room. With fascination, I watch her hips sway as she disappears.

Papa coughs and looks at me pointedly, but I'm not sure why. We return to the room in time to hear Mom ask Nana, "I arrived in pajamas. What do I have for the return trip home?"

Nana holds up a small satchel, the one she carried to London when we stayed over one night there. "You have these," she says laughingly as clothes peek from the edge of the case. Then she pulls out toothpaste and a new toothbrush after she points to the essential clothes inside.

Mom exclaims, "Oh, how thrilling! You are a good mother."

Uncle Brian glances around and mutters, "I have the same problem."

Teresa smiles and quietly confides, "No, actually you don't." She holds up a brown leather bag from which she pulls out a safety razor, soap, and a toothbrush with paste. Teresa adds, "Clothes are inside the bag. I forgot your hairbrush, so you will stay a wild man with a mane of glory." She laughs at him and rubs her fingers through his hair. "My wild man with his hair!" She laughs again as she kisses the top of his head.

Is there a private joke here?

While we are all alone together in Uncle Brian's room, Papa declares quietly and solemnly, "We need to talk." His quiet tone grabs everyone's attention and makes us listen. Papa and Nana tell Evelyn's story. Papa omits the part about the ancestors' interference since Nana doesn't know about that yet. Nana explains anything that Papa doesn't and ends with, "Evelyn is now a patient here."

Papa adds, "Collin is in custody charged with attempted murder, the same charge that Evelyn faces. We are baffled as to motive so far, but the police are investigating."

The police may be investigating, but Papa sort of hid some of the truth.

Uncle Brian and Mom are both horrified, almost in disbelief as they gawk at the speakers. They ask a few questions, trying to let everything sink in and to understand.

After a while, Nana says, "Time to get cleaned up."

In a shorter time than I expected, Mom and Uncle Brian are cleaned up and ready to depart, discharge instructions in hand. Besides a suggested follow up with their doctor, the main recommendation is "don't get poisoned again!" Or words to that effect!

Papa pointedly asks Ian, "Shall we visit Evelyn?"

Uncle Ian almost smiles, focuses on Dexter, and answers, "Yes, I think it best that Dexter check on his mother, and I visit my wife. Each of you may come along if you wish, and I hope that you do." He almost snorts before he adds, "Besides, the hints sent from Dr. Jones indicate that I should. She is one perceptive physician."

The adults, including my parents, agree it is best to see her. Uncle Ian leads the way with Dexter beside him and me trailing.

We spot the guard. Since he is the only one in the hallway, this must be her location. My uncle approaches the seated constable, who stands defensively. Uncle Ian identifies himself, and by way of introduction, names Nana's law firm and Papa's full title to the officer.

Somewhat uncertain, the constable responds, "We usually limit the number of visitors in these cases to prevent an attempted escape." He looks over each of us, seems somewhat relieved, and then adds, "But I suspect we are fine here with a lawyer and a member of the House of Lords." Then he laughs to himself as he motions us to the door and adds, "I hope I'm not relieved of duty for letting this many inside."

Stepping inside, we find her alone in a fairly large room that is a somewhat isolated but with its own bathroom A male nurse almost instantly appears, glances over our number, and asks somewhat anxiously, "Are you all relatives and friends of Lady Wadsworth?"

Uncle Ian says, "I am her husband, and this is one of her sons. The rest are in-laws and cousins."

The nurse says, "There is a rule of two visitors only, especially in this type of legal case. However, the room is a little out of the way and large enough for this crowd. Besides, Lord Ian, I heard you talking to the constable on duty. In view of the unusual circumstances, you may all stay." He gazes toward Papa with eyes getting wider and wider and then tentatively asks, "And are *you* Earl Poppycock?"

Calmly and politely, Papa answers, "Yes, that is correct. Silly name, isn't it. I prefer to be called John Wadsworth." He extends an open hand to the nurse and asks, "And your name?"

The poor nurse is flummoxed by Papa's unassuming manner. He turns bright red as he shakes Papa's hand and answers with faltering speech, "Marty. I'm Marty … Marty Coxsworth."

Papa responds, "I'm pleased to meet you, Nurse Coxsworth." Papa looks knowingly at Uncle Ian.

With that prompting, Uncle Ian adds, "Yes, indeed. Thank you for breaking the rules for us."

Marty's eyes flit over the eleven of us before he begs, "But please, don't all ask for chairs." Then his red face chuckles while he adds with a sly smile, "Now, don't tell on me."

Uncle Ian replies, "We shan't, sir." Papa glances toward his son and suppresses a giggle. He smiles broadly at the nurse, recognizing both his attempt at humor and his previous embarrassment. With time, Marty Coxsworth responds by returning to an almost a normal color.

The nurse checks the IV pump while we gaze at Aunt Evelyn's left wrist, handcuffed to the bedrail with an intravenous line running into her arm high above the handcuffs. Her hair is in disarray; she clearly needs a shower. Despite transfusions, her face is pale and wears an expression of poorly contained fury. Her left leg is heavily bandaged with a small tube sticking out, which drains bloody material into a small plastic bag.

Susanne and I look at this ugly thing immediately. The nurse sees our startled gaze and understands our silent question.

He points and explains, "That's a drain bag to take away any blood accumulating in the wound. It's one way to prevent a collection of blood, a hematoma, that could get infected." Nurse Marty tentatively smiles at us and nods his head slightly as he leaves us alone.

Uncle Ian quietly asks, "How are you, Evelyn?" She looks at Dexter standing tight against his father. She says nothing to either, drops her gaze, and then deliberately keeps her eyes tightly closed.

Uncle Ian repeats his question. Eventually, she slowly and deliberately moves her eyes up and glares at him. She angrily spits through clenched teeth, "How do you *think* I am?"

Nana realizes that the scene is going to become ugly very quickly. She asks quietly, "What may I bring you that you would like? Clothing? Toiletries? A hairbrush? What may I do to help?"

With eyes full of contempt and loathing, Evelyn now glares at Nana. She tersely declares, "Sure, Nana. Try to be helpful. Why don't you bring me a good big bottle of high-class booze?"

In exasperation, Nana's eyes flit away to the distance. Her jaw is silently moving, but no sound is created. Her eyes flash angrily back to Evelyn, then turn away before she glances toward Dexter. Her jaw clenches over and over during her silence. Nana is clearly fiercely struggling.

Papa queries, "Evelyn, surely there is some help we may offer?"

Evelyn's eyes scan Papa up and down before she laughs right at him. With a sneer, she demands nastily, "Sure thing, big boy, Sir-Lord-of-the-Manor. Get rid of the handcuffs."

Papa bites his lip, regards Evelyn sadly, but controls his tongue. His eyes flit to Dexter, afraid of what Evelyn may say next.

Dexter's expression pleads with his mother. "Why, Mummy, why?" Tears start flowing briskly down his cheeks, but he stares, wide-eyed, right at his mother. "I have always loved you. Why couldn't you love me, even a little?"

Auntie Evelyn looks at him as if for the first time, like he is an exhibit in a museum, a curiosity that she doesn't know how to use. Finally, she answers her desolate child sharply and without mercy. "Why couldn't I love you? I will tell you why. You are a weak, soft, simpering waste, no use to me, you little bastard! Now look what you have done. This is *your* fault."

The room is silent. No one knows what to do or what to say.

My heart bleeds for Dexter. I cannot imagine the pain he is feeling right now.

While I stand paralyzed, Susanne's mouth is open in disbelief. She gazes toward Mom, who is quietly crying, and then at Uncle Brian, who appears so angry that I am afraid he might hit Evelyn. He keeps his hands at his sides, but his fists open and close rhythmically. *Scary!* Teresa's face registers disbelief at Evelyn's words, but she has the presence of mind to gently touch Uncle Brian's arm to prevent him from acting. With pity on her face, Susanne glances at Uncle Ian before her eyes finally fix on Dexter. Phoebe's features appear actually distorted with rage—astounding! Like a tigress, she seems ready to pounce to protect her offspring.

Dexter gazes up at his father as they interlock arms. Uncle Ian extends his other hand to cover part of Dexter's arm and hold it tight. Dexter looks down at his father's hand and smiles slightly.

Dexter glances up at his father again. With his dad's slight head nod of silent support, our cousin stares fiercely at his mother and declares, "Drunk and rotten as usual, you were trying to kill my father. You shot yourself. You *alone* caused all this!" Poor Dexter pauses to catch his breath before he continues, "You are always nasty to Dad. I'm not welcome around you. Collin is your favorite because you two are both alike. Both of you are coldhearted killers, willing to do anything to get what you want and not caring about anyone else. I never want to see your face again."

Then and later, I would repeat inside my shocked head, *Careful what you wish for!*

After he says this, Dexter breaks into sobs, buries his face in his dad's side, his shoulders shaking with each breath. The room is otherwise silent.

Poor Dexter has said the unsayable.

Time passes in silence until Uncle Ian collects his thoughts with difficulty. Finally, clearing his throat to speak with a crisp edge to his voice, Uncle Ian notifies his wife, "My divorce lawyer will tell you the terms and conditions. I doubt that you will have grounds to contest. Custody of Dexter will be mine alone."

He stops to think and then deliberately continues slowly with clear articulation, "I will find a reputable psychiatrist and an excellent lawyer for Collin. He will be tried as a minor, as he is only fifteen. But I suspect he will be forever housed with the criminally insane."

Nana looks anxiously toward Ian and then at Evelyn, but she says nothing.

Uncle Ian's words open Aunt Evelyn's eyes wide in surprise. Then she squints in anger before she asserts, "Nonsense, that is *not* what will happen. He will be tried as a minor and released at age eighteen. He will be fine."

Nana speaks up, "No, Evelyn. If he has had a psychotic break that caused his actions, then he would be medically treated and undergo rehabilitation. But Ian has raised the possibility that Collin is a true psychopath. I hope he is wrong. But if that is true, then speaking as an informed lawyer, I must tell you that he will be housed in an institution for the criminally insane for the remainder of his life. But either way, he will not be free at eighteen." Tears are forming in Nana's eyes as she speaks.

Aunt Evelyn becomes enraged when she hears this. She swears words I rarely hear. She rattles her handcuffs against the bed so hard that her wrist starts to bleed.

Teresa exclaims, "She's going to really hurt herself! I'll get the nurse." She briskly walks into the hall and disappears.

A few minutes later, Teresa reappears with Nurse Marty who has medication in a syringe. Aunt Evelyn is still lashing out, screaming and damaging herself. There is blood over the sheets from the abrasions and tears she has caused on the handcuffed wrist.

The sedative slides into the intravenous line, and Aunt Evelyn slowly becomes calmer and then drifts off to sleep. The nurse leaves and reappears a moment later with cleaning solutions and a dressing for the bleeding wrist.

Without prompting, Uncle Ian says, "We shall leave now. Thank you, Marty, for taking care of my wife."

"Yes indeed, thank you," echoes Papa.

Surprised, Nurse Marty's eyes flash over Uncle Ian and then Papa. His face flushes. "You are welcome, Lord Ian, and Lord John." His attention focuses again on the bloody wrist. He doesn't see Papa shrug his shoulders, open his mouth slightly, and then close it again.

Papa wanted to say, "Call me John Wadsworth," but he didn't.

After we step outside the room, Papa stops walking, glances toward the seated constable on guard, gazes intently at Dexter, ignores the police presence, and states, "Dexter, I am proud of you for speaking up to your mother. You were right in what you said. While we may be horrified at your words because they are true, we are relieved that the truth is now exposed to daylight."

As we are about to leave the building, Uncle Ian stops our progress and declares, "She shows no remorse, no regret, only anger. Dexter, I am sorry she said those things to you. I love you dearly. You are a good, strong person, which you proved when you spoke up. She cannot tolerate your kindness and strength. Forget what she says. She lies."

Tears still streaming, Dexter leans as tight as he can against his father. Uncle Ian reaches around him and lifts him slightly off the floor in the tightest, longest hug I have ever seen. Ian says into Dexter's ear, "We will heal, Dexter. We will heal, together." That is all Uncle Ian can say to his son. It is also everything that Dexter needs to hear. They stand tight together when Dexter's feet touch the floor again, both poorly controlling their quiet sobs.

Once outside, Uncle Brian breathes the fresh cool air deeply. His nostrils flare with each deep intake of breath in an almost sensual display. "My, it is good to smell the fresh air!" he exclaims as we reach the little bus and Papa's car. He gives Teresa a little hug with his arm over her shoulder. "And good to be away from that one in there," he mutters, nodding toward the hospital. Teresa smiles at him and nods in agreement.

Papa comments, "Fresh air is always wonderful." No one says anything else.

What's to say?

Dad helps Mom into the bus passenger seat up front. "See you at home. I love you."

"Love you more," she replies.

Inside the bus, Teresa sits beside Uncle Brian. She holds his hand tight. He looks like he will never let hers go.

Dexter looks over to his father repeatedly. Is he looking for reassurance that Uncle Ian will not also disappear from his life?

Poor Dexter has a long road to recovery, as does Uncle Ian for that matter.

When we all buckle up, Papa drives away from the hospital. Dad follows in the other car with Nana as front-seat passenger and Phoebe in the back seat. They seem solemn and subdued.

As we drive, I wonder, "Does Susanne want to tell our parents about the help we received from the ancestors?" I'm still pondering when we arrive safely home.

The few remaining hours of daylight and early nightfall pass slowly. No one wants to play games or be amused. Sometimes, Susanne and I read our new books. Other times, we listen as Teresa and Brian quietly talk together, or we talk with Dexter. And for a long time, we three kids sit alone in comforting silence.

But we plan how to be electronically connected even though we live on different continents. Both Susanne and I recognize that without good friends, things could end exceedingly badly for our cousin. He needs support, and we can be his long-distance friends.

It was Susanne, my perceptive sister, who later said, "After all, Dexter is only thirteen. He is the innocent in all this. And while he can be a right pain, basically he is a kind and loving person when given the chance and a little direction. Uncle Ian is finally giving him that chance. And he is no longer following his brother's lead."

In the late and dark afternoon, Papa drives Uncle Ian, Dexter, and Uncle Brian to the prison where Collin is detained. After greetings when they return, we wait expectantly for news. All four remain pale, solemn, and silent. The quiet worries Teresa, who cannot take her eyes off Brian. Poor Phoebe's facial expression screams, *What now?*

Finally, Uncle Ian announces, "Collin shows no remorse. He is not sorry that he did something wrong. Instead, he is mad that he was caught and that the poisonings failed. Furious that he and his mother are not free, he shows no concern for any of the pain he has caused. He described his victims as little people who were not important." Uncle Ian regards each of us sadly as he apologizes, "I am … sorry." A little catch in his breath stops him from sobbing. Tears well up. "There is nothing I can do."

Dexter comes over to his father, sits beside him, and touches his arm. They remain silently glued together for a long time.

Time passes slowly. We eat. We talk. Teresa holds Brian's hand or touches his arm for reassurance—his and hers. Phoebe's eyes bounce between Susanne and me, concerned about the aftermath of everything we have experienced.

When bedtime eventually arrives, we say a good night to all, especially heartfelt to the recent patients. Like robots, we do our usual rituals without any enthusiasm. We are still too shocked to be happy despite our relief that the attempted murders failed. Deep inside, Susanne and I remain frightened. After all, we nearly lost our Mom and uncle. We are all sad beyond words for Dexter and Uncle Ian and terrified by Collin's pathological and unpredictable responses.

Phoebe lets us talk together and takes a long time with each of us at bedtime. Nothing is accomplished, but we have an adult who will listen, and that is worth the world.

Shortly after breakfast the next morning, the police call to arrange a time after lunch that they may talk to us again. Two officers arrive promptly. The younger, thinner, tall one is Officer Jameson. Officer Walden is older, heavier, and somewhat shorter than his colleague. They ask us a few questions when we are all together. We tell them everything we know, except the part about the ancestors. They seem content that the fire alarm went off by accident.

Officer Jameson says, "We are glad the alarm accidentally saved two lives and not from fire."

After they have finished their questions, Officer Walden asks Papa, "May I have a word in private, Lord Poppycock?"

Papa looks around at everyone in the drawing room. Papa replies, "Certainly, Officer Walden, but I would prefer for the family to hear. Is that possible?"

"As you wish," the officer replies with a look of uncertainty, "but some information is rather ugly."

"Then we had best all hear it from the horse's mouth," replies Papa grimly, "so that all know the exact truth."

Teresa asks tentatively, "Papa, should I leave?"

Brian answers, "Papa wants us all to hear, and you are part of the family." Papa nods in agreement.

Phoebe quietly asks, "As the nanny, perhaps I should leave?"

Our parents and grandparents assert in unison, "No. You need to know whatever we are up against."

The officer sees our expectant faces, shrugs his shoulders slightly, and mutters uncertainly, "Well then, no chance for misunderstandings. No chance at all."

He sighs a little before he begins. "Traffic cameras sometimes picked up a red Jaguar present at the robbery scenes, but we ruled it out as related since Lord Ian owned it. We couldn't see how he could be a suspect. From our perspective, the reasons for the robberies were well past anyone's guessing except petty theft. Unfortunately, that was an error." He pauses and shakes his head slightly.

Papa diplomatically adds, "But an understandable mistake."

Officer Walden nods and continues, "We have asked questions here. We have interrogated Collin at the station and questioned Lady Evelyn at the hospital. It appears that your grandson, Collin, and his mother, Lady Evelyn, worked together to do the robberies you have read about in the papers." The officer gazes toward Papa.

There are shocked exclamations from some. Poor Teresa appears horrified.

Nana responds, "Yes, we know about the robberies. Oscar, one of our friends, broke his arm in a tussle with the thief."

The officer nods that he knows. "Yes, that would be Lord Fullerton, one of the injured victims. There was another elderly gentleman injured, a Mr. Bixen." He sees my grans nod in agreement.

Nana persists, "But why were Evelyn and Collin involved?"

Mom asks, "To what purpose?"

Officer Walden continues, "The robberies were a distraction, a cover. The real plan was to create a robbery at Lord Ian's home, a robbery with a difference—a robbery that would result in Lord Ian's death." He pauses for effect.

To some, this is shocking news. For others, it's confirmation. Teresa looks at Brian in disbelief. Phoebe nods her head in satisfaction.

Had she guessed on her own?

"Lady Evelyn is unhappy in her marriage. She wanted Lord Ian out of the way. In her mind, murder seemed a good alternative to the financial and social loss associated with divorce."

Uncle Ian turns pale, and Dexter cries out, "No, she can't!" and then hugs his dad tight. Nana utters a small cry of disbelief. Mom's jaw drops while Dad focuses on his shoes. Phoebe looks like her suspicions have just been confirmed.

Like I said before, I think Phoebe is really smart!

Before he speaks, Officer Walden peers from person to person, his eyes asking if he can safely continue. "Lady Evelyn recruited her son Collin to help her kill her husband. Collin and Lady Evelyn are unusually close. Apparently, Lord Ian has been a distant father, not especially demonstrative or affectionate. It seems that Collin hates his father."

"I think that's the truth," cries out Dexter. "Collin loves Mommy, and she loves him, but she hates me."

Everyone looks at the tearful Dexter with compassion. The room is silent except for Dexter's quiet sobs, smothered in his father's side. Uncle Ian holds the child tight as Dexter does his best to remain calm.

After a considerate pause, Officer Walden continues, "With his mother's plan, Collin recognized the immediate financial gain, but he also recognized his loss of the title and what that means financially. Collin took a longer view than Lady Evelyn. He was quite prepared to kill his father. But he developed his own plan that suited his wider scope. He was fully prepared to murder more people than his father."

Audible gasps from some interrupt the officer again. He pauses and waits till he can safely proceed. "Master Collin originally planned to kill Lord Poppycock since he must die before Lord Ian if Master Collin was to inherit. But Lady Evelyn was getting impatient to be rid of Lord Ian. We think alcohol may have influenced her plans."

Phoebe mutters something inaudibly into her palm.

In the silence that follows, my mind flits back to Collin's words last night. "But you … you stupid woman! You had to get drunk again and get ahead of yourself, didn't you? You stupid cow!" He was right. Aunt Evelyn is an unpredictable alcoholic who went rogue and really mucked things up, at least for Collin.

I leave my thoughts silent as the Officer continues, "The ice storm allowed Master Collin to quickly develop grander plans when loss of power put all potential victims under one roof."

Most of our crowd seem stricken, confused, still not believing what has happened. Nana and Mom are wiping away tears neither can control. Phoebe is solemn and angry. Papa remains stone-faced.

The officer's eyes flit from one stunned face to another. After clearing his throat, he continues, "Master Collin's murder plans started with Brian Wadsworth and Constance Wadsworth Morris. At the death of Lord John Poppycock, each of them is in line for the title after Lord Ian. Master Collin needed to remove heirs presumptive to ensure his birthright, regardless of what Lady Evelyn did!"

By this point, Nana's head is moving side to side as if she cannot comprehend more. Dad seems bewildered and shaken. Phoebe's anger makes her positively grim. Three of us are hearing some of what we had already suspected, but it's still hideous.

Officer Walden notices Nana's shocked face and adds, "Countess Poppycock would always remain safe. Upon the death of her husband, she becomes the Dowager Countess, but the title with its monies goes to the heir presumptive. In other words, she would never be in Collin's way for inheritance of the title. She was never in danger."

Maybe he is trying to reassure Nana, but it's not working! Her tears quietly stream down her cheeks.

Slowly, Officer Walden continues, "Master Collin's plan was to fake a robbery at night, steal some portable valuables, and kill both Brian Wadsworth and Constance Wadsworth Morris in a staged robbery. The drugging was to guarantee ease of shooting without any struggle. He foolishly hoped a sloppy autopsy might even miss the lethal dose of barbiturate if they had been shot before death. With his firearm, Collin was actually heading into Brian's room on the night of the poisonings when the fire alarm went off, which thwarted his immediate plans. Afraid someone might see the bulk of the gun with its silencer, he had to scramble away unseen to hide the weapon and dispose of the barbiturate drug in his mother's purse, one of the two satchels she was carrying at the time, according to eyewitnesses. Despite the fire alarm, he wasn't worried. He expected both to die before help arrived.

Collin's expectations were old news, but there was a silencer? Susanne and Papa stare at me wide-eyed when they learn this. *How did a silencer sneak past Leila and Edgar, and past Mortimer? Wow! That group is not infallible!*

His persistently calm voice rivets my attention. "It was the next night, the night when Lady Evelyn was shot, that he transferred both the gun and the silencer to her purse and went upstairs with her on the pretext of obtaining a headache pill, little knowing that her access to the gun would destroy their future plans."

Officer Walden pauses for a few moments before he adds, "Master Collin had even calculated what might happen in the bedroom if Mr. Sam Morris awakened despite the silencer. Mr. Morris would die as collateral damage."

We all hear Phoebe's immediate intake of air. "How horrible," she utters angrily.

Everyone flinches with this news. Mom's tearfully-sad pale face flushes with rage. Dad turns white and clutches his stomach, as if he wants to vomit. Nana looks at Dad with love and concern mixed with shame. Phoebe now looks livid but says nothing. Teresa and Brian, both ashen, tightly hold hands. Susanne and I are stunned enough to simply gape at each other. Her chin wobbles fiercely, tears start to fall, and she clutches my hand till it hurts. Silently, I wince but let her hold on tight. Papa's face remains a wall of stone.

My thoughts race. *Collin only cares for his mother, and that's a maybe. What's it to him if Susanne and I become orphans?*

The kind officer waits till we have absorbed this news before he adds, "In their plan, Lord Ian needed to live for a while after the deaths of Brian Wadsworth and Constance Morris. Once it is clear that Lord Ian is the only heir left standing, he becomes expendable."

Now Uncle Ian, like Dad before him, becomes a little sweaty and possibly sick in his belly.

Officer Walden resumes, "With the other heirs gone, Master Collin and his mother, Lady Evelyn, can decide at their leisure how Lord Ian will be terminated. Perhaps another robbery or a staged accident or suicide, so long as Master Collin remains the next heir presumptive. Or maybe Lord John Poppycock might die before Lord Ian, depending on opportunity. No chance of missing the title then, but there would be more in death duties."

He waits, eyes scanning, gauging our tolerance for more information. Satisfied, he continues, "And if Lord Poppycock dies much later after Brian Wadsworth, Constance Morris, and Lord Ian, then it's less likely that someone will make the connection that Master Collin caused all the deaths to inherit the title and its monies." As the officer stops speaking, he quietly ponders his deductions with satisfaction. As an afterthought, he adds, "There was no hurry for Lord Poppycock's death with this plan. He might die of natural causes, or if he lingered too long, he could be assisted on his way later. After all, Master Collin is only fifteen. It's better to get the title at twenty-one!"

Susanne mutters, "What a birthday present!"

Poor Papa cringes.

Officer Walden finishes with, "If their plans had worked with the deaths of Brian and Constance, the robberies might continue episodically as a cover. If they needed another killing, another robbery sadly gone wrong would fit an unsolved pattern."

His thoughts are clearly agitating Papa past his limit. By instinct, both officers take notice. Almost shaking, gramps stands and exclaims, "No wonder Collin was unbelievably angry as he held the gun! Everything was indeed wrong, exactly as he said. His mother unraveled their entire plan. Nobody was dead and everything was exposed, all because Evelyn became drunk and acted alone." He pauses, tears forming, eyes surveying his relatives.

"This behavior … our family … how could all this be?" His shoulders shrug helplessly; his body sags in humiliation.

Perhaps fearing where Papa's emotional upset might lead, the younger man, Officer Jameson, rapidly interjects, "We found the bottle of Lady Evelyn's medication that was used."

Despite the horrors she is being told, Nana recognizes trouble ahead. Without a word, she stands beside her husband, touches his arm, and guides him to a place beside her. Her eyes locked on his, she mouths, "An upset is not helpful." Once again scanning the room, Papa controls his outburst, hides his wounded pride, holds tight to his wife's hand, and sits down silently beside her.

Politely ignoring their interaction, Officer Jameson tries to smile but continues speaking without interruption. "The pills were nearly gone even though twenty-two should have remained, according to the date. It was Lady Evelyn's prescription, but the bottle had Collin's fingerprints all over the bottle and its cap."

Learning all the details that the police were able to extract makes me shudder. My heart bleeds to see my broken grandparents. As I listen to what the police tell us, I think back to Barbara, my eight-greats-grandmother. I remember hearing her persuade her husband, James, to agree to the robbery that would accidentally kill Walter Johnson and end in the execution of Great-Uncle Edgar, James's own brother, in 1745. She was a psychopath who married into the family. This time, Aunt Evelyn is the psychopath who married into the family. She is the one who also bred another psychopath who was prepared to kill his aunt, his uncle, his aunt's husband, his grandfather, and his father to secure his goals. What an awful person! What an awful family!

I wonder if this pathological behavior is genetic? After all, Aunt Evelyn's seven-greats-grandfather was brother to the great-granny who tried to murder me!

Once again, my thoughts run riot. *Do I carry bad genes? What will my children be like? How does one choose a mate who is normal? How does one know?*

My wandering attention returns to the here and now as Nana asks the police, "What will happen to Evelyn?" The answer is as expected—charges of co-conspiracy to murder, attempted murder, robbery, and assault.

She is in trouble deep!

Nana asks, "And what about Collin?"

Officer Walden replies, "The answer is less straightforward. He must undergo psychiatric evaluation. But if he is found to be of sound mind, then he is a responsible individual. In that case, we expect that he would be in custody for the remainder of his life, in part because the crimes planned are so many and so serious. From his perspective, the best he can hope for is life in a hospital for the criminally insane." This is just what Nana said beforehand.

Nana pointedly asks another question. "Does Evelyn know what will happen to her son?"

Officer Jameson answers, "Yes, she was informed when we both spoke to her yesterday. When we told her his fate, she became very angry that he would not be tried as a juvenile and was furious that he would not be set free at eighteen."

Papa quietly states, "We had already told her as much. She was reacting to your confirmation, which she did not want to hear."

At the end of this conversation, the police give us clearance to travel back to the United States. My parents smile wanly and say, "Thank you."

After the police leave, I find a chance to talk to Papa alone in the main hall. I remark, "When I think about Barbara in the eighteenth century and Aunt Evelyn now, I feel sad."

Papa nods, opens his arms wide, and enfolds me in a firm hug. He murmurs near my ear, "I'm too tired for questions and there are no ready answers." That's a first. The poor man looks worn out.

When we were gathered in the sitting room late that afternoon, Uncle Ian received a call from the hospital. We could not hear what was being said, but we were able to watch Uncle Ian's calm but stern face. Then a sudden expression of shocked sadness swept over him and now remains. He mostly listens with keen interest, although he does ask an occasional question. "At what time?" he queries, looks at his watch, and mutters "thank you" as the call ends.

Afterward, he remains frozen in place, standing silent for some time. All ears and attentive, we listen carefully when he finally comments, "That was Dr. Mehta, the surgeon from the hospital. Evelyn did something that they didn't catch. She kinked the drain from her thigh wound to allow blood to accumulate."

Nana queries, "For what purpose, Ian? And what result?"

Uncle Ian gestures that he heard his mother's questions. Failing to answer, he requests, "Please, let me continue." After a pause, he resumes slowly, "She behaved well to the nurses and apologized for her previous outburst. For her good behavior, she was given the privilege to use the bathroom with police outside because she insisted that she couldn't use a bedpan to empty her bowels."

He pauses, uncertain if he should continue. He swallows hard and then divulges, "In the bathroom, she used feces to rub into her leg wound and into the area around the drain."

Each of us gasps in horror.

Uncle Ian raises his hand to silence us and speaks again. "Apparently, she somehow swiped a syringe. She made a contaminated paste with the same fecal material. She opened her intravenous line and injected it all." Uncle Ian swallows hard once more before he adds, "You may well imagine that this provided a source of overwhelming infection." He stops.

Shocked time silently passes slowly before he can eventually speak. "She cleaned up quickly and replaced the dressings professionally. With her brief time in the bathroom, no one suspected anything. It all happened yesterday, shortly after the police told her Collin's fate."

He seems momentarily overcome, unable to say anything further. Eventually, he proceeds. "Last night, she spiked a fever. The wounds did not look bad. The staff didn't know that the intravenous line was used to inject liquid stool nor that the blood drain had been contaminated. Appropriately, they wanted to see a pattern of fever or skin changes before starting antibiotics. As you may know, surgery alone may cause a fever."

After a pause, he adds details. "She became seriously ill with a fast heart rate and her blood pressure suddenly dropped. They called it sepsis. Despite antibiotics, her blood pressure crashed."

He stops and visibly shudders before he slowly states, "When they explained to her that she had a severe infection, she laughed at them. She told them how stupid they were and that no one would keep her confined. Apparently, she was smiling as she declared, 'I will escape one way or another—and this is the other.'

"She laughed and laughed as she recounted what she had done the day before. She proclaimed, 'It's too late to save me no matter how hard you try.' She yelled over and over, 'You are all a bunch of losers!'" He falters as he declares, "They did all they could. A few hours after they realized she was really sick, she died. It happened about an hour ago from something they called gram-negative septic shock."

Everyone gasps audibly. Afterward, Phoebe, Mom, and Dad remain stunned into silence.

Nana and Papa utter, "Oh, no, this cannot be."

Dexter runs to his dad, tears flowing briskly as he sobs into his dad's side. Despite the devastation on Uncle Ian's face, he tries to comfort his son. Teresa looks to Uncle Brian for a cue, confused by this family!

The poor girl's head must be spinning! I'm surprised she's not heading out the front door!

Susanne and I remain quiet. What can we possibly say? Through her tears, Phoebe quietly murmurs, "Poor Dexter." She says nothing about Aunt Evelyn.

I don't remember all the things that happened subsequently. The end of a life is so shockingly final that I felt numb and didn't register everything in my head like usual. But I do remember Uncle Ian eventually saying, "She recruited her oldest son into schemes for murder. Both were apprehended. Now, she has left him alone and stranded, taking no responsibility for the mess she created. That is the *ultimate* in selfishness!"

Facing his son and touching his arm, Papa states, "Ian, I am glad you can recognize her actions for what they are."

Uncle Ian answers, "Papa, thanks for understanding." Afterward, he remarks to his son, "Dexter, please understand. Even though she was cruel and selfish, we must forgive. If we don't find forgiveness, we will not survive. But most importantly, you are not like her or your brother in any way. Please believe me, son. You are not like them."

"Thanks, Dad. I will try to forgive, but not yet. Yes, I do understand that I am not like them, but acting on that will take work—I have followed Collin's lead far too long. But deep down inside, I don't want their path." Tears streaming, Uncle Ian holds Dexter tight to him for a few moments, with obvious relief upon hearing his son's words.

Sometime afterward, Uncle Ian declares, "The hospital cannot be held responsible. It is too much for anyone to expect them to know what she was planning."

Later, Uncle Ian with Papa, Uncle Brian, and Dexter decided to go to the prison to tell Collin that his mother had died. When they asked me, I replied, "I do not want to go. It's all been too much for me!"

It is hours before they return. Dexter remains solemn, but he seems to have more confidence than before. Uncle Ian's speech is sadly matter-of-fact. Uncle Brian appears bewildered and Papa, overwhelmed. It took a lot of listening before I could understand the essentials.

Ian recites mechanically, "Collin learned the unvarnished truth about his mother's actions and her death. He was also told how she laughed at the staff and told them they would fail, that she would escape their custody by death." Uncle Ian pauses to glance at his son as he searches for strength and encouragement.

Dexter remains focused on his father. "Please, Dad, tell them everything. They need to know." Then, silent and solemn, he sadly stares at the floor.

While he glances at his son, Uncle Ian nods and hesitantly agrees, "Yes, Dexter, you are right." His eyes flit from person to person before he decides to continue. "Collin listened carefully to what he was told and smiled oddly. After that, he started laughing. He pointed right at me and exclaimed loudly, 'She got you. She really got you! Priceless!' He laughed hard."

Mom states, "That is the most abnormal response to one's mother's death that I have ever heard. It gives me chills."

Dad admits, "I don't know what to think."

Brian declares, "I don't understand any of it."

Papa responds, "It's still almost impossible to comprehend." He becomes silent and increasingly solemn.

Nana, like Papa, is tearfully quiet. Eventually, they both mutter, "So sad, utterly sad."

Teresa and Phoebe are quiet, shocked beyond words.

Brian's face remains a sad but silent question mark. His eyes flit side to side with his inner anxiety, an unpleasant reminder of his facial expressions during his drinking days.

Besides numbness, deep inside I feel anxious, maybe worried, about what Brian may do under stress. Will he drink again? I'm suddenly frightened for Teresa. Even with her help, will he manage to stay clean, off drugs and alcohol? Or, will attempted murders followed by suicide be too much for him?

I am numb. Sunlight has disappeared for the day. Outside, the wind is picking up and the temperature is dropping. We are still on generator power, so the house is slightly cooler than usual anyway. But I feel actually chill!

No one wants food, but Nana insists. We scrounge in the kitchen to make sandwiches with fruit for dessert. Besides our food, cutlery, and plates, I bring in a jug of milk and a few glasses. Likewise, Susanne brings in more glasses and lemonade. We eat quietly, with little conversation. Dexter fiddles with the sandwich Nana has prepared for him, but he drinks his milk. He sits beside his father, glances at him often, and seems overwhelmed.

Out of weariness and exhaustion, we decide to go to bed early. Before we troop upstairs, Dexter asks if he may sleep in his father's room. Uncle Ian answers, "Yes. Please do."

I am grateful to hear that answer.

Dexter almost smiles as he promises, "I'll dash down to grab my things and then be right up, Dad." He gives a good-night hug to each of us before he heads downstairs.

I happily notice that Uncle Ian returns an encouraging smile as he responds, "Take your time, son. Make one trip do it. I'll see you upstairs."

After big hugs from Nana and Papa, the rest of us head to our rooms. From the upstairs hallway, we hear Dexter in his father's room. Despite Phoebe's kiss on my forehead after I am tucked into my bed, sleep evades me as my mind whirls with many troublesome thoughts.

How could Collin have become such a monster, ready to harm good people? Was getting the title of Earl Poppycock that important? Is it so important to have snobs grovel before you and pay attention to you? Then I think about my grandparents. They are good and kind persons, titled and wealthy, but without an unkind or snobby thought between them. Their hearts must be broken. What must be done to help them recover? More importantly, will they recover? My mind draws a blank on that one.

Are Phoebe and my family, including grandparents, the only living people whom I can trust? Are all people one thing on the surface and something else underneath? Depending on circumstances, Uncle Ian and cousin Dexter, like Collin, can be nice or a nasty snob, almost two different personalities. I hope that both Dexter and his father can be guided to permanently change. Besides my immediate relatives, maybe my true friends are limited to Granny Leila, Grandpa Mortimer, Uncle Edgar with his wife Aunt Jemima, and a few other ancestors. But that's a big problem. Excluding my living family, the rest have all been dead for a few hundred years. You don't go far when your best friends are ghosts!

The world is suddenly an extremely lonely place. I'm one person, alone and scared, afraid of what can happen next. Phoebe's nighttime kiss is not enough to reassure me tonight.

Eventually, I drift off to a deep, dreamless sleep.

Chapter 15

RECOVERY

Heavy clouds mar the morning sky. As I part the drapes a little, an occasional spot of sunshine breaks through and dapples my room in glorious patterns of light illuminating colors on the rug and upholstery, making the furniture glow in patches. When I open the drapes wide, that little bit of sun disappears as gray clouds gather ranks and plunge the world into a sad-and-morose gray. Despite enough sleep, I am fatigued by sadness. My aunt Evelyn may not have been my favorite person, but she had life. Now, she is gone by her own willful hand. And she has destroyed Collin's life by leading him into dark pathways that never end well.

Together they have inflicted incredible pain on two innocent people, Uncle Ian and especially Dexter. While Ian may not be blameless, Dexter truly is innocent. And besides harming Mom and Uncle Brian, those two nasty people hurt undeserving innocents, emotionally and physically, with their bloody robberies.

How can our family be involved in such things? Then I recollect what Barbara and James did. In an earlier era without forensic investigation, Evelyn and Collin might have remained undetected. And without the help of Leila, Mortimer, and Edgar, they would have succeeded here. A cold chill runs down my spine all the way to my slippers!

Like most everyone else today, I don't dress before breakfast. Dad and Papa are the only two in street clothes.

Papa and Nana appear disgusted and serious. Dressed in pajamas, Susanne trundles in, slipper heels clacking and housecoat fluttering. She asks, "Papa, why do you look annoyed? What's the trigger?"

"Obviously, you haven't looked outside. Take a peek. You'll understand," his petulant voice curtly replies.

Sensing Papa's supreme irritation, Dad suggests, "Come with me. We've drawn all the front drapes, but I don't know that closed curtains will deter any of them." Susanne and I follow him to the front of the house. He parts the curtains enough to allow a slit of light. The driveway has multiple cars, and there are people with cameras and video equipment milling around. "The paparazzi are here," he mutters.

They notice the movement of the drapes and swarm closer. Dad drops the fabric, and the slit closes. When we return to the kitchen, he closes the light curtains and remarks, "I want to destroy any good shot someone might take through the closed windows."

"They are like vultures!" exclaims Susanne. "Aren't things bad enough? Don't they realize we need peace and quiet?"

Nana responds somewhat bitterly, "Our welfare is not their concern. A scoop on the story, a good photo, now that's another thing!"

I quietly observe, "This is awful! When I was gazing out by bedroom window this morning, nothing caught my attention, but my bedroom faces the opposite side of the house. At least they haven't encircled us."

In acknowledgement, Papa smiles and then eventually updates us with some good news. "The power is on, and we are off the generator, which I shut down an hour or so ago. The ice is melting outside. While the day is overcast, the temperature is above freezing. Rain is forecast, so the snow and ice will soon be gone. Let's hope there is no flooding and no sleet. It has been a long time since we have had such weather!"

Both Mr. Brown and Mrs. Stewart's husband telephone to report they will be in later in the day since the roads are now reasonably open. They both repeat that they never lost power, so they were safe and cozy.

On the phone with Mr. Brown, Nana asks, "Are you able to stay overnight in town for a few nights as you sometimes do? Brian is still using your room."

He replies, "That is an excellent idea, for many reasons." Afterward, he laughs.

Nana answers, "Yes, of course, I thought as much. That *is* good news." Mr. Brown laughs again.

Nigel calls. He is in London and will return late tonight or early in the morning. He and Papa decide that arrival tomorrow will be better, and Papa will see him at the rail station. They arrange the time.

Afterward, Nana tells Teresa, "You will need to vacate Nigel's room and use the spare one Collin and Dexter were using."

Teresa replies, "That is not a problem."

"Good," declares Nana. "If you don't mind, I'll have you supervise Susanne and Jeremiah to provide fresh linens and towels while you shift your belongings. I'm leaving Dexter out of it. He is still coping with cling and mope. Fortunately, Ian is responding well, as a good father should, and tolerating shared accommodations."

As ordered, Susanne and I make up beds with fresh linens and hang new towels, all in a flurry of activity, as Teresa shifts from Nigel's room to the other spare bedroom formerly used by the cousins. We all take great care returning Nigel's room to its pathological tidiness.

When we have finished, Papa and Dad cook breakfast. They decide to splurge, so eggs benedict it is, with fresh fruit salad afterward. The adults have coffee, and the children all drink milk.

While the food is wonderful, I remain sad inside, which cuts down on the enjoyment I usually have with good food. But I eat my share, as does Susanne. I am not surprised that Dexter barely touches anything.

Uncle Ian receives a call. The police explain the procedures that Evelyn will undergo. There will be a forensic autopsy, which means an examination of blood and tissues as part of a criminal investigation. After all that, the body will be released to Ian for burial. He states, "She will be cremated."

There is general discussion in the kitchen about a private memorial service. Uncle Ian comments, "It is for the best that the service be in the country and not in London, where the paparazzi would certainly create a field day. Those vultures are already causing a problem down here but with fewer numbers than in the city."

Papa remarks, "I'll talk to the local vicar. I hope there is no problem because her death was a suicide."

Uncle Ian wants only immediate family, hoping to avoid press coverage. In hindsight, I'm glad that Uncle Ian postponed the service for a month in the hope that coverage by the press would be scant at a later date. He later told us, "Despite my precautions, the press congregated everywhere and coverage was heavy indeed. Gentry killing gentry sells papers and makes for streaming hits."

Uncle Ian calls the prison holding Collin to inquire after his son. They are courteous while they explain that they are keeping a suicide watch in view of what his mother did in her hospital.

Nana had already made calls to arrange for a London psychiatrist to visit Collin, examine him, and to determine if he is mentally stable for trial. We all think she is still hoping he is unbalanced enough that a trial cannot occur, allowing him to remain in psychiatric protective custody with a diagnosis that responds to treatment.

When the phone rings, Nana recognizes the number, identifies herself, and puts the phone on speaker. Gathered in the drawing room, we all hear, "Weatherly here."

"Oh, Roger, thank you for calling us. You are a godsend. Have you finished Collin's psychiatric assessment?" Nana covers the receiver and whispers, "It's Collin's psychiatrist." Her hands wave for us to gather and listen.

And now, which is astonishingly quick in the holiday season, we are all about to learn the results of Collin's psychiatric assessment from the skilled psychiatrist who has called Nana personally after finishing his final report.

Does Nana's name—Iris Wadsworth, Countess Poppycock, London solicitor—move the doctor to action? Or is it their friendship? We all know that Nana is a mover and shaker in her profession, but we are beginning to see the power of her connections. Anyway, we all listen attentively.

He recaps, "I visited Collin in prison, interviewed him privately over several hours, and insisted he cooperate with some written tests."

Nana queries, "How did you secure his compliance?"

"You must forgive me for lying to your grandson, but I told him I was doing an assessment in the hope of securing his release. That was only partly a lie. I was doing an assessment, but the truth is that the results would speak for themselves."

Nana replies, "Slightly devious but useful. Were your procedures, the interview and the testing, conclusive? Is there anything remedial that may be done to give us hope?"

"Iris, I have known you too long and respect you too highly to give you platitudes or false hope. There is only one psychiatric diagnosis. Collin is a psychopath, incapable of feeling empathy and incapable of feeling remorse. This is a horrific finding at age fifteen. What will happen as a juvenile is clear, but management in adulthood remains somewhat uncertain. However, for the foreseeable future, he will be housed with the criminally insane, once the legal system has processed him from his current prison."

Nana's face turns ashen. Tears form in her eyes. She clears her throat before she replies with difficulty, "Roger, thank you for your candid opinion. I had hoped otherwise, but I knew that it was a foolish hope on my part and that you would tell us this." They chitchat for a few more moments, and then the line terminates.

The room remains in stunned silence afterward. Mom nods to Dad. Dexter gazes at his father. Susanne glances at me and then fixes her eyes on Nana. Papa is beside Nana, his arm touching her shoulder. She leans heavily against him. He comforts her when she bursts into sobs. Teresa and Brian sit in stunned silence.

What must poor Teresa be thinking about this tribe?

Susanne is the first to speak. "I'm sorry, Nana, but this is the expected result."

Ever the pragmatist!

Uncle Ian glances at Dexter and then looks squarely at his mom. "This confirms everything I have known for years. I am so sorry, Mom and Dad. Please forgive me, but I couldn't fix him. He was born that way."

His parents nod. Tears streak Uncle Ian's face as he clutches Dexter in a desperate hug.

This news makes me feel listless with sadness. What a waste of a life! After all, he is only a year older than Susanne and now will be confined forever, most likely. But maybe that is for the best since he is capable of such evil when left to his own devices. The whole thing makes me shudder again!

A little while later, Mom and Dad start talking about the return trip home. Dad says, "Thank goodness your school scheduled a later start date this year. Our departure is not till the fourth of January."

I think of all that has occurred. *What an unforgettable trip!*

After a few days, the press realizes that we are staying put. There are only so many photos of Nana and Papa's house that they can use. Without activity worth reporting, they get bored. Like hungry vultures, they seek their carrion elsewhere.

With the improved roads and the return of electricity, Uncle Ian and Dexter leave for home, but they return daily—always for supper and often before lunch. While his room was being used, Mr. Brown was a good sport about driving into work daily instead of living onsite. I'm slightly autistic and never think to ask why sleeping elsewhere suits him fine, so fine that he leaves his now available room unclaimed for nights on end. *Silly me!*

Throughout all this turmoil, Uncle Ian clearly remains at a loss. He never expected to be a single parent with one son in prison and a desperately needy thirteen-year-old younger son seeking his attention and clinging to him all the time. This would be a steep learning curve for anyone, but especially for Uncle Ian.

By two days after New Year's Eve, which we did not celebrate, most of the press had departed. Nadia drives Oscar over for an afternoon talk and a picnic supper in the morning room, our version of a New Year's celebration. Dear Nadia is sympathetic after her initial expressions of horror. Oscar is fascinated that it was Evelyn who pushed him hard enough to make him fall and break his arm. With utter amazement on his face, he remarks, "She sat at dinner with us and looked right at me, knowing what she had done. That gives me the creeps!" He glances at Ian and Dexter as he apologizes, "Sorry, no disrespect to either of you, but that behavior makes my skin crawl. But remember, neither of you is to blame, and we love you both."

Uncle Ian adds, "Well, we all have the consolation that she will never do such a thing again." He sounds angry. No one responds to his statement. Most stare at the floor. What *can* anyone say?

Papa later explained, "I am glad to hear the anger in Ian's voice regarding Evelyn. It means he is processing his grief and is healing. All to the good!" Then Papa outlined the stages of grieving so that I, Susanne, and especially Dexter might understand.

Nadia is blunt with Ian about likely public response to news of the proceedings that are going to happen. Nadia remarks, "There has already been unfavorable press with reporting of the attempted murders, the robberies beforehand, and the death of Evelyn. And you have seen paparazzi here on your own property. They seem to know no boundaries and show no respect for privacy, anyone's feelings, or the need for healing.

"Evelyn has been labeled the ringleader. Collin, her son, is being reviled as a failed serial killer. Be prepared and not surprised by what may happen." Nadia looks sympathetically at Ian and at Dexter. "Try to be strong," she advises as she gazes straight at Nana.

Nana concurs with her friend. "You both must be strong. You are right, Ian, in keeping things low-key. We must struggle through it all." Focusing directly on her British grandson, Nana declares, "And you, Dexter, above all people, must remember that none of this was your fault, exactly as Oscar said."

This dinner is not the most pleasant I have ever had. But Susanne and I, like Dexter, listen attentively to the discussions and conversations, which allows us to gain insight into how people must struggle when they have received a bad blow. Fortunately, people speak candidly. In later years I came to understand how much candor helps with healing. The adults killed hidden agenda. In-your-head-boogey-men couldn't become larger because they were covered over. Instead, they were examined in the open air and, as a result, they shrank.

In due course, I also came to know that not everyone is kind to someone who has been kicked down. Some will exploit or harass the downtrodden. We learned later what subsequently happened to Dexter and what he did about it. But right now, life is all a learning experience and much beyond anything I ever dreamed that I should ever need to know!

On the same night as the dinner with Nadia and Oscar, I slept fitfully, dreaming of our helpers; Leila, Edgar, and Mortimer. They watched out for us this time round, perhaps in return for my helping them when I was ten. In my dream, together they exclaim, "You are welcome!" Jolted awake, I expect to see them or at least glimpse Edgar's smile vanishing near the drapes. Instead, I am alone. The outside temperature drop has made my room feel chilly, so I pull my comforter up around me and soon drift off to sleep again.

Even though Uncle Ian and Dexter took up residence at their home long before the dinner with Nadia and Oscar, our relatives are always here. Dexter is craving stability and routine. Attachment to his grandparents seems to fill one of the many needs he has at present. Fortunately, they live close enough that frequent contact is easy.

Uncle Brian and Teresa stay on as guests. The day of Uncle Ian and Dexter's departure, bedrooms shift again, with Teresa now upstairs. Brian moves from Mr. Brown's room to the spare basement bedroom. However, Mr. Brown leaves his room vacant for a number of extra nights after he was told Brian had vacated. Where is he sleeping? Why? *I hate being autistic.*

These maneuvers of switching bedrooms remind me of the beginning of a Pink Panther *movie, but in slow motion and for extremely different reasons!*

When they thought they were alone, Nana tells Mom. "Brian now helps Papa with estate management. He listens attentively, and seems to be learning, which pleases Papa. Will this develop into something long term? I don't know yet.

"Perhaps of greater import, Brian has been free of cocaine since before he met Teresa. She knows his history and gave him a warning early on. Any cocaine and she is history. He has made his choice. So far, so good."

I slip away after my eavesdropping.

Good choice, Uncle Brian!

When we have a moment alone, I ask Papa, "Have you told Nana about the help we had?"

He replies, "Yes, I have. She was astounded that Leila and some of the gang were back for a return engagement. But Ian and Dexter know nothing."

After a pause, Papa adds quietly, "So far as I know, Ian still thinks the ancestors are in the attic. He was embarrassed back then that he did not try to help. He doesn't need fresh anxiety from an update on the topic, especially now."

Then he whispers like a conspirator, "Do you realize it has been eighteen months since you first met the phantoms, time travelled back with Great-Granny-Leila to 1744 London, were nearly killed by that other ancestor, Great-Granny-Barbara, and helped solve the case against Great Uncle Edgar? Our attic-bound phantoms went to their final destination eighteen months ago. I'm amazed how rapidly time passes!"

He doesn't wait for a reply as he continues, "Brian never knew the ancestors existed. He has no reason to know. Poor Teresa would run away if we told her. I'm surprised she hasn't run away already. Enough said there. But I think your parents need to know the ancestors returned to help. That way there are no secrets and guilt about things not shared. Secrets are too heavy to carry." He gazes at me meaningfully until I nod that I understand.

"You are right, Papa. Susanne already knows the details, so she must help me tell everyone in the family when we are back in the States."

"Jeremiah, that's the best idea." His head moves as if agreeing with himself. "But, right now, let's say nothing further about the help we had in solving the crimes. There is too much on everyone's plate at the moment."

Uncle Ian and Dexter arrive about an hour before our departure. Dexter clings to Susanne and me. He hugs us twice, with tears in his eyes. He pleads, "Please don't abandon me. We have the Internet to keep in contact. Despite everything, I want to be friends." His chin jiggles a little, the same as Susanne's does when she is about to cry.

We both respond, "We want friendship, too. We all need that." Email information has already been exchanged, so I suspect he will soon know more of America than he wants to know!

Before long, we are saying goodbye to Nana and Papa. Nigel and Mr. Brown are trundling our bags from the hall into the little bus.

Nana suddenly declares, "I hate to see my Americans leave." She and Papa give both Susanne and me a long tight hug and plant a lingering kiss on our cheek before another hug.

With his arms around me, Papa whispers, "I am so sorry this happened."

As I finish his hug, I murmur into his ear, "Better here and now, and with the help we had." He squeezes my arm for a moment. I look at Papa again and hug him tight a second time.

Mom hugs her parents tight twice. Dad does the same. Phoebe gets a big hug from both our grandparents.

"Keep looking after your charges. You are doing a good job with both," Nana says as she lets Phoebe go from her arms.

During the departure chaos, the staff arrive to say goodbye. Interrupting her cooking duties, Mrs. Stewart, with splotches on her glasses and no hearing aids, shakes our hands and loudly wishes us a good trip. Nigel gives each of us a big warm smile and a firm hand-shake, as does Mr. Brown. Moments later, Mrs. Stewart is back in the kitchen, Mr. Brown has headed for the garage, and Nigel resumes duties elsewhere. I feel reassured that Nigel will never learn of the return engagement of our ghosts! He would truly be spooked by them!

Once alone again with family only, Uncle Ian hugs us both tight, and kisses Susanne on the cheek. He remarks, "Thank you both. Contrary to your uncle, you knew how to rouse the house during the fire alarm, which saved two lives. I am grateful." Tears well up while he gazes at us intently and pleads with a quivering voice, "Please, we must start afresh. Can you forgive?"

While I nod agreement, Susanne replies, "Uncle Ian, you are loved. What happened was not your fault. You cannot be blamed for Collin and Aunt Evelyn's actions." We both hug him tight without any comment upon his prior bad behavior.

His next insightful words surprise us. "Deservedly, Evelyn was cordially disliked by many members of the local communities. I became tarred with the same brush, and often rightfully. You saw it on Christmas Eve."

Mom asks, "What do you mean? What are you suggesting? What did we see?"

With a nod to his sister, Ian replies, "In church, no one would sit near us, as usual. Think about it. Seats in our pew remained vacant, even when there were no other places to sit in the packed church. People would rather have sore feet from standing than take a seat beside us. That was the community's repeated customary comment."

His eyes stare into our stunned faces. He continues, "Now I must work, and work hard, to overcome and change the reputation I have earned. High and mighty attitudes must die." We are even more shocked when he begs, "Can you forgive my own previous arrogance, coldness, and stupidity?"

Surprised at his most un-British candor and clarity, we nod and pledge, "Yes we can, Uncle Ian."

He murmurs, "Thank you," with his arms around us both.

Uncle Brian and Teresa move toward us. "It is our turn to say goodbye."

Dressed simply and conservatively, Teresa appears sad until new thoughts make her smile brightly. "You have all been so kind, and forgiving. Everything reinforces my love for Brian." She glances at each of us with eyes filled with meaning before she adds, "Healing takes time, but know that Brian and I are on a firm footing, so I will be here to help my ship with its rudder." She winks at Papa as she speaks. Both Teresa and Uncle Brian give us all hugs. Teresa kisses Susanne and me after a kiss for Mom and a second hug for both Dad and Mom.

Teresa asks, "Brian, did you tell them the news?"

We all look, wondering what the news could be.

My mind is racing in a riot of possibilities, in endless directions.

Uncle Brian faces his father and confides, "While Teresa and I have been staying here, Ian and I have been talking. He is hiring me for a trial run in his firm, responsibilities to grow as I learn the ropes.

I am determined to improve and to stay clean." Teresa flashes an approving glance. Pointing impolitely to his girlfriend, he declares, "She spelled out ground rules long ago. I've made my choice. I'm sticking with Teresa, not with Mistress Cocaine, or Master Alcohol."

With a nod to Teresa and his sons, Papa exclaims, "Well done, all of you. May this new year bring you success!" Initially, Papa's facial expression flashed sad, but he changed it immediately to happy. Most everyone missed the change. Autistic me didn't.

My guess? He's disappointed that Brian won't remain working with him on the estate.

Uncle Ian adds, "Brian may need to return to school to get the degrees involved. But he can do that part-time and at night school. He is a quick study. The right motivation will get him through, and he has that. Besides, I need help. Who better than my younger brother?"

Teresa regards Brian proudly and contentedly smiles. Then she turns to face our other uncle and states, "Thank you, Ian. The opportunity is everything."

As we pile into the minibus and buckle up, Mr. Brown climbs behind the wheel. We all wave to Nana and Papa, blow kisses, and repeat, "I love you, keep well."

I glance around the inside of the minibus. Our bags are taking up the remaining seats! Those piles of luggage may create extra baggage charges at the airport!

The engine starts; still waving, we head down the drive and onto the roadway. I glance back. The house and our grandparents have disappeared out of view.

Concentrating on what we all must do to safely arrive home acts as a distraction. I am happy to have seen my grandparents and their friends. I feel that I have known Nadia and Oscar forever, even though they are actually new friends to Susanne and me. But I also strongly feel the sadness and grief of loss. Evil took away so much.

What's the recovery time from this trip to England? I haven't fully recovered from the last one!

Chapter 16

THE NEXT CHAPTER

Our return flight was uneventful. School will resume two days after our return. All of us are sad and solemn most of the time. This is something new and ugly in our home that I don't like. And our secret, the repeat encounter with our ancestors, weighs heavily on me, and I suspect on Susanne. Papa says that secrets are heavy loads to carry. He is right!

Phoebe is quiet during the return trip and for most of the first day at home. The evening before school starts, she convenes a family meeting. Phoebe's eyes land on each of us in turn before she states, "I must speak candidly. Everyone is still shocked by what happened. We need time to recover, but we must move ahead." She pauses and then declares rather firmly, "This is a new year. We must turn a new page."

She glances at my parents, who let her continue. "We need a plan so emotional recovery does not get suppressed or buried. Each of us has been too self-contained, quiet, and sad, which is not the road to healing. We must deal directly with our feelings as they surface. It is understandable and acceptable to have a sad day. It's okay to talk about feeling blue or down. If we don't talk about all this emotional baggage, too much will be repressed. Do not tiptoe around sad feelings, for that will create problems later. That's not allowed!" She adds, "Three years from now is not the time to dig into buried emotions, especially when the difficult work required can be handled now."

This gives me a sense of relief. I have been afraid to say anything to anyone since everyone suffered the same blow. Susanne has relief written all over her face, as do my parents. We all clear the air as we express our feelings. Mom cries a little while she sits close beside Dad. He holds her tight within his long arms. When she has finished with her tears, she asserts, "That good cry made me feel better, which shows we cannot keep emotions bottled up. Let's agree to talk and share feelings, good and bad."

This also seems a good time to tell my family everything. Kept secrets—unwanted—weigh heavily on me and Susanne. After I catch Susanne's eye, she nods back. "Go for it, Jeremiah."

I hesitantly begin, "There is something else all of you must be told." Questioning faces pivot toward my direction. Glancing from person to person, I add slowly. "Papa, Nana, and Susanne know, but no other *living* person does."

Suddenly, I have their attention with all eyes on me. Probably, the word *living* does it. Mom and Dad remain seated on the sofa. Phoebe, who stood up after Mom finished talking, lands in a nearby chair. They obviously remember the summer when I was ten.

"I have been waiting for you to talk," confesses Susanne. She plops into an armchair sideways, her long legs over one arm. Fortunately, she is wearing jeans. She is sometimes a little lax about adequate coverage. Nonchalantly, she adds, "I may butt in."

"Anytime you want, "I reply.

I explain, "Leila and Edgar warned me that there was danger. Leila surprised me when she appeared one night. I jumped up, hit my head on the bedrail, and fell back smacking my noggin on the headboard."

For Mom, my words are an epiphany. She exclaims, "Good heavens! So *that's* what happened. It wasn't a dream."

"You are so right. That was no dream. It was living nightmare time again!" I pause and then continue, "I was cranky after hitting my head because I was sleep deprived, had a headache, and needed you out of the room, Mom. I pretended to fall asleep in order to talk to Edgar and Leila."

Mom eyes me quizzically and nods with clearer understanding.

Susanne explains, "Leila, Mortimer, and Edgar get a day pass from heaven. Saint Peter prefers that Leila travel because she asks him so many questions." I hear giggles.

"That fits," gulps Dad as he chokes on his laughter.

Slowly, all the facts Leila and Edgar gathered are revealed. Susanne and I tell how the three dead ones discovered that Aunt Evelyn had a gun and how they knew Collin was involved. Susanne confirms, "It was Edgar and Leila who had the information to help us all. We were lost without them."

I chip in my two cents to emphasize Susanne's words. "It was Edgar, Leila, and Mortimer who really saved Uncle Brian and you, Mom. Without them, all of us would have slept through, and you two sleepers would never have wakened." As my voice cracks, I glance quickly at Mom and then stare down sadly. "Edgar gets credit for saying that we needed to rouse the house by something that could be explained. Triggering the fire alarm came to my mind. Then I used the whistle."

I laugh a little as I recount, "Edgar used a lighted candle to trigger the fire alarm, but the sound was so loud that he dropped his burden when he jumped back mid-air." Laughing, I describe his long arm swooping to catch it.

Probably to help ease the tension, Susanne smirks and interjects, "Now that's a visual!"

Everyone chuckles, which is what I think she wanted.

I continue, "It was Edgar who unlocked the door as Aunt Evelyn held the gun on Uncle Ian. Without his interventions again, the outcome might have been entirely different." I shudder a little as I finish.

The three adults sit silently for a moment. Phoebe seems bewildered, Dad perplexed.

Finally, Mom says, "Thank heavens they knew to help. I owe my life to Mortimer, Leila, and Edgar." She catches my eye and adds, "As you know, Papa often repeats, 'Secrets are indeed heavy to carry.' Are you glad you told?"

I smile contentedly. "Yes, Mom, I am. Inside, I already feel lighter and happier."

Dad chimes in after a smile at me and Susanne. "A good lesson has been learned. Remember, we love you both. You are safe to tell us anything, on any topic!"

Smiling, Phoebe comments, "I didn't realize you two were doing battle again with the help of dead ancestors on a day pass from heaven. And last time in England, I worried when you were riding on horses! Silly me!"

A little project is assigned at school the next day. The title is "How I Spent My Christmas Vacation." The typed pages are due in three days. I am terrified at the prospect, but I can only handle my fear by acting like it is all a joke.

At home that night, I read my draft aloud, with a preamble. "With our policy of sharing and free-ranging discussion, I want to share my mixed feelings. I can cheerfully write that I went to visit my grandparents in England. Here's how it will go."

With a little cough, I clear my throat and hold up my messy page. Trying to be funny, I recite everything in a rhythmic sing-song voice. "Prior to and during our visit, my older first cousin named C, and his mother, my aunt named E, robbed numerous rich old people and broke the arms of two elderly souls. This was a preliminary to the attempted murder of my parents and my uncle named B.

"Afterward, they planned to kill my grandfather and my other uncle named I, who is the husband of my murderous aunt E, and father of my murderous cousin C.

"My cousin C was caught along with the one who started the whole process, my aunt called E.

"All ended sadly when my aunt was in hospital for treatment of her gunshot wound accidentally inflicted by her younger son, D. She caused her own death by putting feces in her bloodstream while she was a patient in a British hospital.

"As for my cousin C, he is safely tucked away in a lunatic asylum for the criminally insane. He will remain there forever since he is a thwarted psychopathic serial killer, aged fifteen."

Maybe my attempt to be funny helped push me through. Lordy knows, it's the only tool I have, and it hurts too much to be serious!

Everyone looks at me quizzically as I add, "Do you think my story will play in Peoria?"

Dad retorts, "You don't live in Peoria."

Mom states flatly, "You could do that, but you might be embarrassed by how you are treated." Mom is a lawyer and right now, she sounds like one!

"Yah, I guessed that," I reply glibly.

Susanne asserts, "Well, I have the same assignment. No one needs to know what happened. Keep quiet about it, Jeremiah, or Collin will seem like a pussycat!"

Phoebe opens her mouth to speak, but Susanne interjects, "Our name is different from Uncle Ian's and Papa's. Only a small number of people know how we are linked to Papa's title. I am hoping few make the connection between the news, the tabloids, and our family, and that those who do ... wisely decide to keep quiet." She looks around from person to person, searching for agreement.

Susanne stares at me and swears solemnly, "I do hope I don't need to silence you. Do you want me to commit homicide on this side of the Atlantic?" She giggles, "I could call Collin for pointers."

Phoebe states, "That is the wisest." She stops when she realizes what she actually said.

Dad and Mom blurt, "What? Whatever do you mean, Phoebe?"

She continues, "What I mean is, 'Least said, easiest mended.' That's what my Spanish grandmother often said. I suggest not making all this public. And no homicide!" She laughs at her own gaffe. "And certainly, don't call Collin!"

Dad interjects, "I do thank your grandmother from Spain for that wise advice. And wise advice it is."

By family consensus, Susanne and I do our reports. We don't lie about anything. But the omissions could cover pages—perhaps entire chapters.

Fortunately, the press coverage is scant on this side of the Atlantic. The connection to us is mostly missed. However, Papa's family has to face coverage in Britain. Collin is portrayed as mentally ill and his dead mother as the ringleader, also mentally ill. Sympathy for the survivors runs high. The coverage is intense but fortunately brief and limited, for which Papa and Nana are grateful. Uncle Ian and Dexter sometimes mention the press in their frequent emails.

It is early March when a package from the Silver Vaults arrives addressed to Jeremiah Morris. I am surprised and befuddled, and I say so.

Dad and Mom watch me as I handle the package. Susanne mutters, "Oh, good, it's finally here."

I ask, "What is finally here?" After a moment's reflection, I utter in confusion, "I didn't request anything from the Silver Vaults and I didn't buy anything."

Dad replies, "But you did return over and over to one special thing."

"Yes, you did indeed," echoes Phoebe.

Susanne mutters, "I'll say. I thought it was going to be your present from Mr. Claus, the way you kept returning to it."

My mind flashes to the inkwell with the second glass container used for sand, both sitting on a long gleaming silver tray. Imagine my surprise when I carefully undo the protective wrappings to discover the inkwell and sand containers. The tray and two lids shine brightly. A new six-sided silver pen, engraved with the original pattern, somebody's initials, and a date now sits with its gold nib in the long groove. The initials are J.M.B. with the current year. Except for the new date, everything looks authentic to 1732.

I exclaim, "This is beautiful! I was told that in the eighteenth century there were two glass wells, one for ink and the other for sand to dry the paper."

Dad asks, "Do you think the initials and the dates have any significance?"

Struggling for a moment, I gaze at the original date, the same as in my memory, and at the new engraving. I read, "M.W.J. 1732," out loud, pause, and then add, "So the inkwell belonged to someone whose last name started with a J. Maybe Johnson or Jones or something like that."

What difference does that make?

Staring at the contents of the package, I murmur, "The tray belonged to someone we don't know. But it is still a lovely thing."

I continue to stare at the two containers and to ponder the initials. In confusion, I remark, "The inkstand is beautiful. But the pen belonged to someone whose last name starts with a B. Maybe someone called Bennett or Benson or whatever. But … I'm confused … is the pen new?"

Mom starts to laugh uncontrollably. "Oh, my dear. The pen is new and is inscribed with your initials."

It takes a minute for her to stop laughing before she explains, "When a monogram is done, the first letter of the last name goes in the middle. The first name initial is to the left and the middle name initial is to the right. This is your monogram. Jeremiah Brian Morris is monogrammed as J.M.B. And the date is now. It's new for you!"

I stare and point at the original monogram. With rising excitement in my trembling voice, I ask, "Whose initials are those?"

Phoebe answers, "Now that is the million-dollar question. Shall I tell him all?"

The three others nod for Phoebe to continue.

She begins, "I noticed that this inkstand attracted you. The dates made me wonder." After a pause, she queries mischievously, "Do you recall I have a certain knack for finding things at the Silver Vaults?" Her eyes sparkle while she smiles.

Still staring at the monogram, I try to speak calmly. "Your talented eye found the silver rabbit, one-half of a pair, that became reunited with its frog-mate at the trial of evil James and Barbara, two people who still make me shudder. That purchase helped convict them."

Phoebe continues, "Correct, Jeremiah, that purchase did make a difference. Anyway, I told Papa about your interest. The initials immediately fascinated him. He called the proprietor and asked questions. The provenance of the inkstand is well-known. It was sold in 1753 after the death of the owner and later his wife, in 1752. The heirs apparently had no interest in his personal items."

I state quietly, "I have forgotten what *provenance* means."

Dad answers, "*Provenance* means the history of an object. If you know the provenance of something, then you may know who owned it or its origins. That helps to decide if the object is real or a forgery."

"Thanks, Dad."

Phoebe continues, "Papa found out that in 1753, the next owner of the inkwell was a prosperous merchant. His family treasured him and his possessions. The family kept it until recently. The last person in that line to own the inkstand left no family. Everything in the estate was liquidated.

Before I can ask, Susanne tells me, "*Liquidated* means everything was sold. There was no one who wanted anything that belonged to the deceased."

"Apparently, that was the case," states Phoebe. "It seems sad, doesn't it?" We all nod in agreement.

Phoebe continues, "Anyway, the merchant family represented by the last owner still had documentation relating to the purchase. It was a high-ticket item on its first sale, and this family apparently documented everything. I guess that comes with the merchant blood."

My heart is beating faster, and I'm breathing more rapidly, too excited to speak.

Dad asks, "Do you remember meeting Mortimer Wadsworth last year at the trial?"

"Yes, Dad, I do." I glance toward my father. "We also talked within the last few weeks," I add off-handedly, trying to act casual. After all, Grandpa Mortimer has been dead for 268 years, but we talked together only last month!

Dad smiles broadly.

Funny man, my dad!

Susanne silently stares steadfastly out the window at something that apparently fascinates her.

Dad remarks, "During our investigations, Papa's investigations really, we learned Mortimer Wadsworth had a middle name that began with J. His middle name was Jeremiah. Who knew? And this was his inkstand!"

The rush of love and happiness that washes over me almost makes me burst into happy tears. It certainly leaves me speechless. Finally, I sputter, "This gift is totally unexpected. And there are really two gifts—the inkstand and the shared name *Jeremiah*. Both are totally amazing!"

I am overcome. It takes takes a few moments before I can resume. "To have something that my nine-greats-grandparents used in their home is totally awesome! To discover that Mortimer and I share a name is overwhelming!" Those tears of happiness do spill.

Dad adds, "And we have something that almost never happens. We have the bill of sale from 1753. It came with the tray." He pauses, eyes on me. "Are you still with us?"

I nod my head and reply, "Yes, Dad, I am paying attention. You also have the original bill of sale." I haven't yet fully understood the significance of this.

He continues excitedly, "It documents that the piece came from the estate of Leila Wadsworth, known as Countess Poppycock, who died after her husband, Mortimer Wadsworth, known as Earl Poppycock. It goes on to name the silversmith who made and sold the article originally. It enumerates the four pieces—an inkwell with silver lid attached, a sandwell with silver lid attached, a tray engraved and dated 1732, and a fine quill pen." Dad pauses to let me absorb all this information before he adds, "So Mortimer and Leila were very *au courant* as Nana would say. They used the most up-to-date writing tools, a quill!"

Through my tears, I exclaim, "Wow! This is unheard of—a bill of sale from 1753."

Dad continues, "But you understand what it means that the bill of sale is from 1753."

My mind is blank. "Where are you going with this?"

Mom clarifies, "There is a downer in all this. Barbara, then Countess Poppycock, arranged the sale. James Wadsworth, newly the Earl Poppycock, received the money. We have both their signatures on the bill of sale."

My, I was slow on the uptake!

We all stare silently at the centuries-old piece of paper. To own a document signed by my eight-greats-grandparents is fantastic. To know that both tried to kill me is horrible and makes me shudder.

"This thing is interesting to see," I observe, holding the paper far away from me and quickly returning it to my father.

It's all that I can say!

Dad replies, "I had the bill of sale sent over registered mail, separate cover. It arrived before the parcel. I don't want that document lost, so it goes into the safety deposit box."

I sputter, "Agreed. Please, keep it away from me. I don't want reminders of those two!" Uncontrollably, I laugh with relief knowing I am safe from them.

Suddenly curious, I ask Mom, "When you named me, did you know that Mortimer had a middle name of Jeremiah?"

Dad nods at Mom, wondering what she might disclose.

She answers, "No, Jeremiah, I knew nothing much about Mortimer and Leila. I was unaware of his full initials or his middle name until Papa's investigations before the purchase."

After a pause, she continues, "But while you were *in utero*, I somehow knew you were a boy. The name Jeremiah popped into my head and would not leave, like a song that sticks in one's head. Don't they call that an earworm?"

Phoebe nods yes.

Mom declares, "When you were born, you were indeed a boy. With that name so persistent in my head, Jeremiah you became!" She laughs. "If you had been a girl, I am not sure what we would have done! What is the feminine of Jeremiah?" She laughs out loud. "I am sure it would sound awful!"

"Still not convinced, I persistently inquire, "Did you *really* have no idea that Mortimer had a middle name of Jeremiah?"

Eyes on me, Mom giggles as she confesses, "Well, dear boy, I do not have your knowledge of the extended family. Happily, I have no regrets regarding my first-hand ignorance of the behavior of its people." She laughs out loud. During a lengthy pause, she stares at me intently before she quietly adds an afterthought. "In fact, my money says there are times you wish *you* didn't have so much knowledge about the family tree, or how the family behaves!"

I return her gaze and reply, "You are right. But something positive must come from what has happened. Somehow, it must all be to the good."

We are all silent for a moment, each alone in his or her thoughts. Susanne seems pensive as she gazes down. Mom and Dad focus on each other for a moment before returning their eyes back to me. Smiling, Phoebe sits a little to the side, but remains silent.

Then I think about Susanne and how she must be feeling. I have just received an expensive gift, and she hasn't received anything. That's not fair to her.

I ask rather abruptly, "But did you get something for Susanne? We all did well at Christmas, but this gift is overwhelmingly awesome and probably expensive. We need to be treated the same."

Mom laughs. "You didn't think that the pearls she got from Nana were of no value, did you? Money not changing hands doesn't mean value didn't change hands. Before this, you were badly short-changed, if the money involved is what we are talking about."

Phoebe laughs. "Yes, indeed."

Susanne nods in agreement as she admits, "I made out like a robber princess! Actually, I'm still way ahead."

Surprised, I confide, "I hadn't thought about the dollar value of Susanne's pearls. They were her great-great-grandmother's, which was the value. But Papa did say they were costly." With a sly smile and a nod to my sister, I add, "Congrats, Ms. Robber Princess." After glancing around me, my focus returns to my beautiful ink well and silver tray. I excitedly exclaim, "I shall use this treasure forever!"

I hug each in turn before I declare, "I must write to Papa and thank him for doing the homework on this gift, and Nana too. I shall use this pen to write them."

Dad observes, "Your grandfather certainly was the go-between to arrange it all. "He found the silversmith who executed the design on the newly-created pen to match the engraving on the inkstand. That was no easy job, even with Nana's support. You had best write a good letter!" He laughs.

"The best ever," echoes Susanne.

A few days later, I purchase special thick paper with envelopes to match and blue ink to fill my *new* inkwell. In my letter to Papa and Nana, I write how much it means to me to have something used by Mortimer and by Leila. It's a thank-you-with-love-and-gratitude note only. Writing about other things is too painful, and far too early to do.

The night after posting the letter, I had a dream that I remember vividly, right to this day. During the dream, Leila and Mortimer were in my room in Manhattan watching me sleep. They reviewed all that happened during the last two trips to England. They natter about how excited I was to receive the inkstand. Mortimer remarks, "I am so pleased he saw my writing tools at the Silver Vaults. Thank you for directing him in that direction."

Leila answers, "Of course, Mortimer. I'm rather good at guiding the living. Directing his father for his Christmas gift purchase was really rather easy. Jemima is pleased that her pendant is back in the family. And Nadia didn't need much coaxing to part with the earrings—simply a reminder, although her mind is difficult to penetrate. The *odd* thing was I decided many years ago that Nadia's father needed to buy them, but I didn't know why. Maybe I have a partial gift of prophecy as well." She laughs out loud.

Mortimer chuckles. "I know you have many gifts. I'm not surprised you knew what to do so many years ago." He looks like there is something he doesn't understand or perhaps didn't fully hear and wants to ask about, but he waits to ask because his wife is speaking again.

Leila continues, "And I persisted with Jeremiah because I knew that you wanted him to have your writing tools. It stayed for a long time in the same family after it left ours. But once it was on the market again, it certainly needed to be Jeremiah's."

Leila pauses before she adds, "James and Barbara inherited everything after my death. It was a pity that they cast your pen with its accoutrements aside. James had no interest, probably from guilt. Your initials engraved on the inkstand was too much of a reminder of your integrity. He didn't like the contrast." Leila becomes pensive, then displays an almost sarcastic smirk. "And of course, he was *happy* with the money. The sale fetched a handsome sum."

Then she produces a revelation that still surprises me, even years later. "Jeremiah is much like Edgar in personality. He reminds me of the son we lost too soon in life." She pauses thoughtfully, as if letting me absorb all this. Eventually, she resumes more brightly, "What

Edgar should have inherited is now the property of Jeremiah. That seems fitting and suitable. I am *most* satisfied."

In my dream, she pauses and becomes pensive before she speaks. "I am glad his dear mother was receptive to my persistent thoughts during her pregnancy. She has some of my perceptiveness but not to the point of mind reading like me. Maybe that is just as well, for the gift can be a burden.

Long before her confinement, I realized her fetus was a boy and wanted him to carry your middle name. However, Constance is harder to guide than most. Her mind is intensely strong-willed and poorly suggestible, a blessing for her and a curse for me—more work!"

She touches her husband's face and comments, "Not to be unkind, my love, but the name Mortimer would be too much of a burden in the twenty-first century. But Jeremiah: well, that fits rather nicely!" They both giggle.

Mortimer responds, "Right you are!" He pauses and contentedly gazes at her quietly. "To have this connection span a few hundred years is such a blessing." Leila nods her head vigorously in agreement.

Mortimer continues, "Jeremiah has really proved himself, now twice over. So has Susanne, for that matter."

"Yes, indeed." Leila's eyelashes flutter.

"But you said something that old Mortimer did not catch, my dear. What did you suggest to Jeremiah's father as a Christmas gift and for whom?"

Laughingly, Leila replies, "Oh, darling husband, I thought you noticed. That's why nothing was said. My dearest sweet, I do apologize! I directed him to buy Nana's Christmas present, a brooch that was once a pendant belonging to our daughter-in-law, Jemima. As I recall, the fastening pin to create a brooch was added by a Victorian owner long after Jemima's time. There were earrings to match, but she wasn't wearing them the day both were finally accepted into heaven. Observant Jeremiah noticed her wearing the pendant immediately before their final departure, and he was only ten.

"The set was dispersed after her death. Rather blindly, because I didn't fully understand the reasons at the time, I helped Nadia's father purchase the earrings for his wife decades ago. When I tracked down the brooch, I simply suggested to Sam that he should travel to the Silver Vaults. Once there, I then suggested that Nana needed that brooch as a thank-you gift. While Sam is a lovely man, he follows suggestions easily, so unlike his wife. That took no work at all!

"Nadia, a generous sort, had been thinking for a long time of giving the earrings to Iris, her true sister in thought. I helped her decide that this was the right Christmas. It took a lot of work to get into her mind, much more work than Sam required. Like Constance, she's a harder nut to crack!" Leila starts to laugh uproariously and then proclaims, "But as you know, Mortimer, I always succeed in the end."

Mortimer laughs out loud for a long time. Then suddenly, he becomes quite serious, glances toward his wife, stares directly at me, and asks, "How do you think Jeremiah will do with what is ahead?"

Leila quietly replies, "That question is extremely hard to answer. Besides his near-perfect recall of details, he is extraordinarily perceptive. Case in point, he realized that we knew nothing about silencers, also called suppressors.

"I must confess to a gap in my knowledge. Evelyn's gun seemed rather long, but then I recollected our pistols were lengthy too. However, I forgot that ours loaded rather differently from modern firearms. Did I tell you I've studied silencers since I read Jeremiah's thoughts?"

"No, you didn't." Mortimer bursts into laughter. "I had never heard of a silencer either, although they might have come in handy for the ears in our day."

She continues, "And he has now recognized that we are not infallible." It's her turn to laugh. "But to answer your question, he is young and still growing. He will mature into the challenges ahead."

Mortimer declares, "Of course he will do well. He has a capable mind, with your memory, brains, and some of your perceptiveness. He will figure out what needs to be done and which path in life to take." After a pause, Mortimer seems self-satisfied as he announces, "He has my name and my inkstand as a talisman. We mustn't worry that he sometimes has difficulty understanding people. I expect his form of autism may actually turn into a gift. He is truly all set!"

Leila breaks out in bell-like laughter. It is the happy laugh of delight.

In the dream, my great-grandparents watch my sleeping form and smile. Leila giggles a little and blows me a kiss. I feel her departing hand slide along the side of my face, which makes me shift slightly at the touch.

Awakening a moment later, I fully expect to see Mortimer and Leila in my room, but I am alone.

Were they truly here? Was this all a dream? My only clue is a bit of green thread on the carpet, but is it from Mortimer's waistcoat? Without any fragment of yellow fabric caught anywhere, is one green thread sufficient to form any opinion? *Enough with the speculation!* Besides confused, I am sleepy, exceedingly sleepy.

Despite my fatigue, I ruminate upon the dream. My ancestors said something more might happen. *Not interested. This boy has had enough!* Their visit was a dream and not real, period! I can't deal with any other answer. I mutter lamely, "Of course, I *would* dream about them. It was overwhelmingly exciting to receive the inkstand of Nine-Greats-Grandfather Mortimer Jeremiah Wadsworth, known during his lifetime as the Earl Poppycock."

But why did I dream of the Christmas gift we gave to Nana? I mostly remember the pendant Jemima wore with her miraculously new clothes immediately after Edgar's name was cleared, and they were both heaven-bound. Could Nana's brooch once have been Jemima's?"

As I pull up the covers, I recollect the feelings I had at Christmas as everyone was gawking at the earrings and brooch. Back then, I thought that the brooch had been Jemima's, but I decided to stay silent.

There was too much mental overload at the time. Dad sometimes describes what his friend goes through with post-traumatic stress disorder or PTSD. At times, that's how I felt at Christmas.

I coped by not caring and sometimes defiantly muttered to myself, "I'll never know the true story about that finery. So what?"

Thinking back to Christmas, I assert somewhat sarcastically, "WTMI." I giggle to myself and then mumble, "Sometimes, Leila provides way too much information! Or her dreams do." I curl up comfortably and fall into oblivion.

Over the following months, we learn that Uncle Brian has a real knack for Uncle Ian's business. He is succeeding in his educational courses online and in his life with Teresa, mostly because he remains sober and drug-free.

Socially, Dexter struggles in school because some of his schoolmates are not kind and used the news about his family as a branding iron against him. However, Dexter spoke up. To fix the problem, he agreed to report every episode of bullying, and he did. That takes backbone! Soon the school attracted attention as a place where once bullying was tolerated but is tolerated no more. This received as much press as the attempted murders, and that was all to the good. From his emails, Dexter feels like a leader in a new movement.

Rampant bullying is being curtailed across many schools as a result of Dexter's willingness to stand up and be counted. The press interviews probably gathered people to his cause. His efforts became a rallying cry and helped many other kids in similar situations. We saw one of his press interviews. He pulled no punches about the family situation, his mother's attempt at murder, her suicide, and his brother's assistance with her murderous plans. He talked about the effects bullying might have on any fragile individual who is trying to heal. People responded well to him, maybe out of pity, or perhaps because he posed the issues rather elegantly. Whatever the reason, he has become a voice for the weak and vulnerable. His spreading influence is wonderful to witness.

One of Dexter's texts reads, "Dad works hard to duly note and comment on my work. To have my beloved father's attention means much."

Our cousin's steadily improving self-confidence visibly grows in his weekly and rather lengthy emails to us in America.

Additionally, in Uncle Ian's correspondence, we witness him becoming the man we want him to be—kind, considerate, without a trace of the mean snob he once was. *Good work, Uncle!*

We love those emails! Together, Susanne and I always answer them promptly and carefully. We make comments so he knows we have read and discussed what he has written. We now are developing ties between us that will never break.

*****

It is now late April, almost May. The phone rings and Mom answers. She talks to her mother for a few minutes before she waves to us to come closer as she puts the phone on speaker so we may all hear. She requests, "Let people gather, Nana. I have you on speaker." A moment later, all five of us are huddled together, listening.

Nana uses a voice that tries to be matter-of-fact but which still quavers despite her efforts. "The media frenzy during the trial was horrendous, but it is all over now. A decision has been made about Collin: the courts have determined that he is truly a criminal psychopath. Consequently, he will remain in an asylum for the criminally insane as a juvenile and then will be transferred to an adult facility, where he will stay for the rest of his life. Not a happy ending, but there was never to be a happy ending for Collin. That was his choice."

The room is quiet as her words sink in. No one knows what to say. Our unspoken relief is almost palpable.

Breaking the silence, Nana announces, "Ian wants to speak." There are noises as the phone is handed over.

Uncle Ian states, "I see Collin regularly." He pauses and his voice almost breaks as he continues, "Collin is furious that he failed with the murder attempts on Brian and you, Constance. He remains unrepentant that he tried to kill. Without remorse, his only regret is that he was caught, which is the only source of any sadness he may feel. How did he become such a monster? Oh Constance, how could I fail so badly?"

Mom declares emphatically, "Ian, it is not your fault. There isn't anything you could have done to make any difference. That's the way he is, period."

My inclination is to tell Uncle Ian everything I know about the ancestors in the attic and the psychopaths we know about in the family tree. Perhaps he might think about the genetics involved and realize it was never his fault. Collin arrived already programmed.

It is all too complicated! Too unreal!

I let it go. No one wants to come across as another lunatic.

Papa has told only Nana about the vital work done by Leila, Mortimer, and Edgar during this Christmas mayhem. Papa decided, and Nana agreed, that Uncle Ian would not gain anything and might be embarrassed if he knew. Susanne and I told only Dad, Mom, and Phoebe. On this side of the Atlantic, there are no secrets from the nearest and dearest.

After our phone call finished, I emphatically declare, "I wanted to explain about Aunt Evelyn's ancestors to Uncle Ian so he could stop blaming himself about Collin. But that might have been tactless and maybe not helpful. I remember Papa's words, 'For some, it is a little too unsettling to know that one may have a day pass from heaven and materialize here on earth, even if for the greater good. That is too much information. No one can predict another's reactions.'"

After intense debate, we all side with our British grandparents' opinion that Uncle Ian might not react well. With a smile, Susanne remarks, "Least said, easiest mended."

Phoebe murmurs, "As my granny used to say, wise woman that she was."

I interject, "Nana also once said, 'People outside the family would think we are loony. Day passes from heaven? Really, are you nuts?' Besides, we all said goodbye. I will probably never see Mortimer, Leila, and Edgar on earth again. That's my assumption!"

After another lengthy discussion, we all agree. This tale with its phantoms is too whacky to ever share outside the family. Intervention from dead ancestor spooks? Unbelievable!

In the meantime, Mortimer, Leila, and Edgar are safely in heaven with the other ancestors and their relatives. They all may be given a day pass, but Leila's requests are especially favored! Wow!

Saint Peter, good luck with my great-granny. You are earning your halo!

Chapter 17

CONVERSATIONS WITH SUSANNE

That is how we all left it. No one outside the family was to know what actually happened nor about the help we had. The rest of the story was public and covered by the press but not the bit about the ghosts helping us. Decade after decade has come and gone, almost six decades actually, without strangers knowing about our interactions with dead ancestors.

Papa and Nana, Oscar and Nadia, my parents, and even Phoebe have all joined our ancestors. Susanne and I, along with Dexter, are among the few remaining who were part of that story.

Waiting for Susanne to ring the bell, I patiently sit in my study sipping a small evening scotch. I daydream, recalling many adventures, all wonderful stories that might yet be told. This is the second story my sister has forced me to write. She will decide if this tale will be shared. The bell rings. Ambling toward the door, I yell, "Coming!" The door swings wide. "Good evening, Susanne." She pecks my cheek and hugs me for a moment.

"I'm glad to see you, Jeremiah. You look well."

Full of energy, she enters with a briefcase. In a few moments, we are sitting in my study. She accepts my offer of a scotch with ice.

We comment on recent news and gossip, the usual small talk. I ignore or deftly side-step inquiries about my tentative health. That would be too morose a topic for an evening's entertainment.

My sister has a new hairstyle. Her long gray waves have been cut slightly below her jawline and shaped nicely, which gives her face a pixie look. The blouse and pants she is wearing over low-slung heels complement her trim figure. She still moves swiftly with grace even though she is over seventy. Time has been Susanne's friend. She looks and behaves far younger than her years, so unlike her brother.

"Did you receive the manuscript that I sent to you in advance?"

"Yes, I did," she replies as she pulls it out from her briefcase. She laughs and then comments, "You don't need to feed me coffee and treats while I plow through the manuscript this time. It has already been marked with my red pencil!"

We discuss her suggestions and note the typos that always sneak in uninvited. Susanne answers my questions efficiently.

She gazes at me fondly with a smile and confides, "I am glad I insisted you write about our second escapade. In our first book, it was a pleasure to relive our old family's mostly ghostly secrets, even though some of the things that happened created nightmares. When you unraveled the mystery in that first book, I knew you had to tell the rest."

"Well, yes, but I wrote *solely* at your insistence. Otherwise, all our family secrets and ancient mysteries would have remained unknown." Her words make me want to roll my eyes as was her wont, and famously, as a teenager. With trepidation, I ask, "But surely, you don't mean that *all* our adventures should be shared?"

"Yes, I do, if only for me to read. Your tales take me on a wonderful journey."

Trying to hide my unhappiness at this news, I take the manuscript that she hands me. From under my heavy brows, I stare down through my thick glasses. Using my gnarled fingers to hold pages flat, I glare at all her lethal red slashes, circles, and proofreader's marks that correct spelling and punctuation errors.

Smiling, she reassures me, "This is all the usual stuff expected from an early draft. I like the content. It's a go!"

I sigh with relief. "As a reluctant author, I am glad you approve of the story you demanded be told." We both laugh together. "I find writing difficult and have never been sure that any of our secrets needed to be shared."

"Jeremiah, the story needed to be told. It truly was yuletide mayhem. I think everyone involved would be pleased with your story, except for Aunt Evelyn and Collin. But even they might be happier knowing how close they came to succeeding!"

We both become ominously silent at *that* prospect. Susanne remains solemn, while I feel a chill of fright despite the passage of all the years. Finally, I ponder, "Think what their success could have done to our lives!"

Susanne bites her lip, nods that she understands, and briskly declares, "But they failed. And our lives were not scarred as they could have been. I've always been grateful for that."

She seems thoughtfully quiet for a moment and then asks, "Have you started the third adventure tale yet?"

"Actually, I have an outline in my mind. But I have not committed pen to paper yet," I reply as I think of the electronic devices that save so much penmanship labor.

Susanne demands emphatically, "But you must! During that third adventure, we finally had perspective and learned how much risk we really had during the second story. It was then that I realized that it was only Collin's youth and inexperience that saved us. Terrifying!"

As my mind flashes to our cousin, I add, "And there was some degree of resolution there." I shudder and become silent.

With malice aforethought, I turn the conversation slightly as I ask, "What about Dexter? Does he mind that we are spilling the beans about his closest kin, his mother and brother? We should get his agreement before publication, don't you think? We would be in the wrong, and it might become awkward if he wasn't happy with publication."

Susanne smiles sweetly, tilts her head slightly, and suggests, "Well, let's put things in perspective. We tried to tell him beforehand about the first book, but he was traveling and missed the messages. But, dear boy, he did read *The Unraveling*. He called me and asked, 'What is true and what is fiction?'"

I respond ruefully, "I feel bad. We should have delayed publication and warned him beforehand that we were sharing information about the spooks."

Susanne continues, "He pretended to be horrified when I declared, 'It's all true. And we are finally blabbing about ghostly ancestors.' That made him chuckle. But, from my recollection of my *faux pas* with Uncle Ian years ago, he already knew all about the phantoms in the attic." Lost in recollections, she pauses, then quietly chortles.

Moments pass before Susanne rouses herself and adds briskly, "But this time, I told him the story line and checked that he was okay with the second book and all that it divulges about his nearest and dearest. He replied, 'We are all good.' Jeremiah, we're over that hurdle!" She smiles broadly.

Intrigued, I ask, "What did he say exactly?"

Like a schoolgirl, Susanne giggles. "What did he say? He declared, 'No wonder Jeremiah seemed so smart. He was cribbed by spooks.' Then he laughed uproariously! Finally, he admitted, 'I've come to terms with my hideous relatives. Let everyone know.' And then he laughed again!"

"That's a better response than I expected," I admit honestly.

She pauses in thought before she asks, "Do you remember what you once said? Years ago, you said, 'But someday, perhaps, I shall write it all down. Time will tell. There may be some people out there who will understand and believe.'"

I reply, "That was years ago when I was filling my notebooks with each of our adventure stories, a notebook for each one. I never expected to do anything more than squiggles in a notebook."

Susanne quietly responds, "You were preparing yourself for the final version. You know as well as I do that the story is worth telling. All the stories are worth telling."

"Slave driver," I quip.

The rest of our conversation was limited to the daily this and that—nothing significant. However, I always feel better when my sister visits. Even her small talk perks me up.

After a time, Susanne says, "It's getting late, and I must be up early tomorrow." She kisses my cheek, gives me a gentle hug, and commands, "Make the corrections. I'll help you with your publisher."

"Thank you. I always need help there."

And with that, she disappears.

So you see, it took almost sixty years before Susanne was able to persuade me to write down this story, the second of our adventures together. I hope you have enjoyed the reading, for surprisingly, I have indeed enjoyed the writing.

Don't tell Susanne!

Until next time, *adieu*.

THE END

About the Author

Max W. Justus is on his second career. His first? Not important. But writing with purpose and a sense of whimsy is now his passion. Think about it: writing with purpose—that's almost as important as reading with purpose. Humor is the bonus. He has written a series of books that follows the lives of Jeremiah and Susanne throughout their long and useful lives. The reason? He uses his characters to provide a glimpse into what kindness and fair play can do in society. Secondary reason? Let the reader enjoy a romp through the book and then be inspired to lead by example. Is Mr. Justus fomenting a cultural revolution? Not likely. Kindness and fair play are not truly revolutionary; they are ancient customs, almost a lost art. When Mr. Justus tires of these characters, he writes the occasional whodunit for fun. In real life, he's an ordinary bloke who earns a living, loves his wife and kids, and welcomes the grandkids home. Living in rural America, he feels blessed. But do not worry. He's not slacking. His pen is still on paper.

www.ingramcontent.com/pod-product-compliance
Lightning Source LLC
Chambersburg PA
CBHW030346020726
47493CB00003B/714